CW00395030

MIRRORMAN

V I R G I N
W O R L D S

meet the future

Virgin Worlds is a new imprint. Its aim is to showcase the best in British SF and fantasy, and in particular to discover new talent. This is one of the three launch titles. Here is the complete list.

MNEMOSYNE'S KISS
BY PETER J EVANS

In the near future, the world isn't an ecological disaster area. Quite the reverse. But human beings still have the capacity to make the worst nightmares come true. Addicts such as Rayanne Gatita consume new drugs to erase the memories of life on the streets; an entrepreneur such as Cassandra Lannigan can still end up with half her brain shot away when a deal goes wrong.

Lannigan wakes up in hospital, unable to remember more than a whisper of her past. But someone's out to assassinate her – again – and her only ally is the street-girl Rayanne.

ISBN 0 7535 0380 8

HAVENSTAR
BY GLENDA NORAMLY

The Eight Stabilities are islands of order surrounded by disfiguring, corrupting, lethal chaos. The chaos is encroaching.

Keris Kaylen, daughter of a master mapmaker, is prevented by stifling tradition from pursuing her father's trade. When her father is murdered she sets out across the Unstable and is forced into dubious company, including that of Davron Storre, whose secret is his pact with Carasma the Unmaker, lord of chaos – a secret which, as Keris searches for the maps that will save the world, will one day exact a terrible price.

ISBN 0 7535 0390 5

MIRRORMAN

Trevor Hoyle

VIRGIN
WORLDS

First published in 1999 by
Virgin Worlds
an imprint of
Virgin Publishing Ltd
Thames Wharf Studios
Rainville Road
London W6 9HT

ISBN 0 7535 0385 9

Typeset by Galleon Typesetting, Ipswich
Printed and bound in Great Britain by
Mackays of Chatham PLC

To Liz and Laurence James.

With love, admiration and respect.
And hope for the future.

CONTENTS

PART ONE

DARK SHIP

What might have been is an abstraction
Remaining a perpetual possibility
Only in a world of speculation.
What might have been and what has been
Point to one end, which is always present.

TS Eliot
'Burnt Norton', *Four Quartets*

DEATH ROW

Somebody must have been playing tricks on Frank Kersh, because in the very last second of his life he was granted a reprieve from the electric chair.

Kersh lay on the narrow trestle bed in the twelve-foot-by-eight-foot cell, semicircles of damp spreading from the armpits of his blue work shirt. Through the barred window the Louisiana sky was a bright, aching blue. Another lousy perfect day. Kersh wrinkled his nostrils, smelling his own sweat, but what could he do? Let out of this stinking oven one hour in every twenty-four. When a man was going to die in nine days' time you'd think they'd at least leave him his self-respect.

Somebody was wailing down the Block. That was the name some joker had given to Unit F-2, their last permanent residence:

The Block. Chopping block.

Very funny. Kersh might die laughing.

He lay back, hands clasped behind his head, and listened to the Nigra wailing his lament. Another guy joined in with a soft harmonica. Twenty-three blacks and three whites occupied the cells on Death Row. One of the black kids had just turned sixteen. He was pumped full of drugs to keep him quiet. For three nights he'd driven the rest of the inmates crazy, yelling and screaming and smashing his head against the bars. So now they kept him topped up, and he didn't bother anyone.

Kersh wriggled his bare toes. He tried to imagine them sliding into cool black mud. He'd never know that feeling again. Standing up to his shins in the creek. He'd never taste cold beer either. Or touch a woman. The list of what he'd never do again was endless.

What had Jason, the black guy in the next cell, said? 'It don't hurt none, that's what one of the guards told me. It just kind of tickles a little bit. There ain't no pain. That's what he said.'

'How the hell does he know?' Kersh had asked. 'He tried it?'

Jason went grey in the face and shut his mouth.

There was a metal jug and a tin cup on the shelf above the bed. Kersh poured out some lukewarm water and sipped it. Within seconds, sweat popped out all over his body. It trickled down his legs, ran between his toes. Formed pools on the floor. His shirt scraped on his back. Hellfire couldn't be hotter than this. But Kersh didn't believe in heaven or hell. There was nothing. Void. Just empty cold blackness, like cool black mud. Frozen to a pinpoint of nothingness. The Bible-punchers talked about bright light and angels with wings. Or else about eternal damnation, purgatory. Given the choice, he'd go for damnation – who wanted to end up like some goddamn faggot with silver wings on a pink cloud?

A bird twittered on the window ledge.

Kersh pushed the lank fair hair from his forehead and stared up at it with his one good eye, the other a milky opaque blue. It looked dead. People never knew if he could see with that eye, so they dropped their own eyes, avoided his stare. He liked that. He used it brazenly, a leper flaunting an open sore, liked to watch them blink and turn away. He bet some of them were ashamed they had two good eyes.

The bird hopped about on tiny legs as frail as twigs. It cocked its head, observed him with an eye like a glittering bead. Frank Kersh didn't move. The sparrow grew bolder. It hopped between the bars and stood on the inner ledge. Head cocked one way and then the other. It was a scrawny

4

little thing, hardly an ounce of flesh on its fragile bones.

'Hello, little fella,' Kersh said softly. 'Are you thirsty? That's all I got to give you, a drink. Here we go.'

He slid off the bed, holding the metal cup.

The sparrow inspected the cell. Shiny green walls. *Hustler* pin-ups of spread-eagled women. Stallone with scarred biceps toting a machine gun. Dirty Harry with his long-barrelled Magnum. Half a dozen puzzle and crossword magazines, crumpled and dog-eared. The narrow bed with the hard flock mattress. The yellow plastic bucket with a lid, down there in the corner. Just this and the steel-barred sliding door.

Kersh's twelve-by-eight universe.

'Come on now,' Kersh said soothingly. 'You don't like this heat any better'n I do, huh? Take a nice long drink.' He half-filled the cup and stretched out, pushing it with his fingertips on to the ledge. The sparrow retreated and then came back.

Kersh leant against the wall and folded his arms, smiling.

The sparrow approached the cup, pecked at it. Then hopped up and clung to the rim with its tiny feet. Tentatively, it ducked its head, but couldn't reach the water. It looked sharply at Kersh, then tried again. No dice. But it was a trier. Another wary glance and down it went again. Tail feathers stuck in the air.

Slowly, Kersh unfolded his arms – and pounced. His bony hands shot out, one for the cup, the other like a trap coming down on the rim. The grey feathery ball battered against his fingers. Its head poked through. But before he could clamp his hand tight down it had got free, a fluttery blur of feathers, and was through the bars and away.

A dark soaring speck against the blue . . .

The cup clanged against the bars, flung with all Kersh's strength. He nearly kicked at the clamped-down metal leg of the bed, remembered just in time that he wasn't wearing shoes, and smacked his fist into his palm instead.

Kersh dropped to his knees. He reached under the bed and pulled out the wooden box. Carefully, he lifted the lid and peered inside. Slitted red eyes glinted from a dark corner. The thick pelt of fur was smooth and shiny. The black nose and long whiskers twitched, never ceasing, sniffing for food.

The rat drew back, baring its yellow teeth, hissing in its throat, as Kersh bent nearer to see inside. He wanted to stroke it, but some creatures could never be tamed. He'd had it nearly two weeks, feeding it on morsels from his own plate. Maybe in time it would grow to trust him, let him fondle it.

Maybe in time. Nine days. That's how much time he had left.

'Just missed a yummy little snack for you, Manson, old buddy,' he informed the rat. 'A skinny little thing, hardly a mouthful. But a change from beef stew. You could've crunched the bones. Sorry 'bout that.'

The long whiskers twitched; the slitted red eyes watched him steadily. No, it wasn't ready for stroking. Kersh valued his fingers too much.

He winked at it fondly with his milky eye, and then glanced up, frowning. Footsteps. Quickly, he fastened the lid and slid the box under the bed. A couple of the guards knew about Manson, allowed Kersh to keep his 'pet' as a special privilege. But Meacham, the head guard, didn't. And Meacham didn't care that this was Death Row, and all the guys here were terminal. 'What special privileges did the victims get?' Kersh had once heard him ask a social worker. 'You got any sympathy to spare, give it to their families.'

Kersh was sitting on his bed, sipping water, when the footsteps halted outside his cell. Meacham's peardrop-shaped belly hung over his gunbelt. His soft pudgy fists rested on the third tyre where his waist should have been.

'Put your shoes on and smarten yourself up.' Meacham jerked his thumb. 'You got a visitor, Kersh.'

The guard at the control panel operated the electronic door and Kersh preceded the head guard down the Block, past the row of cells with their lounging prisoners. One of them leant against the bars.

'If it's that born-again dame, give her one for me, Frank.'

In the next cell, the black kid was staring at the wall with vacant bloodshot eyes, saliva dribbling down his chin.

Farther along, a black guy rubbed his groin suggestively and licked his lips as Kersh went by. 'That white pussy sure tastes good, man.'

Kersh gave him the finger and got a prod in the small of the back from Meacham's bully stick as they went through the double security doors into the main corridor of F Cellhouse. TV cameras mounted high in each corner swivelled to watch them go. Plastic signs of red letters on a white ground displayed the geography of the Block: UNIT F-1, UNIT F-2, DETENTION, PROTECTIVE MEASURES, VISITORS' SECTION.

Meacham unhooked his bully stick and pointed the way. Kersh knew it already. Meacham just liked handling his bully stick, the fat slob.

Afterward, puzzling over what had taken place, and when, Jeff Cawdor would wonder if it hadn't all started on that particular day – at that particular moment – when he was standing at his office window on the 23rd floor of the Chrysler Building.

New York was shrouded under a thick grey blanket, a phantom city lost in a cloud of sulphuric mist. Lightning crackled like a plague of mad fireflies through the murk. He was enjoying the display from his grandstand vantage point, feeling safe and impregnable (like a child in a secret cave) behind the granite fascia and the tinted double glazing. Plus the fact he'd always, ever since he was a kid growing up in Torrence, North Carolina, relished the play of natural forces, the more majestic and awesome the better.

On that particular day, hands stuffed in his trouser pockets, a dreamy gawping look on his face, he hadn't thought of this storm as being any different. Maybe the difference wasn't in the storm itself, but in him. A couple

7

of times he'd glanced over his shoulder, having that uncanny sense of there being somebody in the room with him. There wasn't, but he couldn't shake the feeling.

The morning had started ordinarily enough. He'd had breakfast with Sarah and Daniella, then driven in from his home in Franklin, New Jersey, his mind a million miles away as he listened to *Scheherazade* on the CD deck. Well, not a million miles, more like three and a half thousand – the distance roughly between Manhattan and Tuscany, where the three of them were to spend their first European vacation together as a family, after a five-day stopover in London. Cawdor had visited Europe many times before, on business, as a senior partner and chief designer for the civil-engineering company UltraCast International. On this trip he had people to see in London and Norwich, during which time his wife and daughter would stay with friends in Shropshire. Sarah had put in some time on her English family tree and come up against a mysterious gap in the late eighteenth century. Now she was hoping to pick up the trail again and trace it back through parish-church records, filling in the missing pieces. Daniella had never been to England, or indeed Europe, at all. She had vague, muddled ideas about England, fed by old black and white movies on TV, and the only place she had expressed any desire to visit was 221B Baker Street. His daughter would be stricken with disappointment, Cawdor reckoned, chuckling to himself, not to see hansom cabs rattling through fog-shrouded streets and to hear in the distance the baying of monstrous slavering hounds.

It was going to be wonderful! Sights, experiences, sensations; a whole new world the three of them could share together for the first time. And not least because he and Sarah would be seeing it all afresh through the girl's eyes. Staring unseeingly at the roiling turbulence outside the window, Cawdor couldn't stop himself recalling their last trip to Europe – his and Sarah's. It had been sixteen years ago, two years after they got married and six months after Rebecca died. Their baby daughter had been another tiny statistic in the files labelled COT DEATHS. A perfectly happy, healthy child, just starting to take notice of the wider world beyond the protective perimeter of her mother's embrace and her father's cuddles and funny faces. A real family at last, which overnight had turned into a small, cold, rigid lump with clenched blue fists lying face down in the crib, and two desolate individuals for whom the planet, the entire universe, had ceased turning. That had been the reason for Europe. They had to do something, anything, go somewhere, anywhere, or go mad. So Cawdor had taken a clear six weeks off work and they had gone in search of other places, any form of distraction to fill the void. And – if such a thing might exist in some remote spot on the face of the earth – to find peace of mind.

But that was in the past.

Rebecca was a dear small memory. She would never be forgotten, and the pain would never ultimately be assuaged, but their life now had meaning and purpose – as well as lots of fun, laughter, and love.

Cawdor shook off the reverie, his dark-brown eyes sharpening into focus. He brushed back the wavy locks of unruly hair from his forehead and returned to his CAD workstation. The storm slowly abated, moving west across the Hudson, as the sky resumed a more tranquil aspect. From behind a ragged fringe of purple cloud a golden shaft of sunlight poured in through the window. Cawdor was distracted once again, his mind basking in warm sunshine from the vaulted blue of an Italian sky, his hand caressing worn, pitted stones that had been put in place 4,000 years ago, the tingle of blood-red Chianti on his tongue, the dry rasp of its aftertaste making his senses glow . . .

Enough, enough. He snapped out of it and concentrated on the job in hand: calculating some stress-load factors for a shopping mall in Lambertville, Michigan. It was pleasant drudgery, punching in the numbers and watching the columns multiply on the green screen as if breeding exponentially like a virus in a fifties horror flick. God, and to think he used to do all this with a slide rule, a pocket calculator and a tattered book of logarithm tables he'd carried with him since his student days at Columbia.

Twenty minutes later, deciding he needed to take a leak, he walked through the outer office on his way to the men's room. UltraCast International occupied two whole floors of the building: the executive offices, administration and design team on this level; the civil-engineering section, site planning and accounts on the floor below. Sixty-three people in all, labouring on projects as diverse as schools, bridges, office blocks, multiple-screen movie complexes, and, currently, a hotel and open-air casino in Florida that was being overseen by Cawdor's fellow senior partner, Don Carlson.

On the way back he stopped for a word with one of the design engineers in the drawing office, then asked Phyllis, his plump, efficient secretary with the dimpled cheeks, to get him a tuna-mayonnaise sandwich, blue-cheese-flavoured potato chips and a Sprite; woolly-headed daydreaming while he watched the storm had put him behind, and he intended to work through his lunch break. This simple request brought a dimpling, sidelong smile from Phyllis. She was always smiling at him from under her eyelashes, as if they shared an intimate secret or a private joke. She had a crush on him, he guessed (no guessing about it: he knew damn well she did) and he shamelessly played on the fact as an angler plays a fish, pretending all the while to be blithely ignorant of the mute adoration shining out of her eyes.

Of course this made her adore him even more, which of course he also knew, and so the circle tightened its silken spiral.

'You don't know how lucky you are, not having to watch your figure,' Phyllis said, reaching inside the desk drawer for her purse.

Oh God no, Cawdor thought. She wasn't going to make some remark about his lean manly physique, was she? He didn't mind silent worship in small doses, but this threatened to become embarrassing. Once he'd overheard her rhapsodising to another secretary about some guy with 'sleepy bedroom eyes and a wicked seductive smile', and then been mortified to realise this guy was himself.

Cawdor gave a weak grin. 'I gotta few pounds I could stand to lose,' he mumbled, speaking the truth. But Phyllis was blind to any – even the tiniest – imperfection in her hero.

'Not that it shows. Take it from me. To say you have a desk job, you're in pretty good shape. Most men your age –'

Cawdor retreated, almost blushing. 'Er, thanks. Nice of you to say so, Phyllis. Still, better make that a Diet Sprite, OK?' He turned and fled into his office.

2

A thick sheet of laminated perspex prevented any physical contact between prisoner and visitor, a series of holes the size of dimes punched in it so they could hear one another. Tubular-metal-framed chairs were bolted to the scuffed floor, separated by narrow wooden partitions to provide an illusion of privacy. Three large fans moved slowly overhead, stirring the sluggish air. In the corner behind a square deal table a guard in a dark-grey peaked cap sat boredly watching the proceedings.

Kersh had been hoping it was Sophie. But it turned out to be that timid-looking dame again, May-Beth, who, it seemed, had embarked on a personal crusade to save his soul. Why him? He wasn't religious. He didn't and never had 'believed'. Hell, he hadn't been inside a church since he was nine years old.

He flopped down and stretched out his lanky legs. Good to get out of that cell though, even if he had to pay the price of being preached at.

The woman watched him, brown eyes blinking, her unpainted mouth curved in a small tight smile. She had soft, rounded, regular features. Wouldn't have been bad-looking, Kersh thought, if only she'd take a little care over her appearance. Dyed and curled that straight mousy hair, for instance. Got rid of that fringe, which put ten years on her. As it was she was twenty-five going on fifty. He imagined her naked, and decided she'd pass muster. She was well blessed, and he liked his women big up there; the bigger the better.

'Hello, Frank. How are you?' She had a shy, hesitant way of speaking. Normally, Kersh didn't go for the demure type, though the notion of May-Beth murmuring sex words to him in that little-girl whisper made his groin tighten.

'How do you think I am? One thing for sure, I'm not taking out a subscription to *Reader's Digest*.'

May-Beth's mouth twitched – as if she knew it was meant to be a joke but didn't get the point. She dropped her eyes demurely, pressed her lips together. 'I thought maybe you'd be glad to see me . . .'

'Oh, yeah? Why?' Kersh pushed his hand through his thinning fair hair. To compensate for its baby-fine sparseness he'd let it grow long over his collar. He lit up a Marlboro, from his third pack today, and slouched back in the chair. It was close in here, metal grilles over the closed windows, the same stale air circulated by the fans. He felt slightly sick as the smoke hit his stomach.

May-Beth gazed at him with those pleading, cowlike eyes. 'I pray for you constantly, Frank.'

'Yeah?' Kersh dragged in smoke and let it trickle from his nostrils. 'Good for you,' he mumbled, staring blatantly at her breasts. He had the itch today, no question about it.

'There is hope. There is salvation. It isn't too late – the Messengers can help you. Believe in them, Frank, open your heart to them, and they'll offer you eternal life.'

'Is that before or after I go to the chair?'

'Do you want to die?'

'You mean I gotta choice?'

'The Messengers will show you the way. All you have to do is trust in them.'

It never ceased to amaze him how people could believe in this salvation crap. Now they were offering him eternal life. Jee-zuzz. He'd killed a dumb kid, fifteen years old, and he was going to burn for it. End of story. Why was she bothering him, for chrissakes?

'Know what he said, the jerk?' Following his own thoughts, Kersh watched the smoke spiralling upward. 'Had his hand under the counter, reaching for his piece, and know what he said? "Make my day." *Make my day!*' His lips curled. 'So I did. It turned out to be his last one.' The glazed, milky eye watched the writhing smoke.

'All for a measly thirty dollars,' May-Beth said sadly.

'You forgot the two bits and a quarter,' Kersh wise-cracked glibly.

That was six years and nine failed appeals ago, though to Kersh it was as near and sharp as yesterday. He blamed the damn car, acting up on him, same as everything else in his life. The Chevy had sounded like it was chewing ten pounds of ball bearings that day and having trouble swallowing them. Then a fart erupted from the tailpipe, making the car jerk forward and suddenly check itself, so that his forehead nearly smashed into the steering wheel. In fury he whacked the wheel with his fist. The Chevy retaliated by swerving off the blacktop and ploughing a furrow with its nearside wheels through the sandy hardfill.

Cursing, Kersh hauled it back, blinking hard against the glare of the setting sun beaming directly into his one good eye.

He'd been on highway 190 – Baton Rouge fifty miles behind him – somewhere between Opelousas and Eunice. This was Cajun country. The 'gator shitkickers of the Louisiana swampland, Kersh thought of them with a derisive snigger. Them good ole boys could neither read nor write and slept with their own sisters. Ate spiced redfish and black beans for breakfast. Ughh! Last thing he wanted was to get stranded out here. They'd bend this city boy over a barrel and pump him raw.

He was heading for Shreveport and had a long way to go. Over 160 miles by his rough reckoning. He hoped to Christ the battered old Chevy would make it. Now, as well as grinding ball bearings to bits, the engine was giving off a high-pitched whine like a hornet trapped in a fruit jar.

As usual a feeling of impotent rage gripped him in its iron claws.

Why always him? Other guys seemed to get the breaks. He was still waiting for his. Nothing ever went the way he planned it. Nothing ever came out right for Frank Kersh. And that included his life.

An hour later, and the sun gone down, he turned off 190 at Ragley and took route 171 north to De Ridder. He really was in wild and woolly hick territory now. The locals probably had tails and howled at the moon. Even though born and bred in the neighbouring state of Mississippi, this was an alien world to Kersh. Literally. They spoke a different lingo – French or some such, somebody had told him. How in hell could you talk foreign and call yourself American, for chrissakes? It was unpatriotic.

He switched on the radio for company, but all he could find on every band was a cacophony of frantic foot-stomping to fiddle and accordion, played so fast it was like one long screech that made his head ache. He turned it off in disgust. Rhythm and blues and early rock 'n' roll was up his street. Something with a solid backbeat; better than this monkey music any day of the week.

Kersh peered through the bug-smeared windshield into the yellow tunnel of light formed by the single headlight and its flickering companion. The Chevy, like him, was one-sighted too. Drooping cypresses hung over the road, with stretches of soggy marsh backing off into the remote interior wilderness. Now and then he spied the dim glow of a homestead. When it had swept by, the darkness returned, a solid and impenetrable wall of night that seemed to close in on him from all sides.

More for comfort than because he actually felt hungry, Kersh stuffed the last of the cold, greasy double cheese-burger and onions into his mouth and flushed it down with a gulp of Carlsberg Export. Eating it reminded him that he'd broken his last ten spot at a truck stop on the outskirts of Baton Rouge to buy it. And thinking that made him glance in panic at the fuel gauge. He was a quarter full – or, according to Kersh's stinking rotten luck, three-quarters empty. With 120 or so miles yet to go. Jee-*zuzz*.

He slowed the Chevy as the faltering yellow beam picked out a sign, white letters on a blue background. LEESVILLE. He missed the population figure underneath, but Kersh didn't need to know it. Another hick town for definite, couple of bars, clapboard church, wooden houses with peeling paint and sagging porches. Couldn't be anything otherwise out here on the backside of nowhere. His hands tightened on the wheel. Question is, buddy boy, Kersh thought, is the gas station slap bang on main street or some ways out? The gas station would be quiet at this hour – after ten – but anything too central would be bad news. And he fretted it might be one of those with a night window: the cashier safe and snug behind toughened wire-mesh glass, an alarm button next to the register begging a thumb to press it and wake the burg from the dead.

It was a bad habit of his, creating problems before they arose – or that maybe didn't even exist anyway. He was freaking himself out without any real cause. Just hang loose, Kersh told himself. Play the scene as it comes, on the wing. Experience had taught him that, if nothing else, in his 32 lousy years of life.

The gas station was on the final bend before 171 straightened out on its approach into town. Not perfect, not ideal by any means, but it could have been plenty worse. Main street was a ragged cluster of lights about half a mile away. A pick-up truck piled high with swollen sacks of grain went by in the opposite direction as Kersh drove in and pulled up alongside the pumps. The Chevy's engine gave an ominous clunk as he switched off. Hope to Christ the bastard would start up again. If it didn't he'd drop a lighted match in the fuel tank and boom the motherfucker out of existence. And serve it right.

A red-haired teenage kid with rolls of flab overlapping his jeans waddled across and unhooked the pump. He had a freckled, moonlike face, big and empty, and dreamy vacant eyes that gently smiled as Kersh told him to fill her up. Watching the kid through the side mirror,

Kersh flipped open the glove compartment and slid the semiautomatic into the inside pocket of his dark-blue windbreaker. No need to check if it was fully loaded: it always was. He got out and performed a show of stretching, arching his back and angling his head to take a general look-see from his good side. No one else inside the cabin, its bare and shabby interior lit by cold blue fluorescents. Coke machine, a rack of magazines, a small TV on a shelf above the counter showing one of the Dirty Harry movies. Kersh couldn't see a cash register, but maybe the place didn't run to one. Same difference if the cash was kept in a drawer or a tin box.

With the kid still busy at the pump, he ambled across and stepped up on to the narrow wooden stoop, letting the screen door bang shut behind him. When the kid came in a few minutes later, wiping his hands on a rag, Kersh was at the magazine rack, his back to the door.

He waited until the kid was behind the counter and then slowly swivelled, one hand inside the windbreaker, the other hanging free at his side. He felt cool and easy. Not even breathing heavy.

'All the cash you have, sonny. Hand it over. Now.'

The red-haired kid was staring at the lump Kersh's hand made inside the windbreaker. Then he did something that made Kersh frown: he smiled a big empty smile. What the hell was this? Did the punk think he was playing games? Kersh took a step forward, hand still inside his windbreaker, and then he gawped.

The kid had reached below the counter-top and was holding a gun in his fat fist. From where Kersh stood it looked like a .41 Magnum. And the damn barrel wasn't even shaking. Kersh felt his bowels loosen. It was a new and unsettling experience for him – situation reversed as he felt the same cold terror the victims of his petty thieving over the years had felt with a gun pointing at them. Could he run? Could he make the door before a blast from that fearsome weapon spread his guts over the wooden floor? No way, not with sweat running from his armpits and legs like jello.

16

And then, more incredibly still, the kid said:

'Go ahead, scumbag –' mouth widening in a grin that revealed a row of baby teeth with gaps in them '– make my day.'

Kersh couldn't believe he was actually hearing this. Who did this shitkicker think he was, Dirty Harry? The younger generation watched too many movies.

Kersh looked up at the screen, where Clint Eastwood was chasing one of the bad guys down a dark alley. He looked back at the kid, who was still wearing the same gawpy grin on his fat face, and as he stared at the gun it suddenly came to him. The kid was play-acting. He had a mental age of five or six, and the Magnum he was holding, for God's sake – was a toy. It was *plastic*.

Kersh found a watery grin. It was one of sheer relief. The sense of relief lasted three seconds, and then turned in a trice to a boiling cauldron of rage. To think that a moment ago he'd nearly crapped his pants! This sub-mental shitkicker with the vacant smirk had made him feel, and probably look, too, like a glazed-eyed bunny rabbit quivering before the dripping fangs of a diamond-back. Slowly, he brought out his bunched fist from inside the windbreaker and spread his hand to show that it was empty, and at the same time raised his other hand and fired from the hip, the slug taking the kid in the second roll of fat above his jeans. Yessirree. The old sucker punch. Nothing inside the windbreaker, sonny boy, except a bulging fist, the real hardware tucked into the back of his pants, the butt very conveniently placed for his free hand as it swept up behind and performed a fancy twirl to bring it on target, a manoeuvre he'd practised a hundred times in the mirror.

A look of surprise replaced the grinning gawp. The toy gun dropped from the kid's fingers, and he clutched himself with both hands: blood leaking from his belly and running down inside and outside his bulging jeans and spreading over the floor. He took a step backward and slithered in it, did a funny shuffling walk in reverse and then tried a cartoon-character backflip which took

17

him down with a crash that shook the floor, smack on to his fat ass.

Kersh peered over the counter. Flat on his back on the wet floor, the kid looked up at him. He was fully conscious and still surprised.

Kersh tapped the barrel of his gun on the counter. 'You gonna cause me trouble, fella?'

The kid just stared at him. No more trouble there. Problem was, the kid – feeble-brained or not – would remember the lank fair hair and bad eye and thin puckered scar down the cheek. It took a long while to die from a gut wound, Kersh reminded himself – if you died at all. He couldn't risk the gamble.

Plus, on top of everything, there was his own feeling to take into account. That he'd quaked in his shoes because a red-haired hicksville cretin with a freckled moon face had pulled a toy gun on him. That rankled. It riled. It fucking inflamed him. Frank Kersh didn't like being made to look a sucker.

So to make amends he popped another through the kid's throat, one into the heaving chest, and finished off the clip with three into the lard-barrel belly.

Should do it. The kid wasn't going anywhere from now on, except maybe (if he'd been good to his momma) to sing with the heavenly host. Have a swell trip and don't bother to write, asswipe.

Kersh didn't want to get his boots all messy in that red swamp behind the counter. At full stretch he plucked out the bills from the cash drawer. Not much for his pains, so he scooped out the nickels and dimes as well. At the end of the counter, next to the window, there was a display of candy bars and lifesavers. Kersh picked up two handfuls of his favourite Twinkie bars and filled his pockets. He shook his head, thinking, Make my day! What a jerk-off. Too much TV; too many movies.

Already pushing through the screen door, he had a sudden second thought. More like a first thought, and a new one. The kid was dead mutton, no doubt about it. But didn't the cops need a body to bring a murder rap? He was sure he'd read that somewhere. You couldn't file a homicide charge on the basis of a body that couldn't be found. Yeah, he was sure that was kosher. Lack of substantive evidence, or some such legal spiel.

Kersh debated with himself for a long time, nearly fifteen seconds.

He didn't look forward to it, what with the awful sticky mess the kid was in, but he was coming to the view that it had to be done. There were swamps all the way along route 171, and that thought finally decided him.

Tasty midnight snack for the 'gators on all that white blubber and it was farewell freckle face.

After wrapping the body in three or four burlap sacks he found in a back storeroom, Kersh got the soggy lump into the trunk and slammed the lid. The Chevy's springs groaned. Fat fucker. On the bright side, he now had a free full tank of gas, and if his old pal the Chevy bastard behaved itself and started he was long gone out of here.

It did, and ten minutes later he was beyond Leesville and heading north through a night as black as the devil's armpit.

'Do you have any regrets about killing that boy, Frank?'

'Is that it, the whole deal?' Kersh sat up. 'They want me to feel sorry for what I done?' He was suddenly angry. 'Listen. That dumb jerk deserved everything he got, trying to act the tough guy. No, I'm not sorry, you can tell 'em that. I stay the way I am – the one and only original Frank Kersh. They can have my soul and welcome, but I don't regret a damn thing.'

'That's all right then.'

There was silence in the hot, still room. The guard had his head bent, reading from a magazine. Somewhere a fly buzzed, battering against a window pane. At least it had a chance, Kersh thought. Find a crack somewhere. Zoom up in the air and over the wall of Louisiana State Pen. If only, if only . . . It was all the dumb jerk's fault for reaching under the counter. There was no need for it. And added to the kid's mistake was Kersh's error in thinking that without a body the DA couldn't bring a murder-one rap. He was wrong. It was Murder Uno. With or without a body. Bloodstains in the car trunk were enough. The blood group and hair matched the dead kid's. End of story.

May-Beth gazed at him calmly, hands folded placidly in her lap. 'There is a way out, Frank.'

He said bitterly, 'Sure, I know that. Hire me a big-shot lawyer. The two-bit shyster they foisted on to me couldn't have proved Snow White was a virgin. What is it with you? Trying to fill my last nine days with some steady sunshine? Hey, tell you how you can help – sleep with the warden and get me a pardon. On second thought, that wouldn't help my chances any. A face like yours could stop traffic.' He sucked the last smoke out of his cigarette and ground it in the tinfoil ashtray. 'I'm coming out of here a piece of burnt toast. There is no other way. So forget it.'

May-Beth said quietly, 'When the Messengers speak of eternal life, they mean it. They have the power to save you. There is a moment between life and death, before the soul leaves the body. You can remain there, frozen in that single instant of time –'

Kersh interrupted harshly, 'You don't freeze when they shoot two thousand volts through you. Ain't you heard? You fry. Your eyeballs melt. Sparks come outta here –' He tapped his temple. His lips thinned as his good eye roamed up to her intent stare. 'It isn't my soul that needs saving, you stupid bitch. It's my body.'

'There isn't much time, Frank. Just say you'll agree to it.'

'They're offering me one extra second, right? I don't reckon much to their eternal salvation if that's how long it lasts. And what do they get out of it? Another soul they can chalk up on the big scoreboard in the sky?'

'They ask for nothing.'

'That's the part I don't like. It stinks. Everybody's on the take for something. Hey,' Kersh sneered at her, 'maybe they want to put my brain in a glass jar! I seen that movie too.'

May-Beth clasped her hands in her lap. Her plain,

unpainted face and dumpy body were like an insult to Kersh. He thought of Sophie, raw stringy hands, chipped nail polish. Eyes smudged with mascara. The girl of a petty crook and three-time loser. Mr Big Shot who'd never had the breaks, who'd never taken his chances, except the wrong ones, and never got away with any of them. He'd never had a knockout of a woman in his entire life. Somebody with class – like his all-time favourite fantasy, that snooty Sue Ellen dame out of *Dallas*. Big goo-goo eyes, moist lower lip, and legs right up to her ass. Instead it was that dumb bleach-blonde Sophie Molosz – or this dried-up stick of an old maid.

Always last in line, Kersh. Never up front with the smart money. He was sick and tired of it.

'The second between life and death can be everlasting,' May-Beth said softly.

He decided to humour her. 'With me frozen in it.'

'Yes.' May-Beth's brown eyes were calm and sure.

Suddenly he had an idea. 'OK.'

It was so abrupt that she was confused. 'You agree to it? You believe?'

'Sure.' He glanced casually away for a second and lowered his voice. 'Take off your pants.'

'What?'

'That's the deal. Do as I say and I'll agree.'

He really had the hots today, and May-Beth was the only relief within a million miles. He didn't think she would, and then his breathing shortened as she reached below the table. He lit up again greedily, his palms damp, and had the pleasure of watching her as she wriggled her hips, squirming in her seat as she tugged her pants off, then stuffed them in her purse. The thought of it made him rock hard. She gave a tiny scared nod to say she'd done what he asked. Lounging back in the chair, Kersh let his hand fall lightly over his aching crotch. 'Nice, honey. Touch yourself. Know what I mean?'

He saw her hand move down, and a moment later she closed her eyes. Her chin started to quiver. Paper rustled as the guard turned a page, but he didn't look up.

Kersh worked on himself through the coarse weave of the blue serge work pants, his gaze never leaving her face. May-Beth's mouth parted a little; her shoulders jerked in rhythm. She opened her eyes and stared into his, her throat moving, little panting breaths making her nostrils flare and contract. Then she gave a sharp sudden gasp and bit her lower lip, her eyes squeezed tight shut.

Kersh slumped back and groaned, and crossed his legs. He hoped the congealed stickiness around his crotch wouldn't show through and betray him.

He sucked in smoke hungrily. They were all alike, these holy-roller broads. Ice on the outside, pure as the driven snow, but actually begging for it.

May-Beth's eyes were bright, her cheeks flushed. 'You agree to it, as you promised?'

Kersh lit another cigarette from the smouldering butt, and shrugged. 'Sure. Maybe that way I'll get to fuck you for real.' Curiosity nagged at him. 'Explain it to me. They strap me in the chair, right? They throw the lever . . . and then what?'

'Don't worry about it.' May-Beth smiled. 'I'll pray for you, Frank.'

'Yeah, sure. Whatever. You do that.'

On his way back to the Block, Kersh wondered what the hell had gotten into him to go along with such a crackpot notion. Perhaps he was more scared than he dared admit, even to himself. The prospect of death put all kinds of weird thoughts in your head. Everlasting life all wrapped up in a single second, for instance. Jee-*zuzz*.

3

Phew.

Cawdor sank down into his swivel chair, wiping imaginary sweat from his brow. It coddled his masculine ego, having a woman find him attractive. Yet if he wasn't careful there was a danger he might send out the wrong signals, and what started out as a harmless bit of office flirtation could end in –

Jeff Cawdor sat bolt upright in the chair. The imaginary sweat on his brow all of a sudden popped up for real: that's how long it took for his autonomic system to react and his glands to respond to the shock of seeing a man sitting in the black leather chair across the desk from him. A dark-skinned man with a hollow-cheeked, intelligent face and large brown eyes that were made to appear even larger by the magnifying lenses of his silver-framed spectacles. His long, slender brown hands were clasped loosely in his lap, the collar of his expensively tailored overcoat, which had seen better days, turned up by his pointed ears.

Cawdor blinked, dumbly confused. How come Phyllis hadn't said anything? Warned him he had a visitor? But that wasn't right either, because he knew perfectly well that his secretary would never allow anyone – whatever the circumstances – inside his private office, where there was confidential information; definitely not while he was absent. That's what the visitors' chairs in the outer office were for. Visitors.

While he was staring and pondering, and trying to recover from his shock, the man said with the ghost of a smile, 'Quite a storm we had. Did you enjoy it?'

His voice was cultured, his tone measured, each word enunciated carefully and precisely.

'My name is Cawdor,' Cawdor said. 'And this is my office. Would you mind telling me who you are and what you're doing here?' It crossed his mind to call Phyllis in, ask her how this joker had managed to bypass her desk. Then he remembered she would be on her way down in the elevator, eagerly carrying out a love mission for her lean, rugged hero who existed only in her head.

'I'm Doctor Khuman. How do you do?'

The Indian leant forward, extending his hand. His nails were long, pale ovals, carefully manicured. 'Clearly you weren't expecting me, Mr Cawdor,' he went on, unabashed, when his offer of a handshake went unheeded.

'Clearly I wasn't. Should I have been?'

'I . . . wasn't sure. It isn't possible, in every instance, to predict. I was hoping otherwise.'

Predict? The word made Cawdor wary. Into his mind swam the vision of an Indian mystic promising to foretell his future in return for a fistful of dollars. His tongue snagged against the rough edge of a metal filling that was working loose, making him wince, which served to sharpen his irritation. What was happening to security in this building? There were guards on duty in the lobby downstairs, plus UltraCast's own reception desk, then Phyllis as the final frontier – and this guy waltzes past the bunch of them.

Doctor Khuman said, 'I'm sorry for my unexpected arrival, but there was no other way. I can see from your expression that you are angry at this sudden intrusion.'

'Not yet I'm not, but give me a couple of minutes. D'you ever hear of making an appointment? Or using the phone, maybe?' Cawdor waved his hand over the cluttered desk. 'Look, Doctor Khuman –' (And what kind of doctor was he, anyway? Psychiatry? Divinity? Flying Saucers?) '– I really am very busy, as you can see. If it's a medical charity or some religious cause, I suggest you write to us stating your business and I'll see how we can help. I have deadlines to meet, so I'd appreciate it if –'

'There isn't time for that, my friend.' The Indian was leaning forward, his thin elegant hands pressed together. He closed his eyes for a moment, two vertical lines creasing his forehead, as if concentrating hard. Silence hung over the faintly humming computer terminal.

He said, 'This is difficult for you, Mr Cawdor, I appreciate that, but even more difficult for me to explain. How can I put this? There is some kind of disruption about to take place, though I sense it only imperfectly. You might call it a dysfunctional element in the flow of events, cause and effect at odds with one another –'

'What are you telling me, that the end of the world is nigh?' Cawdor interrupted. 'I've heard all that before.'

Doctor Khuman's smile was strained. 'I knew this wouldn't be easy,' he murmured, half to himself. He sighed. 'But I had hoped you would be prepared for my visit, you see.'

'No, I don't see. And I really don't have time for this. I've tried to be polite, but you just barge in here and upset my work schedule . . .' He frowned, genuinely perplexed. 'Just how *did* you get in, right past my secretary? No way she couldn't have seen you.'

Magnified by his silver-framed spectacles, the Indian's eyes gleamed large and brown. 'Oh, she did see me, of course, but then she became distracted. Her mind seemed to be elsewhere. In fact, so I believe, she was thinking of you. That seemed to be the general course of her thoughts.'

'If you can read Phyllis's mind, maybe you can read mine also.'

Despite his flippancy, Jeff Cawdor felt his heartbeat quicken. Unsettling that a total stranger should have picked up on the 'secret' shared only between himself and Phyllis; more than that, it was uncanny. He felt as if his innermost private domain had been invaded. Before he could check them, his thoughts took off on their own, raising such demons as blackmail, extortion, threats to his personal wellbeing and that of his family. Doctor Khuman, in actual appearance, didn't embody the image of a blood-chilling spectre or the psychopathic axe murderer who casually walks in off the street, for example – but in the real world people didn't always conform to the popular myths of Hollywood type-casting.

He voiced what was uppermost in his mind. 'Have you come here to issue threats or to warn me about something?'

'It wasn't my intention to do either. You see, strange as it may seem –' Doctor Khuman gave a slight shrug of his narrow shoulders '– it's you, Mr Cawdor, who possesses the real insight into what I fear is a potential disruption. And in your hands alone lies the power to change it.'

Cawdor said testily, 'Change what? How can I do that when I don't understand what you're talking about? If I had this "insight" you've granted me, then presumably I'd know what it is I'm supposed to change. I don't, on both counts.' He got up. 'Seems you picked the wrong guy, doc.

Thanks for the visit. You can find your own way to the elevator. Good morning.' He looked at his watch. 'Or good afternoon – whatever.'

The Indian remained seated. Even now, and in spite of the annoyance he felt, Cawdor had to admire his composure. If in actual fact the man was some kind of faker, or charlatan, he'd perfected it to a fine art. There was a quiet, dignified seriousness about him, a complete lack of melodramatic flourish, that made Cawdor almost accept him as genuine. Almost, but not quite.

'Are you by any chance planning a trip abroad?'

Cawdor stared at him. Again, the sudden quickening of the heart. He resisted the urge to curl his fists, letting his hands hang loosely by his sides.

'As a matter of fact, yes, I am. So what?'

'With your family?'

'Yes –' Cawdor checked himself. 'How do you know I'm married?'

Doctor Khuman stroked his pointed chin, frowning. 'I can't be certain, but there is something about your forthcoming trip that disturbs me.'

What's the pitch now? Cawdor wondered. Travel insurance? 'Listen to me for a second,' he said, the testiness creeping back. 'In place of all these vague hints about "disruptions" and "insights" and how disturbed you are about my welfare, why don't you spit it out in words of one syllable? Then maybe I could extract an ounce of sense from all this. If you're not peddling travel insurance, what *are* you trying to sell me?' He grimaced as the rough filling found the tender spot again, right on the money.

Doctor Khuman had risen slowly to his feet. He said in his gentle, educated voice, 'If I were a salesman, Mr Cawdor, I doubt very much I'd last out the week, do you? You've bought nothing from me, and you believe nothing I've told you.' He spread his hands, sighing. 'I do wish, truly, I could be more explicit. But, you see, I don't know the precise details and exact circumstances. The beliefs that give rise to these feelings, this sense of foreboding, are of a general philosophical nature, not hard scientific prediction.'

26

'What beliefs are those?'

'The Tantric tradition of the Buddhist faith.'

Cawdor suddenly relaxed. He almost chuckled, the relief was so tangible. He hadn't been too far wide of the mark, he reflected, when the notion of the Indian mystic looking for a hand-out had popped into his mind. Except that Doctor Khuman didn't appear to be the panhandling type of religious zealot. Maybe he was genuine after all – a disciple of Buddhism, as he said – though that didn't help Cawdor any. What he knew about Buddhism could be written in large block capitals on one side of a postcard. He recalled vaguely that they believed in reincarnation. You died and came back as a higher or lower order of being, depending on how well or badly you'd lived your life. Or something like that.

'Look, I respect your personal beliefs, OK? You came here with the best of intentions, fine. Can I save us both some time, and say, Have a nice day and don't get run over in traffic?'

Doctor Khuman bowed slightly. 'I'm very sorry to have disturbed your business routine, Mr Cawdor.' At the door he turned and said, 'One last thing. Have you broken a mirror recently?'

In the distance, a rumble of thunder reverberated faintly as the storm moved over New Jersey.

'No, so I'm not anticipating seven years' bad luck.'

When Doctor Khuman had departed, Cawdor stood at the window and stared out at the city. It looked no different from how it had looked thirty minutes ago, except that now the dark clouds had gone and the buildings and streets were bathed in bright sunshine, like a gigantic stage set under the glare of arc lamps.

Nothing had changed; everything was reassuringly the same, or so it seemed.

Baking heat blasting off concrete: the cars in the parking lot of the Louisiana State Penitentiary shivered as in a mirage as May-Beth came through the gate in the chain-link fence. The prison was built on a concrete raft in an area of cleared scrub. Beyond this, the ground became a thin dried crust, liquid mud underneath, with gnarled trees, creepers and decaying vegetation forming a dense, steamy, impenetrable barrier.

Any prisoner unlucky enough to be lost out there had several hundred square miles of alligators and snakes to worry about – a prospect that made escape hardly more appealing than the dead man's walk to the chair.

May-Beth's distorted reflection rippled along the torpedo-shaped length of the silver trailer, its small portholes of smoked-blue glass like the blank stare of a blind man. Sagging on its axles, the trailer was at least thirty years old, and patchworked with the corners of posters long since ripped off, a few faded strips hanging down, yellowed and stiff. May-Beth reached for the tarnished handle, but before she could grasp it the handle turned and the door swung open on creaking hinges.

Inside, after the dazzling glare, it was black as the tomb, and stifling hot. May-Beth slid on to the bench seat, feeling her way, and heard the door click shut. After a moment or two she was able to make out the thin, erect shape directly opposite. Pale-faced, and in spite of the heat clad in stiff black suit and straight-brimmed hat, the man she knew only as Preacher sat with long fingers splayed on bony knees, the folds of material draped from his skinny flanks dusty and worn with age. May-Beth shivered. Whenever he gazed at her with those fathomless dark eyes set in bony sockets, she had the feeling of soft fingers exploring her mind, delving into her thoughts. She suddenly flushed hot, alarmed and mortified that he might be aware of what Frank Kersh had made her do. But he gave no sign: an absence of expression on the gaunt, lined face.

The trailer was moving. May-Beth glanced outside. Through the blue-tinted windows the landscape looked strangely dark, as if underwater, the twisted trees like fantastic growths on the sea bed.

'You seem agitated, my child. Did he insult you in some manner, by word or deed?'

28

May-Beth avoided Preacher's eyes. 'No, not at all – nothing happened,' she said rather too quickly, wishing the blood would leave her cheeks. 'I asked him, like you said, about that boy he killed – if he was sorry for what he'd done. He said no, he wasn't, and never would be. I guess he's accepted it, the fact he's going to die nine days from now. All the appeals have run out.'

'He may die,' Preacher said, 'but some part of him, a tiny fragment, will continue to exist.' He seemed deadly serious. 'If you were able to convince him of the truth of our message.' His eyes bored into her. 'Did you convince him, May-Beth? Did he believe you?'

'I guess so,' May-Beth said evasively.

'And he doesn't repent!'

May-Beth glanced at him then, such was the throaty fervour in his voice. She sensed that he was trembling inside the stiff black suit and the plain white shirt, tieless, buttoned up to the neck. Yet not a tremor passed over his face.

She said hesitantly, 'I just wish I could understand why this man's soul is so important to you –'

'Not to me, child. To the Messengers.'

'I mean, to the Messengers.'

'Should we abandon him, because he has sinned? This man Kersh is a challenge to our faith. He has a mind, devious and cunning, one that dwells in its own psychopathic universe.' He released a thin sigh. 'I could explain it, but these matters are beyond someone of your limited intellect.'

May-Beth's shoulders went back. 'Now that I've done what you wanted, got him to agree, I'm stupid, is that it?' Her lower lip jutted out. 'I may be stupid – I wasn't educated in a proper fashion – but I ain't dumb enough to believe you can save him from the chair in the last second. That's what you told me to say, so I did. Maybe Frank believed it, but I don't buy it. When they throw that lever and pump in the juice, that's him gone. Finito. There ain't time for him to spit.'

She drew breath, astounded at herself. There was a long timeless moment when nothing happened, except the silver trailer continued along the strip of concrete road that ran straight through the swamps. On either side scummy green pools bubbled and belched. Curtains of creeper hung down like witches' hair. In the shallows, on the verge of the road, an arrow of ripples disturbed the surface as a scaly creature glided through the reeds, searching for dinner.

Stating it quietly, as a fact, Preacher said, 'One second, my dear, can be a very long time. Longer than a human lifetime – but it all depends on the particular second.' His eyes narrowed upon her. 'Do you believe this is the only life you have?'

'You mean another life, in the hereafter?' May-Beth wasn't sure she did believe that. She wanted to and, brought up as a Baptist, that's what they'd preached at her since she was old enough to comprehend. Trouble was, she couldn't remotely imagine what such a place would be like. Certainly not angels with harps and God with a long white beard reclining on a fluffy pink cloud. She rejected that childish vision, of course, but could find nothing to put in its place. Common sense battled with blind faith and defeated it every time. No contest.

Preacher inclined his lean body towards her, and again she felt those soft fingers worming into her mind. 'I speak not of the hereafter, but of the herenow. I mean *another life* lived in the here and now. You have yearned for such a thing, May-Beth, desired it in your innermost secret dreams.'

Well, yes, she couldn't deny it. Wasn't everybody the same? Everybody daydreamed of living a life that was more exciting, more glamorous, more intensely felt. It was the human condition to imagine a fantasy world in which mundane reality was pushed aside and secret desires fulfilled. The fact that she'd been born, grown up and lived her entire short life in the small town of Dubach, forty miles away, was an even more compelling reason. Most of the folk from around here never left the state. Employment locally was with the cattle ranches, or they could head further south to the bayou and find work on the shrimpers or the alligator farms. As for girls her age,

May-Beth thought bitterly, ambition wasn't encouraged. Find a fella, marry and settle down, raise a family. The stuff she saw on TV, in the magazines she read, about a legion of strong liberated women forging ahead in a man's world might have been happening on another planet. Sure, she dreamt of what it would be like, wished she could be one of them, but what use was dreaming and wishing when all the chips were stacked against her? Backwoods-educated, no college degree, no special skills or hidden talents, plain of face and round of form; the only thing she possessed was the honesty to admit that such an uninspiring package would take her exactly nowhere – except into a dead-end marriage with a houseful of kids, a thirty-year mortgage and varicose veins.

The unconscious recognition of this grim fate – and an obscure need to rebel against it – had perhaps led May-Beth to feel drawn to the Messengers when they showed up in Dubach the previous summer. They had arrived from somewhere up north in the ancient silver trailer and taken over a derelict chapel with a rusting corrugated-iron roof on Frog Wash Road, about two miles out of town. A closed, secretive sect, they didn't actively seek converts, and it was only by word of mouth that their presence became known. Rumours started to circulate that the Messengers had charismatic healing powers. They didn't hold services nor even have regular meetings. Neither did they solicit donations, and were rarely seen in town except once or twice a month laying in provisions. Along with the rumours, it was this air of mystery surrounding them that had first sparked May-Beth's curiosity. Not that she needed physical healing, but she did feel an emptiness in her life, a kind of aimless despair at having nothing on the horizon to look forward to, and worse still – that this was the best it was ever going to get.

The Messengers hadn't transformed her life (nothing so dramatic) but they had given her the precious possibility of hope. Ever since the evening in late summer last year when she persuaded her old schoolfriend Cheramie to take a ride with her out to Frog Wash Road, May-Beth had felt the – for her – unusual tingle of optimism. A few local people attended gatherings at the chapel, and pretty soon she started turning up on a regular basis, though without Cheramie, who soon lost interest when she met a boy from Farmerville with sideburns and a Mustang GT convertible.

It was Preacher himself, the leader of the sect, who asked if she was willing to visit the state prison. In agreeing, May-Beth had assumed the purpose to be a mixture of providing social comforts and spiritual solace to the inmate population. She assumed wrong. Preacher had in mind only one inmate, whose time on death row was ticking away rapidly towards zero. And why Frank Kersh in particular? To May-Beth he seemed not much different from the other convicted killers she had seen during her visits. Just as puzzling to her was Preacher's insistent, indeed obsessive, demand that Kersh understood that 'in the final second lay his salvation', as Preacher phrased it. She had obeyed, done as he asked, but that didn't make her any the wiser or convert her scepticism into belief.

In the same way, she found herself struggling to understand what he meant by the 'herenow'. Maybe Preacher was right after all. Maybe she was just too plain dumb to grasp his meaning.

'I can promise you another life, May-Beth, the one you secretly desire, if you will come with us on the journey. What is it you yearn for? Beauty? Fame? Power? Sexual conquest? All these can be yours if you believe in the power of our message. Come with us and you will reap your reward, I promise you.'

'Come with you – where?' May-Beth blinked at him in the torpid gloom of the trailer, feeling stupid again.

'Into the mind of Frank Kersh.'

'Nobody can do that, enter another person's mind,' May-Beth said, and then recalled with a shiver the creeping sensation she had of fingers inside her own mind whenever Preacher laid his flat, cold gaze upon her. But that was simply her imagination acting up, wasn't it? Huh?

'The power of belief is everything,' he told her. 'Without

it, nothing is possible. Are you really so content with your life, May-Beth? No desire to change it for another? When there are so many futures to choose from, an infinite number of possibilities. A great shame that your future is already decided and mapped out because belief lies stillborn inside you.'

May-Beth felt the urge to cry out that he was wrong – she *did* want to change her life. She *didn't* want to settle for a drab future already laid out before her in all its dreary, small-town detail. Preacher held out the tantalising promise of a wonderful world in which all her dreams would come true, but the worm of doubt, of unbelief, prevented her from grasping it.

Almost whispering it, she said, 'Make me believe, Preacher. I do so want to.'

The straight-brimmed hat tilted forward, masking his eyes, as he looked down. May-Beth looked down too. On the floor between them lay a canvas sack she hadn't noticed till now, tied at the neck with a drawstring. Preacher reached down, jerked loose the tie, and the mouth of the sack gaped wide. There was blackness inside and, though May-Beth couldn't be sure, she thought she saw the sack move, as if something heavy was slowly stirring within, uncoiling itself.

She sat perfectly still, her mouth dry as sandpaper.

'If you truly want to believe –' Preacher's voice floated towards her as from a great distance '– prove it by putting your hand inside.'

May-Beth stared into the black mouth of the sack. Fear like an icy claw clutched at her heart, squeezing it dry. Was her fear stronger than her desire to believe? It was a test of her faith and willpower, she knew that; of whether she was prepared to accept with her whole heart the creed of the Messengers as the one and only truth.

A simple enough act, really, May-Beth told herself, to put her hand into an empty sack. No harm would befall her – no possible harm, because the Messengers would never gain a single convert to the faith if the act of conversion was of itself fatal.

She put her hand inside.

And something did move. This time May-Beth was certain. The information flashed to her brain. Her brain flashed a message to her hand. But, before her hand could react, it seemed to May-Beth that an aeon elapsed, as if time had frozen in a single instant.

She saw everything with stark clarity.

The passing swampland, gloomy and ghostly through the tinted glass.

The darkened interior with the erect, motionless figure sitting opposite, silent and watchful.

Her own bare arm inside the gaping mouth of the sack.

Biting back a scream, she yanked her arm out. But not quick enough. Two pearls of blood seeped from the puncture marks on the back of her hand. May-Beth stared at them, her throat closing tight with panic. Her body started to twitch and jerk in spasm. Then she was shaking uncontrollably from head to foot. She tried to say something, but her mouth was filled with foam. She went stiff and felt a creeping numbness in her limbs.

The sack had ceased to move, lay blackly gaping on the floor of the trailer. Preacher reached inside and brought out a heavy coil of thick rope. He held it up for her to see. May-Beth fell back limply on the bench seat. She looked at her hand, which was smooth and unmarked, without a drop of blood. Then she glanced quickly at the man facing her, the dark flat eyes set in bony sockets beneath the straight brim of his hat.

His lips moved.

'Do you now believe, my child?' she heard him say, his voice a million miles away.

May-Beth nodded.

The silver trailer moved on along the concrete strip of road that went straight as an arrow into the distance, the scummy green pools on either side belching softly in the heat of the afternoon.

34

Jeff Cawdor took a gulp of sparkling white wine and lay back, eyes closed, against the cushions. Curled up in an armchair, where she was reading a tourist guide to Tuscany, Sarah looked at him over her glasses.

'The Uffizi Gallery. Remember, Jeff?'

He nodded.

'Florence was wonderful,' Sarah mused with a faraway smile. 'I hope Daniella will like it.'

'She'll love the food. Those pizzas in the Via Porta Rossa that melted in the mouth. We ate them in that little courtyard with the roses climbing the trellis, shading off the sun . . .'

'I knew it all along. You're a romantic at heart.' He could hear the smile in her voice. 'You bought a print from a street-seller, remember? The ugly-looking old guy in a red robe, a pope or something, with a huge bent nose done in profile.'

'Was that the print or the street-seller?'

Sarah giggled. 'We had it pinned up in the upstairs hallway for a while. A Michelangelo, wasn't it?'

'Piero della Francesca. It wasn't a pope, it was the Duke of Urbino. You threw it out? I liked that old guy.'

'I took it down years ago, along with your Elvis posters. They're probably all rolled up in the basement somewhere.'

'So that's what happened to them.'

'You can't remain a teenager the rest of your life, Jeff,' Sarah admonished him, peering over her glasses. 'Not when you have a daughter coming on seventeen.'

Eyes closed, Cawdor said wistfully, 'Reminds me of something John Lennon once said: "Elvis died when he went into the army." '

'Smartest career move Elvis ever made.'

'Going in the army?'

'No, dying.'

'That's cruel,' Cawdor said.

'Sure it is. But true.'

Sarah was teasing him, he knew that, but both of them enjoyed it. Stretched out on the couch, he rested the hand clasping the wine glass on his stomach. It sank in an inch or so. He was reminded of what he'd said to Phyllis at the office, one day last week, about needing to lose a few pounds. Damn right he did. He used to jog every morning before leaving for work until he started getting a numbed feeling in his right thigh – trapped nerve or something – and gave it up. These days he did a few laps of the pool in the basement gym of the Chrysler Building, but not enough to constitute a proper exercise regime. Get a grip, he told himself. Thirty-eight is just the right age to start turning into a slob. What really piqued him, however, was that Sarah, without jogging, swimming or any other form of regular workout, never seemed to have a problem with her weight or shape. She wasn't as skinny as those catwalk models, thank goodness, with their needle-sharp shoulders and flat chests and thin legs, but somehow or other she still managed to stay slender and firm in all the right places.

He sipped his wine. The dryness on his tongue reminded him of when he'd been daydreaming about Italy a week or so ago – the day of the storm, standing at his office window. He knew what his mind was hinting at, in which direction it was slyly nudging him. That's how minds worked – ambushing you when you least expected it.

It was the appearance of Doctor Khuman. Of course.

Not that Cawdor had consciously resisted thinking about that strange meeting, but he hadn't positively opened himself to any speculation about it either. And he hadn't mentioned it to Sarah. That was a little odd in itself, because usually they shared their daily round of events, trivial or otherwise. So what the hell, Cawdor pondered, was it all about? Just a crank, then, this Doctor Khuman, a religious nut who happened to wander in off the street? Funnily enough, no; Cawdor found he couldn't dismiss the Indian so easily. The thing that stuck with him, that he couldn't shake, was that Doctor Khuman seemed to want answers from *him* – as if he expected Cawdor to know what he was talking about. What was it he'd said? Something about him possessing insight into a disruptive influence and having the power to change it . . .

And he recalled what his reply had been. Change *what*?

Jeff Cawdor thought of himself as a fairly intelligent, rational guy. He didn't have any strong religious convictions, and his views on premonitions, psychic phenomena, and the whole ragbag of what could loosely be described as 'the occult' were, to say the least, sceptical. The mystery was why Doctor Khuman had touched a raw nerve somewhere. And he had. The fact that Cawdor had been skirting around the subject, never confronting it directly, proved it. Was he scared to? No, he decided, it wasn't fear outright, not of the wet-palms, stomach-churning variety anyway; yet he had to confess to a vague apprehensiveness. A general feeling of unease . . . as if something was wrong, something he ought to know about, and didn't. But what was it, for heaven's sake?

The sound of the TV made him open his eyes. Sarah had switched on the late newscast. It was a regional cable station that covered both national and local news.

'. . . and, with no last-minute pleas for clemency having been received, the sentence is due to be carried out at midnight,' the florid-faced, bow-tied newscaster was saying. 'The execution of Frank Kersh, convicted six years ago of the murder of an emotionally challenged fifteen-year-old boy, will be the fourth this year at the Angola State Penitentiary, Louisiana, bringing the total nation-wide to forty-three. And now some local stories. Students at a school in Somerville, New Jersey, were alarmed to discover a six-foot boa constrictor hiding in . . .'

Cawdor swung his feet down and finished off the wine. 'That's it, honey, I'm turning in. Do you have a broadcast tomorrow?'

Sarah raised one eyebrow at him over her glasses. 'Since tomorrow happens to be Wednesday, what's your guess?'

'My guess would be yes.'

Sarah worked from home, writing feature articles for magazines and national press syndication. Three evenings a week she hosted a phone-in radio programme for WCTC

New Brunswick, dealing with all manner of emotional crises and rocky relationships. Cawdor liked to kid her that she was becoming something of a media celebrity, which happened to be not so much kidding as actually true.

In passing, he touched her hair and she reached up and squeezed his hand. 'Won't be long,' Sarah said. 'I won't disturb you.'

'Feel free.'

Upstairs, he changed into pyjama bottoms and went into the bathroom. He preferred taking a shower at night rather than in the morning – it helped relax him for sleep – but tonight he was too tired to bother, and also a little woozy from the bottle of Frizzante at dinner, most of which he'd drunk. He brushed his teeth and rinsed his mouth. The loose filling had been replaced: it felt smooth and solid. He picked up his shaving mirror in its swivel stand, intending to use the magnifying face to inspect the tooth in question, but as he spun the mirror over, his hands still wet, it slipped out of his grasp. The mirror hit the tiled floor, breaking free of the silvered metal rim and shattering in a burst of glittering fragments.

Earlier that evening, a few minutes after ten o'clock, the barber had shaved his temples and a three-inch strip round his lower calves. Kersh drank two cups of black coffee and smoked a cigarette. The execution was set for two minutes past midnight. At eleven-thirty the warden appeared, escorted by Senior Guard Meacham and three guards with restraint harness, should it be needed.

The Block was silent as Kersh was led away. Twenty-six pairs of eyes watched him go. He didn't mind them seeing his shaven temples, but he felt ashamed, whether they knew it or not, at having to wear diapers. The worst indignity was having the guards examine the sticky-tape tabs to check they were secure before he was allowed to pull up his blue work pants.

Coming into the main corridor of F Cellhouse, the warden turned to the left. The chamber was one floor down, at ground level. Kersh tried to feel some emotion, but nothing came. He wondered if they'd drugged his coffee. Guys were supposed to scream, go berserk, so he had heard. But this was a quiet, dead-of-night walk. He looked straight ahead, noting the shiny patch of scalp through the warden's thinning hair. Meacham and the other guards herded him in close.

In single file the party went down the stairwell. On the steel rail the paint had been worn down to the bare metal by years of sliding hands. They passed through a cinder-block passage into a small windowless room with a buzzing fluorescent light. An electric fan on the wall wafted the sluggish air. Two men rose as they came in. One was short and plump, neatly dressed in a dark suit, with horn-rimmed spectacles and a professionally composed face. He was holding a black bag. The other man, tall and lean in a faded black suit, looked to Kersh like a priest. Though Kersh hadn't asked for one, he assumed it was standard procedure. They had a doctor, so why not a priest?

Meacham opened a further door, which had a porthole of thick glass set in it. Kersh looked through into the chamber. Floor, walls and ceiling lined with cork. The chair, stoutly constructed of wood, was fastened to the floor with metal plates. Rubber seat cushion and backrest. Rubber mat behind the chair, another one in front, for the prisoner's feet. Leather-covered clamps on pivots were fixed to the arms of the chair and there were two further clamps at ankle height.

The warden put on his glasses and took a document from his inside pocket. He glanced up at the clock. 11:43.

They stood in a silent group for two minutes. The doctor stared at his shoes. The priest stood with eyes closed, hands clasped together on his chest. When the finger jerked to 11:45 the warden unfolded the document, pushed his glasses firmly on to his nose, and cleared his throat.

'I now charge that you, Frank Rudolph Kersh, having been tried and found guilty of murder in the first degree, shall suffer the due penalty as prescribed by the Penal Code of the State of Louisiana, namely death by electrocution. I,

Jesse D Taverner, warden of the State Penitentiary, am hereby empowered by the office vested in me to authorise the prosecution of the law to the person above named.'

He put the document away and took off his glasses.

'Have you any last request, Frank, before sentence is carried out?'

Kersh brushed back his thinning hair. Something felt wrong. He realised it was his shaven temples. 'Cheeseburger and fries to go. Pile on the onions, easy on the relish.'

The warden made a small weary gesture and turned away. Two guards held Kersh by the elbows, guiding him through. Meacham waited by the chair, his arms folded. For a moment Kersh stood there, feeling foolish, not sure what was expected of him. He became aware of the priest standing by his side.

'Would you like us to pray together, my son?'

Kersh looked up at the tall, gaunt figure. He tried a shrug. 'Sure. Go ahead if it'll make you feel any better.'

He didn't make the connection right off. Then he did. Sure – all that mumbo jumbo May-Beth had fed him about the Messengers. This guy was one of them, maybe even the head honcho. Was this what they were offering, their Big Deal, just saying a few lousy prayers to spin out his final minutes? His daddy had done nothing *but* pray, and look where it had got him. Kersh blinked hard. Damned if he was going to start praying now, whatever he'd told May-Beth. Whatever he'd promised her in return for getting his rocks off.

Yeah, that's what they'd like to see all right.

Frank Kersh on his knees, sobbing his heart out, shit scared, begging their two-bit forgiveness.

But he wouldn't give them the satisfaction. He'd go like a real man, like Sly or Bruce or Arnie. Afterward they'd say, with awed respect, 'Never batted an eyelid. Nerves of steel, that guy. Terrific guts.'

'Is your soul at peace, my son?'

Kersh looked up into the priest's lined face. His milky eye flickered. He drew breath and held it. He'd been about to say, 'My soul is my business,' but the words wouldn't come. Because he'd been expecting to see bleeding-heart compassion, a glow of gentle forgiveness; and instead he was chilled to the marrow of his bones.

'You believe in life eternal. You do believe.'

The eyes of the priest, set deep beneath bony brows, bored into him. Flat, grey, cold. The face austere, masklike.

Kersh started to shake. He mumbled, 'If I pray, Father, will I be saved?'

'Of course, my son.' The priest gripped his shoulders. 'Even those who pray in the very last moment will be saved. And in your heart you know it.'

Eyes boring into him, hands holding him in a grip of iron.

That's true, Kersh thought. One second can be a very long time. Longer than a human lifetime. Infinite. The words floated through his mind; they seemed utterly convincing, and he believed them.

Meacham shifted his weight. 'Father, excuse me. But we have to get on with this. The utility company schedule the surge for two minutes past midnight. If you don't mind . . .'

The priest's hands pressing down on his shoulders, Kersh knelt before him. He felt strong bony fingers gripping his head, digging into the flesh of his scalp until it was pulled taut.

Kersh bowed his head. And prayed.

When the priest and the warden had left the chamber, Meacham and the guards secured Kersh in the chair, pivoting the clamps and tightening the leather straps over his forearms and shins. The doctor then applied a film of K-Y jelly to Kersh's temples and lower calves and fitted the electrodes.

The doctor stood up, wiping his hands on a tissue. He hoped to God the electrodes wouldn't fall off or burn out. That had happened before. He'd seen flames erupt from a man's head. Sparks blasting out of every orifice. Taken three tries and fifteen minutes to do the job. People wouldn't believe you could pump 2,000 volts through a person and still find a heartbeat. The hell you couldn't.

Meacham was the last to leave. He pulled the heavy door against the rubber seals and pressed the handle home. He went into the observation booth and stood with the others, looking into the chamber through the one-way panel. The lights dimmed to red. Kersh was sideways on to them, head hanging forward slightly. Eyes open.

At one minute to midnight the countdown started.

In the chair, inside the dark-red chamber, Frank Kersh was listening to the only sound he could hear: the thud of his heart. The heavy, thick liquid pumping, pumping. It should have been speeding up, as the ultimate moment approached, but instead each beat was getting slower . . . and still slower.

Something buzzed near his head. A fly hovered and settled on his left hand. Kersh stared at it. If he was going to die, he reasoned, so was the fly. Fried fly. But what if the fly lived?

Thud, went his heart, like a slow, muffled drumbeat.

Kersh watched the fly intently. Shiny metallic blue-black body. Legs splayed out. Feelers rubbing together, like someone fastidiously washing their hands.

Thud. And slower still.

Kersh watched the fly.

At two minutes past midnight the switch was thrown.

Thud.

Cursing his stupid clumsiness, Cawdor knelt down and started to gather up the larger fragments. He frowned, squinting painfully, as myriad dazzling lights seared his eyes, reflected from . . .

Where?

There was only one source of illumination, a single fluorescent strip above the bathroom cabinet. His heart suddenly constricted, as if squeezed in a fist, and his breath seized up in his chest. The fragments in his hands seemed to come alive. They were blazing with an irides-cent rainbow of light and colour and movement.

Cawdor let the pieces fall, or rather they just dropped from his weak, trembling fingers. He shivered, his bare chest chilled with cold sweat. He felt dizzy and faint.

A scimitar-shaped fragment caught his eye, a swirl of images shimmering across its surface, dissolving one into the other and then separating, like several movie films projected simultaneously on to the same screen. He stared, dry-mouthed, and a thought from nowhere flitted through his mind, like a blown scrap of paper down a dark windy street. Behold in this mirror –

Within the scimitar-shaped fragment he saw a sailing ship, moonlight gilding the sails with silver. A man and a boy on deck, the man carrying something heavy and lumpy. A faint splash in the darkness, and then silence –

The image shimmered and dissolved into an exploding flash of white light tinged with crimson. The sheared metal of a gaping hole. An arm in a blue sleeve waving frantically in the searing blast –

And now a face, white, ravaged, leaning back exhausted against some timber planking, the sea rushing and thudding outside. A thin dark figure came down a ladder and stepped into a congealing pool of stinking, scummy water –

The scene dissolved and became a tower block 2,000 storeys high, poking up out of a toxic swamp of industrial waste. At its apex, a glass-roofed penthouse ablaze with light. From the railed balcony a man with thinning fair hair looked down, grinning –

Hunched over, Cawdor gazed numbly at the profusion of images. Each fragment, he now saw – not just the scimitar-shaped one – contained the same fleeting images. Each fragment contained the whole.

Unsteadily, he got to his feet. Swaying, he caught hold of the washbasin and held on grimly, clenching his teeth. The broken images glittered and shifted on the tiled floor, and it was as if the floor itself was moving, and with it the house, the entire world cast adrift from reality. What was happening to him? Had he gone out of his mind? He squeezed his eyes shut tight, hot breath shuddering in his throat. The mirror breaking – he remembered now – it came back to him in a flash what Doctor Khuman had said. Was this what the warning was all about? Had Doctor Khuman known that something like this was about to happen?

Whatever it was, it scared him witless. He daren't even open his eyes in case the floor was pulsating with light and colour and movement. Give it a minute. Get a grip. It's a migraine attack, he told himself: the flashing lights were a classic symptom. He took slow, deep breaths, supporting himself against the washbasin, the cold porcelain comforting and solid under his hand.

'Jeff, what happened? Are you all right?'

Sarah stood in the doorway, her eyes large and worried, one fist curled to her chest. Cawdor allowed his gaze to drift slowly downward to the tiled floor at his feet, to where the shards of glass lay scattered, reflecting the strip of light above the cabinet.

'It's OK,' Cawdor said, breathing deep. 'No panic. I just broke a mirror, that's all.'

Nothing.

Staring at himself in the bathroom mirror, Kersh presses his hand to his chest. No heartbeat. He's somewhere, some*time* between heartbeats. Incredibly – he can't believe his luck – it has all come true, just as the Messengers promised.

And he hasn't even had to sell his soul to the devil.

What is required of him, and for what purpose, he neither knows nor cares. Somehow he's beaten the rap. Better still, he's beaten *the chair*. So where is he now exactly – alive or dead? His last conscious thought had been of that fly on his hand. Thinking, Poor little bastard, you're about to fry. That was it. Fried fly.

He can't see it around anywhere. Must have escaped. That makes two of us, Kersh thinks exultantly.

He comes out of the bathroom, wearing just a black silk bathrobe, his bare feet sinking into the deep pile carpet. Windows surround him on all sides. Above, the glass-domed roof gives a view of the stars. He thinks it would be great to lie back and see a shooting star . . . and, the instant he thinks of it, a bright object arcs across the night sky.

Jesus, he couldn't have wished for a better apartment. It's like a dream come true. Carpeted steps leading down to a central well, with curved bench sofas in white fur. Low tables made of steel, embossed white leather and smoked-blue glass. A central TV, video and hi-fi console that comes up out of the floor when you point the infrared remote at it. On the upper level, a bar with red leather bucket seats on chromium stalks, bottles and glasses and silver shakers glittering under concealed spotlights, reflected in the mirror backdrop.

This is some swell pad. A place like this costs *zillions*. Only the high-rollers can afford it. And he's finally made it. Frank Kersh, all the way from that bug-infested tenement in Brown Harbor, Biloxi, where you can cut the stink with a shovel.

For this, he reckons, they can *have* his soul. And welcome.

Smiling, Kersh strolls across to take in the view. No need for drapes this high up, because there's nothing higher. The window slides silently back and he steps out on to the terrazzo-floored balcony, warm beneath his feet.

The city is spread out below him, a million lights sparkling like diamonds on blue velvet. It's stupendous. It's dizzying. It's the most breathtaking sight he's ever seen in his entire 38 years. The stars above and the lights below fill his universe, horizon to horizon, with dazzling splendour.

Kersh drinks it in. King of all he surveys. He knows, deep down in his heart, that this is everything he ever wanted, and everything he truly deserves. Even before it happened, he knew, positively knew in his bones, that one day it would be his. All that pimping and hustling and scratching around for nickels and dimes was just jerking off. He always knew there was something phoney about it. It just wasn't *him*. Frank Kersh was destined – that was it, fated – to live this kind of life. It was just a matter of time before it happened. A matter of . . .

Time.

Why should that niggle him, like an itch you can't scratch?

He looks at his watch, but he isn't wearing one. Those bastards in the pen took it away from him. There isn't a clock to be seen anywhere. The apartment has everything, Kersh thinks, everything but time. What the hell. Maybe he doesn't need it any more. When you've got all this, who's counting seconds?

He takes a peek over the rail. Down. A long way down. The perspective narrows to an infinite point, deep in the dark canyons of concrete. Too far to see movement, even traffic. But down there, he knows, people are sweating and toiling and scurrying around like ants. Trying to make a buck. Trying to make something work for them. Lifting their snouts now and then to sniff the stratosphere, eyes gleaming with dreams of what it must be like to make it out of the heap, the herd, crawl to the peak of the dunghill . . . and live high up there in a glass penthouse on top of a granite tower.

Many are called, Kersh thinks with gloating satisfaction, but few are chosen. Tough crud, assholes. It isn't that you had it and blew it. You just never had it. And it's terrific. Never know what you missed. Because you ain't gonna get it. Not a sniff. All for me. I've been chosen, so suck on *that*.

Time.

He can't shake off that niggle. It bothers him. It chafes at him. Like something crucially important you've forgotten to do and can't for the life of you remember what it is.

He could use a woman right now. A sweet, warm, accommodating woman.

And there she is (Kersh can hardly believe it), swaying towards him along the balcony. A pale vision swathed in chiffon. Large tearful eyes and quivering lower lip. She's about to ask him something, this drifting vision, and then doesn't. The question hangs on her moist trembling lips. But it never comes. Her eyes are huge, deep, dark, asking the unspoken question.

Kersh leans an elbow on the rail and strokes his chin. He slightly closes his milky eye, both to hide it and as a seductive signal.

'Hi, Sue Ellen.'

'Hello, Frank.'

'You're looking good.'

'Oh, Frank!' she says, clutching her thin white throat.

Kersh straightens up, squaring his shoulders. 'Anything wrong?' he asks with a frown. 'Hey. Come on now.' He draws in his stomach. 'What is all this?'

She gives a convulsive sob.

'What is it, honey? You can tell me.'

'You've always been good to me, Frank. You're the only person I can trust.'

'Sure,' says Kersh easily, grinning.

She comes closer, biting her moist lower lip. She spreads her arms wide, fingers splayed.

'Hold me.'

Kersh pulls her to him, a little roughly, because he knows that's the way classy dames like to be treated. Tough and tender. He breathes in her perfume, a fragrant cloud which makes him desire her, this instant. Right here and now.

But she presses her scarlet-tipped hands to his chest and arches away from him. What's the matter with the broad?

'You a tease or what?' he asks her.

'Oh no, Frank.'

'Come on then. Let's see a little action.'

Maybe this is the wrong thing to say. Maybe he's over-stepped himself, because he feels her stiffen. But her resistance only sharpens his eagerness. He's ready to take her. More than ready.

Kersh rotates his pelvis, watching her face. He loves how these stuck-up types pretend not to know what's going on, yet all the time, underneath that cool, fragile exterior, they're hot as bear-cats, really can't wait to get rutting. It's just that they've got to pretend. They want to be taken by force, overpowered, as if they're bewildered and a little shocked by what's happening. He knows that. He's been around the block a couple of times.

So let her play her little game. He's happy to oblige, knowing the pleasure is going to taste all the sweeter.

'Like something to drink, honey?'

'Uh-huh.' Sue Ellen gazes at him from underneath her

47

lashes. 'Can we go inside, Frank? We're so high up, I get giddy.' She flutters in his arms, glancing down at the million sparkling lights. 'But I'm glad I'm here. I feel safe with you.' She nuzzles her head to his chest. Her whisper is like a sigh. 'Take care of me, Frank. Please.'

Please. Begging for it now.

Kersh intends to take care of her, *damn* sure.

Arm in arm, they step inside. Sue Ellen drifts down to lie on a couch, reclining like a pale-petalled flower with a frail stem, while Kersh goes to the bar. He's so horny it's almost embarrassing, with only the sheer silk robe for concealment. Not to mention a mite uncomfortable.

He mixes the drinks, knowing exactly what she'll like, and takes them down, ice cubes clinking in the tall glasses. They toast each other silently and drink, looking deep into each other's eyes. Expansive and relaxed, Kersh cradles Sue Ellen while he reaches out and thumbs the remote, raising the central TV console, and switches on.

Trumpets ring out. A sombre voice intones, 'Welcome to our satellite and cable subscribers everywhere. May the blessings of the Messengers be upon each and every one of you!'

Oh no. No thanks. Not more of that religious crap. Kersh can't stomach it. He hates to be preached at. These guys just want to take all the fun out of life.

What he'd really like to see, Kersh decides, is a live Elvis special. Beamed in direct from, say, London. Elvis never visited England, but, there again, he oughtn't to have died when he did – and, as Kersh is calling the shots, he didn't.

Kersh switches channels just in time to catch the opening sequence. A spotlight stabs through the darkness and picks out a slim, lithe, young-looking Elvis dressed all in black leather loping on stage. The King curls his lip and flashes his famous leer at the camera. Kersh settles back. With Sue Ellen cuddling close, he dips his hand into the popcorn bowl, curls his lip and leers back at him.

At long last – and about time too – Frank Kersh has it made.

THE VOYAGE OUT

1

The wooden gangplank was scored with deep ruts. Saraheda Cawdor caught the heel of her shoe in one and nearly tripped. The strip of fetid green water below looked uninviting, to say the least. A foul stench rose up from rotted food and other garbage thrown overboard from the ships provisioning in Plymouth harbour. And there were suspicious-looking brown objects floating in it too that she didn't dare examine too closely.

A few yards behind her, Jefferson Cawdor, loaded down with tied and knotted bundles, a leather valise under one arm, a rolled sheaf of architect's drawings under the other, could only look on helplessly.

'Daniel, watch for your mother!' he cried out to his son in alarm.

At the top of the gangplank, the nine-year-old boy turned and held out his hand. His mother grasped it gratefully. Lifting the hem of her coarse broadloom skirt, she unwedged her heel and tottered the final few paces, landing in an ungraceful heap on the deck of the *Salamander*.

Saraheda didn't care for her lost dignity. At least she was safely on board and not in that foul, stinking privy – for that's what it smelt like.

She and her husband piled their possessions in a spare corner. There was hardly a square foot of free space anywhere: bales, barrels, chests, trunks, and all manner of goods and chattels covered the sloping deck. There were wire cages with chickens, and three pigs in a slatted wooden container. From a lower deck she heard the mournful mooing of cows. Were these for the voyage, Saraheda wondered, or as breeding stock in the New World?

'You'd best stay here,' Cawdor said, 'while I go ashore for the rest of it. And keep an eye on my drawings and prints. Without them I'll be back to stonemasonry!' He stood aside for a seaman bent double under a brass-bound chest, and disappeared down the gangplank.

'Daniel, stay close!' Saraheda warned her son, who was already searching round with the gleam of exploration in his eyes. The vessel seemed to her like a helter-skelter madhouse. Men hung high above from ropes. Officers in stiff-collared uniforms shouted and gesticulated from the bridge. Supplies swung overhead on block and tackle. All this clamour and confusion of preparing for a long sea voyage was new and strange: Saraheda had visions of her son vanishing into the wooden bowels of the ship, never to be seen again.

It must surely calm down, she hoped, when they set sail. Three months of this mayhem couldn't be endured.

'Mother, where do we sleep?' Daniel inquired. He had clambered up on a bale for a better look. 'Are there proper beds, with pillows and covers? How do you stop rolling out? All this *stuff*!' he exclaimed, gazing about. 'It's a wonder we don't sink.'

'Please, Daniel. I ask one favour of you. Don't talk of sinking.'

Saraheda made room to sit on a wooden cask, and then changed her mind. The cask stank of pickled herrings. She found another place to sit, fanning herself. 'Your father has told me in great detail about the depths of the vast and mighty Atlantic. Deeper, he says, than the highest mountains. With large fish and all manner of strange creatures. This diverts him. He thinks it wonderful and mysterious. But I do not. And I like even less any chatter about sinking into these depths, wonderful and mysterious though they might be.'

50

'What creatures? With teeth and claws? And a slimy tail?'

Evidently his imagination was as excitable as his father's. They were both, the pair of them, she thought, utter romantics. Jefferson looked upon the voyage to the New World as a great adventure – dismissed the perils, the vast unknown, with a wave of his hand. This was the eighteenth century! The age of discovery! What man alive could fail to be fired by it?

Saraheda liked to attend to more practical matters. She viewed life as a series of obstacles, of snares and traps, that had to be dealt with and overcome, sensibly and pragmatically. But this adventure was of a different magnitude. So far she hadn't had to deal with anything of the size, not to mention the depth, of the Atlantic Ocean.

She said, 'I imagine such creatures would find little boys a tasty tidbit.'

'I'm too big to be little,' Daniel said loftily, with the certainty of nine-year-old logic. He wrestled with an imaginary beast. 'I'd kick its teeth out, throttle it, and swing it round by its tail.'

'Standing on the waves, I expect,' his mother said tartly. 'For you swim, as I recall, like a stone. From top to bottom.'

Daniel scowled at her. She knew that he hated such niggling details to spoil his fantasy.

'See if your father is coming. We must find our quarters and get our things stowed away. I heard someone say we sail on the evening tide.'

Already the sun was quite low in the sky. It had been a glorious August day, with soft breezes pushing white puffs of cloud across a limpid blue sky. Saraheda wondered about the climate of Virginia; she had heard it was as hot as Africa.

Daniel ran to look over the side, which he could just manage by standing on tiptoe. He had to dodge out of the way as two seamen in ragged shirts and grimy breeches charged along the narrow alleyway, lugging heavy coils of rope. One of them swore at him. Daniel knew it was an oath, though he didn't know its meaning.

Just then, a short, stocky, round-shouldered man appeared up the gangway, bowed down with all manner of strange objects – wooden brackets, tripods, iron stanchions, plus a large sack that clinked metallically. He swayed and staggered under his load, face red and wet with perspiration. One of the larger objects – a tubular device three feet long, slung across his back – got jammed between the wooden posts. Daniel, quick to see the man's dilemma, jumped forward, pushed the tube so that it pointed upward, and the man came on in a headlong rush, falling to his knees.

'Phew, what a scrape! Thank you, boy – help me up, I'm done in!'

Back on his feet, the man reverently placed each of the objects on the deck, muttering to himself as he checked them off. He was especially careful with the heavy, clinking sack, treating the contents as if they were finest bone china.

'Holy Saints, nothing broken, I hope and pray. Delicate materials, these, my lad, worth their weight in gold.'

'What are they?' Daniel asked, goggle-eyed.

The man mopped his face and the shiny top of his head with a square of striped cloth, which looked to Saraheda like the remnants of an undergarment. She hid a smile behind her hand. He was younger than she had supposed – his premature baldness had deceived her into thinking him well on in years. Now she saw that he had pale, smooth, cherubic features and large brown eyes, which he blinked slowly and dreamily as he gazed around. Red hair sprouted above his ears and lay in long strands over his collar.

'These, young sir,' he informed Daniel, 'are items of mechanical apparatus for studying the heavens. Some of which are of my own invention,' he added proudly. Delving into the sack, he held up a circular dial made of copper, inscribed with numbers and symbols. 'With this I can compute the velocity and magnitude of the fixed stars, and also predict their courses at any time of year.'

'How many stars are there?' Daniel asked.

'Ah! Now then. How many would you say?'

'Scores and scores.' Daniel tried to think of a sufficiently large number. 'Five hundred or more.'

The man looked smug. 'So far we have observed and catalogued over *seventeen hundred*. And with my telescope here I can observe many hundred more. One day I hope to have a star named after me. Gryble's Star. And to formulate new laws and processes, as my friend and mentor, John Michell.'

'You will find many new stars in the Colonies,' Daniel said. 'All those on the farther side of the Earth.'

Gryble smiled. His face lit up like a full moon.

'Perhaps some,' he conceded. 'But you must remember that the Earth turns upon an axis, so that we view all parts of the heavens available to us in this hemisphere. And furthermore –'

It seemed to Saraheda that Gryble was about to embark on a treatise. She cut in. 'Mr Gryble, sir, we have to find our quarters and stow our belongings. Will you explain these matters to my son, Daniel, at some later time? We have many weeks of shipboard life in front of us, and I imagine many long days to fill. He is much interested, I can see.'

'Holy Saints, madam, I run away with myself. Attend to your mother, boy – Daniel, is it? We'll have ample opportunity for discourse.'

The ship was almost prepared. Already most of the supplies on deck had been taken below. High in the rigging, men were unfurling the vast yardage of canvas sails, which cracked and boomed as the breeze caught them, blotting out the sky.

The *Salamander* began to strain at the leash, every inch of her, it seemed to Saraheda, creaking and groaning like a soul in torment. On the middle deck, where they were shown their cubicle, the noise was so great she thought the walls were about to split and briny water come rushing in.

As they made their belongings secure in various lockers and crannies, she said to her husband reprovingly, 'I thought you said sea-voyaging was a quiet and soothing recreation? What with all this racket, we'll have to stuff our ears in order to sleep!'

'Not once at sea,' said Cawdor, who had sailed twice before, to Ireland. 'When the ship is in her natural element and running free before the wind, she'll quiet down. It's very soothing, I promise. You'll sleep sweetly. Better than with a dose of laudanum.'

She didn't say anything, but privately Saraheda was appalled by their dingy, cramped quarters. She could, quite literally, touch the slanting walls with her arms not fully extended. The bed (so called) was a wooden frame fastened to the floor, with a piece of dirty canvas hooked to each corner. Daniel's was a straw pallet which took up the rest of the floor, and so had to be stowed away when not in use to get the door open. There was no illumination. Candles were not permitted, due to the danger of fire. With the door shut, it was very nearly pitch-dark, suffocatingly airless, and warm as an oven.

And the smell. The smell was like no other stench. Worse than rotting carcasses. Or a pig's boudoir. In fact she tried and failed to identify its several components. A mixture of slaughterhouse and cesspit was her nearest approximation. Within minutes it seemed to have infiltrated every pore, so that she would never be clean again.

That was something else that plagued her. There was nowhere to wash. Not a bucket nor a basin, nor pump for fresh water. Every drop they needed, for drinking and ablutions, Saraheda now stupidly realised, had to be brought aboard and preciously hoarded in casks.

She was thunderstruck by yet another thought: Where in damnation was the privy in this creaking, straining, slanting world?

'Come on,' Cawdor said. 'Let's not miss our leave-taking. We'll not taste the delicate airs and see the green fields of old England ever again in this lifetime.'

He meant it kindly, as a valediction, and was astounded to see his wife burst into tears.

'What's the trouble? Hey, hey, hey – don't weep, woman, we're getting away from the close-minded bigots that persecute us. Aren't you glad?'

'Oh yes,' Saraheda sobbed. 'Oh yes. I am. But it's to the

end of the world we're voyaging, over an ocean filled with slimy monsters, and not a pot between us to piss in!'

Cawdor roared with laughter. He hugged her to him in the cramped, airless cubicle. 'Don't fret, darling wife. They have a place called "the head" for the natural functions. You'll not arrive in the New World with piles and constipation, I promise you.'

He laughed again, and hugged her until she felt her ribs creak, while Daniel shrank into the corner, reddening with embarrassment, wondering about how strange and childish were the actions of grown-up, adult people.

2

They went up on deck and leant against the bulwark, Daniel perched on a coil of rope, watching the jumbled roofs and rising smoky swirl of Plymouth ebb away. It was a soft, balmy evening, the air like velvet, and Saraheda had to clench her fists to check more convulsive sobs.

The last of Old England. From this moment they were exiles. Like others, of different faiths – Catholics, Baptists, the new Methodists – they were fleeing the vehement hatred that had caused houses to be burnt and people to be stoned to death in the streets. Theirs was the Telluric Faith, founded on Stonehenge and Glastonbury, a belief in the pantheistic truths from centuries before organised religion. Before even Christianity. It didn't matter what religion, or what belief you held: providing it was different from the orthodox, that was reason enough, in this golden age of enlightenment, to condemn it and hound it out.

Saraheda had agreed with Jefferson that they must go. Though the tales she had heard of the Colonies were not comforting. Tribes of Red Indian savages, seven feet tall, with hair standing on end, attacked settlements, raiding and pillaging. There was even talk of rebellion by the existing settlers. Not a year ago, in December, a party had boarded a ship in Boston harbour and thrown the entire cargo of Indian tea into the bay. Someone called Patrick Henry, she had heard, had renounced the sovereign rule of

George III over the thirteen colonies, saying he wasn't just a Virginian, but an *American*, and declaring, 'Give me liberty or give me death.'

Now they were leaving for this alien country. Of course they hoped for a better life – Jefferson passionately believed it had to be freer, more tolerant, after what they had endured during the last few years. What he didn't know, and Saraheda was loath to tell him, just at present, was that (by her own reckoning) she was nine weeks pregnant.

Cawdor hoisted Daniel on to his shoulders and encircled his wife in his broad arm. The vessel was turning about, drawn towards the harbour entrance by lines trailing from longboats. The sun struck the sails and suffused them in glowing pink. They billowed out, like the rosy cheeks of a baby.

Saraheda glanced up at her husband. She could tell from the sparkle in his brown eyes beneath the heavy dark brows, from the upward tilt of his jaw, that the scene deeply satisfied him. He was a hard man to read usually, his expression sober and watchful, his emotions held in check. Now, the breeze ruffling the tangle of dark-brown hair that grew thick and ragged on his collar, he was gazing around with rapt intensity as if hoping to retain every last detail. All the passengers were up on deck. At the front half of the ship, marked off by a white line painted across the deck, were the poorer emigrants, travelling steerage. Here were the artisans and clerks and minor officials, plus some religious groups in drab, austere clothing. On the quarterdeck were the quality: gentlemen in coats of blue and scarlet, edged with brocade, wearing silken hose and powdered wigs. Their wives and daughters wore full dresses with delicately flounced lace chokers, and held parasols to shield their white skins from the sun's rays.

Except one woman, standing alone, who wore a shawl of fine black lace thrown casually across her bare shoulders. She didn't look to be of English origin, with her long mane of black hair and tawny complexion. At any rate, she must be of mixed parentage. Apart from her striking brown-skinned appearance, no English woman of her station would dare to be seen in public in such a state of nonchalant disregard for fashion and propriety.

A sharp dig in the ribs brought Cawdor back to his senses.

'You should be more subtle in your ogling,' Saraheda remarked dryly. 'It's a wonder she didn't feel your eyes burning right through her.'

'Looking never did any –' Cawdor began with a boyish grin but, before he could finish, Daniel let out a yell.

'Mr Gryble! Mr Gryble, you're being robbed!'

A grimy-faced urchin of about eight or nine was on his hands and knees, rooting in Gryble's sack. Gryble whirled round from the rail. He made a grab, but by then the boy was up and running, dodging lithely this way and that. With Daniel still on his shoulders, Cawdor stuck out his foot and the boy went arse over tip. Something clattered from his hands and rolled into a drainway.

Daniel leapt down to retrieve it, and as he did so the boy went for him like a wild animal, spitting and snarling and kicking with mud-spattered feet. Daniel went down under the battery. The boy was a ragamuffin, bred and trained in the streets, and it was no contest. Cawdor hauled him off by the scruff. The boy wriggled and jerked like a marionette, letting fly with a string of foul abuse. Then sucked in his cheeks and gobbed in Cawdor's face.

'Throw him over the side!' somebody called out. The passengers nearby were enjoying the commotion. Cawdor was tempted to take the advice. Instead he calmly wiped the spittle away, and then had to veer aside as the boy clawed at him with strangely misshapen hands. The knuckles were bent out of their natural form, jutting whitely, and he had an extra, sixth finger on the outside of each hand, like a withered hook.

'Do you belong to anyone, boy, or are you a foundling?' Cawdor asked.

'Lemme down, lemme down!'

'Not till I get an answer.'

'I shit on yer mother's grave. I piss on yer father's memory. That's yer answer.'

'Give 'im the nine-tails!' somebody shouted furiously. 'Till he's raw. That'll teach 'im a jot of respect for his elders.'

Cawdor turned him upside down and, clamping the struggling boy's ankles firmly in his fist, carried him across to the herring barrel, prised the lid off with his knife, and dropped him in.

'Goddamnation, he'll make the fish smell,' a voice complained.

'And I bet he's pox-ridden,' somebody muttered.

Saraheda was comforting a shaken Daniel, and wiping his bloody nose. Cawdor said, 'Don't coddle him. Next time he'll have to fend for himself.' But he was pleased to see that his son was dry-eyed, and looked more angry than scared. The boy was no namby-pamby weakling. And, at his age, Cawdor doubted whether he himself would have stood much of a chance against the six-fingered ruffian.

The ropes from the longboats were cast free as the ship cleared the harbour. The topsails were now unfurled on the sprit and mizzenmasts, and the *Salamander* surged forward gracefully on the ocean swell. She was a fine ship, of the class known as Dutch East Indiaman, based on the same design as the legendary *Golden Hind* of two centuries ago, though larger and with four decks below instead of two.

With a smile, Cawdor lifted his son up again as the shore receded. He felt in tremendous spirits. A new life in the New World! Freedom from petty corruption and mean-minded bigotry. He was a man with a trade: a mason who'd served his time, with ambitions to become an architect. During the coming months he would apply himself, study his books and work hard to improve his facility at calculations.

The Colonies were virgin territory, ripe for a builder of foresight and daring such as Jefferson Cawdor. Why, he was prepared to take anything on, from a cabin to a cathedral.

Saraheda watched her husband's face, which was broad and ruddy in the sunset. She could tell what he was thinking. Head filled with lofty, vaulting dreams. Eyes fixed on the golden future. While she could only see (and smell) what was under her nose, fret about the privy, and worry about the child forming inside her.

3

They were all three of them, for 75 continuous hours, sick as dogs.

The ship reared and plunged, riding to the top of a foaming crest, then crashing headlong into a deep, glassy-green trough. Then another crest, and another trough –

Foaming crest and crashing trough.

Crest and trough. Crest and trough.

Saraheda felt she had been born, lived her full span, and was about to die in their crazily tilting cubicle. She thought the wall was the floor and the ceiling the door. Not that she minded most of the time. She would have died quite happily. She had never known such torture.

Cawdor insisted that they eat something, to keep up their strength. They forced down watery, lukewarm soup and dry bread, and kept it down for fifteen minutes. Then it joined the seawater sloshing to and fro, ankle deep, in the passageway outside. This was used by everyone the length of the deck for the same purpose.

The privy confirmed all Saraheda's worst fears, and added a few more she hadn't in her wildest imaginings thought of. It was a canvas bucket, suspended on some kind of swivel arrangement, which meant that the contents moved about fairly freely, coming into contact with the person seated upon it. Saraheda employed it twice, and then devised an alternative method when her nerve broke.

On the third day, just after dawn, with the ship pitching and tossing as violently as ever, she struggled weakly out of the cubicle to find the doctor. It was Daniel she was concerned for. During the night he had been ill several times, and then lapsed into semiconsciousness. She was unable to rouse him. Cawdor had tried to feed him soup, but it was impossible.

It took two hours to fetch the doctor. First he had to attend to the passengers in the best berths, nearly all of them prostrate with seasickness, and after that had to be dragged away from the wife of a tobacco merchant who insisted he stay and bathe her brow.

'There's no disease that I can detect. No fever or inflammation,' the doctor said, after examining Daniel, who lay in his parents' bed. 'He's weakened by lack of substantial nutrition, as are many of the others. Keep him warm and as dry as possible. Do you have brandy?' When Cawdor replied that they had, the doctor said, 'Feed him brandy and water on a spoon, every hour or so.'

'Is there nothing more you can give him?' Saraheda asked anxiously.

'I have an extract of opium, but it may be too strong for his constitution.' The doctor, named Chapman, scratched his unshaven chin. His fingernails were rimmed with dirt. He had sad, pouchy eyes and his cheeks were a mosaic of broken veins. He reflected for a moment and then rummaged in his bag.

'Here, try these fennel leaves in a tepid solution. They should prevent the vomiting. But until we hit calmer weather there's nothing to do.'

The three of them were jammed in the lurching space between the bed and the door, Cawdor braced with arms outstretched. Saraheda was clinging to the wooden bedframe.

'And how soon will that be?'

'Tomorrow. The day after. Next week.' Doctor Chapman shrugged. 'This is my third voyage to the Colonies – the previous two being different as chalk and cheese. So far this is about middling.'

Saraheda was aghast. 'You mean it could get *worse*?'

'Oh yes. Quite a deal worse. This is but a heavy swell. Storms are something else. In that event there's nothing to do but bind yourselves to anything immoveable. And if you believe in Him,' the doctor added, with a kind of dour twinkle, 'pray to your Maker.'

'If that happens, we'll all have need of your opium extract,' Cawdor said grimly.

'Jefferson, pay the doctor his fee,' Saraheda said. 'Thank you, sir, for attending to our son.' She had tried to catch the whiff of drink on his breath, and couldn't, and thought that she had misjudged him. From what she knew of doctors, he seemed averagely capable, and certainly willing to do what he could.

'I shall waive the fee,' Doctor Chapman said, fastening his sealskin coat. 'Instead, ma'am, would you be prepared to attend with me, when the time comes, on one of the women in steerage? She is several days off yet – I estimate about a week. I have promised to make the delivery, and I would be glad of assistance from someone of sober disposition.'

Saraheda agreed. They would need every penny of their eleven pounds five shillings in savings. In any case, she had decided that she liked Doctor Chapman, despite his slovenly appearance.

4

Cawdor leant his forearms on the rail of the quarterdeck, breathing in deeply. There was a cool, stiffish breeze blowing, whipping up a few white-caps, but the ship was taking them confidently in her stride. Canvas crackled softly above his head. Timbers creaked in rhythm, as if to a tune of the rolling sea.

Above the spread of sail, Cawdor could see a few faint patches of blue in an otherwise grey sky.

It was a great relief to taste fresh air after the days confined below. He hoped it would blow the reeking stench from his clothing. Sleeping in the cubicle had become almost unbearable.

Daniel was playing with two other children on the deck beneath the rail. They scampered around the hatch in a game of tag. His recovery had been instantaneous: on the first morning of calmer weather he had wolfed down a double ration of mutton, beans, cabbage, cold mashed potato and Gloucester cheese, and drunk two cups of cow's milk laced with brandy. Ten minutes later he was racing along the gangways and climbing ladders. Cawdor had warned him of the parts of the ship to which he was restricted. Their section extended from the quarterdeck to the white line – the area between the quality and officers' decks on one side and the steerage passengers on the other. And of course he had to keep well clear of the rails. The captain wouldn't turn about for drowning boys.

'One of yours down there? Ah yes, I see it now: in the nose and chin. The boy with dark hair.'

'You've got a keen eye,' Cawdor said. By the cut of his coat and breeches, the man appeared to have strayed from the upper deck. But he was dressed carelessly, his neckerchief hanging loosely open, his waistcoat stained, a button missing. Between thirty and forty years of age, Cawdor estimated.

'He looks none the worse for wear following our sport with the elements,' the man remarked. 'Do you take snuff, sir?' He held out a little silver case.

Cawdor didn't. The man inserted a pinch into each nostril. He had no trouble, because his nose dominated his face, bony in the bridge and pendulous at the tip. By contrast, the rest of his features were fine, with friendly, intelligent eyes and a high, noble forehead.

'My name is Tom Paine,' he said, offering his hand. 'A native of Thetford in the county of Norfolk.'

'Jefferson Cawdor of Wells, Somerset.'

'Jefferson! Indeed! You have a famous namesake in the Colonies. Thomas Jefferson, a legislator. He's a leading light in the formation of a congress, objecting to the Tea Act.' He beamed. 'In fact, I hope to meet Mr Jefferson in Philadelphia, where I aim to settle.'

'I have not heard of the gentleman, nor his congress,' Cawdor admitted.

'You will,' Tom Paine said, nodding sagely. 'The government is embarked on a foolish course, with the imposition of duties on our fellow countrymen; while at the same time denying them the machinery of representation. You and me wouldn't stand for it, Mr Cawdor!'

'Are you a politician, Mr Paine?'

'What? Oh no, no . . .' Tom Paine seemed to find this as much insulting as amusing. 'What am I?' he wondered aloud. 'I should say a radical pamphleteer. In other words, a scribbler.'

'What do you scribble?'

'Things that make sense – to me if not to others. Plain common sense, as I see it. Hallo! Our resident wizard of science in pursuit of the secrets of the cosmos, I see . . .'

Daniel and the other children had gathered to watch Gryble, who was fussing around with his tripod and stanchions, setting up some experiment or other. Cawdor didn't have a clue what he was up to. He had heard that Gilbert Gryble was a cosmographer, and he was puzzled as to how the man could study the heavens in daytime from the platform of a heaving ship.

Gryble gave Daniel a piece of apparatus to hold, while he fiddled with something that required delicate alignment. Daniel was proud to be trusted. His face became very sober, and he glanced sternly at his playmates as if to caution them against childish pranks.

'Your boy takes his duties seriously,' Tom Paine observed. 'Perhaps you have there a budding scientist. They call ours the Age of Reason, so m'be he's the coming man. Mind you,' he went on sardonically, 'every age prides itself on its capability for reason. Myself, I don't see much of it. Slavery, barbaric duelling, the torture of dumb animals for pleasure, the practice of medicine by brute ignorance, women treated as unpaid drudges, the fairy tales of religious belief –'

He coughed and shuffled back a pace, as if embarrassed.

'Pardon me, Mr Cawdor, sir. Are you a Christian man, by any chance? I have no wish to offend.'

Cawdor shook his head. 'No. I was baptised a Christian but have since rejected it. My family are of the Telluric Faith, which regards the Earth and its natural wonders as the fountainhead of our belief. They reckon it to be a native English religion, older than Christianity, or so I have been told.'

'So you would regard yourself as a pantheist?'

'Indeed I would,' Cawdor agreed.

The two men stood companionably at the rail, enjoying the brisk sea air, and watching Gilbert Gryble busy himself with his apparatus.

After several moments, Cawdor became aware of a group of figures standing stiff and motionless on the far side of the lower deck. They too were observing Gryble, most intently. All five wore identical dark-grey robes, which hung slackly on their tall, lean frames, the hoods thrown back to show knoblike heads shaven close to the scalp. Behind them lurked a small following of plainly dressed men and women with stony-eyed, unjoyous faces.

A religious order, obviously. Cawdor knew there were various sects on board, though he couldn't put a name to this one.

Without a signal or a word being exchanged, the austere, monkish group of elders moved as one, coming to stand in a silent semicircle, gazing down on Gryble as he crouched over his apparatus. Daniel tugged at Gryble's coat-tails.

'In a minute, boy.'

'But, Mr Gryble –'

'The brass screws on the astrolabe are tarnished to hell. It's this damn salt air. Why didn't I think to grease 'em?'

'Is this infernal contraption of your devising?'

The voice, deep and sombre as a dungeon, seemed to vibrate through the planks of the deck. Gryble started, dropped the handful of screws, and cursed.

'Leave them be!' the voice commanded, as Daniel stooped to collect the scattered screws. Daniel froze.

Gryble had recovered, and was staring up at the gaunt speaker with a mixture of anger and bewilderment. But he kept his composure. 'Excuse me,' he said politely. 'But what business is this of yours? I am a free Englishman, on board one of His Majesty's ships, conducting my own affairs and not harming nor interfering with anyone. May I suggest you do the same?'

'With this contrivance,' the leader said, pointing his finger, 'you are seeking to meddle with forces that the mind of man cannot comprehend.' The finger pointed to the sky. 'It is a mechanical device capable of disrupting the celestial symmetry. And, as such, I instruct you to desist at once.'

'Oh?' Gilbert Gryble said mildly. 'You do? Well there's a nice thing. Hear that, Daniel? I am *instructed*. By what moral right do you instruct me?' he wanted to know. 'Is it *your* heaven and no one else's? Have you been given sole charge of it?'

'Do not add blasphemy to your transgressions.' The leader's voice tolled like a bell, reverberating through the air.

He moved a threatening pace nearer, and the others penned Gryble in. The cosmographer was at least a head shorter, round and plump as against their angular stringiness, and for the first time a shadow of unease passed across his face. The finger pointed down. 'I tell you now, this devious work is against the natural order. It must not, and will not, be allowed.'

'And again I question your right to order me.' Gryble bravely stood his ground. 'You are mistaken, I assure you – this apparatus cannot possibly influence anything beyond itself. See, it is static and inert. For measuring purposes only. No rays or galvanic 'fluence or other harmful emissions –'

'Some knowledge is forever forbidden. It is dangerous for us to know. We interfere with the great beyond at our peril.'

'Balderdash!' Gryble spluttered. 'We are men with brains. We were given brains to make use of them. I am a man of science and it is my profession and calling to carry out investigations.'

The leader folded his arms. From deep inside their bony sockets his eyes bored into Gryble, flat and cold and without pity.

'Then listen and pay heed. You do so at your own risk. You have been given a warning by the Shouters – the first and the last warning we shall give. Very well, ignore it. But, if you do, you must prepare yourself to accept the consequences.'

Gryble flushed and opened his mouth to protest, but the group had gone, again without sign or word passing between them, and disappeared below deck. Daniel held out the screws. Gryble took them mechanically, gnawing at his lip. He came to himself, blinking rapidly, and thanked Daniel with a wavering, uncertain smile.

'Shall I run and fetch some duck's grease, Mr Gryble?'

'Not now, Daniel. I need to – er –' He rubbed the top of his bald head distractedly. 'Yes, that's right, I have to attend to one or two matters. To, er, other . . . pressing details. Yes. You go on and game with your play. I mean play with your game.'

He began to dismantle his apparatus.

'You take my point,' Tom Paine murmured dryly in Cawdor's ear. 'Hardly, would you say, the Age of Reason?'

'Who the devil are those people?' Cawdor said, trembling. Gryble's experiments meant nothing to him, yet he felt himself bursting inside with a great knot of anger. 'They have no earthly right . . .'

'Earthly right, no. Their mandate comes from heaven, or some such mythical place.' Tom Paine shook his head sadly. 'Or so they believe.'

'Gryble ought to complain to the captain. His is the sole authority aboard ship. Not that of the Shouters, whoever they might be.'

'Have you met our master mariner, Mr Cawdor?'

'No. I haven't even clapped eyes on him.'

Tom Paine chuckled. 'I don't believe Captain Vincent would care to intervene, particularly in an affair that involves religion.'

'He's a religious man?'

'Far from it. A vehement atheist, from my brief observation. That's why he steers well clear of any controversy. He's aware that many of the people here – most of them,

66

in fact – hold strong religious views, all divergent. The last thing he wants is to spend three months at sea with a shipload of pious hotheaded fanatics, all at one another's throats. Myself, I have some sympathy for that position.'

'Still, Mr Gryble should not be browbeaten in that fashion,' Cawdor objected earnestly. 'We're off to a land free from bullying, bigotry and persecution, aren't we? That was my supposition.' He scowled. 'Not much of a promising start, I'd say.'

Tom Paine took another pinch of snuff, sucking it in with a sharp implosion up his prodigious nose. 'The New World may be free of such evils, Mr Cawdor, but the *Salamander* exports a full cargo of 'em.'

5

Saraheda and Doctor Chapman crossed the white line and descended to the lower decks. The steerage passengers didn't have cabins, or even cubicles. They were allotted a meagre space on the bare planks and had to defend it. Saraheda was amazed that the ship didn't plunge nose first to the bottom, packed as it was to capacity in the forward sections.

The heat and smell of so many bodies in close proximity was worsened by the smoke of illicit cooking fires. Steerage had its own galley stove, on the middle deck behind the foremast, but the queues were endless; all around, in dim recesses, shadows flickered on blankets strung up on ropes, marking off private kitchens shared by several families.

Squirming through narrow spaces, stooping low under beams, stepping over bodies, Saraheda kept her scarf, sprinkled liberally with rosewater, pressed to her face. Consumption and pneumonia would be rife here, as well as all manner of dread, unknown plagues.

'Here we are, Mrs Cawdor.' Doctor Chapman indicated a dark shape stretched out on a matting of dirty straw. The woman's husband, a narrow-shouldered runt of a man with veined arms, knelt beside her. A girl of about six, indescribably filthy, sat nearby, sulkily sucking her thumb. When she removed it to gaze open-mouthed at Saraheda, the thumb was the cleanest object in sight.

'We need more illumination,' the doctor said, pulling the blanket aside to examine the woman. Her breathing was hoarse and ragged, and she was running with sweat.

'I have just this one small lamp,' the husband bleated, holding up a feeble yellow glow.

'Get more, man. Shape to it. Your wife is near her time.' The husband scuttled off. Doctor Chapman turned to Saraheda. 'See if you can find something for the afterbirth. Any kind of receptacle will do. And, if there's hot water, bring a panful.'

Saraheda gripped the woman's hand. She opened her eyes, cloudy with pain, and Saraheda smiled down at her. 'We'll take good care of you. The doctor is here. You'll soon be fine.'

She went in search of hot water. It was a struggle to get through the gangways, which were piled high with sacks and bundles. Faces peered up at her out of the dimness. Voices whispered and murmured. Somebody was singing in a slurred, drunken drawl. It had all the elements, and atmosphere, of a phantasm. Had she known it would be like this, she would have gladly paid Doctor Chapman his fee twice over not to endure it.

But, now she was here, Saraheda resolved to do her utmost.

Dancing shadows, thrown by a small fire, drew her to a ledge on which bodies lay. There was hardly room to sit up, let alone stand. A blackened cooking pot hung over the flames. Steam drifted up.

'Pardon me.' Saraheda shook the shadowy reclining form. 'I have need of hot water for a woman in labour. Is it possible that you could spare –'

Awakening from a heavy slumber, the man grunted and cleared phlegm from his throat, then shifted his weight and let out a rasping fart.

Saraheda raised her scarf to her face.

'Warrisit? What d'yer want?' He sounded to be in a

stupor. He heaved himself up, wiping spittle from his lips. His bleary eyes focused on the woman. 'Warrisit you want? Eh? Holy Mary, you're a fetching piece of stuff. Come for a poke?'

'She wants hot water, Franklin,' a young voice said. 'Strike a bargain with 'er. You might get a poke in return.'

From behind the man's shoulder there came a cackle of laughter, and Saraheda glimpsed the boy who had attacked Daniel, mouth split wide in a grin of yellow, carious teeth.

'Climb up, sweetheart,' the man grunted, 'and join the happy circle. Edge over, Six-Fingered Sam, m'lad, give the lady room.'

He smiled lazily over his shoulder at the boy. Then suddenly his hand shot out and fastened on Saraheda's wrist. He pulled her towards him roughly, at the same time thrusting his face forward, eyes bloodshot, his breath a cloud of hot, foul gas. Wet lips slobbered against her cheek.

'Climb up and I'll give you a big, hard keepsake. Here, feel it, honey-cup. Got a nice warm purse to put it in?'

'Let go of me, please.' Saraheda's wrist was chafed by the man's rough palm.

'Don't believe I will.' His other hand plucked the scarf aside. His eyes grew large and round. One of them was dead and glassy, with a layer of skin over it. He licked his lips greedily. 'I spy a couple of grand turnips down there – God's teeth, this is a strapping woman, Sam, m'lad. Fit as a butcher's dog.'

Saraheda raised her eyebrows. 'You'd like to be thrilled?'

'Yus, if you please, ma'am!'

The man yowled as Saraheda slid the long hat pin from the tail of her scarf and stuck it straight into his arm. His skull hitting the bulkhead was like the hollow bong of a church bell. Six-Fingered Sam shrieked and giggled. He shut up as a fist hit him in the teeth.

Saraheda went on, ignoring the string of abuse shouted after her along the dark gangway. She pulled her scarf close to her body with trembling fingers.

A hand reached out and touched her, and she almost screamed.

She fumbled for the hat pin, but couldn't find it. A shape rose up, a tall silhouette, and she vaguely made out a raised palm.

'Forgive me, you are startled. I'm sorry, forgive my clumsiness. Do you require help? Are you lost?'

'I need some hot water for a woman – over there – in childbirth. Do you know where I can get some?'

'Surely at once. Of course. I can help you.'

The man's voice was stilted and halting, as if each word had to be pondered over. Saraheda realised why now, seeing glistening brown eyes in a dark-brown, sensitive face. He was Indian, tall and very slender, with lustrous black hair splayed over his shoulders.

'Come with me. Along here. We shall go together.'

Saraheda followed him. He moved easily and gracefully, seeming almost to flow through the cramped spaces. She had difficulty keeping up. An Indian off to the New World! That was a rare novelty: an ancient culture confronting a pioneering frontier.

The Indian led her to the galley, a bedlam of smoke and heat and confusion. Without pausing, he cut through the milling chaos of people. They went on squabbling among themselves, while the Indian quietly and calmly did what he had to do, and within minutes had organised hot water in a large copper pan. No one paid any attention to him.

Almost as if, Saraheda thought, they hadn't even seen him.

His name, she learnt, was Satish Kumar. He had lived in England for five years. Before that he had wandered through Europe, learning different languages and absorbing diverse cultures. He spoke seven languages, not including four Indian dialects.

He said to her, his face long and serious, 'Stay away from that man – the one with the dead eye. His name is Franklin Kershalton. He is a convicted murderer –'

'A murderer! Are you certain?'

Satish Kumar nodded. 'He boasts about the deed. I

listen to him and his small friend, Six Fingers, talking in the night. Kershalton was on the gallows, about to be hanged, and in the final minute he was saved.'

'How was he saved? By whom?'

'I have not learnt how it happened. Nor the reason why.' They moved back through the crowded lower deck, the Indian carrying the copper pan in his cupped hands. 'He had no choice but to flee the country, and take the first ship leaving port. It is bad karma that it should be this one.'

'Karma? What's that?' Saraheda asked curiously.

'Bad fortune. Or, as you would say, unfortunate.'

'Yes,' Saraheda said, reflecting. 'Perhaps the captain ought to be informed of Kershalton's history,' she suggested. 'A murderer loose on his ship . . .'

Something had been niggling at her. Now it struck home as Satish Kumar placed the pan of water, still bubbling and steaming, by the doctor's side. She touched the rim of the pan, and it nearly blistered her finger. *Yet the Indian had carried the boiling water in his bare hands.* She glanced down and saw that his pale palms were completely smooth and unblemished.

Then she became preoccupied and forgot about it as the woman's pains started to come strong and fast. The baby was delivered not long after, a boy, raw-skinned and shiny, slithering out on to the straw like a fat red eel.

And, when Saraheda looked round again, the Indian had gone.

6

Cawdor stood gazing out at the dark ocean. It was a warm night, the wind balmy and soft, and the oppressive closeness below had driven him up on deck. The gentle motion of the *Salamander* was barely perceptible through these placid southern waters.

He turned his head at a sound, and in the deeper shadow of the quarterdeck thought he saw movement. He stepped forward, peering into the darkness. Smiling to himself, Cawdor tiptoed closer.

'What secret rituals are these in the dead of night, sir!'

Gilbert Gryble jumped, nearly upsetting his apparatus. 'Holy Saints, Jefferson, pray don't creep up like that! I thought it was those mad zealots with the shaven domes.' He patted his chest with a fluttering hand. 'Nearly expired of a seizure.'

'An excellent night for star-gazing, Gilbert,' Cawdor said jovially. 'Have you discovered Gryble's planet yet?'

'For that I need to make exact observations, which are not possible on ship. No, my purpose is to compute the alignment of the Great Bear. You see it, there? At these latitudes it is dropping near to the horizon. And, just below, the Polar Star itself.' He went on, his voice quivering with enthusiasm, 'But these are ideal conditions, very excellent! I believe I could discover a new body with the naked eye!'

'The stars do look larger,' Cawdor granted, looking at the magnificent spread of light above the black line of the ocean. 'Brighter too. Is it true, or a trick of sight?'

'Partly true, I think,' Gryble said, adjusting the angle of his astrolabe and squinting along its brass pointers. 'The atmosphere is gentler and seems to sharpen their rays. Each star has its distinct colour, you will observe. See there, the fat blue one. It is named Rigel, in the constellation of Orion.'

'At what distance is that from the Earth?'

'We cannot know, at present. We have no device to measure the particles of light travelling from such a distant object.' Gryble turned the astrolabe to another quadrant of sky. 'John Michell, a very profound scholar of physical nature, has postulated that some of the bodies in the heavens are of such great mass that their light is entrapped, and cannot escape. Thus they remain invisible to us.'

Cawdor frowned as he grappled with this concept. 'Stars blazing light but remaining invisible? How so? Surely we should see them?'

'Not according to Michell. Light is emitted, but is then made to return towards its source by the star's own proper gravity. Providing the star is of a certain density and diameter, that is. Michell computes it as exceeding that of our sun in the proportion of five hundred to one.' Gryble folded the instrument and fitted it into a leather case. 'These bodies would be black in the night sky, and thus rendered invisible.'

'Is light a material thing, then?' Cawdor asked, baffled.

'According to Newton it is certainly affected by gravity, which, as far as we know, is a universal law of nature, affecting all things, including particles of light.'

'Fiery objects in the heavens that cannot be seen . . .' Cawdor mused, shaking his head. 'On quick reflection, I think I'll stick with stonemasonry and architecture. Mundane earthbound subjects, but which a man can grasp with both hands. Your study is too ethereal for me.'

Gilbert Gryble smiled as he collected his bits and pieces together.

'There are men in the Colonies with newer theories, enough to boggle the brain. Have you heard of Benjamin Franklin?'

Cawdor admitted he hadn't.

'The greatest scientific genius of the age,' Gryble pronounced emphatically. 'He has harnessed and transmuted the elemental forces of lightning and thunder, to be used for practical purposes. I hope to make the gentleman's acquaintance and learn to be a genius, too.' He chuckled. 'Us men of science are the coming breed.'

He bade Cawdor good night and traipsed off with his paraphernalia.

Cawdor strolled about the deck, fully alert, his mind filled with a thousand whirling thoughts and fancies. He paused under the mainsail, whose edge cut a curving swathe through the blaze of stars, and climbed up into the lower rigging. He lay back at an angle, feet securely planted, arms outspread, resting in a cradle of rope.

The ship rocked slowly from side to side. The stars slid up and then drifted down with its gentle, rhythmic motion. Cawdor became lost and dazzled in them, their brazen splendour; his senses swam and seemed to leave his body, flying outward and upward . . .

Perhaps Gryble had something. What a study it would make! Their majestic brilliance dwarfed everything else. Their sheer audacity put man in his proper place – an insignificant, squabbling speck with delusions of grandeur.

A woman moaned and made a low, guttural noise – it seemed directly beneath Cawdor's feet. A man grunted, grunted again, and the grunts flowed into a steady, regular syncopation. Again the woman moaned, but louder this time.

Spread-eagled above them in the rigging, Cawdor lay absolutely still and quiet. His chest shook and his stomach ached as he fought to contain the bubbling laughter within. If he moved he would disturb the lovebirds, but if he stayed where he was he would be forced to eavesdrop on their crescendo of passion, and its inevitable climax.

He decided that silence was the better course. Let them get on with it uninterrupted and finish in their own good time, which, judging from the sounds they were making, wasn't far off.

Cawdor chewed savagely at his lower lip. He mustn't laugh out loud. No. He would *not* laugh. How would he himself like it, to be secretly observed in such a delicate situation?

He bit into his lip, almost drawing blood, as a gust of stifled laughter shot down his nose. It sounded to him like the whinnying of a hysterical nag. He held his breath, quivering inside, and then let out a sigh of relief when the noises continued without abatement.

Even if he'd yelled at the top of his voice, it seemed doubtful to Cawdor they would have noticed.

The couple were lost to the world, and it came as much of a shock to them, as it did to Cawdor, when a gaunt figure launched itself from out of the shadows, took the man by the hair, and wrenched him bodily away from the woman.

Faint starlight gleamed on a shaven skull. Eye sockets like black cavernous pits. Lined cheeks and thin compressed mouth, tight as a scar. The leader, or spokesman, of the Shouters flung the man down as if he were a piece of carrion. The stern, granite head was raised up, and for a moment Cawdor thought his presence, suspended above them in the rigging, had been detected. But the leader was looking from the crouching man to the partly disrobed girl cowering in the shadows.

For several moments the figures below remained totally still, as if frozen in a tableau. Then the girl made a pathetic whimpering sound, like that of a frightened animal.

'Paul. Elizabeth –' the voice was toneless and drab, and yet there was a thin, sneering undercurrent to it '– your carnal desires have been apparent to us for some time. Every glance, every touch of hands, every unspoken communication. Noted and set down in permanent record. And now you both have sinned in deed as well as in thought.'

'But we are to be married, Elder Graye. You know that we are already betrothed, Elizabeth and me.' The young man was on his knees, hands clasped together in a writhing knot. 'I beg your mercy. Do not punish us. Show forgiveness, I implore you –'

'It is not for me to forgive. The law is the law and none shall rise above it. You have knowingly broken the commandment to which you both pledged yourselves, hearts and souls, signed in blood. Is that not a fact?'

'For pity's sake, Elder Graye, I beseech you to –'

'*Is that not a fact?*'

The shrill words pierced like a dagger-point. Cawdor himself felt a sharp pain in the centre of his forehead. The young man gasped and covered his ears. The girl cried out as if struck in the face.

'Yes! Yes! Yes!'

This from both the man and the girl, an urgent, terrified litany of confession, of guilt.

Elder Graye pressed his outspread hand to the young man's bowed head. 'Pray with all your might that your sins will be forgiven. Cast out thoughts of sensual pleasure. Reject the weakness of the flesh. Do penance and seek contrition within your heart. Be gone!'

Cawdor watched the young man stumble off into the

darkness. With trembling hands the girl tried to cover herself. Her shoulders were bare, her white breasts exposed. Her fingers fumbled uselessly with the strings of her bodice.

'Your sin is much the greater than his, Elizabeth,' Elder Graye rebuked her stonily, 'because you have wantonly employed your body to entice his manhood and encourage his lechery. You have tempted him with a lustful display of those female parts that quicken a man's nature and cause a portion of him to be engorged with blood. I hope and pray that you have no knowledge of such intimate bodily processes.'

He moved closer, looming over her. 'I hope and pray you have not seen it grow, and touched with your hand the monstrous thing in its full extended state. But if so, Elizabeth, I instruct you now to purge your sin.' His voice sharpened accusingly. 'Have you, child?'

The girl let out a shuddering sigh. 'Aye, sir. I do confess it.'

Elder Graye shook his shaven head. 'I am woefully sad to hear this, Elizabeth. A young, tender, innocent girl soiling herself with such loathsome depravity. Have you no shame, child?'

Elizabeth trembled. She gazed at him, stricken and dumb, tears rolling down her cheeks.

She flinched as Elder Graye placed his hand on her shoulder. He said soothingly, 'I do not mean to be unkind. It is for your own good that I chastise you, Elizabeth. But, if I am to help you, you must have faith in me. You must trust me.' His hand slid down and took hold of her breast, squeezing and moulding it with his long fingers. The girl stood rigid, her throat working.

'You see, child, breasts as full and ripe as these are a sore temptation to man, to his lustful fantasies. Note how your nipple stiffens and rises when it is toyed with . . . your body responds to a firm touch, does it not? You feel yourself grow hot and excited when a hand caresses you here, and here, and lower still . . . *here* . . . and you become wet, as I feel you now becoming.'

76

The thin, dry hands roamed everywhere, exploring every part of her body. The girl tried to move, but she was trapped, stifled, smothered by the crushing weight pressing against her.

'Sir, please don't . . . I cannot breathe.'

'Your soft body betrays you, Elizabeth. Your juices flow. This corruption of flesh and depravity of thought must be rooted out and cast away –'

The words were strangled in his throat. Elder Graye started to choke. He clawed at the arm locked tight round his windpipe. Cawdor increased the pressure, bending the long body backward, and backward still further, until it seemed the backbone would snap.

Elder Graye staggered back and went sprawling full length on the deck, choking and gasping for breath.

Fists clenched at his sides, Cawdor planted himself between them, a barrier between Elder Graye and the girl. He could hear her sobbing. He said over his shoulder, 'You have nothing to fear now. Go below. This long piece of common dog's turd won't harm you again.'

When she had gone, Cawdor said quietly, 'If I hear that you've touched that girl with your filthy paws, or even made advances to her, I'll see to it that you're made to suffer. Is my meaning clear?'

The long dark shape rose silently. Massaging his throat, Elder Graye said hoarsely, 'Your interference is a dire mistake. This is none of your concern –'

'I'll make it my concern. You have my faithful promise.'

'Heathen!' Elder Graye hissed at him. 'Pantheist! Worshipper of false idols!' A dry rattle issued from his throat. 'Your faith won't protect you. We have powers beyond anything you might dream of – older than time and stretching into the infinite future. There is no escape, now and for ever!'

'Would you care to be tossed over the side?' Cawdor asked him, in casual inquiry. 'I can arrange it. Let's see how your infinite powers survive a ducking.'

Elder Graye hurriedly retreated.

Cawdor nodded. 'Ohhh, I see . . . these almighty and

infinite powers extend to terrorising young women, but little beyond it.'

'Do not utter blasphemy or you will pay the price –'

'That threat might work on Gilbert Gryble,' Cawdor said, 'but it won't wash with me.' He rasped through his teeth, 'I tell you to your face what you are, Elder Graye. A craven, cringing, yellow-bellied, loathsome despoiler. Despicable by nature, mean of spirit, and bereft of any decent saving human grace. A foul lecher, religious charlatan, and a detestable hypocrite. To sum up, a long streak of rat's piss.'

Sick to his stomach, Cawdor turned on his heel and, still quivering inside so that his guts felt wrenched apart, made his way down the companionway to his cubicle on the upper deck. Partly, his disgust was aimed at himself. He could have, so easily, choked, *and had wanted to*, the last lingering breath from that stringy, joyless body.

7

'Mr Gryble says he will teach me all the known constellations in the sky!' Daniel enthused, biting off a lump of cheese. He crammed in some bread. 'And says with my sharp eyes I might spot a new 'un and have it called after me –'

'Don't speak with your mouth full.' Saraheda glared at him severely. 'Jefferson, tell the boy. His manners are atrocious.'

Cawdor shook his head.

'What?' Saraheda frowned. 'Why not?'

Cawdor pointed to his bulging cheeks. 'Can't,' he said, munching. 'Not allowed. Mouth full.'

Daniel rolled over on to his side on the bed, squealing with laughter. Saraheda turned her glare on Cawdor, who kept a straight face. 'How can I discipline him if you encourage him? Anyway, it's the father's duty – he's your son.'

'Glad to hear it,' Cawdor said. 'You've relieved my mind.'

'Jefferson Cawdor! What a scandalous thing to say! And in front of the boy, too!'

'What? What?' Daniel bounced up, all ears. 'What did he say, Ma? I missed it. What?'

'Nothing.'

'He did! You just said so. What scand-luss thing?'

Cawdor looked at Saraheda, widening his eyes innocently.

'Well, Ma? You're always preaching that a child should have as complete an education as possible. Answer his question!'

Saraheda glowered at him. Then: 'Little boys should be seen and not heard,' she informed her son primly.

'So now he can't talk with his mouth full, nor when it's empty.' Cawdor sighed and wagged his head. 'Poor little brat.'

'What's "scand-luss"?' Daniel asked, taking another bite of cheese. 'Is it something very bad, like –'

'Don't speak with your mouth full,' Saraheda and Cawdor chimed together, and burst out laughing.

There was a knock at the door. Cawdor was surprised to find one of the ship's officers, the first lieutenant, Mr Tregorath, standing there. Of medium height and ruddy complexion, he was a Cornishman, rather dour and phlegmatic in disposition.

'The captain's compliments, Mr Cawdor. He wishes you to attend him in his cabin, forthwith.'

'This instant?'

'If you would, sir.'

Cawdor fastened his collar and put on his coat, and followed the first lieutenant up on to the quarterdeck and through into the aft part of the ship, the quality end, where usually he was forbidden to tread. He had glimpsed Captain Vincent only from a distance, as Vincent paced the poop deck. A small, round man of hunched appearance, with a hooked nose and dark shaggy eyebrows.

Close to, Captain Vincent was perhaps even more formidable, with a hard, piercing stare which swept around like a lighthouse beam, missing nothing. He was standing, hands clasped over his coat-tails, before the large leaded window that gave a view of the *Salamander*'s creamy frothing wake tapering into the distance.

After removing his cocked hat, Mr Tregorath announced Cawdor and stood formally next to the long, low chart table. Above it, a large, ornate, and highly polished brass lantern swayed to and fro with the slight roll of the ship.

The captain didn't greet him or offer to shake hands. Cawdor wasn't offended, because he didn't know marine protocol. Or maybe Captain Vincent was just plain ill-mannered.

'You're a married man, I see, with a son.' Captain Vincent had glanced aside at a sheet of paper, resting on an open ledger. He looked up. 'Is that correct?'

Cawdor nodded. 'Yes, that's so.' He was half-smiling, in puzzlement more than anything. 'My wife Saraheda and son Daniel.'

'Those circumstances make what I have to say even more distasteful and unpleasant.' The lighthouse-beam stare was fixed unwaveringly on Cawdor, at maximum intensity. 'Allegations have been put against you, Cawdor, I have to tell you. Most serious allegations. Concerning behaviour of a lewd and bawdy nature with a young woman of good and reputable character. Indeed, little more than a girl. I must say that as master of this ship I take it upon myself –'

'Wait. One moment.' Cawdor stopped him with a raised hand. 'Before you take it upon yourself to say anything more, who has made these allegations against me? Or *accusations* it sounds more like.'

'The young woman I have just mentioned; she has made them. First to Mr Tregorath, and then to me, personally.'

'I see.' Cawdor nodded to himself. 'This woman is named Elizabeth, is she not? A dark-haired girl of about seventeen or eighteen.'

The captain threw a sharp glance at the first lieutenant. A glance that spoke volumes. The man corners himself; he as good as admits it.

'That is the girl, and a fair description. She has sworn, on oath, that last night you accosted her on deck –'

'I did so? She identifies me by name?'

Captain Vincent sighed ponderously. 'Yes, by name, sir. That you – Jefferson Cawdor – accosted and interfered with her, and forced yourself upon her intimate person. She has given me graphic detail, and I do not believe for a minute that a girl of such tender, innocent years could invent such gross and offensive practices, as were described to me in the company of my first officer.'

'I agree,' Cawdor said quietly.

'You agree?' Captain Vincent was thunderstruck.

'Yes. I don't believe it either. The question is, who did? Who put her up to this base slander?'

'Put her – *up to it*?' Captain Vincent's eyes bulged. 'Are you actually suggesting that this young woman made these putrid and obscene allegations by rote? Is that your best defence, man?'

'I do not have to defend myself for something I haven't done,' Cawdor said, keeping his voice even. 'The girl is lying. There isn't a shred of truth in what she says.' He paused and reflected. 'Except perhaps there is, involving another party.'

'What other party?' the captain barked.

Cawdor, about to speak, held his tongue. He suddenly recalled what Tom Paine had said about Captain Vincent and his utter detestation of religious factions warring on board his ship. Any counteraccusation that Cawdor made concerning Elder Graye and the Shouters would most likely be viewed in that light. Captain Vincent wouldn't give it house-room. Cawdor would just be seen as a member of one sect, the Telluric Faith, shifting the blame on to a rival religious order, so as to save his yellow skin.

'Well?' Captain Vincent demanded. 'Will you speak? Or do you stand comdemned by your own silence?'

Cawdor stared at the floor. Lifting his eyes, he said, 'I should like to see this girl, Elizabeth, stand before me and accuse me to my face. She is a gentle creature, I believe. Truthful and honest. I don't believe she has the guile to repeat this slander before me. I'll stake my honour and good name on it.'

The captain turned and paced, the short-necked head even more deeply hunched, like a cannonball balanced on a bulging sack of grain.

'I had hoped, Cawdor, that you wouldn't put the girl through that trial. She is distressed enough.' He looked at Cawdor from beneath his beetling brows. 'Do you insist on it?'

'I am left with no other alternative, so it seems. Or am I to be accused and condemned without benefit of natural justice? It is a charge I can refute but not disprove, unless you will grant me the means to do so.' Cawdor met the captain's stare full on. 'Yes, sir. I do insist on it.'

Captain Vincent nodded curtly to his first officer. It became clear that they had prepared for this: the girl was already there, waiting in the captain's private cabin, which adjoined the main saloon. Mr Tregorath brought her in. Captain Vincent indicated a chair. The girl sank into it, while the three men stood, swaying in unison to the gentle tilting motion.

'Elizabeth, is this the man whom you swore on oath accosted you on deck last night? Consider most carefully.'

'Aye, sir.'

The girl was staring at her feet. She hadn't once examined Cawdor's face, nor even glanced fleetingly at him.

Captain Vincent bent forward, hands splayed on his knees. His round, hard belly overhung his white breeches. 'And the details of the episode – which I shall not ask you to repeat – they are true and correct in every particular?'

Elizabeth nodded, head downcast.

'You must say so. Nodding isn't enough.'

'Yes, sir.' Her throat moved as she swallowed. 'They are all true. In every particular. I swear.'

'You realise that these are very serious charges.'

'Yes.'

'And you stick by them?'

She nodded rapidly. 'Yes. Yes. Every word.'

Cawdor forced himself to stay calm. He said, 'May I be

permitted to ask Elizabeth a question?' Captain Vincent straightened up, and gave a brusque nod. 'Were there any others present when this alleged incident took place, Elizabeth?'

The girl's hands trembled violently. She curled them into tight little fists, knuckles showing white. 'No one,' she said, barely above a whisper.

'Look at me, Elizabeth.'

Her dark head jerked up in stages, as if on strings. Her eyes, shiny with pain and fear, were fixed on a spot somewhere beyond Cawdor's left shoulder. All the energy seemed to drain out of Cawdor, leaving his legs weak. He saw that it was hopeless.

He said gently, 'I understand why you are saying this. You have been coerced into it, by a certain person, whom we both know. Will you not tell the captain the true circumstances of what took place, and what has led you to make these charges against me? Your denial is my only salvation, Elizabeth. As your friend and protector I ask you, I beg you, to give a straight, honest account. Will you?'

Captain Vincent was watching her closely, his eyes like penetrating rays, as if they might see into her very soul.

The girl stared glassily past Cawdor's shoulder. She moistened her dry lips. Then, very slowly, she nodded her head.

'Yes?' said Captain Vincent alertly.

Elizabeth raised her finger and pointed. 'This man accosted me on deck last night and made lewd and bawdy suggestions and by means of force overcame my resistance to his advances and against my will interfered with my intimate person.'

'Enough.' Captain Vincent made an abrupt gesture of dismissal.

Mr Tregorath took the girl out. He returned and stood by the chart table, his cocked hat tucked under his arm. The captain observed the swooping, squabbling sea gulls for a short while with a brooding gaze. He then pivoted on his heels, hands clasped over his uniform coat-tails, head lowered like a charging bull.

'For this misdemeanour, Cawdor, I could have you put

in irons and fed on water and hard tack for the remainder of the voyage. I shall not do so. Not for your sake, I hasten to point out. But you are a family man, and, as far as I can ascertain, of previous good character. It is for these mitigating reasons – principally for the sake of your wife and son – that I have decided to take no further action, nor to broadcast your disgraceful and unmanly behaviour to the ship's company and passengers.'

His eyes bored into Cawdor's face, which under its weathered tan was pale and immobile.

'But this is your one and final warning. There won't be another,' Captain Vincent pronounced grimly, 'be assured of it. If I hear that your conduct falls, even in the slightest degree, below the exemplary, you shall answer to me for it. As master of this vessel you have my earnest assurance on *that* point. You may go. Get out.'

Cawdor turned and went.

8

The days on board the *Salamander* were long, hot and hazy. The ocean lay flat and pearl grey beneath a sluggish vapour. They had now been at sea nearly five weeks. Shipboard life had settled into a familiar, easy pattern. To Cawdor, it seemed as if he had never known any other life but the one of this creaking, rocking world.

In fact, it occurred to him to wonder why all seamen weren't stark mad.

For they lived in a different element from normal men; inhabited for months on end an alien environment, cut off from every cosy sight, sound and sensation. No houses, streets, people, horses, taverns, churches; no family and relations; no long walks in the countryside; no *getting away*, even for an instant, from this floating wooden cask.

Everything here was familiar and routine, and yet strange and other-worldly. Relationships remained the same, but subtly changed, heightened, more intense. The usual rules didn't apply, but there were other rules, even stricter, more rigorously enforced.

It was all very odd and unsettling.

One hot and sultry afternoon Cawdor was reading in his cubicle. It was a treatise on the dreaded subject of materials' stress-to-height ratios, with which he found great difficulty. He must have read the same page a dozen times, and still couldn't grasp the argument. Saraheda was in the galley, preparing food with the other women. He didn't know where Daniel was, but was unconcerned. The boy had become accustomed to the seagoing life, and sensible to its potential dangers. Probably, Cawdor thought, he was off in a quiet corner somewhere, discussing cosmogony with Gilbert Gryble.

A sound from above suddenly disturbed his concentration.

There it was again. Cawdor sat up. He'd never heard anything like it. Was it a human cry? Or some monstrous squawking sea bird?

The voice – if it was a voice – cried out again. Others joined in. Even down here, through the thickness of the deck planking, the sounds were penetrating and painful. They merged into a sustained, insistent chorus.

Cawdor tossed his book aside and went up.

Other passengers, also alarmed by the strange noises, were appearing on deck. Twenty or so already lined the rail to the quarterdeck. Cawdor pushed through to look. By now the screams – cries – were deafening. Some of the passengers had their hands to their ears. Others were backing away, faces screwed up in pain.

Below, the five grey-clad figures of the elders stood in a tight circle, facing inward. One by one, they ducked their shaven heads into the centre, and from each gaping mouth came a bellowing scream that rent the air. Down went each head, mouth agape to its widest extent, and from it blasted this horrendous unhuman sound.

Their followers stood a few paces back in a bowed group, eyes fixed on the deck. Faster and faster the heads ducked down, a continuous rotation that was dizzying to watch, like the whirling movement of a spinning top.

The Shouters. This must be the ritual whereby they got

their name, Cawdor realised. Though what it was meant to signify –

The next instant he was staring in horrified disbelief.

There was somebody inside the circle.

Between the thin, grey figures Cawdor glimpsed the curled-up form of a man, his arms wrapped protectively round his head. With each bellowing scream his body jerked convulsively. And now Cawdor saw blood spurting from his nose, mouth and ears – even the tears rolling down his cheeks were tinged with red. The blood was running freely from between his fingers and dripping thickly to the deck.

As Cawdor watched the man being ceaselessly and mercilessly battered by the solid wall of sound, he understood the purpose of the ritual and what was happening to the poor wretch.

He was being shouted to death.

People were turning away from the rail, sickened and disgusted. But no one was doing anything to help. It wasn't wise to intrude upon the arcane rituals of a religious sect – and of that sect in particular. The Shouters were feared throughout the ship. They kept to themselves, ate their own kind of food, worshipped in their own mysterious fashion. The elders ruled their 'flock' with an implacable, unyielding rectitude that would not tolerate any lapse or deviation, and, least of all, interference.

Cawdor looked up to the poop deck. There were two officers on duty, one of them Mr Tregorath, the first lieutenant. He saw Cawdor looking up, and quite deliberately turned away. The other officer, holding a brass telescope in the crook of his arm, gazed blandly out to sea.

Captain Vincent's sentiments, it appeared, were shared by his officers; in religious matters, the policy was to look the other way. Nobody was prepared to lift a finger.

Cawdor shouldered people roughly aside to get to the companionway. Somebody grabbed his arm. Cawdor tried to shake him off.

'Jefferson, don't be a damned fool!' Gilbert Gryble had

to shout at the top of his voice in order to be heard above the ear-splitting cacophony. He hung tightly on to Cawdor's arm, his eyes wide and fearful in the round moon of his face. 'For God's sake, man, don't interfere. It's none of your concern!'

'Then whose concern is it?' Cawdor demanded, thin-lipped.

'If anyone's, the captain's –'

'The captain doesn't give a tinker's toss. Neither, it seems, does a single one of these good, pious folk. Let go!'

He shook Gryble off and leapt down to the lower deck. Booming waves of sound battered Cawdor's eardrums. They reverberated inside his skull, sending needles of pain through the soft brain tissue. It seemed to Cawdor that his brain was being violently shaken, as a terrier shakes a rat.

The elders were too preoccupied with their deadly work to notice him. In – out, in – out, in – out went the knoblike heads, lips drawn back, mouths black holes, hurling screaming lumps of sound at the man writhing on the deck, blood pouring from every orifice.

BOOM!
BOOM!
BOOM!

Like a battering ram, hammering away without respite, rendering him insensible.

Cawdor staggered and fell to his knees. He reached out at full stretch, got a slimy hold on the man's shirt, sodden with blood, and dragged him from the grey circle.

The suddenness of the silence was almost as painful as the sound had been. Cawdor's head shrieked with it. His ears rang. Black spots swirled before his eyes. He got to his feet and swayed dizzily for a moment. He became aware that the grey circle had surrounded him and was closing in. Blindly, instinctively, he swung his arm, and had the satisfaction of feeling his fist connect with one of them. He hoped to God it was Elder Graye. But he couldn't be sure: his blurred vision was only now clearing, and, when he blinked and got his eyes into focus, the circle had broken apart.

Cawdor glanced down at the man slumped at his feet. His face was a mask of blood. Slowly, Cawdor recognised him. It was Paul, the young man who had been dallying with Elizabeth.

'Come on – try and stand.' Cawdor lifted him up and supported him. 'Let's get you to Doctor Chapman. Move out of the way,' he grated at the grey line of elders; and, when they didn't, snarled, 'I said shift, boneheads. Now. This instant.'

Elder Graye barred his path. Veins like blue worms were throbbing in his hollow temples. 'You have committed the most grievous sacrilege by this interference in our sacred –'

Cawdor stuck the flat of his hand in the bony chest and pushed him out of the way. 'No time for all that twaddle. Say another word and it will afford me the greatest pleasure to snap your spine. And that is not a threat; it's a promise.'

Elder Graye clamped his mouth shut. His slitted eyes in their deep bony sockets went black.

Cawdor half-carried the young man to the bottom of the companionway. A row of faces stared down. Some frightened, some timid, a few curious and puzzled. One of the faces Cawdor registered, not because it was flawlessly beautiful, and framed by a mass of tangled black hair, which it was, but because it was smiling. The Spanish Woman – as everyone referred to her – was smiling down on Cawdor as if they shared a private joke. Yet he didn't get the joke, nor much care for that cold, mocking smile.

Gryble had scurried down the steps to lend a hand. Together they carried the bleeding, semiconscious form up to the quarterdeck.

'I have to say it, Jefferson,' Gryble panted. 'I think this a grave mistake on your part. How do we know what he's done – broken some sacred oath, m'be, or transgressed the tenets of his faith? Perhaps he deserved the punishment they were meting out . . .'

'They weren't punishing him,' Cawdor said angrily. 'They were killing him.'

'All the same . . .'

'All the same *what*?' Cawdor snapped. 'You'd have let him die, would you? I don't care much for your cosmogony, Gilbert, if it permits you to watch a man killed, right there in front of you, and you don't lift a finger to prevent it.'

'Of course I would wish to prevent it. If I could,' Gryble mumbled, shamefaced; and added, 'Even though cosmogony admits of no moral philosophy.' He sneaked a scared watery glance over his shoulder, just in case the elders had overheard him. 'Naturally I would.'

9

'Naturally,' Saraheda said bitterly, 'it would have to be you and no other, wouldn't it? No one else but you would be so foolish as to intervene in such controversial affairs. What about the captain? What about the officers? Where were they?'

'Busy turning a blind eye,' Cawdor said wearily. 'While a blameless young man bled to death.'

It was late evening, and a refreshing breeze had sprung up. Cawdor had been enjoying it, after the heat of the day, strolling with his wife on deck, until this subject had reared its ugly head. He had tried to avoid it, and then make light of it, but Saraheda would not be deterred or humoured.

'You don't know for certain he was blameless.'

'You sound as bad as Gilbert Gryble.'

'What do you mean, "as bad as"?' Saraheda said testily. 'I'm not "as bad as" anyone. I'm stating my opinion. I'm allowed to do that, ain't I? I'm not simply and merely your "chattel", Mr Cawdor. Wife, mother, cook, washerwoman, servant and drudge rolled into one – yes, I am all that, granted – but I also hold views and opinions.'

'No one has ever suggested –'

'And am *allowed*, I think, to express them.'

'Yes, madam, of course you are,' Cawdor said placatingly.

'Do not, sir, patronise me. I know that tone.'

'What tone?' Cawdor said despairingly.

'Insinuating that my views are to be aired only under sufferance from my lofty lord and master.' Saraheda's voice deepened to a gruff bass: 'Let the little woman have her say. That's the easiest course. One can ignore it, as one always does. After all, it's only the female way of thinking – the product of a shallow feeble mind.'

Cawdor remained silent. They were on a new tack now. The original difference of opinion had been subverted, lost and forgotten somewhere along the way. They had entered upon a circular argument that he had less chance of winning than a cat surviving in hellfire.

The sun was ebbing over the horizon. From it stretched a path of light, like glittering golden fish-scales. At this point, Cawdor reflected, they must be very nearly in the plumb centre of the Atlantic. Over a thousand miles of ocean either side. Several weeks away from the nearest scrap of dry land. It wasn't a thought to dwell on, with nothing but a few planks of timber separating them from the briny deep. And he had heard someone remark that typhoons were common in the waters they were now entering.

Saraheda too had fallen silent, perhaps in contemplation of the rosy sunset. Speculatively, to test if their row had been forgotten or not, Cawdor drew her close to him and kissed the side of her neck, which was invitingly warm. He felt her body resist for a second, and then relax and mould into his. He murmured in her ear. It tickled her, and she rubbed her head against his shoulder in a lazy, feline movement.

Trying to tease her, Cawdor was about to murmur some more, when he suddenly tensed and stared.

A pale shape was flitting towards them. For a heart-stopping moment, because it moved so silently, Cawdor could have sworn it was a ghost, until he heard a soft footfall on the deck. The shape came directly up to them, dressed in a long, straight, white garment. Eyes and teeth gleamed in a dark face.

'If you will permit it, I must speak with you.'

Satish Kumar placed the palms of his hands together and gave a slight bow. Cawdor knew about the Indian from Saraheda: she had mentioned the help he had given her in bringing the hot water.

'What do you wish to say?'

Kumar made a graceful motion of his hand, beckoning them to step down into the deeper shadow of one of the lower gangways, or waists, as they were called, which ran lengthwise along each side of the vessel.

'I have become an untouchable,' the Indian explained, teeth flashing in a grin. 'From across the white line. I must be careful not to be observed in this part of the ship. Good evening, Mrs Cawdor.'

'Good evening,' Saraheda replied, amused by his formality.

Cawdor said, 'Then it must be important for you to take the risk of breathing this exalted air. Tell me, does it taste any better here?'

'Oh yes, much,' the Indian answered gravely. 'As soon as I crossed the line the air was scented with roses.'

'What does it smell of over there?'

'Cowslips,' Kumar said promptly.

Cawdor chuckled. 'You're more English than the English, Mr Kumar. So why put yourself in jeopardy? What's to do?'

'Nothing, I hope. The man is a bag of wind, boasting of this, that and the other. Some of it has a grain of truth, perhaps, but most of it is vain bragging. He –'

'Wait. Wait,' Cawdor said. 'What man is this?'

'Why – the man who insulted your wife,' Kumar said, blinking his eyes wide. 'The one called Franklin Kershalton.'

'Yes. I see,' Cawdor said evenly. 'Go on.'

'Ah . . .' Kumar gave an elaborate shrug, spreading his slender hands. 'Forgive me, Mrs Cawdor, for placing you in this position. I had assumed your husband was aware of what had befallen you. My humble apologies.'

'Never mind,' Saraheda said. 'He has an inkling now.'

'Tell me about this man Kershalton,' Cawdor said tightly. 'And what his bragging has to do with us.'

'Kershalton is an evil man, Mr Cawdor, a cutthroat, a thief, and a rogue by his own admission. He boasts of evading the gallows for a foul crime.' The Indian's voice became hushed. 'Some little time ago I saw him in company with Elder Graye – though I know Kershalton is not a member of their sect. Later I overheard Kershalton, in drink, conversing with his young companion, the one named Six-Fingered Sam. He spoke your name and laughed.'

'He spoke my name. Is that all?'

'It was the manner in which he spoke it. And his laughter.' Kumar's eyes were bright with anxiety in his swarthy face. 'He is the kind of man who would commit any base deed for a gold sovereign or two. I have lived within earshot of him these past weeks, Mr Cawdor, and I know his heart is black –'

'You also say he is a vain braggart. Why should I have to fear a drunken scoundrel?'

'Listen to Mr Kumar, Jefferson.' Saraheda's voice was husky with trepidation. 'Ask yourself why Kershalton should make mention of *your* name. He's been put up to something. Don't, I beg you, assume a brave face for the sake of manly pride.'

'You'd rather I crept around, jumping at shadows?' Cawdor asked sardonically.

'I'd rather you weren't so pig-headed, but showed a jot of sense, and listened hard to Mr Kumar! You well know the ill-feeling that exists between you and the Shouters – never mind now the reasons for it. You did what you did. Too late to cry over spilt milk. But for heaven's sake, and for mine, pay heed!'

Cawdor put his arm round his wife's shoulders and kissed the top of her head. 'Very well,' he said simply. 'I shall.'

Satish Kumar touched the palms of his hands and bowed. 'It saddens me deeply to be the bearer of this disturbing news. But I should not sleep easy in my bed, having neglected my duty.'

'Duty?' Cawdor said, puzzled. 'Why duty?'

'It is the duty of all good men to resist evil, Mr Cawdor. If we did not, then the world would be in an even sorrier state than it is now.'

Cawdor smiled. 'You seem very sure that I'm a good man, Mr Kumar.' There was a gentle hint of mockery in his voice. 'Can you see into my heart too?'

'No. But I have observed your actions. Today you saved a man from certain death – while others stood by. It was a good thing, a noble thing, and a brave thing.' Now it was his turn to smile. 'No, I do not think my judgement is faulty in this respect.'

'I take it you are a religious man?'

'Yes. As we say in my creed, "No God, no soul".'

'And what is your creed?'

'I follow the teachings of the Theravada.'

'I do not know it,' Cawdor confessed.

'It derives from the original doctrine of the Buddha, the Enlightened One, comprising the Three Signs of Being, the Four Noble Truths, and the Noble Eightfold Path.'

'You don't want for theology, it seems,' Cawdor said with a smile. He had vaguely heard of the Buddhist belief, and it intrigued him. Satish Kumar, the man, interested him, too. He couldn't say why. It was an intuition that Kumar held within himself many secrets; held them comfortably and securely, without strain. And thus – unlike most men – had no need to blurt them out in order to appear better, or wiser, than his fellows.

'We have several weeks left of this voyage,' Cawdor said. 'I should like to learn more of your creed, and discuss it with you – if you are willing.'

Kumar bowed. 'I would be most honoured, Mr Cawdor.' He glanced up with a mischievous smile. 'Providing I can cross the white line and am permitted to breathe in this exalted atmosphere.'

They watched him glide silently away, a pale blur in the deepening purple twilight. Saraheda slid her hand into her husband's and squeezed it tightly. 'Mr Kumar was right and I was wrong. Good, noble, and brave. Yes – what you did, Jefferson, was all of those things.'

VIRTUAL FUTURE

1

With a sudden start, Jeff Cawdor sat upright and then slowly subsided on to the bed. The sheets felt damp. His hair was stuck to his forehead and warm trickles of sweat made his scalp itch. He lay there, panting slightly, as the images ebbed and faded away. That was some weird dream. What had he eaten last night to dredge up such a lurid fantasy? Something about . . .

What *had* it been about? Even now, moments after waking, the dream was floating away and dispersing into the air like mist in the morning sunlight. Cawdor struggled to remember, getting tantalising glimpses of a vast ocean, a sailing ship, a warm night under a swaying spread of fat bright stars scattered from horizon to horizon. But, the harder he tried, the more diffuse and ethereal they became, until he was left clutching at nothing.

Cawdor gave up. No wonder he couldn't remember: his head was tight and muzzy, and his throat parched raw as if he'd been yelling in his sleep. Some dream all right.

Beside him, Sarah stirred drowsily. The dim light filtering in through the blinds gave her face a ghostly translucent quality. Cawdor reached out and lightly touched her shoulder. The flesh was reassuringly soft and warm and solid. She moved again at his touch, and he withdrew his hand in case it might wake her. He had no idea of the time, though he sensed it was early by the raw quality of the daylight.

Being a sound sleeper, he very rarely woke at this hour. He let his gaze wander about the dimly lit room as if it might alight on something different or unexpected; but everything looked just the same. For some reason this gave him immense relief. The bedroom was just as it always was, with his wife sleeping beside him, and his daughter asleep also in her room three doors along the railed landing. His life, in other words, was proceeding normally. In a little while he would get up, shave, take a shower, and sit down to a breakfast that Sarah had prepared – maybe his favourite of French toast with a round hole cut in the centre to hold a sizzling fried egg, coated in Worcestershire sauce.

Funny how such little, unimportant things brought comfort. The whole crazy planet might be in turmoil, yet French toast with a fried egg restored his world to one of cosy domesticity.

Cawdor slid out of bed and padded through to the bathroom, taking advantage of his early start by having a leisurely shave. He'd always been a hot-water-and-razor man, enjoying the ritual of lathering and scraping as much as anything, never feeling an electric shaver quite did the trick. His face ballooned in the magnifying side of the mirror as he bent towards it, the blade cutting a satisfying swathe through the foam, like a snowplough clearing a drift. Why some men found shaving a chore he never understood: it always revived his spirits, honed him physically and mentally for the day ahead . . .

Then he found himself staring not into the mirror but *at* the mirror itself. He looked down at the tiled floor. In his mind's eye he saw a heap of broken glass, the mirror's base and stainless-steel rim among it. Hadn't he smashed this mirror? Clearly he hadn't, because he was using it to shave with. Then was it maybe a lingering remnant of the dream that had shocked him awake? He tried to remember, but no good – it was gone, every last scrap of it.

By the time he was dressed he could hear Sarah in the kitchen and smell coffee and the mouth-watering tang of bacon on the air.

He went to fetch the morning paper, which was still damp from the dewy lawn, and sat reading it at the breakfast table while he took his first sip of coffee. Sarah slid a plate of bacon and French toast in front of him and bent to kiss his cheek. At the last moment he quickly turned his head so that she kissed him on the lips instead.

She smiled. 'You were up early. What happened to my morning cuddle?' His arm encircled her waist, and Sarah removed his straying hand from her buttocks. 'You want your daughter to walk in and find us rutting over the breakfast dishes?' she asked primly, gliding out of reach.

'Where is she? It's getting late,' Cawdor said, gnawing at a strip of bacon. 'Doesn't she have school?'

Sarah laid aside a piece of buttered toast and wiped her fingers to open her mail. She couldn't face anything cooked in the morning. 'You forget? She's in the end-of-term play, doesn't have to show till mid-morning.'

'Still in her room?'

Sarah nodded. 'Some programme on cable that all the kids are into. You don't watch it, brother, you don't rate *at all*. Might as well emigrate to Outer Mongolia.'

On the portable TV a lean young man, long dark hair trailing over the collar of his dazzling white suit, was darting along a line of people in the studio. He thrust the mike at a fat teenage girl who was awash with tears because she felt unattractive and boys didn't want to date her. The dross they filled the airwaves with, Cawdor thought sadly. Sarah had half-turned to watch it as she refilled his mug from the thermos jug.

'Daniella's hooked on TV trash, is she?' Cawdor remarked with a sardonic grin. 'Welcome to the club.'

'What?' Sarah wrinkled her nose. 'No, I don't go for this stuff! Stupid show for even stupider people.'

'Careful, it's like junk food. You might get a taste for it, honey.' The hot coffee was like balm to his rasping throat. That must have been a lulu of a dream if he'd been shouting himself hoarse in his sleep. But then Sarah would have nudged him awake; she always did when he snored after too much late-night fraternisation with Jameson's Irish Whiskey.

She put on her glasses to read the letter she had opened and looked at him reprovingly over the tortoiseshell rims. 'And, by the way, I promised Daniella we'd go see her in the play, all right? It's very short, about thirty minutes. You *might* even enjoy it.'

Cawdor held up his hand. 'OK, OK. Anything for a quiet life.'

Theatre-going wasn't his favourite recreation. Of the arts, he preferred classical music, and even a Broadway show, to heavy drama. He had once sat through a four-hour performance of Eugene O'Neill's *Long Day's Journey Into Night*, receiving sharp digs in the ribs from Sarah to stop him dropping off.

'Well, if it's only one act,' Cawdor conceded generously. 'And parents should take an interest in what their kids are doing, support them.'

'You've been at the Doctor Spock again. I warned you about that.'

Seated across from him, Sarah cradled a coffee cup, taking little sips. The sunlight streaming in from the window behind her made a halo of her silvery-blonde hair, which was uncombed and still a bit tangled from slumber. Without the benefit of mascara and pencil-liner, her eyelashes and eyebrows were like filaments of gossamer. She looked wonderfully, nakedly, innocent. At this moment, sitting peacefully and domestically facing each other, Cawdor felt incredibly fortunate to love and be loved by this woman.

Sarah pushed her glasses more firmly on to her nose and read the letter. She sighed and made a clucking sound with her tongue.

'What is it?'

Sarah held out the letter. 'It's from Bill Benedict. Wanna read it?'

'Not particularly.' Cawdor looked at his watch, checked it against the wall clock, and took a gulp of coffee. 'Better get moving.'

'He's got a nerve. Listen to this – he says the programme's been taken by another six stations, which makes thirty-seven in all, but my fee stays the same.' She tossed the letter aside. 'What a skinflint that guy is. He'd take the gold fillings out of his grandmother's mouth.'

'What if she had false teeth?'

'He'd take them instead.'

'Does it really bother you, not getting paid more?' Cawdor asked, thinking he ought to show at least a token interest. Bill Benedict was the owner of WCTC New Brunswick, the radio station that broadcast Sarah's late-night phone-in programme, *Take Five*. 'I thought you did it because you liked doing it.'

'Yeah, that too,' Sarah agreed, 'but I object when my efforts are taken for granted. My fee should be adjusted pro rata to the audience share. That's only fair.' She bit into the slice of toast, leaving smears of butter at the sides of her mouth. Cawdor rose and leant over to kiss her. His tongue flicked out and licked away the butter. Sarah munched on through a big grin.

He went out waggling his fingers; and she waggled back, still grinning as she turned to watch the TV.

Today was beautifully sunny with clear blue skies. Total contrast to a week ago, Cawdor thought, remembering the spectacular thunderstorm raging over the towers and canyons of Manhattan.

Phyllis was there to greet him, as ever, with her dimpled smile and fluttering sidelong glance, the coffee percolating on the hotplate behind her desk. She brought him in a cup, set it down, and waited in front of his desk, briskly rubbing her chubby little hands in keen anticipation of anything, any small service, she might be called upon to provide. Later he'd have some letters to dictate, Cawdor told her, but there was nothing he needed right this minute, thanks very much.

With a pert nod of her tight curls, streaked blonde at the tips, Phyllis dimpled a smile and bounced out.

It was nearly lunchtime when Don Carlson tapped on

the door and popped his head in. 'Spare a minute?'

'Sure.' Cawdor pushed the swivel chair away from the VDU and got to his feet, arching his back. 'Going cross-eyed anyway, staring at that screen. Think I might need an eye test.'

Cawdor's fellow senior partner at UltraCast International was tall and rangy with thinning sandy hair brushed forward in an attempt to hide the prematurely balding truth. While Cawdor was the engineering brains behind the outfit, Don was the front man who spent much of his time selling their design service to corporate clients right across the States. They had formed the partnership eleven years ago, and it had proved the perfect match: Don's confident boardroom technique and easy social banter allied to Cawdor's flair for innovative ideas and new techniques in architecture and construction.

'You got a vacation coming up, right?' Don tilted his head in that quizzical way he had. 'How soon?'

'Uh, let me see. About four, five weeks away.'

'Hey, that's OK then.' Don was suddenly animated. 'Hows about a trip to Albuquerque? We need to get somebody down there within a couple of weeks – not a problem exactly, just to iron out a few teething troubles.'

Cawdor rubbed his jaw. 'I'm not too familiar with that project. Conference centre, isn't it? The Grace Corporation?'

'Grace MediaCorp. Auditorium with TV facility. Thing is, Jeff, it's technical, otherwise I'd handle it myself. I mean, I know I'm better looking and have nicer manners than you, but I'd just stand around being decorative and charming, with a dumb look on my chops.' Don gave an exaggerated shrug of appeal. 'Take a couple of days per-haps, three at most. Listen to their gripes, if any, baffle 'em with science, the usual bullshit. You'll run rings around 'em.' He raised his sandy eyebrows in another appeal, more hopeful this time.

'I could make it a full week,' Cawdor suggested with a grin. 'I've never been to New Mexico, could spend some time sightseeing, start my tan off before I go on vacation . . .'

'Hey, let's not go overboard,' Don said, raising both hands. He was jesting, but not totally. 'Can do?'

Cawdor nodded. 'I'll need to bone up on the technical spec first though, so's I don't look a complete asshole.'

'Great.'

Mission accomplished, Don Carlson departed, leaving Cawdor with the rueful feeling that somehow or other he'd just been bamboozled by an expert.

Soon after lunch the technical spec landed on his desk. It comprised two loose-leaf binders, each three inches thick.

Cawdor heaved a sigh, draped his jacket over the back of the swivel chair and sat down at the CAD keyboard. Even though all blueprints were generated by Computer-Aided Design, and could be called up by any workstation in the office, the reams of technical data were in the form of hard copy, which was still the most convenient way for easy access and cross-referencing.

The design brief was for an auditorium seating 5,000 people, with a large stage area which also doubled as a television studio for live transmission and recorded programmes. This complex infrastructure of lighting and sound systems, control booths, the maze of air-conditioning plant, plus a host of backup services, was housed within a pyramid, and here, Cawdor realised, was the nub of the problem. How to support all this – and a large public space – inside such a structure was a difficult engineering task. Probably what the people at Grace MediaCorp were most concerned about. He decided to give the mainframe number-cruncher another crack at the stress factors and load parameters – just to make sure the math came out right and he didn't make a complete babbling idiot of himself when they tossed a fizzing bomb into his lap.

The brief didn't specify the type of TV programmes the company produced; not that it mattered. But that was one helluva size – 5,000 – for a studio audience, wasn't it? Rock concerts, maybe, or Las Vegas-style spectaculars. Or even, he thought with a shudder, one of those damn confessional shows you couldn't escape from nowadays:

partners and lovers revealing their most intimate thoughts and shameful secrets on prime-time TV. He speculated idly for a moment about why they chose to put themselves through such an ordeal. Of course, to them it *wasn't* an ordeal. That was the point: they found it quite easy – hell, compulsive – to blurt out loud to 50,000,000 people what they found impossible to whisper behind drawn shades to their nearest and dearest.

Cawdor couldn't figure it. Unless this public act of revelation and contrition, it occurred to him, had taken the place of religious confession; perhaps that was the reason.

But then it was not much different from what Sarah did on her radio phone-in spot for WCTC New Brunswick. Callers rang in with all kinds of personal and emotional problems, some of them harrowing, many of an explicit sexual nature. They needed to talk them out, unburden themselves, and it seemed that the warm, friendly yet disembodied voice of someone with a degree in psychology and behavioural social science provided the ideal conduit. But Sarah was always very cautious about making her advice too specific. Advising a battered wife to seek professional help was one thing. Telling her to take the kids and leave the brutal sonofabitch was verging dangerously near a law suit, or, even more directly, a drunken irate husband hammering on the door of the radio station and threatening to tear the head off that feminist ball-breaking bitch who was destroying his marriage.

And it was true that Sarah had received a few scary phone calls from the bulging-eyed pointy-head brigade who wrote anonymous letters in jagged green capitals. Thus far, thank God, none of these cranks had managed to get within arm's reach.

Bang on the dot, 3:15, Phyllis brought in his coffee. Never a minute early, or a minute late. Black, one spoonful of sugar, already stirred. She placed it by the keyboard.

'You seem ... I think the word is "fraught".' She regarded

101

him with a tiny frown, head on one side, like a reproving mother hen.

'You got it in one, Phyl,' Cawdor said, knowing this would please her, and it did. She blushed with delight. It was cruel, leading her on like this, but he meant no harm. Anyway, she seemed to enjoy it.

'Anything for me?' Phyllis asked. 'Any letters?'

On her large bosom was a silver pin he hadn't noticed before, in the shape of a butterfly, or was it the outline of a bow tie? Hard to tell.

'How's the Donleavy report coming along?' Cawdor took a sip. 'You get those photo references from Research?'

'I checked and they didn't have them. So I called the Engineers and Mechanics' Library in Rockerfeller Center. They had! Phyllis beamed at him, and he was tempted to pat her on the head. 'They promised *faithfully* to fax them by noon tomorrow. Don't worry, I'm on the case.'

She bounced off, winking from the door as she went out.

Dumpy, dependable Phyllis. In some ways, he supposed, she was quite attractive. If you went for the fuller figure. Certainly, if large breasts and a big behind turned you on, Phyllis was the woman with all the equipment. Those demure, cuddly types with the dimples were probably seething with passion, could smother a man with an abundance of soft white flesh. And, to be honest, there had been times when he had been tempted – or at least the glimmering of temptation had flitted through his mind. She had a habit, for instance, when she brought his letters in to be signed, of standing beside his chair and leaning over the desk, balancing on one leg while the other curled up coquettishly so that her tight skirt was hitched up over her solid thighs. While Cawdor tried to concentrate on reading through the letters and signing them, he was very much aware of the opportunity for his hand to stray downward and touch the inside of her calf. From there it was a logical, and entirely natural, progression – without either of them acknowledging it was happening – for his hand to slide upward until it was trapped in the heat and smoothness of her bare inner thighs, because, as he well knew, Phyllis preferred stockings and suspenders to panti-hose. As she leant further over the desk, sorting the letters to be signed, and while still maintaining her poise as the brisk, efficient secretary, Phyllis would shift her weight in order to part her thighs and permit access for his fingers to delve even higher. Had anyone entered the office unexpectedly they wouldn't have noticed anything out of the ordinary. A secretary standing by her boss's chair as he signed his letters. A misleading impression, this normal, everyday business scene, because by then he would have edged aside the damp narrow strip of material and inserted three fingers inside her. Phyllis would be leaning right over, her round belly resting on the desk, legs straddled wide, capacious rear end thrust out as he worked at her. By now of course her cheeks would be flushed, her breathing coming in fast and shallow gasps, her huge wobbling breasts straining the buttons of her blouse as she moved back and forth in response to the fingers sliding with silky smoothness in and out of her. His fingers, almost his entire hand, would be immersed as she opened up wetly and slackly to him, yet he would pay no attention to any of this, cursorily skimming through the typed letters, signing his name, moving the sheet of paper aside, skimming through the next letter as Phyllis jerked and moaned beside him.

She would come explosively, knuckles white as she gripped the front edge of the desk, bucking frantically with her gigantic rear end as she sought to quicken the pace and bring that sweet searing pain to the very edge of the precipice until she was over it, over it and beyond, a hot flushing wave of pleasure washing over her and through her like a blood-heat tropical deluge so that she felt drenched inside and out.

The white knuckles on the edge of the keyboard were his own, Cawdor saw, staring at them with shock and amazement. He looked down at the hard bulge in his trousers. Incredible –

He was having a masturbatory fantasy about Phyllis Keets!

Never before, never once, had he entertained such thoughts about her. She didn't appeal to him in that way. Or maybe she did and he didn't know it: the state of his arousal gave lie to his denial. He had damn well near climaxed, right then and there, sitting at the computer.

Cawdor swung round in the swivel chair and got to his feet, embarrassed by the hard shape pushing out the front of his trousers even though he was alone in the office; in truth he was embarrassing himself. He was convinced that the next time he came face to face with Phyllis he would blush for shame. The image of her lying gasping and jerking across his desk was so vividly erotic that it would hover in the air between them like a hologram, a kind of ghostly shadow play forever repeating itself.

Even more bizarre – why such an idea had entered his mind at all. It was like an alien thought. As if somebody other than Jeff Cawdor had planted the fantasy there. And goddamnit, he'd gone right along with it, lived through every moment, and enjoyed it too – his erection proved that even while his conscience backed away and held up its hands in horror.

The mind in the skull was easily tricked, but the cock had a mind of its own.

2

This was one of Sarah's evenings at WCTC New Brunswick, and she had already left for the radio station to prepare her broadcast. A note on the kitchen counter told him that Daniella had a rehearsal at school for her one-act play and would be home about seven-thirty. She would hitch a ride with Sandy, a schoolfriend helping out backstage who lived three streets away, and whose mother would pick the girls up.

Cawdor took a Michelob from the fridge, unbolted the French doors, and stood on the patio drinking, letting the quiet sounds of the peaceful evening soothe him.

It had been a late spring, with unseasonal frosts, and the shrubs and trees and Sarah's carefully tended flowerbeds were two or three weeks from achieving their mid-May glory. The lawns, which were his job, needed cutting.

Inside the house the phone rang, and he was so jittery he spilt beer down his chin and on to his shirt. But jittery about what? Nothing he could put his finger on; he just had this obscure feeling of unease deep within, a weird sense of . . . displacement. Cursing his clumsiness, he mopped up with his handkerchief, then stepped back into the kitchen and unhooked the portable from its wall cradle.

A familiar, slightly nasal voice squawked a cheery greeting.

'Hi, Jeff! It's Gil. Thought you wasn't home. Weren't takin' a shower or somethin', was you? Did I disturb ya?'

For a man with a doctorate in particle physics – and a research fellow at Columbia University to boot – Gil Gribble had the quaint grammar and twanging delivery of a New York cab driver. Or how New York cab drivers used to sound before the East Europeans and Asiatics took over.

'Hi, Gil, good to hear from you. I was out in the garden, relaxing with a beer. Pleasant evening here. Everything OK with you?'

'Sure, hunky-dory!' Everything Gil Gribble said seemed to be punctuated with exclamation marks. And he was the only person Cawdor knew who stuck to outmoded expressions like 'Hunky-dory'. 'How's Sarah and the sprog?'

'They're both fine.' The 'sprog' – a word Cawdor had heard no one but Gil ever use – was Daniella. 'They're both out at the minute. It's Sarah's agony-aunt spot on New Brunswick.'

'Right, yeah. I don't think we can catch that in New York, can we?'

'It's syndicated,' Cawdor told him. 'Not sure about Manhattan, but over thirty local stations carry it. They play the old Dave Brubeck number as intro music.'

'What old Dave Brubeck number?'

' "Take Five", remember it? That's the title of the show as well. *Take Five*. Each caller gets five minutes to discuss their problem, then they have to make way for the next one. Keeps the thing rolling along and stops the cranks and sad sacks hogging the line.'

'Hey, that's a neat idea! Who came up with it – Sarah?'

'Yeah, she thought of it,' Cawdor said, smiling to himself. Trust Gil to be so vague, even after Sarah had discussed her radio show many a time with him. Gil just didn't live in the ordinary world: he inhabited another plane of existence. Half the time he wandered through the crazy quantum world of particle physics where you could meet yourself on the stairs, turn into your own grandfather, die before you were born, etc. The other half he spent creating video games of mind-blowing complexity and fiendishness, purely for the intellectual challenge and amusement of himself and his circle of computer nerds. There was a story told about Gil Gribble, which Cawdor could believe was true and not apocryphal, that one time he forgot where his second-floor apartment was situated (116th Street, two blocks east of Broadway) and had to go into a phone booth and call the operator to find out his own address. The wonder of it was, Cawdor marvelled, that he was able to remember his own name, and hadn't spent hours with the phone in his hand sorting through the amazing junkyard of his brain until he stumbled across it.

'How's the Beast these days?' Cawdor asked, using Gil's pet name for the sprawling computer system that was taking over his apartment.

'You won't believe it, Jeff. Absolutely amazing! Teamed it with VR three-dimensional hologram graphics. It's a first, never seen it done before. Jeez, it's so damn real,' Gil enthused. 'Buildings, objects, even the people – you swear you can touch them. Right now I'm working on an interactive program I've christened "The Zone" where the player can create his own virtual reality as he goes along.'

'Doing all this for fun seems a bit of a waste. Couldn't you market it, sell it as a package? I'm certain there are commercial and industrial applications galore. You could make yourself a fortune.'

'Yeah? You reckon?' Gil Gribble's response was unsure.

'Why'd I wanna do that?' he then asked, genuinely baffled.

'Yeah, right, why would you?' Cawdor realised it was a dumb suggestion. Making money didn't even register a zero on Gil's list of priorities. Employing his creative and inventive faculties for their own sake was what mattered. The joy lay in exploring the boundless possibilities all around him, in setting up fiendish technological puzzles and solving them with the old grey matter. It occurred to Cawdor, not for the first time, that people whose only goal was to make a stash of money rarely succeeded for the simple reason that making money was their only goal. Those who *were* successful had a passion – a crusading zeal to bring something new and better into the world. When they achieved it, the money came along too, kind of tagged along for the ride as it were.

Gil was the perfect example. His ideas were probably worth millions because they really mattered to him, whereas the accumulation of wealth didn't rate a passing thought. Gil was sitting on riches, didn't know it, and didn't give a hoot anyway.

Cawdor reached across for his beer, only half-listening as Gil chattered on about his wonderful new toy. That was another thing about Gil: he flung himself body and soul into whatever fascinated him at the time, no half-measures, nothing faint-hearted.

'You can create your own landscape, your own city, your own people, that's the beauty of it. In fact "The Zone" is anything you want it to be. Like dreaming in a sense. It's your personal vision, unique to you and no one else. On top of which you can interact with it, play out various scenarios, and every time it comes out different, so you can never predict what's gonna happen next. Tell you, Jeff, it's kind of amazing. Real humdinger.'

'Humdinger'. Cawdor hadn't heard that in a while either. Something snagged at him, as if he sensed a flaw, a subtle contradiction, in what Gil was saying. 'How come it's different every time if the user creates the vision in the first place? And how can it be unpredictable when they're your own thoughts you've put in there?'

'Probability,' Gil said, slightly puzzled, as if it was the obvious answer to a dumb question.

'Huh?'

'Yeah, it's built into the program. An infinite progression of probable consequences – this way, that way, any which way.'

'I see,' Cawdor said, who didn't really. 'And who or what decides where these probable consequences lead to?'

'Well,' Gil said, sniffing. 'Nobody decides. Strictly speaking, nothing decides.'

'*Nothing* decides?'

'Yeah, it's random. Probability decides. You got a beer in your hand right this minute?'

Cawdor frowned. 'Yes, I just picked it up off the counter.'

'If you hadn't picked it up, the beer would still be sitting there, wouldn't it? Well, in parallel time it still is. You didn't pick it up. It's on the counter, not in your hand.'

Cawdor looked at the bottle of Michelob. 'But it is in my hand.'

'Sure, in that strand of time it is. But in another strand of time it's on the counter and you're standing there without a beer. That's probability.'

'This beer I'm not drinking sure tastes good though,' Cawdor muttered dryly, which made Gil Gribble chuckle. He went on, 'Could be we're not even having this conversation . . .'

'You got it, that's right, maybe we're not!' Gil agreed enthusiastically. Cawdor was being facetious – that was his intention at any rate – but by the sound of his voice Gil plainly wasn't.

They said their goodbyes and hung up. Cawdor finished off his beer and decided he could eat something. He looked at the clock. Daniella would be home soon, and in all probability she'd be hungry as well.

Probability. That damn word again.

They ate in the kitchen, the French doors open to admit a cool yet pleasant evening breeze. Cawdor had made a bolognese sauce, steamed and strained a large scoop of spaghetti, and chopped some tomatoes, cucumber, apples and iceberg lettuce as a side salad, sprinkled with grated walnuts. From the oven he took a sliced baguette wrapped in foil, basted lightly with garlic butter. He opened a bottle of chilled Californian Chardonnay, which Daniella was permitted to drink fifty-fifty with mineral water. She ate well enough, but he thought she looked paler than usual, and she was quiet, not bubbling over as expected about how rehearsals were going, the fun they had had with missing props, falling scenery, forgotten lines.

Just turned sixteen, his daughter was losing the gawky, gangling knobblyness of adolescence. Six months ago Daniella had reminded him of a yearling colt, tottering about on legs like sticks, so painfully thin that her ribs showed through her tank top. Now she was filling out, having grown to almost her adult height, was even developing a figure as distinct from a flat-as-an-ironing-board body. She took after Sarah, with her fair hair, pale colouring and fine bone structure. Her skin was flawless, almost translucent in its perfection, with a delicate gossamer down on the sides of her neck and the backs of her forearms.

Cawdor felt a pang. That too brief interlude of teetering between girlhood and womanhood was the most exquisite age, he believed, the vitality of life positively bursting into full bloom.

He added some wine to her glass and topped it up with mineral water.

'We need tickets for this play or just show up? And when is it – next week sometime?'

'You really want to come? Sure?' Her long lashes blinked at him, grey-blue eyes wide and steady.

'Don't you want us to?'

'Well, yeah, I don't mind.' Twich of the shoulder in a half-shrug. 'She said you weren't a big fan of theatre plays. You always fall asleep, snore all the way through, she said.'

' "She" is the cat's mother,' Cawdor said, stung by his daughter's discourtesy. 'I suggest you call her by her proper name.'

'Yeah, yeah. *Mom* said – OK?'

'Sarah told you that, huh?' Cawdor gave a heavy mock sigh. He held up a finger. 'I did it the one time, and I've never been allowed to forget it. And that play was over four hours long. Seemed more like ten.'

'This is thirty-five minutes.'

'That's my kind of play, Tonto,' he said, raising his glass. He clinked hers and grinned. Daniella gave a rather wan smile and sipped her wine. It was a game they had played since she was seven or eight, this Tonto–Kimo Sabe routine. Usually she would have responded, and they would have batted it back and forth. But not this evening, apparently.

He was trying to jolly her along, and not making too good a job of it. She might be feeling down because of her period, but he didn't know if it was that time of the month – and he certainly didn't intend raising such a delicate subject. If it didn't embarrass her, it definitely would him.

He tried another tack.

'Hey – vacation not far off. Looking forward to it?'

'Yeah, I guess, sort of . . .'

'It'll be fun. Lots of places to see. You've covered ancient-Roman history in school, haven't you? We'll stop by in Rome, tour the Coliseum, take a trip to Pisa and the leaning tower – and wait till you see the little villages of Tuscany, perched on the side of mountains.'

Daniella pushed her plate aside. She had apparently found something interesting in a stray breadcrumb and flicked it across the table. It bounced off the wine bottle.

Outwardly, Cawdor remained calm. Inwardly, he was infuriated by his daughter. He would have preferred her to come straight out with a flat statement: No, I'm not looking forward to it. I don't want to go. What's to see in Italy except a pile of broken statues?

More than anything, he hated the kind of lazy teenage indifference she was displaying. It was neither one thing nor the other. It was that manner some young people had of patronising their elders, of bored compliance with their wishes because that was the easiest route to take without giving offence to the old farts. The puzzling thing, however, was that Daniella had never behaved in such a truculent fashion before. She was a lively and intelligent and curious creature, not a sulky and tiresome and ill-mannered brat. Was the hormonal change she was undergoing the end of childhood – goodbye to Tonto and Kimo Sabe – and the beginning of the moody teenage phase? He dreaded the prospect.

No sense in prolonging a conversation that wasn't going anywhere. Not a conversation, he corrected himself, more a game of ping pong with only one player.

'Let's clear away. Then you can get an early night – you look tired to me.'

'No, I'm not,' Daniella contradicted him.

'OK, fine, you're not tired.' He wasn't going to argue the point.

In silence they stacked the plates and glasses in the dishwasher, and, while Cawdor stretched clingfilm over the salad bowl and put it in the fridge, Daniella returned the condiments to their shelf and wiped the table with a damp cloth.

'*Take Five*'s on in fifteen minutes,' he said, glancing at the wall clock. 'Gonna listen?'

Daniella shrugged indifferently. On her way to the door she tossed her head, flinging her long hair back over her shoulder in a gesture that was both arrogant and dismissive. He had never struck her physically, would never, ever have dreamt of doing such a thing, yet he felt like hitting her now.

'Daniella?' Cawdor said, his infuriation boiling up into real anger. 'What's got into you, for heaven's sake?'

'No, guess I won't listen to her – to Mom – if you don't mind. I'm gonna watch *The Lovebeams Show* in my room instead. If that's OK with you. Thanks for the meal and the wine, Dad.'

She went out, and a few moments later he heard her bedroom door slam upstairs.

Cawdor stood alone in the kitchen. The heavy silence Daniella had left behind her was disturbed only by the faint hum of the refrigerator. The gleaming white surfaces seemed to be glittering all around him, reflecting the overhead spotlights into his eyes. He pressed his eyelids shut against the painful glare.

He couldn't begin to imagine what was the matter with her, why his lovely sweet-natured daughter had been transformed into this sulky arrogant creature he didn't recognise. Moving to the cupboard, he reached for the bottle on the top shelf and poured a measure of Irish whiskey into a Waterford-crystal glass.

Credits were rolling up the TV screen. The final soaring chords swelled and then died away as the screen faded to black.

Cawdor lay back with his head on the cushion. He was palpitating and perspiring. He knew from past experience that his dreams were always much more vivid if he happened to fall asleep on the couch than if he dreamt in bed at night. His imagination seemed more excitable, and certainly more capricious. As if his mind was trapped in a kind of limbo.

But what relief, deeply heartfelt, to wake up.

He took a drink in celebration and felt the whiskey burn a molten path right down to the root of him. It was so good he took another and then rested his head, eyes closed, the glass on his chest.

The images floated up from his unconscious, like poisoned fish. It now struck him as funny, ludicrous even, to have imagined the sexual episode with Phyllis in his office. How in God's name had such a bizarre notion entered his head? If you believed Freud, it might mean that unconsciously he actually desired such a thing to happen. That he secretly lusted after her. Cawdor mulled this over, and came to the conclusion that if it *was* true, it was buried so damn deep there was no chance of it ever coming to the surface.

He opened his eyes and gazed across at his wife, glasses perched on the tip of her nose as she leafed through a brochure, the leaning tower of Pisa on its cover.

'Remember the last time we went to the Uffizi?' Sarah said, glancing up at him.

112

Cawdor nodded and smiled. Even though it was many years ago, he could see the golden light of that afternoon in Florence bathing the honey-coloured stonework of the Palazzo Vecchio... could feel the heat from the worn paving slabs through the soles of his shoes. The memory of it seemed like yesterday.

He felt content and relaxed, the warm glow of whiskey spreading through him. The liquor had gone straight to his head; his senses were spinning, his vision unsteady. He tried to remember if he had eaten earlier that evening, but couldn't. Hence the reason he was feeling woozy, drinking on an empty stomach, Cawdor supposed.

Another movie had started, some kind of prison drama. A hollow-cheeked runt of a guy with thinning fair hair was being strapped in the electric chair. The usual scene, with prison officers, a doctor and a priest, standing by with grim faces. The camerawork was terrible, the quality of the print even worse, grainy and badly processed, with blotches of light and shadow. Maybe it was a documentary, Cawdor thought, except they would never show a man actually in the electric chair, about to be fried. Standards in television had slipped, but not to that extent.

'... the appeal for clemency was rejected,' a voice was saying, 'and the execution will take place as scheduled. We now take you over live to join our reporter, Cal Parker, as the final minutes tick away.'

Cawdor squirmed round to look at the screen. Was it a movie or was it for real? This was totally unbelievable. Making a public spectacle of executions was a return to the Middle Ages. If not for real, it had to be a spoof, part of a sick game show – that was the only explanation he could think of. But there was none of that hysterical audience laughter, no jovial host egging on the contestants to make complete jerks of themselves.

'The condemned man has been shaved at the temples, as you can see,' a hushed voice said. 'Also, his lower calves have been shaved and K-Y jelly applied to aid conductivity. Thirty minutes ago, in his cell, he was made to don diapers, a necessary precaution because of involuntary dysfunction of the colonic system when the switch is thrown and the juice flows. The event itself is not a pleasant sight to view, so, if you're of a nervous or sensitive disposition, prepare yourself or maybe look away for a minute or so. I'll give you the countdown, so be ready for it.'

Despite himself, and even while feeling repugnance, Cawdor craned forward. To watch a man die, live, on nationwide TV, was an event of such momentous historical significance that he was bereft of thought or feeling, beyond that of morbid curiosity. He felt numbed and mesmerised by it, his emotions on hold. He sneaked a glance at Sarah, to see if she was as gripped as he was. She was turning the pages of that damn holiday brochure, smiling to herself. A man was about to die and she was lost in daydreams of Tuscany.

Cawdor stared at the screen. The man was slumped forward as far as the restraining straps would allow. On the wall behind him, a thin red hand swept round the big white face of a clock, marking off the final seconds. There was a kind of fuzziness above the man's head, vapour hanging in the air, like a faint blue halo. What was that – static electricity? Had the execution taken place and the blue halo was a discharge from the body? No, not yet – Cawdor could plainly see that the man's eyes were open, and he was staring down at his left hand.

On the big white clock the seconds swept smoothly away, and the long black hand jerked suddenly to two minutes past midnight. The man sat motionless, the fuzzy blue patch hovering above his head, waiting with incredible calmness for the ultimate event. The image on the screen seemed frozen in time, stuck in the last eternal moment.

Leaning forward on the cushion, unblinking, Cawdor swallowed so hard that his throat hurt. He felt a sour burning sensation and started to cough, and then to choke.

He opened his eyes to find himself covered in sweat.

He looked at the TV. The screen was blank. And he was alone. There was no one sitting in the armchair.

On the coffee table next to him stood a bottle of

Jameson's, almost empty. The Waterford-crystal glass lay on its side, the spilt whiskey making a trail of bubbles on the varnished surface. A glistening bead of amber liquid formed on the table's edge and dripped to the damp patch on the carpet. Another slowly gathered and hung there, trembled, and fell.

He sat up, his head throbbing, a hollow sickly feeling in the pit of his stomach. Christ, but he felt dreadful.

Light from the table lamp glanced off the bottle in splintering fragments that pierced his brain like needle points. He attempted to look at the time, but the rectangular face of his wristwatch wouldn't stay still.

Upstairs, from Daniella's room, he heard the muffled sound of applause and cheering. She had walked out of the kitchen and gone upstairs to catch *The Lovebeams Show* less than an hour ago. Had he practically finished the bottle and drunk himself into a stupor in so short a time?

It came back to him then. In his dream he had been dreaming – a dream within a dream. In that dream he had been lying here on the sofa watching the man on TV about to be executed. He had awakened from that dream too, to find himself lying on the sofa. It wasn't possible that this was a dream too, was it, and he had yet to wake up?

3

It was two days later, on a warm peaceful evening, that Sarah dropped the bombshell.

They were in the garden. Sarah was kneeling on the grass, her hands caked with earth from the Lavatera Silver Cup – grown from seedlings – which she was planting in rows along the edge of the flowerbed. He had uncoiled the water hose and was adjusting the jet to a fine spray when Sarah turned her head to look at him. Her silent stare made Cawdor stop what he was doing. The silence stretched out, like pulling a rubber band to breaking point.

Then she said, 'Jeff, I've got something awful to tell you. Daniella's on drugs.'

Cawdor's mouth fell open. 'What? I don't believe . . .' He frowned at her. 'You mean you caught her smoking a joint or something?'

Sarah lowered her eyes to the earth she was kneading between her fingertips. 'That I wouldn't have minded, I guess. Kids her age smoke grass, I know that.' She dusted off her hands and rummaged in the back pocket of her jeans. 'I found this in her room.' It was what looked like a candy wrapper, a square of waxed paper bearing a red 'M' in a black circle. 'Any idea what this stuff is?' Sarah asked. 'What the "M" stands for?'

Cawdor shook his head. 'Have you asked her about it?'

'Of course I haven't.'

'Why not?'

'Because she'd have gone absolutely apeshit over my prying into her personal things. I remember when I was a teenager and wanted to keep things secret from my parents. They respected my right to do it, but once a kid feels that trust has been broken it's a hopeless cause trying to win it back.'

Cawdor knelt down on the grass beside her. He hadn't thought to mention Daniella's strange behaviour a couple of evenings ago; in fact it had passed clean out of his head. He kept his voice low, because Daniella was in the house somewhere. 'Sarah, honey, she's already broken that trust herself, hasn't she? The trust *we* had in her. What are we supposed to do? Ignore it, pretend nothing's wrong, just because you peeked into her personal stuff?'

'We won't get anywhere by antagonising her,' Sarah said obstinately. 'We charge straight in, raising the roof, it'll turn her against us. Let's try and think this through, Jeff, the best way to go about it.'

'So what is the best way? You thought of one?'

Miserably, Sarah shook her head. She picked up the trowel and stabbed it into the flowerbed.

'Maybe the stuff doesn't belong to her,' Cawdor said.

'The wrapper was hidden away, stuffed down the side of the mattress.'

'Why didn't you tell me about this before?'

'Before when?' Sarah said. She was busy with the trowel again, scooping out shallow holes to take the seedlings. 'I only found out myself yesterday.'

He recalled how pale and quiet Daniella had been during their spaghetti dinner in the kitchen, and how she'd then become sullen and insulting, totally out of character. Something occurred to him.

'If you weren't prying in Daniella's room, how come you know the stuff was there?'

'I didn't say I wasn't prying; I said it would be a big mistake for her to think I was.'

'So you went in there with the intention of looking for something?'

Sarah gave a tight nod.

'What?'

'Videos. Not the regular kind,' Sarah added with a side-long look. 'You know the kind I mean. Sandy's mother said they're being passed around in school.'

'Daniella watching that stuff? You sure?'

Sarah gave him a thin, pitying smile. 'Come as a surprise that your sixteen-year-old daughter is interested in sex?'

'No, course not . . .' That was true. More shock than surprise. 'You find anything?'

'No. I didn't want to disturb all her things, so I left it. But I found the wrapper – and that was even worse than I feared.'

Taking drugs and watching blue videos? Cawdor's mind accepted the facts but his heart and soul rebelled. Not Daniella, his own sweet, pure daughter. He couldn't believe it. Yet the hollow, sick feeling inside gave the lie to his disbelief.

Phyllis wasn't at her desk as Cawdor strode through to his office the next morning. Usually she was there to greet him, coffee percolating on the electric ring behind her desk, already reaching for the mug to pour a steaming brimful.

Cawdor checked the time: 9:07. No coffee and no Phyllis. Was she off sick? He couldn't remember the last time she had been away from work, it was so long ago.

But this morning, of all mornings, Phyllis was the least of his worries.

His mind elsewhere, Cawdor swung his chair to the computer and switched on the CAD system. He had a mountain of work and he'd better get on with it. Worrying over whether or not his daughter had a problem with drugs wasn't going to resolve anything. He and Sarah had to work it out together, decide between them what action to take.

About mid-morning, Don Carlson appeared in the main design office, where Cawdor, with the help of one of the electrical engineers, was trying to pinpoint a glitch in a thermocouple circuit layout. The look on Don's face was enough to tell Cawdor that something was up.

Don jerked his head to indicate he wanted a private word. They walked together past the rows of desks and workstations with their flickering green screens. Don went ahead into the office and remained standing by his desk while Cawdor shut the door.

Don's angular face with its prominent cheekbones was a stony mask. 'I don't know how to say this, Jeff, but . . .' He stared down at the carpet, Adam's apple working.

'Not like you to be stuck for –' Cawdor's breath failed him. He stopped dead. Something had happened at home. Sarah. Or at school – Daniella. The police had called Don to break the news to him. That's how bad it was. Don's air of distress was proof of that. Had one of them been hurt in an accident? A fire at the house, a car smash, a 747 falling on them from the skies?

'It's . . . Phyllis,' Don said, looking as wretchedly embarrassed as Cawdor had ever seen him.

A wave of relief swept over Cawdor. Thank God it was her (that's right, she hadn't shown up for work) and not them. The ugly thought almost made him blush with shame, but the relief was still there.

He found his voice again.

'What's the matter, Don? Is she unwell?'

'She's been on the phone to me.'

'Then she's OK? She isn't hurt?'

Don turned away, shaking his head. Cawdor started to get annoyed. He actually was very fond of Phyllis, and he wanted to know how much of his sympathy this was going to take.

'Phyllis has made a serious allegation . . .' Don was looking away, his gaze hovering aimlessly as if it couldn't settle. 'She can't decide whether to report it to the police or not. Jeff, the fact is, she's made an accusation against you.'

Cawdor went suddenly cold. He knew what was coming. He knew what Don was going to say before he said it.

'Of sexual assault. When she brought some letters into your office for signing.' Don glanced up, spreading his hands as if in apology. 'That's what she told me, and she went into some detail too. According to Phyllis, she was standing next to you at the desk, leaning over, and she felt your hand on her leg. Then you moved it right up and touched her – intimately. That's how she expressed it. She came out with this stuff over the phone, very explicit, not like Phyllis at all. Incredible that she could have invented such a story.'

'Meaning she didn't,' Cawdor said grimly.

'No, I didn't mean it *that* way.' Don still wasn't, Cawdor noticed, looking him squarely in the eye.

It was more incredible than Don Carlson supposed: that Cawdor had fantasised about just such a sexual episode, and then Phyllis had actually accused him of doing that very thing. How was that possible? That his fantasy seduction had somehow zapped through the ether and implanted itself in her brain? That didn't make any sense, but nothing else he could think of made any sense either.

He said to Don, 'She called and told you this a few minutes ago?' Don nodded. 'And when did all this take place, or she say it took place?'

'Yesterday afternoon. When she brought your letters in.'

'Why didn't she report it then?'

'I asked her about that. Said she was too shook up. She couldn't believe you'd do such a thing; it totally shocked her.'

119

'So she went home and brooded about it – is that her story?'

Don nodded. His face bore an expression of mingled pain and bewilderment. 'I didn't know what the hell to say to her. She was crying as she came out with all this stuff. I couldn't stop her. I mean, anyone but Phyllis, and there'd be a question mark –' He snapped his lips together as if the words had escaped when his intention had been to keep them under guard.

'And you believe her, do you, Don?' Cawdor's voice was steady and cold.

'I – I don't know.'

'Did I fuck her?'

'What?'

'You heard. Did she say I fucked her?'

Don shook his head. He edged his narrow flanks on to the window ledge and rocked foward, his agitated hands clasping and unclasping. 'If you want to know, she said you put your fingers, then your whole hand, inside her while she was face down on the desk. And you just carried on signing letters as if nothing was happening. That's what I can't get over, she went into every detail – like, you know, describing something that had really happened to her. She didn't just say, "He raped me," or "He assaulted me," but gave it the whole works, chapter and verse.'

Cawdor's eyes drifted off his partner to take in the hazy Manhattan skyline through the large plate-glass window. He didn't know what to say. He couldn't tell Don that he had fantasised the exact same scenario, with Phyllis a willing participant, because Don would instantly, and understandably, jump to the conclusion that Cawdor was inventing this pathetic lie to cover his tracks. In fact, the truth of what had happened – the seduction taking place inside his head, and *only* there – was the one thing he could never reveal to anybody. People would simply shake their heads and give him a withering look of scorn and pity: that the best you can come up with, you degenerate sonofabitch? Take advantage of a young female employee and think you can get away with it by giving out this cock-and-bull story? What kind of a cowardly slimeball are you?

'What am I supposed to do now?' Cawdor said. 'Sit and sweat it out while Phyllis makes up her mind what action she intends to take? And what about you?'

'Me?' Don gave him a sharp, furrowed look. 'What d'you mean?'

'You're involved in this because Phyllis chose to tell you about it. Why'd she do that if she didn't expect you to act on it?'

'I am acting on it,' Don said, nettled. 'I called you in and told you, didn't I? What else am I supposed to do? Christ, Jeff, give me a break, this isn't easy for me. If you want to know, it's the hardest fucking thing I've ever had to do.' He sucked at his lower lip. 'I keep asking myself, Why? Why would she say such a thing, for what reason? She's a sweet kid, a good worker, been loyal to us. Trustworthy. Can you think of any reason?'

For the life of him, Cawdor couldn't.

Don folded back the doors of the walnut cabinet and poured out two hefty shots of J&B. He added ice from the miniature icebox and the two men drank silently in an atmosphere that was palpably thick with tension, as if a potent nerve gas had been siphoned into the room. Side by side at the window, staring out, they tried in their separate ways to come to terms with the situation, and to figure out what could be done about it.

'We'll have to hope she doesn't go to the police,' Don said eventually. 'No question the press will get hold of it then for sure.' A thought struck him. 'Could that be it, d'you think? Blackmail? Does she have money problems? She want a payoff to keep her mouth shut?'

'That isn't Phyllis,' Cawdor said. 'Not in her nature. I can only think it's some kind of . . .' He hesitated.

'What?'

'Nervous breakdown.'

'She been acting strange?'

'No, goddamnit, she hasn't. We get on really well together, I like her and she likes me.' Cawdor felt himself

121

reddening. 'I mean – What I mean is, we have a good working relationship.'

He seemed to be digging a hole for himself, stumbling over ordinary blameless phrases that had become suddenly pregnant with sinister meaning. Don patted his shoulder. 'I know, it's OK, I know what you're saying. We'll work this out somehow. It'll come right in the end.'

Cawdor finished off his drink in a gulp. He was deeply shaken by this, naturally, but he couldn't tell Don *how* deeply. To be accused of sexually assaulting a female colleague was bad enough; to have your secret fantasy turn into horrifying reality was even worse.

Maybe it wasn't Phyllis at all, Cawdor thought crazily, who was having the nervous breakdown. Maybe it was him.

The visit to Glen Cove wasn't strictly necessary; in fact it wasn't necessary at all. The contract for a development of luxury condominiums on the headland overlooking Long Island Sound hadn't yet been awarded, although UltraCast had pitched for it and was included in a short list of three. Cawdor told Don that he needed to take another look at the proposed site because he was worried about the mix of shale, sandstone and rock, and he wondered if their costings had taken full account of the geological substrata.

It was a weak pretence, which Don recognised of course, but he simply nodded and said, 'Sure. Go out there, take another look.'

Cawdor came off the two-lane blacktop and steered the Oldsmobile down a deeply rutted sandy track towards a flat natural basin about 300 yards from the water's edge. Tall, rattling reeds and wind-blasted bushes were dotted sparsely about, struggling for survival in the sculpted dunes, buffeted by the constant westerlies whipping up clouds of salt spray. Already Cawdor could taste it on his lips. He stood by the car, facing into the wind, thankful to be out of the office and away from New York for just a short while.

Almost in a daze, he found himself walking towards the sound of unseen waves crashing against rocks, his hands bunched inside the pockets of his jacket. On the promontory he stood for a long time watching the ceaseless motion below him, his face becoming numb from the wind and sea spray. He was actually getting a soaking from the flung droplets, but it was of no importance. There was a small craft of some kind, a fishing boat perhaps, pushing steadily through the crests and troughs to the open sea. He watched it until it was a hazy speck, and carried on watching even when it had dwindled to nothing more than a faint smudge on his retina.

One word kept spinning through his head. The word that Doctor Khuman had used. That word 'disruption'.

That was how it felt exactly – as if his routine, peaceful, happy existence had been violently disrupted by an unknown force, something out there in the vast darkness of his ignorance and incomprehension. Doctor Khuman had talked of cause and effect too, he remembered, of events not being allowed to follow their proper course. Was this what was happening to him? Somebody or something meddling in his life?

Thinking back, he tried to pinpoint when it had started. Certainly after Doctor Khuman's visit, he was convinced of that. Daniella behaving strangely when they were having dinner in the kitchen . . . No, before that, his sexual fantasy about Phyllis, which had now come full circle with her accusation that he had actually done the deed. And, of course, Sarah finding evidence of drug-taking in their daughter's room. If these events were connected in some way, Cawdor hadn't the faintest notion how, or what the whole crazy farrago was supposed to mean.

But he was forgetting something. The dreams he had been having during the past – what, week, ten days? Ever since Doctor Khuman's appearance in his office, when the guy had hypnotised Phyllis or some damn thing and waltzed straight in.

Cawdor screwed his mind tight, focusing his concentration on what the dreams had been about. But dreams, of their nature, were elusive and transient will-o'-the-wisps, powerfully vivid at the moment of dreaming and then just as quickly forgotten, consigned to the trash can of the unconscious, where they came from in the first place. Come on, come on, he raged at himself: it was you that dreamt them, dredge 'em up again from that soggy grey mass you call a brain.

An image shimmered tantalisingly at the edge of his mind, wrapped in a kind of vague blue haze. It resolved itself into a blue halo. Cawdor edged slowly and cautiously towards the image, scared that if he approached too fast, pressed too hard, it might suddenly vanish. And then, instantaneously, the whole picture came to him of a guy strapped in the electric chair, the blue halo hovering a foot or so above his head. There was a big clock on the wall behind him, the thin red hand sweeping round the face. The guy was in a trance, staring down at his left hand. In his dream, Cawdor remembered, this had been happening on TV – that's right, he'd been watching a movie, so he thought, or a gruesome fly-on-the-wall documentary.

OK, he'd dreamt of somebody about to be fried in the chair. A stranger he'd never seen before. So what? That was two or three evenings ago, lying on the sofa, after finishing half a bottle of Irish whiskey. In that state, small wonder his unconscious had conjured up so macabre a scene. He'd recalled it, great, and yet was none the wiser: its meaning or significance – assuming it had one – eluded him.

Hands clenched in the pockets of his jacket, Cawdor arched back as the wind sent a stinging wet slap of spray into his face.

The physical sensation acted upon his memory, as if that too had received a mental slap, and the buried dream shot to the surface of his consciousness. In it he had been on a sailing ship bound for America. His wife and son were with him. The ship was packed with emigrants, mostly poor people, with a few skilled tradesmen like himself. Cawdor could almost smell the reek of humanity crammed below decks. He could feel the heat of the sun in mid-

Atlantic burning his shoulders through his broadcloth shirt. There were several religious cults on board, and the dream now yielded itself up so vividly that he knew the name of one of them – the Shouters. And see them too: a circle of tall, austere figures in dark robes punishing some poor wretch for a transgression of their dark serpentine faith.

For several minutes he stood there, remembering, finally aware that his clothing hung heavy, saturated with spray.

Cawdor turned from the shoreline. Heading back to the car, he moved slowly along the sandy track winding through the dunes. Don Carlson's reaction to Phyllis's accusation troubled him. If Don, his partner and close colleague of ten years or more, had doubts about him, what would others think? Suppose Sarah got to hear of it? Even if she rejected the whole thing as absurd and accepted his plea of innocence (already he was on the defensive, having to *plead* his innocence) the niggling, wriggling worm of suspicion would be at work inside her. That was human nature. No smoke without fire. That's what people would say, giving one another sly knowing winks.

Yeah, course the bastard did it, took advantage. Sure as God made little green apples.

Inside the car he discovered he was shivering. The square green quartz clock in the leather fascia told him it was four-thirty. He backed the car round and drove up the rutted track to the two-lane road which, six miles further on, linked up with 107.

Traffic was light as far as Roslyn Heights, after which it got heavier, but it was heading towards him out of the city. The shortest route home was directly through Manhattan. He knew he had to talk to somebody, and the somebody he had in mind lived on 116th Street, two blocks east of Broadway.

The dolls and fluffy toys that had been her childhood friends and companions, but which she no longer played with, were arranged on three corner shelves above the unit with its tier of drawers that served as a worktop for Daniella's dress designs and fashion sketches. Patterns and intricate shapes cut from sheets of brightly coloured paper were scattered about; they were intended to form an ensemble of ideas for tops, skirts, dresses, casual wear and complete outfits, but had lain on the worktop, untouched and forgotten, for the past fortnight.

Wearing T-shirt and shorts, her long brown legs tucked under her, Daniella reclined on the bed, propped up on a bank of pillows and cushions. The screen threw a green wash of light over everything, making the pink bed covers a sickly purple. She'd half-closed the blinds, dimming the light that was already fading as evening came on. There was no lock on the door, but her mother wouldn't enter without knocking. Sarah respected her privacy, knew that her daughter liked to remain secluded in her room. She sucked on the round lozenge that had rather a bittersweet taste. All the kids at school were using them. They were passed from hand to hand, given away as freely as candy. The wrapper, bearing a red 'M' in a black circle, was screwed up in the pocket of her shorts. Daniella wasn't too sure what the 'M' stood for, though Sandy had told her it was something called 'melibrium'. And God, yes, she'd have to remember to flush the wrapper down the toilet – she had found a wrapper pushed underneath the mattress a couple of mornings ago, and panicked that she might have left other wrappers for her mother to find. If that happened, the shit would really hit the fan, and how!

The stuff was working, she could feel it now, as if *redness* - that's the only way she could describe it – was pulsing through her body in slow undulating waves. It was like floating languorously in a red ocean, the sky above kind of yellow. No, more like ochre, as Mrs Sullivan, her art teacher, would describe it.

Daniella sighed luxuriously and sank into the pillows, absorbed by the image on the screen. His face was lean and pale, and he had burning soulful eyes with long black lashes that penetrated right to the core of her being. She loved the way the two curtains of hair swept back over his

126

ears; the thin, curved sideburns that emphasised the fine cheekbones and shadowy hollows beneath.

It was Ricki who had first told her about the *Beamers of Joy* video. In class one day she'd rolled her eyes and said in a throaty whisper, 'Gotta watch it. You'll come like Niagara with that hunk, babe.' In truth, Daniella had been shocked at the crudity of Ricki's language, but what she said was a living fact. You could really get it on with this guy. And what seemed to make it even more exciting was that he wasn't your regular tanned musclebound jock; more the slim and lithe type, dark eyes throbbing into yours with the promise of sweet and tender understanding . . . and yet lurking in their depths was that hint of devilment that sent chills down her spine.

Oh yes, absolutely – Yessss! the hit was on line now – she was afloat on the red ocean under the ochre sky with this gorgeous guy, the two of them locked together like true soul mates, the thudding bass rhythm of the soundtrack beating in time with her heart. His eyes seemed to contain a secret message for her and her alone. It was in the music too, an urgent voice whispering repetitively in her ear –

Messiah Wilde loves you

– and the harder Daniella stared at the screen, which now and then seemed to flash with faint symbols –

I love Messiah Wilde

– the more she felt to be sliding into another realm while the world around her became airy and insubstantial, like a ghostly shadow play.

The walls of the room had turned dark red and were starting to bulge inward. It was getting hotter too. The dark eyes on the screen seemed to glow with scorching heat she could feel on her skin. Daniella stretched out her legs, shiny with sweat, and arched back against the pillows as the undulating waves of redness coursed through her body. She felt to be burning up with fever. There was a tingling sensation in her breasts, and her thighs were on fire. Her mouth parted in a dry gasp, and the words moaned out of her, 'I love Messiah Wilde . . . I love Messiah Wilde . . . I love Messiah Wilde,' until they

127

became a chant that pulsed inside her to the beat of the music and the bulging dark-red walls. She pressed her hands to her breasts and pushed her palms down her sides to her waist. Her damp fingers fumbled with the buttoned fastening of her shorts, and she raised her legs to slide the shorts and her pants off together.

Daniella opened her legs wide to the dark burning eyes on the screen. He could see her, she knew it, and the thought of brazenly displaying herself to his gaze made her shudder deliciously with a thrill of wanton wickedness. She longed to have Messiah Wilde lying beside her on the bed. To feel his lean body close to hers, to submit to the touch of those slender graceful hands. He would be very gentle with her, Daniella knew, and also very masculine and hard, both tough and tender, fully understanding how it must be handled as she ceased being a girl and became a woman.

But she was alone in the furnace heat of the dark-red room. No one there to caress her . . .

Looking into his eyes and chanting his name, she could imagine it was him doing it, his long tapering fingers slipping inside her, her moistness responding to his urging, quickening tempo. She writhed on the bed, uttering little moans and whimpers, while around her the room pulsed waves of heat and the beat of the music pounded on relentlessly from crescendo to climax.

4

Gil Gribble pushed back the mop of frizzy ginger hair from his eyes and fitted the helmet-like VR sensory unit to his head. With the padded shoulder braces fitting snugly, it transformed his appearance to that of a small, potbellied man with the shiny black head of a gigantic beetle.

Suddenly muted, the braying horns of gridlocked traffic coming through the balcony windows sounded to his ears even softer than the usual subdued hum of the central processing core. Gribble settled himself. The Beast was his baby all right. He'd cannibalised a dozen or more systems to build it. The control console alone took up a complete workbench, cables and wires trailing off to six shelves of a ceiling-high metal rack that held the peripherals and power transformer feeds. The memory store could hold half the contents of Columbia University Library, whose tall narrow windows directly faced his across 116th Street.

Reaching up, he tweaked a control on the side of the headpiece, then, like a blind man, with outstretched hand fumbled for the master switch on the panel in front of him. The central processing core chuntered to itself for a while; there came a series of clicks and beeps and electronic burps; and then the program locked in.

He was in business.

A black void filled his vision. At the centre of which was a glowing orb the size of a dime, pulsing with varied colours. Gribble leant forward, a pugnacious frown contorting his face behind the visor. He was visualising the billions of neurons zapping through his brain which formed his consciousness and controlled his autonomic system, and attempting to make just a tiny handful of those neurons interact with, and thus affect, the image he was seeing. Similar experiments had been done in the University's Department of Parapsychological Studies – he himself had witnessed them – in which human control subjects could impose a pattern on a random number sequence by the use of mindpower alone, without any physical connection to the apparatus. They'd done it also with atomic clocks, slowing them down or speeding them up by nanoseconds. The infinitesimal degree of success didn't matter. It was the proof that it *could* be done, that it *was* possible, that excited Gil Gribble. The principle had been established, and he intended to take it a step further; well, one huge, great, gigantic leap forward – if it worked.

One small anomaly was vexing him, however, which had nothing to do with getting the Beast to work. It was that, whenever he put the headpiece on, the same set of images kept flashing before his mind's eye, as if the electronic signals generated by the software were interacting with

129

the neurons in his brain. In other words, the exact reverse of what he intended was happening: it was the computer calling the shots, controlling *his* mindwaves instead of his imposing his will on a bunch of integrated chips and germanium circuitry. Now this wasn't on. He'd built the hardware piece by piece, created the program, bolted the contraption together with his own two hands. There wasn't a single byte in the hard-disk memory store that he hadn't put there. So how come it had a 'mind' of its own? No matter how sophisticated they were, machines couldn't think for themselves. They didn't possess innate intelligence and therefore couldn't figure out something that was beyond their ken.

There had to be a gremlin or a glitch lurking somewhere in the system, Gribble reckoned. He'd track it down, root it out, and strangle the little bastard. No damn computer was going to tell *him* what to think.

Hands gripping his knees, cut off from the outside world inside the beetle-like headpiece, his entire attention was focused on the glowing orb of shifting, mingling colours. The orb began to pulse and expand, resembling the primeval atom at the birth of creation, the big bang that kick-started the universe into being. Fine so far. He was in control. Easy does it. Not too fast. The orb was expanding now like a slow-motion explosion, filling the black void with light and colour and movement. Gribble blinked, stared, fingers digging into his knees. He couldn't believe it. The same thing was happening again. The same crazy images as before . . .

He was in a vast auditorium filled with thousands of excited people keyed up to a fever pitch of anticipation. A drum roll sounded and a spotlight stabbed through the air, forming a silvery disc at the centre of the curved stage. The audience seemed to rise up all around him as a tall; lean, lithe figure strode out from the side of the platform. As the figure stepped into the spotlight the noise became deafening. Glistening black hair swept back from long sideburns, smouldering dark eyes, almost a contemptuous sneer on his full lips, he swung his guitar round and struck

130

a pose, legs braced apart, one shoulder dipped, head thrown back, and let it rip –

Gil Gribble blanched. He couldn't believe this.

Elvis singing 'Heartbreak Hotel'. Or rather, not singing it, but mangling the words between his adenoids and grinding out the result in strangulated hiccuping falsetto.

Gribble tore off the headset. He held it at arm's length, in two minds whether or not to dash it to the floor. The one singer he hated most in all the world. Never had liked his voice, his appearance, his music, his movies. Never liked him, period. If this Pandora's box wanted to play fun and games with its creator, why couldn't it have brought on stage a real singer, somebody he would appreciate and enjoy – Billie Holiday, say, or Nat King Cole – instead of a hip-swinging truck driver with tortured tonsils?

Muttering to himself, Gribble placed the headset on the table. He felt a movement and glanced down to see Schrödinger, his scruffy white and marmalade cat, brushing herself against his leg. He picked her up and stroked her back, which undulated under his hand. She made a low growling purr.

'Wonder what you'd see,' Gribble mused aloud, 'if I tried it out on you? Tom and Jerry? Or a cat's universe, huh? Whatever that looks like? Yeah, an ever expanding bowl of milk.'

Schrödinger had endured enough stroking. She squirmed free and bounded to the floor, tail whipping to and fro.

The door buzzer sounded. Gribble padded down the hallway in his laceless sneakers and squinted through the peephole. His face lit up. Swiftly he slid the bolts back, released the three locks, lifted the angled iron strut out of the way, and finally opened the door.

'Hey, Jeff! Come on in, come in.' He grabbed Cawdor by the elbow and felt dampness. 'Is it raining?' he asked, puzzled.

Cawdor shook his head and proceeded along the narrow hallway into the organised chaos of the front room. After a few moments of relocking and rebarring, Gribble followed him in, rubbing his hands and beaming.

'Hey, it's great to see you, man. Didn't think I would so soon, not after we talked on the phone and you said you was busy and stuff. You want something to drink? I got beer, I guess, and, er . . . that's about it.'

'I could go a beer,' Cawdor said, looking around for somewhere to sit. Gribble shifted a huge stack of computer magazines, academic journals and junk mail from a chair on to the floor, where it threatened to topple over. Cawdor sat down on the tubular kitchen chair with the plastic back faked to look like wood.

Rubbing his hands briskly, Gribble went bustling off to the tiny kitchen. Halfway there he paused and turned, frowning. 'You OK, Jeff? You seem kinda . . .'

'Get the beer,' Cawdor said. 'Then I'll tell you.'

'Jeez, that's a real humdinger, Jeff.'

Gribble's tongue performed a slow rotation, licking off the dewdrops of beer clinging to the fringes of his beard. He straightened up in the chair and pushed the frizzy mop of hair back from the high dome of his forehead. It immediately flopped down again.

'Is that it, the sum total of your considered opinion?' Cawdor muttered dryly. ' "A real humdinger"? Thanks, Gil.'

'Well, the woman's a crackpot obviously, wouldn't you say? It's all up here –' he tapped his temple '– a fantasy plain and simple. She can't prove anything, can she? So?'

It was all Cawdor could manage to stop himself grinding his teeth in frustration. Though he'd started off by telling Gil Gribble about the episode with Phyllis Keets, he found it impossible to hold back on the other stuff, and out it all came. Seeing the man in the electric chair with the blue haze hovering above him. His dream of the sailing ship, centuries ago, with its cargo of fetid humanity. He even mentioned his daughter's odd behaviour at dinner the other evening that had so baffled and alarmed him. Gribble had listened impassively, blinking now and again in a perplexed fashion as he tried to make the connection between these disparate events in this disjointed narrative. Therein lay the puzzle: there wasn't any connection. None that Gribble could see, anyway, and Cawdor had to admit he couldn't either.

The bit about Phyllis, however, had registered more strongly with Gribble. Although he had never met her, she and Gribble had spoken a number of times on the phone when he had called Cawdor at his office.

Even so, his conclusion was wide of the mark, and Cawdor told him so.

'You're missing the point, Gil.'

'I am?' Although he had no need of spectacles, Gribble gave the impression of myopia with his owlish large brown eyes forever blinking.

'It wasn't her fantasy – Phyllis's – it was *mine*. I told you, these weird sexual images just popped up out of nowhere; I had her over the desk and I was ... you know, touching her, my hand right up inside. Nothing, I swear to you, like that happened. Nothing. Yet she calls Don and describes in detail the very same experience. If it never happened – and it didn't, except in my mind – how come she knows about it?' Cawdor took a swig of beer and belched. 'Got a quantum theory to fit that? Can't you run it through the Beast – the Darth Vader's helmet there – and see what it comes up with?'

He gestured with the beer can to the headset among the clutter on the workbench, with its jumble of cabinets connected by skeins of cables to the equipment on the metal shelves. He wasn't being serious; at least not intentionally so.

Apparently Gil Gribble thought he was. 'You're welcome to try, but I ain't got the glitches ironed out yet.' He sighed gloomily. 'Somethin' screwy goin' on I can't figure out.' He gazed off into space, biting his bottom lip. 'Could be the probability curve's out of kilter. Even so, that don't explain it. Couldn't stand the guy. Never a *real* singer, you ask me.'

Cawdor was positively not tempted to ask him what he meant by this. With even a hint of prompting, Gil would launch into a complicated, impenetrable spiel peppered with 'temporality' and 'synchronicity' and 'acausality' and other words ending in 'ity' that gave Cawdor a headache just listening to it, never mind trying to understand it.

'Sarah any idea what's been goin' on at the office?' Gribble asked.

'Nothing's been going on at the office.'

'I mean – Ya know what I mean.'

'Don just told me today, Gil. I haven't seen Sarah yet.'

Gribble fixed Cawdor with his big, brown, earnest eyes. 'Know what I think? I think if I was you I'd tell her. S'pose she hears it from somebody and you *ain't* told her? She's gonna suspect somethin' fishy's goin' on even if there ain't. She might think, Jeff's got a guilty conscience, that's why he kept quiet about it. If there was nothin' to it, you'd tell her, right?'

That made sense. Except that he hadn't revealed to Gil his deeper fears, the sickly foreboding he had of things falling to pieces. In some obscure way Cawdor felt himself trapped in a downward, ever tightening spiral that was sucking him deeper and deeper into an unknown yet ultimately terrifying darkness. He could sense it, feel it in the marrow of his bones. But he was unable to stand back and see the thing whole. And he felt powerless to do anything to stop it happening. That was the most frightening thing of all.

'What say we step out and get somethin' to eat?' Gil Gribble proposed, finding a space in the workbench's clutter for his empty beer can. 'There's a halfway decent place just round the corner. You like Italian food, don't you?' He smacked the palms of his hands together, trying to lighten the sombre mood. 'Hey, that is if you don't have to get on home . . .'

'No, I don't,' Cawdor said. 'Not right now.'

He felt a sudden lurch in his stomach, like a physical blow from a heavyweight's glove, and a voice in his mind said, Yes, you do. Right now. He stood and said, 'I have to go.'

It was Sarah. Something about Sarah. It was the next link in the inevitable downward swirling spiral. Oh Jesus no! Had something happened to her?

Gribble was blinking at him, puzzled, from under tangled reddish eyebrows. 'Huh? Which is it, Jeff? You just said you was stayin'.'

'I've changed my mind.'

Right now!

'I have to go, right now. Sorry, Gil.' He looked around for his coat, the one he hadn't brought with him.

Gil Gribble followed Cawdor along the hallway. Gribble had to push past him to attend to the various bars, bolts and locks. Cawdor waited with shoulders tensed, clenching and loosening his fists repeatedly. He was white as a sheet. At long last Gribble got the door open and edged back in the cramped space, a small, humped figure with a comical fuzz of beard, gazing up with wide, spaniel-brown eyes. 'You OK to drive? Sure now?'

Cawdor went past him, muttering, 'Gotta get back. Sorry, Gil, don't ask me why.'

Gribble watched him go down the steep stairway. The guy was suffering some kind of mental trauma, that was obvious. Battling a terrible inner turmoil. He'd never seen Jeff this way before. It was perplexing and worrying, and it frightened the living shit out of him.

North of Grant's Tomb he came on to the Hudson Parkway, heading for George Washington Bridge. The rush-hour peak was over, but even so it took him an agonising 45 minutes to cross the bridge and get on to interstate 95. Then it was a matter of keeping his foot down, cruising at a steady 70. It never occurred to him to check his mirror for speed cops or to even think about helicopter patrols and radar traps.

Cawdor's suit had more or less dried out at Gil Gribble's, but now he was just as wet underneath, tension and fear and a crawling dreadful premonition bathing him in sweat, so that he had to turn on the air conditioning to prevent the windows getting fogged up.

135

The needle crept up to 75, then nudged 80. I-95 became I-80. He was on the outskirts of Paterson now, and soon would be on the lookout for the road to his right that linked up to 202. That route eventually became 23, which would lead him directly home to Franklin.

Cawdor gripped the wheel, narrowing his concentration to the strip of blurred tarmac directly ahead.

It started to rain. He switched on his wipers, and then the headlights, as the cars coming towards him switched on theirs. The oncoming lights flashing by were splintered into dazzling refractions by the raindrops hitting the windshield. He squinted his eyes to see through them. Instead he found himself looking not through them but *into* them. Into the fragments of light themselves.

To his shocked amazement, each fragment contained a separate and distinct image.

A black tower 2,000 storeys high, above it a thin slice of moon stuck to the night sky like a piece of silver paper. The feeble glow it gave off was swallowed up in the dark streets hemmed in by tall buildings of granite and glass. At the peak of the tower he saw a penthouse blazing with light, and from the balcony a thin runt of a man with lank fair hair gazing out over the city –

The images flickered in front of his eyes as the headlight beams broke up in the raindrops, sparking off in all directions. Strange and disturbing images that filled him with mind-freezing horror.

And one that almost made his heart stop beating.

It was Sarah. She was stretched out naked on a rough wooden floor, surrounded by a circle of gaunt, shadowy figures, their faces hidden inside shapeless hoods. A thin hand emerged, white as a fish's belly, and a bony finger pointed down. Sarah tried to squirm loose from the hands that were holding her wrists and ankles. She opened her mouth to scream, but a thick rope had been coiled several times round her neck so that she was barely able to draw breath. The figures moved closer, crowding in shoulder to shoulder, shutting out

136

the dimly flickering light and enclosing her in a circle of blackness –

Memory came back to Cawdor, making him grip the wheel so tight his knuckles ached. He had seen these images before, and he remembered where. In the fragments of his shaving mirror smashed to bits on the bathroom floor – the mirror that mysteriously the next morning had been intact. The broken mirror had been part of the dreams he had forgotten. In that particular dream he had been kneeling on the tiled floor, the holographic images from the shards of glass searing his eyes. Sarah had appeared in it too, standing at the door, eyes bright with alarm, her hand clasped to her chest. It seemed so real to him, Cawdor knew it wasn't a dream, had actually happened, and yet the morning after Sarah hadn't mentioned the broken mirror, and the mirror was still on its shelf, unbroken.

Dream or reality?

Earlier that afternoon, while out at Glen Cove, Cawdor had tried his damnedest to discover when and why recent events had started to go awry; to pinpoint the exact moment and possible cause. Now he had the answer. The night he broke the mirror in the bathroom. That's when it had happened. Before then his life had belonged to him; after that, he was cast adrift on a dark mysterious ocean of the unknown.

The sign for 202 flashed by, and almost too late he spotted the turn. In the few seconds it took the fact to register, the slip road was nearly upon him, and he had to ram the brake pedal with both feet and wrench the wheel round, sliding the Olds sideways for ten yards before the car shuddered, shimmied its rear end, and regained its traction. There was a smell of burnt rubber and a jolt that made the suspension groan as the car bounced over the concrete lip before straightening up and resuming the direction he was steering it in.

Leaning back in the seat, Cawdor blinked stinging sweat from his eyes. Even though the interior of the car was cold, he was soaked through, his shirt clinging to him like a clammy second skin.

Smashing up the car, and himself with it, wasn't the brightest of ideas. The object of the exercise was to get home quickly and preferably in one piece. The same awful sense of suffocating panic he had experienced in Gil Gribble's apartment took hold of him. Like choking to death in a confined, airless space.

Once again, the demons of his fevered imagination were let loose.

He pictured the living room trashed, the walls and furniture covered in bloodstains. A trail of blood where his wife had dragged herself, cowering in the corner as the psycho with the mad gentle smile and empty gleaming eyes crawled towards her on hands and knees, humming a little tune under his breath.

Too late, Cawdor tried to obliterate the scene from his mind. It had sprung full-blown in all its gory horror before he had the chance to censor it. He pushed it away, twisting his head from side to side to physically shake free of it – and at once it was replaced by another, as if the sly demons of his buried subconscious had any number of such ghastly scenarios in store, lurking to ambush him.

In this one the house was on fire, and Sarah was trapped in the bedroom, her nightgown ablaze. With blistered hands she was beating frantically at the flames that were licking and writhing like orange-tipped blue tongues around her body. Then, as abruptly as a film cuts to another scene, she was lying concussed in the bathtub, her long fair hair swirling in the soapy water as she feebly tried and failed to raise herself before sliding down limply below the surface.

Cawdor shook his head violently and stared through the windshield at the circles formed by his headlights on the blacktop rushing towards him. They appeared stronger now, more sharply defined as dusk was shading into night.

Flat open farmland was spread out on either side. Lights glowed in the clusters of homesteads dotted along the highway. To his left, a few faint gleams were reflected on the dark placid surface of the Oak Ridge Reservoir. Franklin was less than six miles away.

He was nearly there, thank God.

Almost home.

Cawdor entered the house through the ground-level garage. A door at the rear of the garage gave on to a short passage, at the end of which was a bare, windowless room with the washing machine, dryer, and a cupboard containing household and kitchen supplies. Next to the utility-room door a flight of open-tread wooden steps led up to a small rear lobby adjoining the kitchen.

Silently, Cawdor ascended and stood listening at the head of the stairs. At first he could hear nothing above the hammer thudding in his chest and the blood pounding in his eardrums.

He stepped softly towards the wooden arch and the three steps of waxed oak leading down to the living room. The heavy brass lamp with its green fringed shade on the bureau threw a dull sheen across the parquet floor. The floor itself was spotless, not a speck of blood to be seen. As was the back of the ivory moquette couch, when it came into view. The gently smiling psycho rapist of his worst imaginings hadn't struck; he could be thrown back into the locked lumber room of Cawdor's murky subconscious.

The TV was on: he had been hearing it for several moments, Cawdor realised, without actually being aware of it.

She was curled up on the sofa. Wearing jeans and a loose, pale-lemon jumper with baggy sleeves, feet bare, her hair spilling over her shoulders, Sarah was completely absorbed by what was happening on the screen.

Cawdor was torn between relief and bewilderment. Not a thing was wrong. Everything was fine, perfectly normal, just as it should be. No calamity had befallen his wife, and for that he was profoundly thankful. At the same time he was baffled that his premonition of some dreadful catastrophe had turned out to be groundless. The panic churning in his guts had convinced him the danger was both real and imminent. He had nearly killed himself in a car smash to prove it.

A voice boomed out, 'And now, please give a warm welcome to the star of our show – Messiah Wilde!'

The camera panned across a sea of faces, eyes wide and mouths hanging slack in hushed anticipation. Some were blinking back tears of rapture. A glittering staircase splashed with a swathe of stars led up to an archway of what seemed to be white granite, white smoke billowing forth. Through the smoke stepped a figure dressed in black. Tall and slim, his face lean and pale, he had long black hair that fell away from a centre parting and draped his shoulders. His eyes were dark and soulful, fringed by dark lashes. His appearance brought an instant storm of applause. One hand raised gracefully to acknowledge the reception, Messiah Wilde descended the sparkling staircase, the faintest hint of a smile on his lips.

The applause died away to total silence.

'Lovebeams from my heart to your hearts.' He crossed both hands over his heart and then spread his arms wide.

It came as a surprise to Cawdor that his accent was English; the voice was low, intimate and caressing, with underneath the trace of a softer lilt.

'And I can feel your lovebeams coming right back to me.'

He smiled, basking in the warmth of their adoration.

'Have you got it?' he breathed softly.

'We got it.' The response was a breathless whisper.

'What have you got?'

'The Message.'

'Didn't hear you.'

'The Message!' The response grew louder.

'Say it again.'

'THE MESSAGE!'

'One more time.'

'THE MESSAGE!'

A large letter 'M' flashed up on the screen. The shape of the 'M' peeled off and attached itself to form an upside-down version of the original.

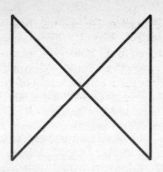

The symbol might have represented a butterfly, or a bow tie, or perhaps two beams radiating from a lighthouse. Cawdor wasn't sure which, but it did occur to him that the shape was similar to one he'd seen before. Very similar, in fact, if not identical, to the silver pin he'd seen Phyllis wearing.

His presence in the doorway went unnoticed by Sarah, who was watching the TV with a rapt, faraway expression, leaning forward on one elbow, chin propped in her hand, a dreamy smile on her lips. His predominant feeling, Cawdor realised, was that of an intruder into a private moment – even an intimate one – as if he had no right to be there. Like a jealous husband snooping on his wife because he suspects her of infidelity.

Unaware of his arrival, neither did Sarah register his departure.

At the bottom of the open-tread staircase next to the utility room, elbows on his knees, Cawdor sat with a cloudy look of bemusement on his face. The panic at Gil's – rushing off with hardly a word – the mad dash in the car – dire premonitions of something truly awful happening to his wife. All that for nothing. Damn near killed himself in a car wreck for no good reason.

A faint burst of applause came from the living room. Cawdor raised his head, listening, and ran a hand through his unruly hair. He knew what he ought to be feeling. Profound relief and everlasting gratitude at finding Sarah secure at home watching TV, safe and unharmed. But any such feeling was absent, and he couldn't figure out why.

Kersh sips his drink and stares across the penthouse apartment to the wall of sliding glass. He can't see the city from here, the millions of lights spread out far below like a glittering carpet, but he has an uneasy feeling about it. He senses danger: old instincts die hard. He's survived on gut feeling for 38 years. Like an animal sniffing out water, hiding from predators, gobbling down the weak and unwary, his instinct for self-preservation is the only one he trusts.

And now he has much more to lose – all this. His empire. Riches. Luxury. The woman of his dreams.

If he's been given all this, Kersh reasons, he must also have been granted the power to keep it. To protect it. At all costs.

Rising, he freshens his drink at the bar and goes out on to the balcony. A misty crescent moon is stuck to the black sky. It reminds Kersh of a silvery sail attached to an invisible ship, the wind-filled sail puffed out and straining but unable to shift its burden by so much as an inch. In fact nothing moves. The lights below sparkle; the stars above glitter coldly; but nothing ever changes.

Time stands still.

Perfect. Just the way it should be. No movement; no change; everything stays like it is this minute. Except there is no minute, he reminds himself, starting to grin. That's right, Frankie boy, you've done with all that crap. 'As time goes by' don't mean a thing no more, not up here. Here you stay the same for ever, never ageing a single second, because seconds have gone the way of minutes and hours – down the tubes – along with weeks, months, years. He throws back the drink in one, and the liquor burning his throat feels good. Life is good. In fact, *this* life is fucking great!

Leaning on the rail, Kersh grins into the abyss, and can't help snickering at such sweet fortune.

'What's so funny, Frank?'

Kersh spins round.

Something is crawling across the tiles towards him. Something that might have crawled out of one of his own nightmares. A stunted torso on feelers. It drags itself nearer and squats on its rump, looking up at him – a smooth, bland, cherubic face, lidless eyes, the pale and hairless head of a radiation victim.

Is this mine? Kersh wonders, staring down at it.

'Everything's cool, Frank,' Baby Sam says, scratching his belly with a claw. 'Don't worry about a thing. So what about that drink you promised your old pal?'

They go inside, Baby Sam lurching and slithering along behind him. He leaves a slimy brown trail on the carpet, Kersh notices. Baby Sam grips the legs of the barstool and crawls up, feeler over feeler, and perches on top. His head swivels; the lidless bloodshot eyes look round admiringly.

'This is a neat setup you've got here, Frank. I always said you had great taste.'

'Thanks.' Kersh slides the glass towards him. Baby Sam extends a feeler and grips it in a claw. The stringy muscles are cratered with blue punctures and covered in weeping scabs and lumps of hard scar tissue. There's barely a square centimetre that hasn't been injected.

'Here's to you.'

Kersh drinks to that. He wipes his mouth with the back of his hand. 'How are things below? Any problems?'

Baby Sam grins, showing raw red gums. 'Like I said, not a thing to worry about. Tight as a nun's cunt. You're sitting on top of two thousand floors, Frank. What could be safer?'

'I guess you're right,' Kersh says worriedly.

'Sure I'm right! Have I ever let you down? Listen – if you go, we all go, so the crew's pretty keen, you can imagine. Anyhow, the guy's lost, working in the dark. He don't know jackshit.'

'Guess that's so.' Kersh nods. He stops nodding, stares with his one good eye. 'Who don't know jackshit? What guy's that?'

'Relax, old pal, you got Cawdor flapping around like a

headless chicken.' Baby Sam chuckles. 'Poor sap don't know his ass from his elbow.'

Kersh feels a chill creeping through his gut. Back there on the balcony he couldn't put his finger on it, but his sense of danger was bang on the money – and this disgusting bag of weeping pus has confirmed his instinct was dead right. Fact is, Kersh now realises, that's what Baby Sam is and why he's here – as a kind of go-between, linking Kersh to events on the outside. Maybe a form of protection too, alerting him to any bad shit that might come down before it comes down. The notion comforts him. Is he bombproof and fireproof or what?

'Anything we need to do about this creep?' Kersh asks, suddenly more confident, his panic already a fading memory.

'Naw! Like I sez, Frank, he's up shit creek without a paddle.'

'He don't know about me, right? That's so, ain't it?'

'Well, yeah, that's right.' Baby Sam squirms a little. 'And no, it ain't . . .'

'Can't be both, scumbag. Which? Spit it out.'

'Don't ask me how, he's seen you in the chair. He musta tapped into something, gotta flash of you hanging in there. But, for chrissakes, so what?' Baby Sam shakes his hairless cranium dismissively. 'Cawdor's got plenty troubles to keep him busy, Frank. His whole world's falling apart. Naw, he won't bother you.' Sagging forward on the barstool, Baby Sam winks lewdly by squeezing one lidless eye shut. 'Hey, the chick, how she rate? She deliver? Gives good head? She's got the mouth for it all right.'

Kersh leans moodily on the bar. 'She's a ten. Even came up with a coupla things I hadn't thought of before.'

'Yeah? What?' A whiteish substance dribbles from the corner of Baby Sam's mouth.

'I'd better not say. It'll stunt your growth.'

'Ha fucking ha. Anyway, when you've done with her maybe you could . . .'

'I'll think about it,' Kersh says shortly. He has to keep these punks in check, stop them getting uppity. This is *his* penthouse, *his* tower, Kersh tells himself. Give 'em an inch, they'll take a mile. Never let them forget they're living between *his* heartbeats.

Baby Sam's feelers hold out the glass. 'Gimme another shot.'

'You've had enough.' Kersh finishes his own drink and bangs the glass down. 'You'd better go. I'm tired. I want to sleep.' Baby Sam flops to the floor with a squelchy sound. A disgusting smell escapes from him, as if his insides are rotting, which they probably are.

He slithers off, leaving a glutinous trail.

If that's what I picked to protect me, Kersh muses, why didn't I go for something seven feet tall built like a brick shithouse?

He goes through into the bedroom and sprawls out on the black silk sheets. Acres of stars shine down on him through the glass roof.

The crescent moon hasn't budged. The silvery sail impotently pulls the immobile ship.

His mind's too tense, too fraught, to think straight. He'd like to unwind by taking a little nap, but – truth is – he's scared to sleep. Yeah, OK, he admits it. Because, whenever he sleeps, he dreams, and in his dreams time moves on. Visions of the electric chair loom before him, only a heartbeat away. And he knows the next heartbeat – should it ever come – will be his last. It doesn't bear thinking about. Kersh shrinks from thinking about it. It makes his brain hurt. Like a fist squeezing the juice from an orange until the pips squeak.

Forget all that. Forget, Kersh tells himself grimly, you even thought of thinking about it.

He wishes now he hadn't sent Baby Sam away. They could have chewed the fat, traded dirty jokes, got smashed together. Kersh doesn't want to sleep any more. That's the last thing he wants. If he falls asleep and dreams, God knows what he'll dream about – there's stuff floating around in his brain even *he* doesn't know about and is none too keen to find out.

Back in the main suite he fixes himself another drink and pads down the three steps into the circular well and flops down on the curved couch. Automatically, he reaches for the remote and switches on the TV. His hand is shaking. The panic he thought was under control rises up again, gnawing at his throat. Not the chair this time – Kersh can live with that. It's Cawdor. That's where the real danger lies. The Messengers have delivered on their promise, installed him in splendour, been ungrudging with his every comfort, but they had failed to warn him that all of it might be threatened from outside.

Kersh doesn't know how yet; living by his wits, he senses the danger, and that's plenty good enough for him.

Suddenly he's hit by a bolt from the blue. Maybe they haven't warned him for one simple reason – they don't know. It's down to him to warn them.

No sooner has the notion entered his mind than he sees on the TV screen a dark chamber with a high conical ceiling fading into deep shadow. Figures shrouded in black robes kneel in a semicircle, chanting with bowed heads. They raise their eyes and look up. They are looking directly at him. Goddamn. This is a mighty shock, and with it comes a thrill more intense than sexual orgasm as Kersh realises who is the object of their devout worship and humble supplication.

The one and only him.

The Messengers are praying to Frank Kersh.

RITUAL IN THE DARK

1

It got hotter. The sails were becalmed. The *Salamander* drifted on a flat, colourless sea in which the sun was reflected like a brass gong. The drinking water, stored in casks in the deepest part of the hold for coolness, tasted brackish. Many of the passengers complained of stomach cramps and vomiting, and a rumour swept the ship that an epidemic had broken out.

During a single night there were two deaths in steerage, which Doctor Chapman pronounced were both due to natural causes – a statement greeted with private scepticism but which no one publicly had the nerve to question. Panic was feared almost as much as plague. It could devastate the ship just as effectively.

Captain Vincent issued a proclamation which was nailed to the main mast, advising that anyone found crossing the white line did so on pain of instant quarantine in the aft hanging magazine. This was a vertical wooden shaft sealed off from the rest of the ship, used for storing powder, cartridge and shot when the vessel was employed as a man-of-war. From this, Cawdor deduced that the captain was deeply concerned that a contagion would spread from the crowded forward quarters and infect the middle ship and, worst of all, the 'quality' end.

'I don't think Captain Vincent cares overmuch about those poor souls forward of the main mast,' Cawdor remarked to Saraheda. 'But he lives in mortal terror that the fine ladies and gentlemen might contract the pox. They have influence, and the captain doesn't wish to lose his mariner's certificate.'

'If I had my way, he'd lose more than that,' Saraheda said darkly. She lay on the bed, a damp cloth across her forehead.

Cawdor knew her mood, and from the stubborn set of her jaw guessed what she was thinking. He had told her of his interview with the captain, leaving nothing out. Saraheda had been all for finding the girl, Elizabeth, and shaking some sense into her and the truth out of her. And she was outraged at the 'justice' Captain Vincent had dispensed. But Cawdor had been sanguine. Under the circumstances, what else could the captain do? The girl stuck by her story, wouldn't be budged from it; it was Cawdor's word against hers, and the captain had chosen to believe her.

'You should have told him what you saw on deck that night. How you intervened to save the girl. And then –' Saraheda sat up, her eyes wild '– how she had the nerve to accuse *you* of the act you prevented!'

'If I had, what then?' Cawdor shrugged. 'It would have been my word against the girl's and Elder Graye's. Two against one. No, it was the better course, Saraheda. Or at least the best I could make of a bad job.'

Saraheda shook her head. 'I'll tell you what the best course would be.'

And proceeded to do so, involving a carving knife honed to razor sharpness and a certain portion of Elder Graye's anatomy.

Cawdor awoke, streaming with perspiration, the smell of the privy in his nostrils. He lay there for a minute, feeling nauseous. He couldn't endure this stifling heat an instant longer.

He put on his shirt and breeches and went up on deck. There wasn't a breath of wind, but at least he was free of that noisome stench. Gratefully, he sucked in a lungful of air. It was a moonless night, black as pitch, the ship in darkness except for a single lamp on the poop casting a feeble yellow glow. Even the spread of stars appeared dull and misty.

No Gryble tonight, Cawdor thought. And (he prayed) no young lovers either. Cawdor was in no mood to play the knight in shining armour, and to be slandered and severely castigated for his pains.

'Have no fear, Mr Cawdor. My honour is not in jeopardy.'

It was less the unexpected voice than that his innermost thoughts had been pried into that made Cawdor spin round, his mouth dropping open like some country bumpkin's. He felt a flush rise to his cheeks. The Spanish Woman was smiling at him, the same ironic, mocking smile he'd seen before, as if they shared some complicity – which damnit all they didn't! He'd never even spoken to the woman.

'That's an odd statement to make, madam,' Cawdor blurted out, at once confused and suspicious. 'What prompted it?'

'There has been talk about you.' Despite her accent, her intonation was clear and precise, and she spoke the words casually, as if quite at home with the language. 'At the dinner table. An officer said that you had been wrongly accused. I agree with him.'

'Mr Tregorath?'

'Yes, that is the gentleman.' The Spanish Woman came closer, and Cawdor was enveloped by musky perfume. She wore a lace shawl across her shoulders, but otherwise, as far as Cawdor could make out in the darkness, they were bared to the warm air. And there seemed a good deal of flesh.

'If that is Mr Tregorath's opinion, why didn't he speak out before? He might have, yet he stood silent and did nothing –' Cawdor paused to control his breathing. He was angry and inflamed. 'And I do not much care to be the subject of dinner-table tittle-tattle. Is that how you make your entertainment on the upper deck?'

'That isn't my notion of entertainment, Mr Cawdor.' The Spanish Woman gazed up at him through her eyelashes. 'I prefer other diversions.'

Cawdor felt his stomach tighten. He breathed in her perfume, and his senses seemed to come adrift. He felt drowsy and at the same time aroused. Her breasts were luminously pale, rising and falling above her low-cut gown. They seemed to beg to be caressed.

'And, as I said,' the Spanish Woman went on softly, 'my honour is not in jeopardy. You need have no fear of that.'

They stood facing one another in the silent, pressing darkness. She reached up with both hands and pulled his head down. Cawdor tried to resist. He told himself then, and afterward, that he tried to resist, though whether he did or not the outcome was that he slipped into her embrace, feeling her breasts rise up voluptuously out of her gown as they flattened against him and her lips mould themselves hotly to his in a hungry kiss.

Saraheda dreamt she was being suffocated. It was so real that she kicked out and fought with all her strength. She wanted to scream, and couldn't, because her mouth was filled with cloth. She could smell liquor on someone's breath. She could even identify it.

Rum.

She could smell rum.

And hear a man's laboured grunts.

The dream was too real.

She was being carried, bound and gagged, over the man's shoulder, along the passageway, down a flight of steps, his hard shoulder banging into her stomach with each step.

Where was Jefferson? He couldn't have slept on while she was attacked in her own bed. Because she *had* kicked. She *had* struggled. He would have felt it, surely to God. But he hadn't, otherwise he would have done something when the man hoisted her over his shoulder and carried her out.

The breath was being jolted out of her body. She tried to suck in air but the gag prevented her, and now she started to choke. Her body arched and bucked as convulsions racked her. Her eyes streamed with tears and strings of mucus hung from her nose. She was about to vomit. If she did she would choke to death. With all her willpower she fought against the sour bubbling and frothing that was erupting in her stomach. But the hard, jolting shoulder kept striking her and forcing the sour mess into her throat.

The possibility entered Saraheda's mind that she was actually going to die – that she would be tossed into a dark corner somewhere and allowed to choke on her own vomit. Her struggles were mere weak twitches now. Her consciousness ebbed and dwindled away until it became a solid pounding roar in her eardrums.

Where was Jefferson?

Where was he?

Where?

2

'Set her up. Remove that bond. And the rag from her mouth. But be ready, lest she cry out. The ceremony must not be violated by unbelievers.'

A smoky yellow flame threw its flickering light over Elder Graye's face, deepening the hollows underneath his cheekbones. The other elders stood beside him, two on either side. All five watched as Kershalton released Saraheda's hands and unwound the knotted cloth from her face. She choked something up and spat it on to the floor.

From the corner, sitting cross-legged on a pile of straw, Six-Fingered Sam gazed with bright, unblinking eyes at the young woman, who was dressed only in a thin nightgown that was already torn at the neck. His mouth hung crookedly open in a wet, vacuous grin. Now and then he giggled.

'As your lordships commanded,' Kershalton said, standing by Saraheda's shoulder. 'My part done and delivered, without so much as a squeak or a whimper. You're all witness to it. A promise made and kept. In good faith, you'll keep to your side of the bargain.'

'Yes. We will keep to it, to the letter, when the final act

is accomplished. Mark what I say: the final act.'

Kershalton made a fulsome low bow, hand to his heart, as a courtier to his king. He winked at Six-Fingered Sam. 'Trust me, your lordships. I'm the man to do it.'

Elder Graye laced his long fingers together and held his hands devoutly to his chest. 'Saraheda.' His voice was deep, full of trembling reverberations. 'Saraheda. A very pretty name. And a fine figure of a woman. I can see from your appearance that you are a woman capable of giving great pleasure. No doubt you have done so, many times, with numerous randy gentlemen. And some not so gentle, eh?'

Saraheda's flesh chilled. Something cold crawled in her belly, like a snake uncoiling. She gathered up the phlegm which burnt her throat and spat it at his feet.

Elder Graye sighed and shook his head. 'You do not know your place. Nor your function. We shall teach you.' He smiled. 'You'll know it then. This I promise. And you'll never forget it.'

The boy, Six Fingers, sniggered into his grimy fist.

Elder Graye unlocked his hands, took hold of Saraheda's nightgown and tore it apart down the middle. Kershalton was ready and, before Saraheda could react, he grabbed her wrists from behind. Elder Graye ripped the torn shreds from her and threw them away. His eyes travelled slowly from her face and down the length of her body, lingering on her breasts and pubis.

'The flesh is evil and must be purged,' he intoned. 'All women are sinful, being formed and shaped for the purposes of temptation and the weak indulgence of sensual desire. Being shameless and wicked, they must be punished and abased, until they become meek and contrite, and seek forgiveness for their harlotry and despicable lust.'

'Your religion suits you,' Saraheda said. She stood facing the five elders, proud and unashamed. 'A warped and twisted theology, the product of depraved minds and empty souls. You would be contemptible were you not so pitiful.'

Kershalton gave a gruff chuckle. 'This one's a real vixen,

worthy of your lordships' most severe chastisement.' He leant forward and peered over Saraheda's shoulder, ogling her breasts, one eye gleaming, the other drab and sunken with its dead layer of skin. 'I could give it a good, sound shafting m'self.'

'When the ceremony of the Fall from Grace is over, you may do as you please.'

'I can have her then, can I?' Kershalton gloated. Spittle ran down his chin and dripped on to her shoulder. 'I have in mind a trick or two her husband never taught her. She has a very soft mouth.'

'My husband shall deal with you in good time,' Saraheda said. There was a tremor in her voice that she couldn't control; her body had started to tremble, nervous spasms twitching in her neck and arms. 'He won't wait on the captain's justice again, I promise you that.'

She stared straight into Elder Graye's impassive face. Then her throat welled up for a scream, which was stillborn by Kershalton's rough palm clamped hard across her mouth. Saraheda tried to bite into it, but her head was wrenched backward until she thought her neck would snap.

'Now, now, none of that,' Kershalton grunted in her ear. 'Nary a peep or a squeak, or you'll get a throttling, Mrs Cawdor. Be still now. Quiet as a church mouse.' He slid his hand from her mouth and clasped it lightly round her throat.

Six Fingers rocked to and fro, hugging his knees, giggling.

Elder Graye stepped forward.

'For your lewd sins, woman, and for the blasphemy of your husband, Jefferson Cawdor, there is a price to be paid. You shall now pay that price in full and exacting measure.'

Towering above her, he parted the front of his garment and revealed himself – the bulbous tip of it reared up, an inch or so away from Saraheda's white belly.

The breath fluttered in Saraheda's nostrils, and, against all odds, feeling herself lost and abandoned in a bottomless pit of fear, she found a withering smile. 'Is that the

153

best you have to offer, sir? You ought to equip yourself with a decent instrument before you venture to play a tune. Yours is a penny whistle.'

Six Fingers stifled his giggles.

In the smoky flickering light the stringy cords of Elder Graye's neck stood out, taut as bowstrings. Under the bony ridge of his brow, his eyes were hidden in deep black sockets. He was incapable of speech. When eventually he managed it, his voice was hoarse with a consuming and remorseless rage.

'We shall see how readily you jest and make sport of us, woman, in a little while from now, when you have been split asunder.' He gripped his erect penis. 'Hold her fast!'

The eyes of the Spanish Woman were green and flecked with gold, like splinters of sunlight through green leaves. With an effort Cawdor looked away, blinking, not seeing the cabin with its pools of light and darkness, the oak beams curving down where they formed a rounded corner of the vessel. He was dazzled by the woman. Mesmerised. He didn't seem to have any power over his own faculties, as if he had entered into a dream state, all proper motion suspended in time.

He felt to be a stranger to himself.

She patted the bed beside her. 'Why are you suddenly so restless? No one observed us coming here. Are you frightened that *your* honour may be compromised?' The idea amused her, and she laughed, her teeth very white against her dark skin.

She arched back, pushing the tangle of black hair from her face, a languorous movement that raised her breasts and made the valley between them deeper and more shadowy.

Against his will, Cawdor was drawn back to stare at her, a compass needle aligning itself to some mysterious planetary influence it couldn't resist, much less comprehend. His chest felt constrained with the air he couldn't expel. His heart beat leadenly.

'Is it any man you want, or is it me?' The words tasted

foggy in his mouth. 'I've seen you watching me, several times, as if you knew what the upshot between us would be. Is that a true fact, or did I imagine it?'

'You are generous in granting me the powers of the mystic, *señor*. Do you believe the future can be foretold?' She shrugged expressively. 'Perhaps so, perhaps not. But no, I simply looked at you as a woman looks at a man, reading the message in your eyes, as you read it in mine. That much of the future can be foretold.'

'I wasn't aware that my eyes transmitted any message.'

'That is the statement of a fool, whether or not you believe it to be true.' She sighed, examining her nails. 'It isn't necessary to play the role of the good, honest Englishman, of fine principles and straight conscience. The part is a parody, as well you know.'

'I don't know that I do know,' Cawdor said distractedly. 'I seem to know less and less. My wife . . .' He faltered.

'What about your wife?' The Spanish Woman raised her eyebrows, which were as fine and artful as a water-colourist's brushmarks. 'She is Señora Cawdor today; she will be Señora Cawdor tomorrow, in spite of all. I am most discreet in these affairs. Your reputation is safe with me.'

Cawdor knew that she was mocking him. He was quite clear and rational about that. But another part of him had taken over, was now in charge. Something instinctive and compelling from the very root of his being. A deeper, darker strain of emotion sweeping him along in its current, and against which he felt weak and powerless.

Especially when her green, gold-flecked eyes were fixed upon him, as they were now. Black curling lashes. Dark complexion and the vivid redness of her lips. Bare shoulders and the swelling softness above her gown, rising and falling, bathed in a sheen from the lamps which made her flesh glow.

Cawdor moved towards the bed.

Her eyes and lips filled his world, from horizon to horizon. No other thought, no other person, entered his head.

The Spanish Woman watched him standing before her.

No longer smiling, no longer mocking, she unfastened

the front of her gown, down to the waist. She moved one shoulder, and then the other, easing herself free. The material collapsed in folds around her. She placed her hands under her heavy breasts and lifted them slightly. Her thumbs touched her nipples, teasing them, until they grew stiff and jutted out, casting shadows which rippled like waves over her fingers.

'Give me your hand.'

Cawdor put out his hand. The Spanish Woman guided it to her breast and pressed her hand over his, increasing the pressure until his palm was full to overflowing. Reaching out with her other hand, she traced the hard shape of his penis with the tips of her fingers, then took a firmer grip of it through the material, pulling him forward.

'Come, *señor*,' she breathed. 'Come to me,' and Cawdor tumbled dizzily down and down into the depths of her green eyes flecked with splinters of golden sunlight.

3

Surrounded by the elders, Saraheda was made to kneel in front of Elder Graye. At his bidding, Kershalton held fast her lower jaw while Graye forced himself into her mouth until she gagged and choked and almost fainted away. To revive her, Kershalton slapped her neck with the back of his hand, four or five times, raising bruises and drawing blood. He was jumping up and down, beside himself with frenzy, having watched with growing impatience the young woman being dispassionately used as a receptacle. This excited him beyond measure – the fact that Saraheda wasn't a common whore, but a respectable married woman. And Cawdor's very own wife to boot! That upright, decent, smug self-appointed defender of the weak and the righter of wrongs. God's teeth, this was supreme justice indeed, and with a vengeance! Kershalton did a jig. He was aching to get at her, to such an extent that he had to undo his flies and hold himself tightly, all the while in agony as he fought against a premature finale.

It was like an oven. The trapped heat between the

straw-littered floor and the low bulkhead was heavy and pungent with the smell of sweat and other bodily fluids. Six Fingers watched in rapt silence, his quick eyes darting everywhere, missing nothing.

Elder Graye thrust himself in grunting rhythm into Saraheda's mouth, his face a wet, stony mask. Surrounding her in a close circle, the other elders bucked to and fro, jabbing at her head, rotating their hips to strike her across the face, blunt truncheons smacking with a flat, glutinous sound.

'Wanton temptress!' Elder Graye panted, his body shuddering as he drove into her.

'Brazen sinner!' He thrust again, panting.

'Lewd defiler!' And again.

'Blaspheming bitch!'

'For your sacrilege –

'You shall be anointed –

'With the sacred seed –

'Cleansed within and without –

'Until your lures and snares –

'And lustful thoughts –

'Are swept out –

'And washed away –

'As on a flood –'

He groaned and quickened his pace.

'Cawdor's bitch wife!

'Cawdor's lewd wife!

'Cawdor's whore wife!

'Now! Yes, now! Now! This instant –

'NOW!'

He grunted and released himself, as did the others, simultaneously, in accordance with his instruction. The deluge erupted. Saraheda was coated. Her hair was stuck to her head and glued in slimy strands to her shoulders. The stuff bubbled from her mouth and hung from her chin. Blindly, she raised her head, as if to cry out, and Kershalton struck her a stinging blow that knocked her sideways. She lay sprawled, moaning insensibly, on the filthy matting of straw.

'My turn, my turn,' Kershalton gibbered. Falling to his knees, he forced Saraheda's legs open to take her from behind. He heaved at her thighs, raising her buttocks into position. 'Feel that, my little lovely honey-cup,' he crooned, sliding in. 'I'll give you good firm measure. What a snug little home, Mrs Cawdor. Tight as a sword in its scabbard. On my oath, what a sweet little snatch!'

In less than a minute he flopped back, having spent himself.

Elder Graye was anxious to complete the ceremony. He pushed his foot under the inert body and lifted it over on to its back. Saraheda's elbows and knees were bleeding from having been scraped on the rough boards. Her nose had been broken from Kershalton's last blow.

'Come here, boy.'

Six Fingers scrambled up at Elder Graye's bidding.

'Make water.' Elder Graye indicated where, and the boy gushed a stream of steaming yellow piss over her face and breasts.

'Drop your breeches, boy, and squat.'

Six Fingers doubled over, the white moons of his buttocks almost resting on Saraheda's face.

'Empty your bowels, boy.'

Six Fingers strained, farted, and ejected a long thin turd. It lay curled like a soft brown snake. Elder Graye pushed the boy away. He took a piece of splintered wood and used it to smear the ordure over Saraheda's face, poking some of it in her mouth. He then daubed her body, dragging the sharp point so that it snagged her flesh, raising bloody weals. With the blood he scrawled symbols and words across her breasts, stomach and thighs. His face was ashen, the lines etched deep, eyes black as pits.

'Whore!' Elder Graye spoke the words as he scratched them, working himself into a demonic rage. 'Harlot! Slut! Bitch!' The straw on which Saraheda lay became a bloody mat. Weakly, she tried to fend him off, which gave Kershalton the opportunity to wrench her arms backward and stand splay-footed on her wrists.

Elder Graye inserted the sharp point between her legs

158

and thrust it in with all his strength as far as it would go. He straightened up, clasping his hands to his chest, and intoned solemnly:

'I call upon you all to witness that this woman, Cawdor's wench, has been cleansed and purified. Her wanton lust will never again defile our creed. Let her be cast away, in shame and ignominy, and never more offend our sight.'

He made an abrupt gesture of dismissal.

Saraheda's legs were raised and forced down either side of her head. A rope was tied round both calves, looped round her neck and pulled taut, so that she was trussed up like a fowl, hands bound tightly at the back of her thighs. Six Fingers went to find a sack. The woman was shoved inside, and the sack fastened securely with strong rope. Kershalton did most of the work, and by the time he'd finished he was pouring with sweat.

'Don't say I haven't earned your favours, your lordships. I'll wager I have – in spades!'

'Yes, yes.' Elder Graye nodded his shaven head, impatient for an end to the business. 'We do not make promises we cannot keep. Now listen – the ocean is calm, a splash will attract attention. Lower her in by degrees. You will need a weight to sink her deep.' He raised a warning finger. 'And take care you are not observed by the night watch.'

'I know my business,' Kershalton said, grunting as he hoisted the sack over his shoulder. He glanced back at Elder Graye, one eye glittering, the other a dulled fishy stare. 'I trust i' faith that you know yours as well, your lordships.'

4

Had he dreamt it? Daniel wondered.

Scuffles and hoarse breathing and footsteps fading away.

In the dream that perhaps wasn't a dream, Daniel remembered raising himself on one elbow and trying to listen through his tiredness. Then he'd yawned; his head had lolled forward; and he had curled up on the straw pallet and fallen fast asleep.

Had that been minutes ago, he puzzled, or hours?

He was wide awake now, sure enough, heart thudding wildly in his chest, eyes straining through the darkness. The bed was empty. Both his parents gone. He threw the covers back to make sure and ran his hands over the lumpy mattress, as if his mother and father were lying there invisibly and he could make them reappear by willing it.

Cold.

Daniel opened the door and crept barefoot into the narrow, creaking passage. The ship was asleep. Hugging his elbows to his sides, he climbed up the companionway, a thin pale ghost in his long nightshirt. A voice in his mind was telling him to be calm. The reason his parents weren't in bed was perfectly simple, if only he could think of it.

'They're with Mr Gryble, looking at the stars,' he said aloud to himself. This was comforting, so he repeated it. He thought of another explanation. 'They're having supper with the captain!' But this was less satisfactory, because Daniel well knew that the captain didn't associate with anyone from the middle part of the ship.

His heart started its furious beating again. It drowned out the quiet, calm inner voice. Tears started to sting his eyes.

On deck, despite the torpid warmth, he shivered, feeling clammy and cold. Visions of scaly sea serpents with eyes as big as dinner plates reared up in his imagination. His mother and father had been gobbled up. They were in bits and pieces, chewed and mangled in the beast's belly, at the bottom of the ocean.

Of course they weren't. Daniel laughed to convince himself what a ridiculous notion that was. But the laugh came out weak, more a nervous gasp, a quavering giggle. It only made him feel worse.

Then he found himself smiling, with immense heartfelt relief. Yes, he was sure of it – he could see his father standing at the rail, holding his mother in his arms. Two dark shapes silhouetted against the black sky and faint winking stars. How silly and childish he had been – getting fretful over nothing! He felt ashamed, disgusted with himself, but also very glad. The world was a friendly place again. All was bright and beautiful!

Light of heart, Daniel jumped down into the gangway and skipped towards them, smiling.

The night was perfect. Inky black. Moonless.

Kershalton swung the sack from his shoulder on to the rail. The sack nearly slid over of its own accord, and Kershalton had to make a quick grab. It was soggy, that explained it, blood seeping through. He'd have to remember to wipe the rail clean. Come the morning, his lordships would inspect the ship for signs from end to end.

'Hurry it along.' Kershalton spoke out of the corner of his mouth. Crouched at his feet, Six Fingers was threading the rope through the iron lug in the canister of lead shot, and taking his time about it. 'Come on, Sam, come on! Let's to our beds.'

'Franklin – hist!'

'What's to do?'

'Someone's coming.'

Kershalton clutched the soggy bundle to his chest. He daren't let go. On such a peaceful night the splash would cause an alarm. Hell's teeth, the watch would have to be deaf as posts not to hear it.

He squinted over his shoulder with his good eye.

Six Fingers gave a low whistle of surprise. 'Mary's bastard! Look who comes, sprightly as a lamb in spring.'

Then Kershalton made him out. Cawdor's brat, a chip off the old block. He couldn't help grinning. Double helpings. Two for the price of one. He murmured sideways, 'Keep down. Get a march on him from the rear. Not a peep, Sam!'

Daniel had stopped a few feet away, peering uncertainly into the darkness. Kershalton kept his back to him, concealing the sack.

'Father?' Daniel said hesitantly. It seemed then as if he had second thoughts. He shuffled his feet and backed off a pace. 'I'm sorry, sir, I mistook you for my father, Mr Cawdor. Have you seen him hereabouts?'

'Not tonight. But I've seen your mother.'

'You have, sir? Where – where is she?'

Kershalton choked on his laughter. 'In the near vicinity. Not an arm's length away.'

Daniel looked around. 'I don't see her.'

'You don't? That's strange.' Kershalton hugged the sack to him as he felt the contents squirm and struggle. God's teeth, she was trying to break free! He tightened his grip, afraid he might drop it. 'By chance I had intercourse with your mother not many minutes ago.'

Daniel frowned. The word seemed to perplex him. 'You had intercourse with my mother?'

'We exchanged pleasantries. Bade each other a peaceful good night and sweet dreams. Now I expect she has retired.'

'Oh yes,' Daniel said with evident relief, the obscure made plain, it seemed. 'I expect she has. Thank you, sir.'

He turned away with a shy, grateful smile. Six-Fingered Sam rose up silently behind him and locked his arm round Daniel's neck. There was a dull thud as the two of them fell to the deck, locked together, and rolled over into the gangway. A figure turned on the bridge, the yellow lamplight glinting on brass buttons. Kershalton's eyes widened in alarm. He stared down into the black well of the gangway, from where scuffles and grunts and the slithery sounds of bare feet issued. To him it sounded like pandemonium. He thought at once of lights going on and hatches being slammed back, people surging up from below. He held his breath, waiting for it to happen, thinking he'd drop the sack overboard, weight or no weight, and make himself scarce. But no lights went on; no people appeared.

The buttons winked out as the figure on the bridge turned away.

'Sam!' Kershalton hissed it into the black well. 'D'you have the snotty brat? Get him by the bollocks, boy, and be done, afore you wake the ship –'

One of them let out a strangled cry. Kershalton strained to see, but it was a dim, hopeless confusion of limbs and threshing bodies. Evidently the Cawdor boy was tougher than he looked. He was certainly tougher than Kershalton had reckoned on, because it was Daniel, and not Six Fingers, who staggered to his feet. The boy tottered to the rail, holding his head in both hands, shaking it muzzily from side to side.

Keeping one hand on the writhing sack, Kershalton curled the other into a huge knotted fist and delivered a roundhouse that exploded in the dead centre of Daniel's forehead. The white nightshirt billowed to the deck as if filled by a gust of wind; the gust of wind died suddenly away, leaving the nightshirt crumpled and still. 'Drag him here,' Kershalton snarled, as Six Fingers raised himself wearily. 'You're getting as soft as a tart's snatch.'

Kershalton looped the rope several times round Daniel's bare legs, jerked it tight, and lifted him up under one arm. 'Get the weight.' He lowered the struggling pulpy sack over the side, then the dangling boy, then the canister of lead shot, taking the strain now that both hands were free. One by one – sack, boy, canister – they went under, causing barely a ripple. Then, leaning right over, Kershalton let go of the end of the rope. It snaked into the darkness, making the faintest splash.

PART TWO

TEMPLE DEEP

The quantum principle shows that there is a sense in which what the observer will do in the future defines what happens in the past – even in a past so remote that life did not then exist.

John Wheeler

BEAMERS OF JOY

1

The headquarters of Grace MediaCorp dominated the flat Florida landscape. Reclining in the deep plush seat of the limo that had been waiting on her arrival at Miami International, Mara BeCalla caught sight of the structure from highway 441 just north of Fort Lauderdale: a majestic and imposing glass pyramid way off in the distance, flashing the rays of the sun for miles around like a giant heliograph.

This time of year was as much in between seasons as ever it got in the Sunshine State: the winter vacationers from the northern states long gone, the tourists from Europe yet to arrive in appreciable numbers. It was Mara BeCalla's first visit, and she was less than impressed. To her right were the hotels, the apartment blocks, the fancy condos, the restaurants and bars, bingo parlours and garish stores which catered for the holiday crowds. On her left the drab landscape alternated between scrubland bleached by the constant sun and large tracts of marshy quagmire with pools of brackish, stagnant water filmed with green and yellow slime. The Everglades lapped right up to the thin strip of civilisation along the coast: primordial swampland cheek by jowl with sun-seekers' paradise.

Quite definitely not *her* idea of where to spend a vacation.

Twenty minutes later she was standing in the marble-floored reception hall. Mara BeCalla was surprised, indeed taken aback, by its elegant proportions and overall splendour. Against a backdrop of dark-veined marble, a huge silver 'M' and its inverted image stood proud of the wall. Suspended at an angle from the ceiling, a bank of forty television screens replayed sequences from *The Lovebeams Show*. It was Grace MediaCorp's primetime programme, Mara BeCalla knew, though she'd caught maybe only five or ten minutes here and there. Something of a TV celebrity herself, hosting a talk and entertainment hour for a cable station in Pittsburgh, she found *The Lovebeams Show* an oddball mix of style and content. Part stageshow extravaganza, with dancers and musical acts, part soul-baring confessional – teenagers mostly revealing their tortured relationships and romantic growing pains – it was also imbued with a peculiar kind of religious fervour. Not that the show promoted a named movement or any one creed, as far as Mara BeCalla could tell. Nonetheless, there was a distinct aura of new-age evangelism promising a golden future of sunlit tomorrows.

Striding towards her, a clean-cut, broad-shouldered young man with an even tan and a set of perfect teeth presented the image of wholesome wellbeing. A silver pin – a tiny replica of the symbol on the wall – glinted in the lapel of his dark-blue blazer. His thin-striped tie, stone-coloured chinos and polished black shoes reminded Mara BeCalla of a tour guide. As a one-word description, she rejected 'humourless' and settled on 'robotic'. After a few words of welcome and a perfunctory handshake, he conducted her towards a square core of stainless steel and smoked glass containing four glass-sided elevators that rose up through the centre of the pyramid-shaped building. Like layers in a cake, each level was revealed to its furthest depth on all four sides as they ascended to the nineteenth floor. The building was a hive of open-plan offices divided into workstations, with rank upon rank of employees dutifully toiling at VDU terminals. Above their heads, lenses in rotating domes of blackened glass kept a constant vigil. Mara BeCalla bet herself a month's salary that not so much as a pencil ever went missing from Grace MediaCorp.

She voiced what was on her mind.

'This is one sweet setup. All this to produce a TV show?'

The clean-cut young man raised a disdainful eyebrow. Apparently she had betrayed her astounding ignorance. 'Television production and broadcasting is but one division of Grace MediaCorp,' he informed her in clipped tones. 'What you see here embraces all forms of mass-media dissemination.'

Even talks like a robot, Mara BeCalla thought.

'We have a suite of twelve sound studios for radio broadcasts and a recording division for CDs and tapes. We have a video production unit, five publishing imprints handling books, magazines, brochures, and other types of promotional literature. There is a department of two hundred and seventy-three people creating and servicing websites on the Internet. In addition to this facility here in southern Florida, we have several others in the process of design, development and construction in Minneapolis, Dallas, Albuquerque, Denver, Seattle and Sacramento. When completed, Grace MediaCorp will have the technical capacity and resources to beam our programmes twenty-four hours a day via five satellite channels worldwide.'

Mara BeCalla felt the least she could respond with was a 'golly-gosh', or even a 'wow!' She resisted and merely said with a limp smile, 'Silly old me.'

The clean-cut young man proved himself a humourless robot, too. His air of disdain turned to frank disapproval, as if she had compounded her appalling ignorance with unforgivable flippancy.

On the nineteenth floor, he led her from the main elevator to a smaller, private one. After seeing her safely inside, he went on his way. Mara BeCalla wasn't sorry to see him go.

'This is level twenty-seven. Alight here for Mr Graye's executive suite,' a female voice murmured softly from the speaker grille as the doors slid open. 'Mind your step. Thank you. This is level twenty-seven. Alight here for . . .'

Mara BeCalla came out into the hallway. Concealed lighting gleamed on black marble, and her high heels resonated on the polished granite floor as she strode towards a door inlaid with bronze panels. In the absence of any receptionist or personal assistant, she grasped the ornate handle and entered without knocking.

A tall spare figure with a narrow shaven skull was standing with folded arms, gazing out through the slanting wall of tinted glass. The office suite was at the apex of the pyramid, two faces of the outer façade forming a vaulted triangular enclosure like that of a chapel. A sultry sun burnt low in the sky, filling the room with light the colour of blood.

Isolated on the expanse of granite floor, Mara BeCalla waited as Graye turned from the slanting glass wall, letting his arms fall to his sides. His suit of fine black pinstripe hung slackly on his gaunt body like an empty sack.

He motioned her to an armchair of dark-blue velvet and sat down opposite her, lacing his long fingers between sharp knuckles. His hooded eyes in their cavernous sockets possessed the quality of a clinical incision, assessing her with icy objectivity. If his scrutiny was meant to be intimidating, it didn't work with Mara BeCalla. Supremely confident about her appearance – the mass of tumbled black hair and smooth dark complexion, huge green eyes flecked with starbursts of gold, voluptuous body under the creamy silk blouse and tailored jacket – she looked fabulous, and knew it.

She relaxed into the velvet armchair. For a moment she considered lighting up one of her thin, liquorice-paper Spanish cigarettes, but refrained. Not for Graye's sake; of far more importance was her need to maintain a strong inner sense of cast-iron discipline and control.

'I am pleased that you accepted my invitation, Miss BeCalla. It is a pleasure to meet you at last.' In contrast to the polite sentiment, Graye's voice was flat and rasping.

Mara BeCalla gave a slight shrug. 'You paid for the trip, Mr Graye. And your proposition, I have to say, sounded intriguing – at least the outline of it in your fax did – otherwise I wouldn't be sitting here now.'

Graye raised his sparse eyebrows. 'A global audience of millions has its attractions, does it not? I sense that your ambition stretches further than a few thousand cable subscribers. Grace MediaCorp has satellite channels reaching a third of the world's population, and more are presently in development. We also have several radio networks, a publishing division –'

Mara BeCalla interrupted him. 'I've already had the guided tour, Mr Graye. One of your young men here gave me the rundown. And yes, before you ask, I was impressed. I'm also familiar with *The Lovebeams Show*. Let's take it from there, shall we?'

Apparently, Graye wasn't used to being interrupted, and plainly he didn't like it. He sat ramrod straight in the chair, his neck a thin, veined column, an artery beating in the hollow temples.

He spoke in a low, harsh tone. 'If you wish to join us, Miss BeCalla, you must understand the nature and purpose of our enterprise. Grace MediaCorp is not a communications empire for mere financial reward. We are motivated and inspired by profound and sacred beliefs whose origin lies in ancient days.'

'Is it necessary that I understand?' Mara BeCalla asked him. 'Even if I don't share your beliefs?'

'With understanding will come belief; nothing is more certain.'

'What if I choose not to?'

'You will believe, gladly and sincerely,' Graye insisted, 'when you understand the nature of our ultimate purpose in this world.'

'So what is your ultimate purpose?'

'To disseminate the Message and make converts of those millions who watch our programmes, through the grace of our Saviour and Redeemer, Kersh. With His help we are able to influence the course of history and set both past and future on the rightful path.'

As a sceptic, Mara BeCalla might have laughed in

his face. She didn't. Instead, a stab of apprehension penetrated through her heart. It was the name Graye had uttered – *Kersh* – that struck within her a strange chord of remembrance, and with it the icy chill of fear.

'What do you mean, "the rightful path"?' she asked less confidently.

Graye regarded her with his hooded eyes.

'Past, present and future are linked together, following a certain course. But it must be one of our choosing.' The deeply etched lines of his face creased in an austere smile. 'As an unbeliever, you will be ignorant of the fact that many alternatives exist. However, the Rule of Infinite Parallex tells us that the present we inhabit is but a single refracted image of all other existing presents. Thus it is vital that the rightful path is of our choosing.' Graye's thin lips affected a superior smile. 'But don't tax your brain, dear child, with such difficult concepts –'

Mara BeCalla stiffened in the chair. 'Don't patronise me!' she snapped. 'If you were as all powerful and all knowing as you pretend to be, you wouldn't need me to help you. And I think you do need me, Mr Graye. I think you do.'

Graye sat with his hands locked tightly together. A distant light gleamed in the dark eye sockets, as if, Mara BeCalla thought . . . as if at some secret knowledge he was withholding from her. The tension in him was apparent in the flaring of his nostrils.

There was a secret and thrilling power there, Mara BeCalla had no doubts about that. It was the dark nature of that power that intrigued, tempted, and yet also frightened her. She wanted nothing more than to taste it for herself: to savour it as one savours a delicious, forbidden fruit. But not to be devoured by it.

Mara BeCalla arched an eyebrow, flawless as an artist's brushstroke. 'Tell me, Mr Graye.' She leant forward. Her green eyes glittered. 'What would happen if the rightful path, as you call it, was not the chosen one?'

'We would lose control. The world – this world – would be changed.'

'This world?'

'This world,' he repeated stonily. 'The one we presently inhabit.'

'I see.'

'You don't see. But you shall.'

The two of them faced one another, the silence trapped between a rock and a hard place.

After a moment Graye rose to his feet, his domelike head bathed red in the rays of the setting sun. 'There is no danger of that happening while we protect, and in turn are protected by, our Saviour and Redeemer Kersh. One day, Miss BeCalla, you will come to understand that.'

Her curiosity was aroused. 'The way you speak of Kersh . . . as if he has ultimate power. What is he? Who is he?' The sound of that name on her lips made Mara BeCalla shudder, as if something slimy and cold had crawled over her skin. When Graye didn't immediately respond, she said, 'An actual living person . . . or someone from the past?'

'Kersh isn't dead.'

'Then he must be alive.'

Graye shook his head.

'He isn't dead,' Mara BeCalla mused aloud, 'and neither is he alive . . .'

'Kersh is in another place,' said Graye solemnly.

'I didn't think he was in the next room. Then where?'

Graye had no humour, and didn't indulge it in others.

'The City of Perpetual Night.'

'Sounds pretty lonesome, stuck there in limbo. What's he find to do all day – or should I say all night?'

Graye ignored her flippant tone. 'Kersh has plenty to occupy Himself, Miss BeCalla.' He turned away. The meeting seemed to be over. But, as Mara BeCalla got to her feet, Graye turned again. They faced one another in the rosy twilight of the vaulted room. For a moment the masks of pretence were stripped away, the naked ambition of each mercilessly exposed. Mara BeCalla didn't fool herself that she had any grasp at all on what Graye, in his supercilious manner, had revealed to her. Nor could she

173

give credence to his beliefs – this talk of 'the rightful path' and 'the chosen way'. As for the fantastical figure of Kersh, who existed and yet didn't exist in some lonesome night-time limbo, he was less real to Mara BeCalla than Santa Claus.

But some things she did understand, and believed in fervently. Fame, wealth, and power were real and knowable to her, as tangible as her own fingertips, and she craved them with an insatiable lust more powerful than sexual desire.

Graye curled a finger. 'Come with me. Let me show an unbeliever what we have to offer, all of which can be hers.'

The elevator descended rapidly, the levels zipping by in a blur. Mara BeCalla tensed her knees, anticipating the sudden braking as the indicator lights flicked down the panel to the first floor. She was caught off guard. The elevator kept on going. The lit levels vanished into darkness.

'There are ten sub-basement levels,' Graye said, in answer to Mara BeCalla's startled look. 'The studios are located below ground to minimise external sound and vibration.'

The elevator slowed and stopped, and a red panel marked STUDIO 7 lit up.

From a small lobby, they passed through heavy double doors into a dimly illuminated corridor with large observation windows along one wall. A sound like the far-distant rush and rumble of waves on the shore filtered in. It was the murmur and buzz of a huge and excited crowd, muted by the thick glass. Mara BeCalla caught a glimpse of them through the observation windows, sitting in a steeply raked semicircle which rose from the stage and vanished into the shadowy depths way up near the roof gantry. The tall figure of Graye strode ahead, and Mara BeCalla followed him into a viewing gallery which was open to the auditorium.

At once the distant rush and rumble became the roar of

174

one vast wave crashing down. Perched high in the studio, as if on a cliff edge, the gallery overlooked the sea of faces lifted expectantly to the stage area bathed in a curtain of light. Cameramen with lightweight shoulder cameras, the sound crew, and a dozen technicians were making their final preparations. The floor manager was talking to the control booth through his miked headset. Mara BeCalla followed his gaze to the angled windows on the opposite wall of the studio where heads and shoulders, partly in silhouette, were hunched in front of monitor screens.

For the first time, Mara BeCalla took in the audience. What struck her immediately was that they were all young, fresh-faced kids, average age seventeen or thereabouts. And they were as excited and pepped up as if at a rock concert. As she gazed down upon all this youth and vibrant energy, her attention was caught by a girl of about fourteen with spiky red hair, cheeks flushed, eyes bright and joyful. She saw the girl slip something into her mouth. She then took a gulp of diet soda, head tilted back, her slender white throat rippling. Another kid further along the row did the same. Now that she was consciously looking for it, Mara BeCalla saw at least a dozen more unwrapping small round pink tablets and swilling them down with diet soda. The wrappers had a red symbol on them which she couldn't make out from this distance.

From the corner of her eye, Mara BeCalla looked at Graye in the padded, high-backed chair next to hers. His hands were clasped reverently together, the long planes and hollows of his face suffused with a dreamy reflection. 'A median share of forty-three point six every day of the week, Miss BeCalla,' he murmured with gloating satisfaction. 'Over six hundred million worldwide. And just the beginning.'

The lights in the main auditorium began to dim, and a huge collective sigh passed over the packed rows. The audience seemed to sink into a state of trancelike hypnosis. All eyes were fixed unblinking on the stage, which was revolving. Slowly, the long curved staircase with its myriad dazzling lights came into view, the white arch at the top outlined against a deep-purple backdrop sprinkled with stars. Smoke billowed forth, and a voice from up above boomed out like the tolling of a bell.

'To our friends everywhere, brothers and sisters the world over, may the blessings of the Beamers be upon each and every one of you. Welcome to our daily hour of celebration, beaming joy into your hearts. And tonight . . .'

There was a roll of drums accompanied by a tumultuous fanfare of trumpets.

' . . . the Beamers are proud to present to our millions of satellite and cable subscribers everywhere – the Chosen One. Yes, friends, somewhere in our audience here tonight is a very special person, given the honour and privilege to step up on to the stage and become the Chosen One! And now please welcome your host . . . Messiah Wilde!'

A shudder of ecstatic anticipation rippled through the audience like an electric charge. Despite her hard-edged professional cynicism, Mara BeCalla thrilled at the spectacle.

This was power! To hold the hearts and minds and dreams of people in the palm of your hand! To sway them, make them laugh or cry, to play with them and control them, and see the light of adoration shining in their eyes . . .

The fanfare swelled as a figure dressed in black materialised through the billowing smoke. He paused there for a moment, dark eyes in a pale and solemn face, his long black hair sweeping over his collar. A slender hand raised in graceful greeting, he came down the curved stairway to the stage. The trumpets died to a silvery echo in the sudden hush of breathless silence.

A spotlight stabbed on and circled over the audience, seeking out the honoured and privileged person on tonight's show. Messiah Wilde stood at the front of the stage, his pointing finger following the beam of light round and round as it swept over the restless sea of heads in the darkened auditorium.

Suddenly his arm shot out, his finger aimed like a dart. A sigh went up like a swooning breeze. The spotlight settled and narrowed its beam to focus on a girl of about sixteen with long flaxen hair draping her shoulders. Her complexion was unnaturally pale, her eyes wide and glazed as if she were in a waking dream, or else in shock. A clean-cut young man in a dark-blue blazer was helping her out of her seat.

Over the speakers came the deep bass chords of a guitar, and the audience started to clap in time to the pounding rhythm.

Messiah Wilde was holding both arms wide in a gesture of welcome. And as if bestowing his personal benediction upon her. In the depths of his dark eyes there was that teasing gleam of sardonic humour that his millions of adoring young fans loved to see. He winked complicitly at the nearest camera, a wink he shared privately with each individual viewer, a bond between the two of them alone.

'Lovebeams from my heart to your heart.' Messiah Wilde took the girl's hand as she came up on to the stage, and he pressed it between both of his. Although his accent was unmistakably English, there was a gentler lilt to it, soft and lyrical. 'On behalf of the Beamers, welcome to our very special guest, the Chosen One on tonight's show.' He drew her forward. 'Will you tell us your name?'

'Josie,' the girl said in barely a whisper.

'Would that be Josephine?' Messiah Wilde faced her towards the camera. Her eyelids fluttered and she almost swooned as his arm encircled her shoulders.

There was something about the girl, something creepily unreal, that Mara BeCalla found perplexing. Her face was artificially white, her eyes outlined and lips drawn in with an expert's touch. She didn't wear T-shirt and bluejeans, or a skirt, like most of the other girls in the audience, but a long, champagne-coloured satin dress and matching satin slippers. In fact, Mara BeCalla realised, the girl's appearance reminded her very much of a bridesmaid's. All she lacked was a posy of flowers.

'Your own global television show,' Graye hissed in her ear. 'That's what you want, isn't it, Miss BeCalla?'

Mara BcCalla nodded, her eyes fixed on the spectacle

below. Fame. Wealth. Power. Yes. She wanted them all. And Grace MediaCorp could offer them to her. Beaming her face and voice into millions of homes around the globe . . .

It came to her then, in a flash, why Graye needed her. Watching Messiah Wilde down there in the spotlight, basking in all that female adoration, Mara BeCalla realised that she was required to fill the same role for the young males in the audience. The sexual magnetism of *The Lovebeams Show* had to appeal to both sexes – and the gays too. For there were, she noted, quite a number of young men in the audience whose eyes were shining in adoration as they followed every move of Messiah Wilde's lithe body clad in black.

'I believe I now know, Mr Graye, what it is you want.' She turned to him. 'And I think I can deliver.'

Their eyes locked together. Then a faint smile brushed Mara BeCalla's lips when she saw him nod.

The deal was done, the bargain sealed.

2

Phyllis Keets had yet to put in an appearance at the office – today was her third day of absence. Don Carlson had tried calling her, several times, as had Cawdor, but the phone hadn't been picked up, nor was the answering machine switched on. They had debated what to do and come up with nothing decisive.

Cawdor was keenly aware that Don was having one hell of a problem with the whole situation. The crux of it was: who to believe? His partner of eleven years or a faithful employee who had been a rock of probity and a person of impeccable virtue? Maybe the easiest and most obvious answer was that Phyllis had tripped a circuit and was living on the planet Zarg. Trouble was, Cawdor didn't entertain that scenario for a minute, and neither, he suspected, did Don Carlson.

It was an effort to drag his mind back to the calculations on the CAD screen flickering before him. With his brain on autopilot, he watched the endless columns scrolling upward, pressing the appropriate keys as and when necessary, without conscious mental activity.

When three-fifteen came around he almost expected Phyllis to walk in with her dimpled smile, bringing him a mug of freshly percolated coffee. He actually stared at the door, willing it to open and admit her, restoring normality to its proper place and banishing the weird dislocation of events in which he was trapped. After all, if he imagined it hard enough (as he had imagined, too vividly, his sexual assault on her) then it was bound to happen. Simply a matter of willpower. Phyllis would enter the room with his coffee and everything would be fine, just as it should be. The fraught meeting when Don had disclosed Phyllis's accusation against him never took place. Today was a normal day, the same as any other.

The door remained closed. No phantom Phyllis appeared.

All that happened was that a wretched Jeff Cawdor continued to sit before the console, gazing blankly at the rising columns of figures, the passage of time marked by his thudding heartbeats.

Suddenly, and for no accountable reason, his heartrate quickened. Then it was racing – pounding inside his chest, palpitations making him breathe hard and fast as if from extreme physical exertion. For, right on the edge of his conscious awareness, glimpsed as it were from the corner of his mind's eye, there hovered a fragment of the dream he had dreamt last night. The most terrible, most frightening dream yet. On waking this morning, a sensation of dread had lingered on, sour as the taste of bile in his mouth. But the substance of the dream, its actual content, had evaporated into space even as he was lying there, staring at the ceiling and squeezing his brain to retrieve it.

Now, hunched at the console, there flashed an image as clear and sharp as a beam of sunlight caught in a mirror.

A hot black night on a creaking deck. The gentle lisp of ocean under the stars. A man carries a trussed-up dripping bundle across his shoulder. Beside him pads a ragged barefoot boy with a coil of rope. The man halts at the gunwale, breathing hard, shakes the sweat from his eyes.

179

The boy fumbles with the rope, and then in the silence a soft splash as the bundle is lowered into the water.

And the ship sails on under a moonless sky.

It was only a fragment of the whole, Cawdor knew. Elsewhere in the dream lurked deeper, murkier horrors which he sensed with a shiver of repulsion, but which stubbornly failed to materialise. They were locked inside his skull, and he didn't possess the key to release them. He wasn't sure he wanted them released. This time it was as though his mind's eye had deliberately averted its gaze in order to shield him from particular loathsome images far beyond anything he could have imagined taking place in the devil's own domain, in the very pit of hellfire.

Cawdor leant back in the chair. His breathing slowed, his heartbeat steadied. Right this minute he could have used the coffee the ghost of Phyllis hadn't brought in.

With the orderly processes of thought that suited him to the job of design engineer, Cawdor invariably pursued a methodical approach – the application of *logic* – to any knotty problem that confronted him. But logic had no purchase on the shifting, transient realm of dreams. He just didn't know where to start. Dreams were composed of symbols, he had read somewhere, representing deep-rooted hopes, desires, anxieties, fears that the waking mind suppressed. So what were these dreams, these hidden symbols, supposed to mean? What relevance did they have to his life? Why him? Yet applying his famous logic to discover the answers struck Jeff Cawdor as not only pointless but absurd. Like using differential calculus to explain the fragile beauty of a butterfly's wing.

He pressed the PAUSE key, then SAVE to back up the work carried out thus far, and pushed the chair on its roller balls away from the console. It was impossible to concentrate with his mind in such confusion and turmoil. Surely somebody somewhere could make sense of what was happening, help him sort out this mess. The constant nagging frustration and feeling of helplessness was driving him crazy. That's what he needed all right. Help.

* * *

Clad in a long swirling white robe, with nothing underneath, Messiah Wilde stepped from the brightness of the elevator into subterranean gloom. The flaxen-haired girl in the satin dress – Josie – lurched against the metal wall of the elevator as she tried to follow, and required the assistance of Messiah Wilde to help her stand upright. 'Whoops-a-daisy.' He gripped her by the elbow. 'You feeling OK?'

She nodded hesitantly and looked along the bare concrete tunnel stretching dimly ahead. 'Where are we going?' The words jostled each other into a single slurred sound.

'Why, I've told you already,' Messiah Wilde said, breathing a small sigh of impatience. 'You are the Chosen One, and you're coming with me to the Temple. How many more times?'

'Huh . . . oh, yes,' Josie murmured vaguely.

It was stiflingly humid down here. She had to lean on him as they moved along the tunnel. This was the very lowest point of the sub-basement – five levels below the television studio, nearly 200 feet underground. The main elevator shaft didn't come this far; the only access was by two small elevators with restricted code combinations. The corps of security guards aside, not many people in the building knew of its existence.

The tunnel ended in a door thickly padded with fibreglass insulation held in place by wire mesh. Messiah Wilde heaved it open. Even though the chamber was wide and high, the conical ceiling sixty feet above taking up three levels, the atmosphere was if anything even more oppressive. The stench of putrefying vegetation hung on the air like sickly incense. An animal of some kind gave a lazy yawning croak, and there was the sluggish rippling of stagnant water. The smell and the heat and the mysterious unknown of the large dark space made the girl pause on the threshold, and she stumbled forward from a push in the back.

'Don't block the passage,' Messiah Wilde chided her, 'or I'll be tempted to block yours. Move on, they're waiting for us.'

He bared his teeth in a smile. His hand gripped her shoulder, the long tapering fingers digging in. He propelled her forward over the flagged floor.

Six dark shapes knelt in a semicircle before an altar of large stone slabs, erected to form an 'M' ten feet high. The shaven heads bowed in unison, the sound of their chanting a mumbling drone that vibrated the air like the sombre bass chord of a pipe organ.

> In Your tower of granite and glass
> Keep us safe and protected in this world
> Our Saviour and Redeemer Kersh.

Swaying a little, Josie stood beside Messiah Wilde, his tall robed figure a blur of white in the darkness, his hand kneading the soft muscle of her shoulder. The air was thick, like hot syrup. The monotonous chanting dirge went on, the circle of heads bowing each time the sacred name of Kersh was uttered.

> Warn us of the dangers to our faith
> From unbelievers who seek to destroy us
> Our Saviour and Redeemer Kersh.
> Through Your dreams reach out to us
> And guide us by Your divine wisdom.
> Our ears are ever open and waiting
> For Your thoughts to enter and enlighten us
> Our only Saviour and Redeemer Kersh . . .

The voices died away to a silence broken only by the sluggish lapping of water. Heads raised in an attitude of listening, the circle of kneeling figures stared up beseechingly to the altar of stone slabs. For several minutes no one stirred. In the deep silence the smallest whisper would have been heard, amplified by the cavernous chamber.

But there was nothing.

The attentive, straining circle listened in vain.

Messiah Wilde leant over Josie, his mouth close to her ear.

'Aren't you the lucky one. How many young girls, I

wonder, would love to be where you are now, about to experience the sublime ceremony performed by the Messengers of the Fall from Grace? You're happy, aren't you,' he said, an affirmation rather than a question, 'to have been chosen out of so many. So happy and so . . . filled to overflowing with gratitude.'

His hand slipped from her shoulder to the hollow of her slender back. Then it slid down over her buttocks. Josie struggled to resist, but the stifling heat of the chamber was like a soporific gas, making her movements sluggish. Now Messiah Wilde was lifting the hem of her dress, his long fingers touching her thigh. She tried to move away, raising her arm as if to ward him off, and would have fallen over if he hadn't caught her.

Messiah Wilde chuckled. 'Whoops-a-daisy. Not too clever on our dainty little feet, are we, pussikins?' His voice turned to coaxing sympathy. 'Oh it's such a shame, little girl, and you so young and pretty. You know I could eat you? Gobble you up from top to bottom.' His hand slid lower, his palm cupping and squeezing. 'Starting here, and lick you all over –'

A shape rose from the circle, gaunt and austere, and whirled around in its black robe.

'Remember, we require a virgin, not a slut despoiled at your hands!' Elder Graye thundered. 'Have you interfered with this child?'

'Not yet. I haven't had the opportunity.'

'She must be pure and unsullied –'

'I haven't laid a finger on her,' Messiah Wilde protested mildly. 'You think I don't know the rules?'

Elder Graye placed the bony claw of his hand on Josie's blonde head. His long eyelids drooped shut, and his head was raised high. 'Let not this child harbour unclean thoughts and fancies. Keep her free from temptation and sin so that our Saviour and Redeemer Kersh may bestow his blessings upon us.'

Messiah Wilde bowed his head and mumbled, 'All glory to our Saviour and Redeemer Kersh.' He flicked back a strand of hair. 'Amen to that.'

'I need to speak with you,' Elder Graye said. He beckoned to one of the elders. 'Show the girl our little pets. It will keep her amused.' He patted Josie on the cheek. She was led away across the dark bowl of the chamber. The two men moved to a leather couch in a small alcove. Graye lifted the top of a cabinet and a bright dazzle lit his face from below, sparkling off bottles and a mirror shelf. He poured drinks, added cubes of ice, and handed a crystal tumbler to Messiah Wilde.

'What does she think will happen to her?' Graye asked.

'She has no idea. Maybe thinks she'll get to fuck me and that'll be it.' Messiah Wilde smiled as he drank.

Graye remained standing, a frown creasing his face. 'Your levity displeases me. Also your behaviour towards these creatures. They are not to be treated as your personal sex toys. I have mentioned this before.'

Messiah Wilde stretched out his long legs beneath the white robe. On his pale feet he wore sandals of soft kid leather. The robe concealed the puncture marks and broken veins on his thighs. He sighed and said wearily, 'Don't you know it's the sexual bit that pulls in the ratings? If they didn't have the hots for me, the TV show and all the videos and websites would be less popular than a presidential press conference. "Sex is Power" – that's the Message, isn't it?'

'We don't wish to disseminate the Message to our flock so blatantly,' Graye said sternly. 'Our credo is to beam health and vitality, clean minds and loving hearts. The Message is understood but *unspoken* – you should know that.' He swirled his drink, brooding into the glass. 'The ceremony will have to be delayed.'

'What on earth for? She's ready.'

'Because there are more important, more vital matters to be dealt with first!' Graye was visibly trembling, overwhelmed by anger at Messiah Wilde's nonchalant manner. 'Why do you suppose we are trying to communicate with Kersh? Already, once in his dreams, he has warned us of Cawdor and the danger he presents. But he hasn't told us when or how this might happen – under what

184

circumstances. We must learn all we can before Cawdor himself realises the significance of past events.'

As he took in what Graye was saying, Messiah Wilde's indolence vanished. His dark eyes became troubled. He said, 'I don't see how Cawdor can possibly know anything. How the hell can he?'

'He might not. If the past remains a closed book of blank pages, he will not have any genetic memory of what has taken place. In his ignorance, the future will unfold according to plan, and he will be powerless to change it. But the warning from Kersh must mean something – the threat of disruption, perhaps – and we cannot ignore it. We must act to prevent it.' Graye's knuckles whitened as he gripped the glass. His thin breathing sounded like a breeze rustling through dry reeds.

Messiah Wilde lounged back on the leather couch. 'Well, I guess that's your department. I've tried, but I can't hear Kersh the way you and your boys can.'

'No,' Graye said through thin lips. He finished off his drink in a single gulp and banged the glass down. 'I shall leave the sexual charisma to you; leave the safeguarding of the Beamers to me. I have a long history of doing precisely that.'

On the far side of the chamber, Josie and the elder were walking slowly along the wall of thick, greenish glass, her slender shoulders enveloped by the flowing sleeve of his black robe.

She understood now why it was so hot down here, and the cause of the fetid, cloying smell. The reason was the swampy jungle behind the glass, with its closely packed trees and hanging vines surrounding a large pool of water flecked with green slime, everything steeped in a mist that dripped on to the floor of rotting vegetation.

High above, powerful halogen lamps mimicked a tropical sun, filtering through leaves and branches to form a green miasma.

And the reason for the thick glass was obvious too. The jungle was alive. Alligators snoozed on the sandy edge of the pool, snouts partly submerged in the water. Looped along the branch of a tree she saw a boa constrictor, twenty feet long and thick as a man's waist, its unblinking eyes like pebbles of polished glass. Other creatures rustled in the dense undergrowth, and she heard the chirping of birds and the raucous cries of macaws.

At first – seeing the cameras – she'd wondered if it was an elaborate film set. There were two movie cameras on moveable dollies and another on a rotating platform high up near the sloping roof. But of course that wasn't possible, Josie realised. Far too risky putting live actors in there with the alligators and reptiles. She gazed through the glass wall, squinting because her eyesight was kind of bleary. Then she was staring. Half-buried in the sand at the edge of the water was a skull. A human skull. She spotted another, and then a third, wrapped in a tangle of weeds, scummy water lapping in the empty eye sockets.

There were bones as well, pale and gleaming, picked clean as a whistle.

One of the alligators stirred and yawned wide, the rows of teeth white against the pink fleshy interior of its jaws. Josie tried to back away, but the arm round her shoulders held her firm.

From across the chamber came once more the chanting dirge as the Messengers prayed to their saviour and redeemer:

> Through Your dreams reach out to us
> And guide us by Your divine wisdom.
> Our ears are ever open and waiting . . .

3

The elevator doors opened and Gil Gribble went staggering, expelled into the corridor by the pressure of people eager to get out. Students streamed past him on either side: Herculean boys and Amazonian girls who made Gribble feel like a pygmy in a land of giants. What did they feed kids on these days? Ball bearings?

Mopping his brow with his handkerchief, Gribble trailed after them into the refectory. The place was like bedlam. Confronting the din of voices and banging of trays and clatter of cutlery took physical stamina, as if battling through a shock wave of noise. He skirted the long straggling line waiting to be served at the counter and trotted towards the faculty dining room at the far end. As the double doors closed behind him he closed his eyes for a blessed moment, feeling carpet under his feet, savouring the relative peace and quiet of murmured conversation, the subdued tinkling and clinking of civilised adults eating a leisurely lunch. Not that he disliked the students here at Columbia (the kids who attended his Theoretical Physics seminars were a lively and enthusiastic bunch) but he had no desire to observe, even at a distance, the frenzied feeding of the five thousand. Reminded him too much of pigs with their snouts in the trough.

He shuffled into the short, dignified line of fellow academics and admin colleagues and peered over their shoulders to see what was on offer. Gribble wasn't a gourmet, but he loved his grub. The pork chops and gravy with mashed potatoes and green beans looked tempting. A side salad with Italian dressing to go with it. And, for dessert, apple-and-blueberry pie with two scoops of mint-chocolate-chip ice cream. To round it off, a slice of Brie and crackers, and a tall glass of iced tea. It was as he was turning away from the cashier's desk with his tray that he spotted her. In fact it was her blaze of red hair, boyishly cut close to the scalp and razor-trimmed around her white, pointed, pixie-like ears, that caught his eye; in the sober shades and hues of the room, Annie Lorentz stood out like a beacon.

His inward rush of pleasure showed itself in a beaming grin as Gribble hurried over.

She was finishing a plate of Waldorf salad, leaning forward with her elbows propped on the table, reading a thick, leather-bound volume with dusty yellowing pages supported at an angle on a pile of students' workbooks. Close to, the contrast between her white skin and cropped red hair was even more startling. On her lips was the faintest blush of lipstick, but she wore no make-up on her silvery eyebrows or lashes. Rather than disguise it, the woollen plaid shirt and baggy, grey cord trousers seemed to emphasise how slender she was, shoulders wide and angular, long legs crossed at the ankles under the table, comfortable flat brown loafers on her feet.

Her eyes, as she looked up at Gribble's greeting, were of the very palest blue. He had worshipped from afar, and closer to, ever since she had joined the faculty one year and three months ago. He had not the faintest idea how he stood with Annie Lorentz, and lacked the courage to find out.

'Hi, Gil,' she said with an easy smile. 'Grab a seat.'

'If I'm not in the way.' Gribble tried to indicate her book with his loaded tray. 'You ain't preparing or nothin'?'

His voice died away as he saw Annie Lorentz gazing at the food on his tray. He looked too – or rather gawped. In place of the pork chops and mashed potato there was a double cheeseburger with bacon slices and a heap of greasy fries. Instead of a healthy salad he had chosen a side order of griddle cakes with ham sausage. For dessert there was coconut-cream pie topped with frozen yoghurt. Plus (and here Gribble goggled in disbelief) a couple of Twinkies.

'Better put that mountain of animal fat and cholesterol down before you collapse under it,' Annie Lorentz advised him. She watched with a little twinkle of amusement as Gribble manoeuvred himself and his lunch between two chairs and finally settled opposite her. He was red in the face and drops of sweat were trickling down from under the frizzy mop of hair that flopped over his forehead like a bedraggled squirrel.

'Glad I ran into you,' Gribble said, unfolding his knife, fork and spoon from his napkin. He stared at the plates of food as if seeing them for the first time. Cheeseburger and fries?

With a quick, shy smile he said, 'Ain't seen you in a month of Sundays. You bin away?'

'Yeah, got back Tuesday from a field trip. Three weeks

in Washington State studying the Haida tribes. Went across to Vancouver Island mid-trip for four days. You ever visited that part of the northwest, Gil?'

Gribble admitted he hadn't.

'It's amazing. Wonderful country!' Annie Lorentz pushed her plate away and closed her book. 'The Haidas still carve traditional totem poles up there. Eighty, ninety, some over a hundred feet high. I brought one back for you.'

Gribble nearly choked on a mouthful of cheeseburger. 'You brought me back a hundred-foot-high totem pole?' he spluttered, wiping his mouth.

Annie Lorentz delved into a canvas drawstring bag and produced a totem pole of carved wood, painted in bright colours, about nine inches tall. She stood it on the table in front of him. 'For you. Look good on your mantel. Have you got a mantel?'

Gribble said he had, which was true, though with the amount of electronic paraphernalia and other junk in his living room he couldn't remember where it was. What did that matter? Annie had thought of him – had thought *enough* of him to bring him back a present from her travels.

'Hey, thanks, that's really nice of you,' he mumbled, a delicious warm flush spreading through him. 'Appreciate it a lot, Annie. It'll have pride of place.'

'That's OK.' Annie Lorentz tugged open the neck of the canvas bag to reveal a dozen or more totem poles. 'They were having a sale, so I bought a job lot. Know anybody who'd like one?'

'Not right off the bat, no.' Gribble's attempt at a valiant smile was as bleak and watery as a sunset seen through a storm cloud. 'But I'll ask around if you like.' His appetite seemed to have deserted him. He jabbed a fork into the heap of fries and stuck them into his mouth.

'Do you want me?' Annie Lorentz asked.

The fries went down in a single gulp. 'Huh?'

'I thought maybe you wanted me for something when you said you were glad to have run into me.' She cocked her head. 'No?'

'Yeah . . . um, that's right, I did.'

'What was it?'

Gribble had to think. His mind was in its usual clutter, and the proximity of Annie Lorentz added to his confusion. 'Uh, a friend of mine, Jeff Cawdor, he's . . .' Gribble frowned, wondering how to begin. How *did* you explain to someone the weird, unsettling problems Cawdor was experiencing? 'You know about mental stuff, don't you, Annie? You studied psychology, am I right?'

'Social anthropology, Gil.'

'Oh.'

'With particular reference to tribal arts and customs.'

'Ain't the same, I guess.'

Annie Lorentz leant back, folded one arm across her chest, pulling at the short red hair curling behind her left ear. 'About the same as asking a cosmologist what the stars foretell for tomorrow.'

Gribble saw her point. He dabbled with the griddle cakes. 'Aw, well, my mistake.'

'Something wrong with your friend up here, Gil,' Annie Lorentz advised him, tapping her head, 'he ought to see a psychiatrist.'

'He's not *crazy*, Annie. It ain't that kind of mental problem. He keeps getting flashes of stuff – like, you know, *visions* – just come out of nowhere. He didn't actually say as much, but he's worried sick, I can tell.'

'Visions of what?'

'He told me a whole bunch of things.' Gazing into the middle distance, Gribble smothered a burp. 'Lemme see . . . a sailing ship from way back long ago. Then a guy about to be fried in the electric chair. And this really weird daydream, I guess, about seducing his secretary at the office. Tell you, Annie, he's in a bad way –'

'Whoa. Whoa. *Seducing his secretary*?' Annie Lorentz was shaking her head. 'Hey, come on, Gil, that's not a vision; that's a male lust fantasy. He has the hots for her, so he lies in bed imagining what it would be like to fuck her and playing with himself.'

Gribble felt himself blushing. She had a forthright and

190

uncompromising way of expressing herself that, although he would never confess it, Gribble found shocking. He chewed on some burger, which refused to go down, and kept on chewing.

'Nothing strange about that, Gil,' Annie Lorentz said mildly.

Gribble finally and thankfully got the damn thing swallowed. 'It ain't that of itself that's strange. Cawdor was honest enough to admit such thoughts *had* popped into his head.'

Leaning back with folded arms, legs stretched out, Annie Lorentz listened as he told her of the imagined sexual encounter which then – so Cawdor's secretary claimed – had actually occurred. Her shrewd pale-blue eyes fringed by silvery lashes were slightly narrowed as if she were weighing the credence of the story each step of the way, testing its validity.

When he had finished, she was silent for a moment, head on one side. 'Your friend Cawdor, he asked you for help?'

Gribble shook his head. He could tell she was intrigued. 'Not straight off. What I think is, Jeff needed somebody to talk to, so he talked to me. But I can't figure it out, can you?'

'And when he says he never made any play for this woman – Phyllis – you believe him?'

'Oh yeah, absolutely, one hundred per cent.' Gribble felt vaguely offended that she should question his friend's honesty. 'I mean, why would Jeff even tell me about it if he had – you know, if he'd messed around with his secretary? Why mention it in the first place? He'd have kept his mouth shut.' He shrugged. 'We'd be none the wiser, would we?'

'That's true,' Annie Lorentz conceded. 'Yeah, that is odd, I have to admit.' She picked up her canvas bag, yanked the drawstring tight, and pushed back her chair. 'Gotta go.'

Gribble watched as she stood up, hooked her finger under the collar of a denim jacket and tossed it over her shoulder. Now was the moment, if he was serious, to ask her out to dinner, or at least to have a drink with him after work. In the normal run of things he wouldn't see her again for days, even weeks. He took a breath.

'As a matter of fact I do know somebody, Gil. Not sure he'd be able to help your friend, but he'd be willing to listen and take him seriously. Doctor Khuman is interested in that kind of thing. Want me to ask him?'

Gribble let go of the breath he'd been holding. 'Thanks, Annie. Yeah, sure. Is he on the faculty?'

'No, he has his own private research institute, the Troth Foundation, in upstate New York. Like me to call him?'

Gribble nodded, bereft of words. Annie Lorentz was already moving off. He watched her tall, rangy figure threading through the tables to the door, a small glowing smile on his face. Gribble felt suddenly happy. He had an excuse now – a legitimate one at that – to keep in touch with his dream woman. And he'd be doing his friend a favour into the bargain. He hoped and prayed Cawdor would see it that way.

Bill Benedict leant towards the mike, crinkled eyes on the sweeping hand of the clock, and flicked the talk-back button.

'Stand by, Sarah. Red coming up in ten seconds. Nine ... eight ... seven ...'

Behind the thick glass window of the control booth, inside the tiny studio with its walls of oatmeal-coloured soundproof tiles, Sarah made a circle of her finger and thumb and held it towards him – OK. Fed through the large floor speakers, the opening chords of Dave Brubeck's 'Take Five' tinkled in the air as the mixing engineer eased the slide control on the panel. Bill Benedict gave Sarah a nod and encouraging wink, the close crop of his white hair like a skull cap atop his ruggedly handsome weatherbeaten features.

Sarah saw the red light wink on and brought the swivel mike in its sponge glove close to her mouth. 'Good evening and welcome to *Take Five*, WCTC New Brunswick's intimate late-hour confessional of soul searching and breast baring, with me, your friend and confidante, Sarah Cawdor.'

She had a wonderful mellifluous voice for radio, low-pitched with just a hint of huskiness. The theme tune faded away. Sarah smiled at Bill Benedict in the control booth. She raised one finger, listening over the headphones as he cued her in to the first caller of the evening. Then she launched in:

'Hello, Alice, welcome to *Take Five*. Say what you have to say and we'll do our best to give you good advice.'

'It's my kid, my son Paul. He's kinda changed. I dunno how to explain it.' A thin nasal whine, the voice of the struggling, ill-educated underclass. 'He was such a sweet boy, kind and thoughtful, and in the last few months it's like – I dunno – like Jekyll and Hyde, you know?'

'How old is Paul?'

'Fourteen.'

'Is he doing well in school?'

'Well, yeah. I guess so. I mean, I don't really know – he never tells me nothin', you know? Never talks to me or nothin', like I don't even exist, and when he does say somethin' it's like, you know, just abuse and stuff, no respect –'

'Remember you only have five minutes, Alice. Then we have to move on. So what's the problem with Paul? Is he drinking? Taking drugs? Antisocial behaviour? Is he violent?'

'No, no, he ain't aggressive, least not to me. About drink and drugs and stuff, I wouldn't know.'

'What does his father have to say about this?'

'We split up, six years ago, me and Ron, and he don't come around too –'

'You and Ron were divorced.'

'We couldn't get divorced 'cause we wasn't married. No, the sonofabitch – excuse me, slip of the tongue – bastard run off with a bleached blonde with big feet and bad breath. Tell the truth, Sarah, I ain't seen him from that day to this. An' I don't want to, believe me, that guy treated me like dogshit – excuse me, pardon my French –'

'Five minutes, Alice, remember?'

'Oh yeah, sorry.' There was a sniffling pause, and faintly in the background the gulp of something liquid. Then: 'I'm at the end of my wits with that boy, Sarah. Paul, I mean. Wha'd'ya reckon I ought to do? He's too big to be chastised. I tell you, honestly, I just don't know how to handle him.' Another loud sniffle.

'A lot of kids – most kids – go through a rebellious stage, Alice, at Paul's age. It's perfectly normal and natural. But you do, I feel – and I think you'll agree – have an additional problem here with the absence of a father.' Sarah's voice was calm and reasonable, uncritical, not apportioning blame. 'I think discipline is the key here, Alice. Paul needs guidance; he needs direction, positive goals to aim for and attain. And that's where the Message can make a real difference. Do you understand what I'm saying?'

'Well, yeah, I think . . . What's that again?'

'Does Paul ever watch *The Lovebeams Show*?'

'Uhh . . . dunno . . .'

'Get him to watch it, Alice,' Sarah insisted. 'Young people are crying out for a guiding light in this world of confusion and corruption. Values have been tossed on the scrap heap or made a mockery of, and it's high time we got back to our basic, core beliefs that made this country great. *The Lovebeams Show* can get Paul started on the right path. Will you give it a go?'

'Yeah, I guess, if it'll do him some good.' The tired, defeated voice hesitated. 'What is it exactly?'

'Oh, it's a fun thing, Alice, he'll enjoy it. They have music, games, prizes, pretty girls. Paul likes girls, doesn't he? And they don't preach at you: they beam the Message into the hearts of everyone prepared to receive it.'

Sarah nodded to Bill Benedict, acknowledging the countdown coming over the headphones. She said, 'Your five minutes is nearly up, Alice. Take my advice and try it with Paul. The change in him will amaze you, I promise. OK?'

'Thanks, Sarah. Just one more thing –'

'My pleasure, Alice, and thanks for calling *Take Five*.' She sat back in the padded chair as the theme music swelled up, reaching for her cigarettes. She just had time to light one and take a deep pull before the next caller was on the line.

'Hi, Trish, this is Sarah Cawdor welcoming you to *Take Five.*' Smoke gusted from her mouth and nostrils. 'The floor is yours.'

'Oh, Sarah, I want to say how much I agree with the advice you gave the last caller!' This was a trembly, lisping voice belonging to a teenager or young woman. 'You wouldn't believe the difference it's made to my life!'

'Maybe I would, Trish, and glad to hear it. What's your problem?'

There was a quivering sigh. 'It isn't *really* a problem, not as such . . . It's, well . . . Oh, I don't know if I can say it!'

'If you don't or can't, Trish, we'll have to say bye-bye.'

The voice suddenly gushed forth: 'It's this tingling I get – it feels right but I'm not sure – every time I see Messiah Wilde coming down the *Lovebeams* stairway. Kinda hot and can't catch my breath, and, like I said, tingly. When you see his dreamy brown eyes real close and that little crooked smile he has, like he's sharing a secret with you, just you and him, nobody else. And I feel kinda . . . Ooohh.' She gave a moaning sigh. 'I never, ever felt that way in my entire life before.'

'What age are you, Trish?'

'Fifteen. I'll be sixteen November eighth.'

'Nothing to fret about,' Sarah said with a smile in her voice. 'You're a healthy young girl and your feelings are perfectly natural and normal. You're of an age when your hormones are budding and blossoming, like sap rising in a young tree, and you suddenly discover emotions you never knew you had.'

'There's nothin' wrong with me, then?'

Sarah chuckled. 'No, just the opposite. Everything's *right* with you. Relax and enjoy it!'

'It's his eyes, Sarah, and that curl of his lip. I get goosebumps all over.'

'Well, who wouldn't!' Sarah sounded amused in a rather arch, coquettish way. 'Take it from me, Trish, it isn't only girls your age he has that effect on. I love his smile, too, and the way he casually tosses back that long black hair of his. And have you noticed he has the most beautiful and expressive hands I've ever seen on a man, very slender, with long tapering fingers? Stirs up my imagination even talking about them. Just as well I'm a happily married woman, or who knows!'

'Oh, thank you, Sarah, I'm really glad now I called you and had the courage to say what I did. I thought it might be, you know, kinda wrong or maybe unhealthy, thinking as I do.'

'Nonsense, nothing wrong in it at all. Nice talking to you, Trish. Bye.'

Brubeck's muted chords swelled again. Sarah took a deep pull on her cigarette and tilted her head back, letting the smoke dribble from her nostrils.

In the den that also served as his workroom, across the landing from the master bedroom, Jeff Cawdor sat in the penumbra beyond the circle of light thrown by a table lamp. The temperature in the room was about average, not at all cold, yet Cawdor's fingertips were frozen, his stomach shrivelled up as if it contained a block of ice.

'No, that's true, a lot of people have difficulty grasping it at first. But when it happens – when the Message gets through – it hits like a shock wave running right through you. You'll know it when you feel it, I promise. No mistake.'

'Was that how it happened with you – all at once, straight out of the blue?' The voice was young and male, reedy and anxious. 'It don't just creep up on you gradual like?'

'Don't worry about it, Gavin. Any day now, when you're least expecting it, you'll experience a chill down your spine, as if someone's walked over your grave, as the saying goes. That's the first sign. Then you'll know it's coming, and you'd better prepare yourself, because when it *does* happen it'll knock you straight into tomorrow.'

The voice was Sarah's, there was no doubt about that, but the words coming over the radio belonged to someone who was a total stranger to him. Someone who bore no resemblance to the woman he was married to, yet who was using the gentle, intelligent, familiar voice of his wife to spout this utter quasi-religious, pseudo-spiritual garbage.

Sitting tense and upright in the leather armchair, Cawdor felt physically sick.

In the past week or so, while eating breakfast, he had caught the odd five minutes here and there of the show Sarah was now praising to the skies. Certainly he'd seen enough to spot a mile off the fake sentiment about 'lovebeams' that the slimy host, Messiah Wilde, had been spouting. Even worse, Cawdor felt, was the way the show pretended to understand its youthful audience and to sympathise with their emotional problems, when actually it was manipulating their natural doubts and insecurities to make cheap and salacious entertainment. In short, a cynical media exercise in naked exploitation of a vulnerable age group.

But that Sarah, of all people, should be taken in by it! The listeners to her radio programme, and the millions who watched *The Lovebeams Show*, might possibly believe themselves to be a joyful band being led by Messiah Wilde towards the golden, sunlit uplands of a better, happier life. Yes, he could accept that; what he couldn't accept was Sarah's complicity in the fraud.

The block of ice in his stomach seemed to grow like a malignant black tumour. Because he knew – would have staked his life on it – that his wife would never be hoodwinked by such blatant gimcrack fakery.

And yet, incomprehensibly, she was.

God knows how he kept off the whiskey while he waited for her, but he stuck to his promise to himself, determined to face her calmly and straight up front, his brain unfogged by alcohol.

Sometimes Cawdor waited up for Sarah, sometimes not, so she wasn't surprised to find him in the living room, sipping at a mug of coffee, the latest issue of *National*

Geographic spread across his knees. Sarah swung her shoulder bag on to a chair and smiled at him through a yawn. She patted her mouth.

'Oh! – pardon me. It's the drive home, I guess, knocks me out. I felt fine leaving the studio.' She paused then, seeing his face so pale and stiff, his brown eyes hard as stones, unblinking.

'You don't look too good, Jeff.' She came round the sofa towards him, her eyes clouding. 'Aren't you well?'

She halted in mid-stride as Cawdor held up his hand.

'I'm sorry, Sarah, but I'm having a real tough time understanding this. I hope you can explain it to me.'

'Explain . . .?' She shook her head a little.

'Or have you just lost your senses? Suddenly gone crazy?'

'Jeff, what are you talking about . . .?'

'The crock of shit I heard on your programme tonight. Telling people to watch *The Lovebeams* TV show. How it would change their lives once they received the Message – whatever *that* is. And then drooling over that huckster charlatan with the shy smile and expressive hands and long black hair he throws over his shoulder – the so-called "Messiah Wilde" and his freak sideshow.'

Cawdor threw the magazine aside and stood up. His mouth had a taste of battery acid. He stared into her face.

'Where'd you *get* that stuff? How can you possibly believe any of it, and, even worse, broadcast the crap and encourage other gullible saps to be taken in by it? This isn't you, Sarah. It isn't *you.*'

She stared back at him, her eyes wide and bright. He tried to see into their blue-grey depths, to find the woman he loved residing somewhere deep inside. But all he could see were bright shining orbs containing a look of resentment, hostility even.

'Thank you for your opinion.' Sarah kept her voice calm and low-pitched. 'It just so happens I have a mind of my own and can think for myself. And I *have* thought about it, long and hard, and I believe in what the Beamers are trying to do, that they're a power for good. People in the world today have no direction, no purpose; they're crying out for guidance, for something positive to give their lives meaning and fulfilment.' She raised her eyebrows and went on in the same quiet, moderate tone: 'You're free to believe or not believe anything you want, Jeff. I demand the same right. That's fair, isn't it?'

'You thought about it long and hard,' he croaked in a rusty voice, 'and never said a word to me? Why not?' He jerked his thumb towards the kitchen. 'When you were watching that stuff on TV and I asked you about it, you dismissed it as foolish nonsense. A stupid show for stupider people you said –'

'Maybe I did say that; I don't deny it.' Sarah turned away from him. As she did so, the light glinted on something above her right breast. Cawdor had been so intent on her face that he hadn't noticed till now the Beamers' silver symbol pinned to her cashmere sweater.

'That's all I thought it was at first, until I began to really listen and pay attention to what they were saying.' Sarah took a pack of Stuyvesant from her bag and lit one. 'Then I talked it over with Bill – he's been watching their show too – and he agreed we should carry the Message on the late-night show, because a lot of our callers are young people who are emotionally confused in one way or another and don't know which way –'

'I'm not following this,' Cawdor broke in, his voice hollow with incredulity. 'You talked it over with Bill Benedict but not with me? You value his opinion, do you, more than mine?' He stared. 'I can't believe it's you, Sarah, saying these things.'

'I purposely didn't talk it over with you, Jeff, because I already knew *precisely* how you'd react.' Sarah sucked in a lungful of smoke sharply. She looked at him defiantly. 'And I was proved right, wasn't I? I knew you'd put me down, make a mockery of it. Not even bother to listen.' Her mouth twisted in a thin bitter smile. 'It can seem rather sad, you know, a man your age being jealous of someone like Messiah Wilde just because he's young and good-looking and charismatic.'

Charismatic? Cawdor thought. That wasn't one of Sarah's words. He'd never heard her describe anybody as charismatic in all the years he'd known her. But this woman he didn't know. She was a stranger to him.

Cawdor felt suddenly very frightened.

There was a torrent of feeling dammed up inside him. As well as fear, there was bewilderment and incredulity, but above all a deep anguish that she was slipping away, and a yearning to bring her back. He tried to break the dam, let the torrent pour out, but couldn't. One look at the expression on Sarah's face – a mixture of scorn and amused pity she didn't bother to conceal – and he was struck dumb. Anything he might say would be treated with contempt, as someone making a crude and pathetic effort to salve his wounded ego, and at the same time mock her beliefs. The very thing she had a moment ago accused him of doing.

Sarah stubbed out her cigarette and slung her bag over her shoulder. 'I'm tired. I'm going to bed.' She went up the three wooden steps to the hallway. Motionless, Cawdor stood listening to her weary tread ascending the staircase, feeling as cold and abandoned as a corpse.

4

Gil Gribble's spine went rigid with shock as he watched Doctor Khuman stick a hatpin laterally through the thumb of Cawdor's left hand.

'Tell me what you feel,' Doctor Khuman said in a gentle, modulated voice.

Gribble turned to look at Annie Lorentz, questions dancing in his eyes. She was too mesmerised to notice him, sitting on the arm of his tattered, bulging sofa, one leg drawn up, hands clasped round it. She had a faint bemused smile on her face, and was shaking her head slightly, as if she couldn't believe what she was seeing. Gribble turned back to stare; neither could he.

'Nothing,' Cawdor said.

'No sensation at all?'

'No.'

Cawdor was sitting on a cheap kitchen chair that Doctor Khuman had positioned next to the windows, facing into the room. The coned metal shade of the desk lamp had been angled so that one half of Cawdor's face was brightly illuminated, the other half in shadow. His eyes were open, looking straight ahead with an expression that was slightly out of focus, quite placid and untroubled. Not a hint of any pain.

Doctor Khuman withdrew the hatpin. It shone clean and bright, not a trace of blood to be seen. There was no blood on the thumb either, as Doctor Khuman placed Cawdor's hand back in his lap. He slid the hatpin into a leather pouch and put the pouch away in his inside pocket. Then, perched on the edge of the workbench, he clasped his slender brown hands together and raised his head and gazed at the ceiling through silver-rimmed glasses that magnified his already large and luminous brown eyes. Except for the distant rumble of traffic two blocks away, the room was silent.

What happens now? Gribble wondered. Do we meditate? Join hands and contact the undead? Spriritual shenanigans of this nature left him on the cusp between deep scepticism and irreverent mirth. Again he looked to Annie Lorentz, who this time reacted, glancing towards him with raised eyebrows and a waggle of thumbs clasped to her knee.

Gribble hadn't actually seen Doctor Khuman *do* anything – that was the thing that perplexed him the most. No hypnotic stare, no gold watch swinging to and fro like a pendulum. No chanted gobbledegook or numbers counted backward. All he had done was place the fingertips of both hands on the sides of Jeff's neck, with the lightest of touches, for five seconds, no longer. And Jeff had stayed exactly the same. He hadn't slumped forward or moaned or turned into a zombie, nothing like that. His eyes had gone a bit fuzzy . . . and that was it, as if his mind had floated off somewhere.

And then Doctor Khuman stuck the hatpin through his thumb.

Christ, Gribble thought, what if, instead of saying, 'Nothing,' in answer to Doctor Khuman's question, Jeff had leapt up yelling, 'Yes, it hurts like fuck, you stupid bastard!' What then?

It had been a day of surprises right enough, starting that morning when Annie had called him the minute he arrived at his office in the Theoretical Physics department. At first, he assumed it was coincidence that the phone was ringing as he stepped through the door and hung up his leather jacket, but no, it was so urgent that she had been calling every few minutes for the past half-hour. The man she had told him about, Doctor Khuman of the Troth Foundation, was in town, and had agreed to meet Gil's friend. But it had to be today, Annie insisted, because Doctor Khuman was leaving later that evening. Saying he'd try to arrange it, Gribble had put the phone down with a horrible sickly feeling. There was a tiny complication in that he hadn't, as yet, mentioned any of this to Jeff. What the hell was Jeff going to say? Not only had he, Gil Gribble, discussed Jeff's personal business with a third party, Annie Lorentz – he'd also fixed up some kind of damn consultation with a doctor (doctor of what? Gribble had no idea) to discuss matters confided to Gribble in a private conversation between friends. It crossed his mind not to call Jeff at all – just forget the whole deal – and then spin a small white lie to Annie that his friend was out of town or something. In the end, however, he had called him. As he pressed the dialpad, Gribble had been rather desperately thinking up a long litany of apologies for betraying a confidence. Then the biggest surprise of all. Jeff had listened and quietly asked who this person was who Gribble wanted him to meet. Gribble had told him. There followed a long silence. Clenching his teeth and waiting for the thunderbolt, Gribble heard Jeff's calm voice at the end of the line say, 'Yeah, I'll come. I can get away about five. At your apartment?'

Gazing at the ceiling, Doctor Khuman spoke in the cultured tones of a high-caste member of his race, worldly and intellectual.

'Tell me about your thoughts, your dreams, your worries, Mr Cawdor. Anything that has troubled you recently, or perhaps merely puzzled you. I do not ask you to reveal anything you wouldn't ordinarily, were we speaking together on a professional basis. Do you understand?'

'Yes.'

Doctor Khuman looked down. 'Very good. Proceed.'

When Bill Benedict broke the news to her, Sarah thought she was going to faint.

She was on her way to the studio on the second floor when the shorn white head was thrust into the corridor and he beckoned urgently to her. He propelled Sarah inside his office and strode past her to the desk, smacking his meaty, sunburnt hands and chortling under his breath. He was wearing a short-sleeved shirt of black and salmon-pink stripes, its pink buttons straining over his beer belly, the open neck revealing tight little white curls beneath the hanging brown pouch of his throat. He jabbed a blunt finger at the chair in front of the desk, nodding briskly at her, eyebrows like bushy white caterpillars against his craggy, tanned forehead.

'Better siddown, Sare. Somethin' to tell you, girl!'

Sarah looked at her wristwatch. 'I don't have much time, Bill. I'm on air in forty-five minutes and there's a mountain of mail I have to sort through. And I mean *mountain* – we had five sackfuls come in this morning alone.'

'I know, I know. Siddown, you got time. It's like we breached a dam when we introduced the new format. Like there's a hunger out there – people are going wild for it.' Bill Benedict cocked one of the white caterpillars at her. 'And, before you say anything, I'll say it first. You were right all along. I was wrong to hold out against the idea; I didn't have the faintest notion of the potential we were tapping into. Just damn glad you persuaded me!'

Sarah gave him a smile and a teasing wink. 'It took a while, but the Message finally got through to you, hey, Bill?'

'Did, sure 'nough,' he acknowledged. 'And have I got a message for *you*.'

Sarah waited. He was spinning it out, she realised, relishing every minute. He sat back in the leather chair and pointed at arm's length to the phone.

'Guess who I bin talkin' to, not ten minutes ago. You'll never guess in a million years, Sare.'

'The President?'

'Hah! Better'n that.' He leant towards her, lowering his voice to a throaty whisper. 'Somebody from Fort Lauderdale, Florida. Now who'd ya think that might be, huh? Huh?'

Sarah felt her heart quicken its beat. She was suddenly impatient to know, to have it confirmed. Bill Benedict saw the look in her eye and a slow, devilish smirk spread across his beefy face. He was teasing her now, keeping her in an agony of suspense.

He spread his hands, as if bestowing a benediction. 'He called me himself, person to person, on that phone, I swear to God. I just talked, Sare, to Messiah Wilde in the living, breathing flesh!'

'I don't believe it, Bill,' Sarah said, heart pounding. 'I can't . . .'

'True as I sit here. An' lissen, if you find that part of it hard to believe, girl, there's no way you're gonna believe the next part. He says to me, "Bill, please be sure and pass on my respects and thanks to Sarah Cawdor. That show of hers is terrific, so please tell her so from me." He didn't actually say "terrific", as I recall; I think what he said was "superlative" or some such phrase. How 'bout that, Sare?' Bill Benedict punched the air. 'A ringing endorsement from the main man hisself!'

Sarah was sitting weakly in the chair. She licked her dry lips. 'I find it incredible that he even knows about the programme, way down there in Florida. Our outreach doesn't extend that far, does it?'

'Not into Florida itself, but all through the midwest, and a station in Memphis covers a swathe south to New Orleans. You saw the figures, Sare; I showed you the charts. We got an umbrella that throws its shadow over twenty-five million people. The Beamers must've gotten feedback from scores, hundreds, hell, *thousands* of listeners to the show. An' they love it – the Beamers, I mean – they think you're doin' a swell job.'

Bill Benedict was as tickled pink as his shirt.

Sarah was shaking her head in wonderment, smiling as if privately, inwardly, purely for herself. 'And he took the time to call you to say how much he liked the programme. You talked to Messiah Wilde in person.'

'Yeah, sure did,' Bill Benedict said, wearing a broad grin. 'And now he wants to talk to you.'

That was the moment when Sarah thought she was about to faint. She gripped her knees through her jeans to hold on to some semblance of reality. Deep inside, in the very core of her, she felt her uterus contract. Juices started seeping out of her, and a warm tingling spread upward from her thighs and bathed her in tropical heat.

'You're blushing, Sare.' Bill Benedict's eyes narrowed to slits, a mischievous twinkle in their depths. 'You got the hots for that guy, huh? Huh?' He wagged his head and tutted. 'An' you a respectable married lady with a family.'

'Don't be silly, Bill.' Sarah recovered her breath. 'I'm just very flattered. Did he say why? I mean, did he give a reason?'

'Didn't ask him. Maybe he wants to thank you hisself, in person. Told him you'd be through just after eleven, so he's gonna call you then.'

'You mean here? Tonight?'

'Right.' Bill Benedict clapped his hands. 'Don't just sit there like a moonstruck calf, girl: go get the show on the road!'

He watched, grinning, hands laced behind his head, as Sarah left the office in a daze. She went along the corridor to the studio, her hand dipping in her purse. Just as she arrived at the heavy door with the small square window, a white sign with red lettering on it saying STUDIO PERSONNEL ONLY, she glanced both ways and, seeing there was no one about, slipped the round candy-sized lozenge into her

205

mouth. She wadded the wrapper with the red 'M' in a black circle and shoved it to the bottom of her purse, opened the door and went in.

Some of it Gribble had heard already. Before, though, when Cawdor had visited the apartment, his account had been so rambling and disjointed that Gribble couldn't make head nor tail of it.

Under Doctor Khuman's gentle prompting and guidance, he now recounted a mysterious tale about a sailing ship in the middle of the ocean under a moonless sky. And a very high tower block in a blighted futuristic cityscape of desolation and poisoned urban sprawl. Then a complete switch to something quite normal and everyday: Jeff at the airport, heading off on vacation to Europe with his family. There was also the dream – if that's what it was – that remained most vivid to Gribble, of the man strapped in the electric chair, a hazy blue halo hovering over him.

Oddly enough, the one incident Cawdor didn't once refer to was Phyllis Keets's accusation of sexual harassment. Gribble was perplexed by its omission, because Cawdor, he recalled, seemed to have been more shocked and dismayed by it than anything else.

Each of the other episodes he described with exact clarity, embellished with specific details. He mentioned names too – the Shouters, Kershalton, *Salamander*, Cobb, Elder Graye – some of them several times over. How much of this Cawdor was consciously aware of, Gribble wasn't sure. Maybe not too much at all; it was locked inside his brain and could only be released during this trancelike state. And afterward? Would he retain it? Or would these images sink back into the swamp of his fevered unconscious?

Gribble's attention continually flicked between Cawdor, sitting there with his hands resting in his lap, speaking in a low, unemotional voice, and Doctor Khuman, head slightly bowed, listening intently as he examined his pale, elongated fingernails. He never at any point interrupted Cawdor, or led him along a particular path, and only asked a question when there was a natural pause in the flow of monologue.

After about half an hour, when a couple of times Cawdor had closed his eyes as if growing weary, Doctor Khuman brought him out of it. Again there was no dramatic clapping of hands or snapping of fingers, none of the stage hocus-pocus Gribble had expected. The Indian merely leant forward and took Cawdor's wrist, holding it in the palm of his hand, and murmured in his ear, 'Thank you, Mr Cawdor. That is all. Come back, come back.'

At that, Cawdor straightened up and worked his shoulders as if to relieve some stiffness from having sat immobile for such a long period of time. He eased his neck from side to side. He smiled at Gribble. 'I'll have that beer now, Gil.'

Gribble went to the kitchen to get the beer he'd offered when Cawdor had first arrived, and which he had refused, and returned with four cans of Coors in case anyone else was thirsty. To his surprise, Doctor Khuman accepted the beer, opened it, and tilted his head back to take a good long drink, not even asking for a glass. Gribble realigned the desk lamp and switched on a table lamp in the corner. There was a couple of hours of daylight remaining, but the sky was low and overcast, the light outside the window a drab steel grey.

The four of them drank in silence, Cawdor sitting on the kitchen chair, Doctor Khuman leaning against the workbench, Annie Lorentz perched on the arm of the sofa; Gribble stayed standing, moving his weight from foot to foot. He was watching Cawdor's face, and Cawdor in turn was looking at Doctor Khuman with such intensity that Gribble found it rather unnerving, though the Indian was apparently oblivious.

'Satish?' Annie Lorentz said, and, when Doctor Khuman glanced at her, one eyebrow raised in inquiry, she burst out impatiently, 'Well, come on, for Pete's sake, what's the verdict? Does all this stuff mean something? Or nothing? Or don't you know?'

The long lean planes of Doctor Khuman's face relaxed

in a smile. 'I was just wondering . . .'

'Yeah, what?'

Doctor Khuman turned to Cawdor, the cone of light from the desk lamp winking on the thin silver frames of his spectacles. 'Are you a religious man, Mr Cawdor?'

'By that you mean, do I believe in God?'

'Not necessarily . . . God. Have you read the novel *Siddhartha* by Hermann Hesse? In it he speaks of the unity of the world, how all events, large and small, form a single unified whole. He expresses it as belonging to the same stream, obeying the eternal laws of cause and effect – or karma, as Buddhists would say. But the hero of the novel, Siddhartha, is disturbed by the notion that this perfect, embracing wholeness is broken in one place. There is a gap through which strange disruptive forces can enter. *Or –*' Doctor Khuman held up a finger '– one can use the gap oneself to enter into a strange, different world. Another level of existence.'

Cawdor shook his head. 'I've never read it.' He was sitting upright in the chair, and Gribble could see the tension in his body, the way he was gripping the beer can so tightly that his knuckles showed white.

'You don't really believe that to be true, Satish,' Annie Lorentz said. 'I mean, it's a metaphor, isn't it, for some form of spiritual experience? Not something that could actually "happen" in the literal sense of the word.'

'I'm not at all sure it couldn't,' Doctor Khuman said.

'So what's the deal? These dreams, visions – whatever they are – they're a snapshot of some other level of existence? Is that what you're saying?' Annie Lorentz said.

'Snapshot!' Doctor Khuman was nodding and smiling with genuine pleasure. 'That's an excellent way of putting it, Annie. It's a single glimpse of an underlying reality. In some way we don't yet understand, Mr Cawdor has been afforded the opportunity to –'

'Doctor Khuman.'

Cawdor's voice was hushed, yet charged with such trembling emotion that it seemed to Gribble as if he was in the grip of fever. His chest rose and fell and there were bubbles of sweat on his forehead.

Now it was Doctor Khuman's turn to stare at Cawdor. A shadow passed over the large, liquid brown eyes behind their magnifying lenses. 'What's wrong, Mr Cawdor? Are you unwell?'

'You don't remember . . .'

'I'm sorry?'

'Meeting me . . . before today.'

'Have we met before?' Doctor Khuman asked, so quietly that the words barely escaped his lips. Two vertical lines cut deep furrows through his forehead.

'You really don't remember the day you came to my office? There was a thunderstorm that day, lit up the whole sky.' Cawdor blinked up at him. 'You came to warn me that some kind of disruption was about to happen.'

A subtle yet startling transformation had come over Doctor Khuman. His face had gone taut, a pulse beating in his temple. In a soft, hoarse voice he said, 'But that is quite impossible, Mr Cawdor. I don't know where you work. I don't even know what you do for a living. Annie gave me your name, nothing more.' He glanced towards Annie Lorentz, as if seeking confirmation.

'When was this, Jeff?' Gribble asked.

'Ten days . . . two weeks ago.'

Doctor Khuman was shaking his head. 'It can't have been. My last visit to New York was last fall. Could it be that you met someone who resembled me, a case of mistaken identity perhaps?'

'Possibly,' Cawdor was prepared to concede. 'But one hell of a coincidence that his name also happened to be the same as yours. Are there two Doctor Khumans?'

'Good God,' Doctor Khuman murmured. His brown face had turned ashen.

'Maybe you dreamt that too,' Gribble suggested, before he realised that to dream of someone you'd never met, and then to meet that person in real life, was just as incomprehensible.

Annie Lorentz hugged her knees, her pale-blue eyes

wide as saucers. 'I can't get my head around this, Satish. Jeff remembers and yet you don't? How in hell's that possible?'

'Read *Siddhartha* and you will understand,' Doctor Khuman said, though it was a distant response, as if his thoughts were circling far and away beyond this cluttered apartment on 116th Street.

Cawdor finished off his beer and wiped his mouth. When he took his hand away there was a wry, bitter smile lurking there. 'I came here looking for answers, Doctor Khuman. I assumed you remembered me from before, that you could help me figure out what's been happening. And what you've done is dump another mystery on me.' The smile vanished as his face darkened. 'The dreams are only part of it. My relationship with my wife, with my daughter, a woman I work with – everything's falling to pieces for no reason, and it's got me scared. I know – that is, I *feel* – all this stuff is connected somehow, even the dreams, but I just can't make sense of it. I don't know how.'

He looked up, and there was no mistaking the naked appeal for help in his eyes.

Doctor Khuman said, 'Let me put this proposition to you. Come and spend a few days at my research institute, the Troth Foundation. It's located near Griffin, which is thirty miles west of Glens Falls in upstate New York. Annie's been many times; she knows the place well.' Doctor Khuman slid off the workbench and straightened up, a lean dark form with pointed shoulders. 'Please give my proposal serious consideration. I will not be so rash as to promise I *can* help you, Mr Cawdor, but I shall do my utmost. That I *do* promise.'

'Thanks. I don't ask for anything more.' For the first time Cawdor was able to conjure up the ghost of a real smile. 'And who knows, Doctor Khuman . . . maybe I can help you too.'

'Oh? In what respect?'

'To remember the last time we met.'

The Indian's magnified brown eyes, large and unblinking, were fixed on Cawdor. 'I am by no means certain,' he said in his precise, modulated tones, 'that I do wish to remember it.'

Bill Benedict had let Sarah use his office and left her alone to take the call. She sat in his chair staring at the phone, continually glancing at her wristwatch in between working her hands nervously in her lap. Her breathing was rapid and shallow, and she hoped to God she could articulate a few simple sentences without the sounds getting strangled in her throat.

She didn't jump when the phone rang. Her reactions were dulled by the second melibrium, sucked like a sweet during the programme, and her head felt to be floating away from her body; only the restless, fidgeting hands betrayed the turmoil of emotion buried under the layers of her drifting dreamlike state.

Sarah picked up the phone. She held it to her ear and took a deep breath. 'Hello?'

'Is this Mrs Cawdor?'

'Yes.'

'May I call you Sarah?'

'Yes.'

'How good it is to speak with you, Sarah. This is Messiah Wilde speaking.' The rich, bass voice that she knew so well flowed over her like golden syrup. She could see his lean dark face and the burning soulful eyes that seemed, even on the TV screen, to penetrate right down to the innermost secret recesses of her soul. And now, in this actual moment in time, he was speaking to her and her alone in all the world. Her very own name on his lips!

'Mr Benedict has conveyed to you, I trust, how much we admire your wonderful programme, *Take Five*, and how truly grateful we are to you for spreading the Message to your radio audience. But I wanted to say it to you, personally, Sarah, and to thank you, on behalf of the Beamers, for the magnificent work you're doing. Thank you.'

Sarah's body was melting into the chair. Beyond the bright circle of light, it seemed to her, the darkened room was whirling around, faster and faster, and she gripped the edge of the desk to keep from whirling with it.

'It's what I believe in ... to be right ... give people inner peace they seek ... hope for the future ...'

Her halting speech was almost incoherent, but she couldn't help it. She felt herself trapped and suffocating in some primeval heat. Her loins were on fire. She said huskily, 'I must tell you, Messiah Wilde, it's your presence on *The Lovebeams Show* ... when you appear it's as if a golden aura surrounds you ... I confess I get excited as a schoolgirl, that's what you do to me ...'

From 1,200 miles away a low chuckle came down the line, as intimate as if he were close beside her. 'Thank you most kindly, Sarah. How very nice of you to say so. And, since you're so brave and honest in confessing it, let me make a confession too. Your voice on the radio has a beautiful, calm – no, a – how shall I say? – a *serene* quality. It moves me deeply when I listen to you.' There was a pause, and she could hear him breathing. 'If you understand my meaning.'

'Yes,' Sarah said, suddenly feeling calm and serene, 'I think I do.'

'There is another reason for my calling, Sarah, in addition to thanking you most sincerely. As a mark of our appreciation, I'd like to invite you down here in order to participate in *The Lovebeams Show*. I wonder if you would be willing to do us that honour. As our guest, of course. Flight, hotel, all expenses paid.'

Sarah clutched the desk tightly as the room spun out of control.

There was a long pause filled with his measured breathing.

'Is that possible, do you suppose?' Messiah Wilde said, his deep voice softly cajoling. 'Bring your daughter along as well, if you like. Daniella. You would both be most welcome.'

'I'm – I'm –'

'Lost for words?' A low rumbling chuckle vibrated the receiver against her ear. 'May I take that to mean you accept?'

'Yes.'

'I'm so pleased. Tomorrow I shall e-mail the travel arrangements for the two of you. Thank you, Sarah. I look forward to meeting and getting to know you. Sleep peacefully. Good night.'

'Good night,' Sarah said reverently, her head floating up towards the ceiling. 'And –' the line clicked and went dead '– thank you, Messiah Wilde. Thank you so very much.'

5

Jeff,

We don't and never will see eye to eye about this, but I have a right to my opinions and beliefs, whether you agree with them or not. Believe me, I've thought about and considered this seriously – *very* seriously. It isn't just a frivolous fad or fancy that will pass with time. When you found out about the radio prog I knew how you'd react, and it convinced me I was right not to discuss it with you before I made my decision.

Well, I've made another decision without consulting you – and for the same reason – because I know you'd raise objections and we'd have a fight over it, so when you read this it'll be too late for you to do anything about it. I feel very privileged to have been asked to take part in *The Lovebeams* TV show and they very kindly invited Daniella to come along with me. She was so thrilled, especially when I told her we'll be in the presence of Messiah Wilde Himself.

We're taking the eleven-thirty morning flight to Fort Lauderdale, and they're sending a limo to take us to the studio. We may be gone a couple of days. I'm not sure of the final arrangements.

Sarah

PS Please don't, I beg you, do anything to spoil this for Daniella and me. I'll never forgive you. I hope and pray that one day you'll receive the Message, and with it will come true understanding.

Cawdor read it through, and then read it again, shaking his head as he did so because at first his brain refused to take in the meaning. And then, when he did finally understand, carried on shaking his head with a creeping numbness of disbelief.

The neat, rounded handwriting in blue felt-tip dissolved into a blurred scrawl on the white sheet of paper. He crumpled it in his fist and leant against the counter, where he had found the note the minute he walked into the kitchen, folded and propped conspicuously dead centre next to the spice shelf.

With a dulled gaze, Cawdor read the time on the wall clock: a little after seven-fifteen. Their flight would have arrived in Fort Lauderdale earlier that day, around two o'clock in the afternoon, while he was at the office. When had all this been planned? Sarah had said nothing to him at breakfast about the invitation. But she must have known then that she and Daniella were flying out of JFK later in the morning. Of course, he realised, he was being stupid; the note told him in so many words why she had kept it from him: 'I've made another decision without consulting you.'

Bars of gold and black were imprinted on his face from the light of the evening sun streaming in through the Venetian blind. A bird twittered out in the garden, and was answered by another. The trees and bushes were a luxuriant dark green in the deepening twilight. Everything around him seemed peaceful and quiet, normal and comfortingly suburban ... and yet the paper scrunched up in his fist made a mockery of it all. Wrenched normality out of shape, gave it the dark twisted form of nightmare.

The evening before, at Gil Gribble's apartment, Cawdor had at last glimpsed, so he thought, a chink of daylight, the promise of renewed hope. Something about Doctor Khuman had inspired in him the belief that help was at hand. All day at the office he had been carried along on a wave of optimism, his spirits uplifted, thinking that he might now have the chance to unravel the hopeless tangle of dream and reality, to finally restore his life to what it had been, one of reassuring domestic normality.

He'd been a naive fool. The note in his clenched hand killed that dead. Snuffed out any glimmer of hope.

The agony that pierced him most fiercely was the dread feeling that Sarah was drifting further and further away from him – as if obscured in a fog, beyond his grasp no matter how hard he strained to reach out to her. A kind of insidious evil had entered into his wife and taken possession of her. What on earth was the nature of this influence the Beamers were able to exert over people? Through the 'presence' of Messiah Wilde they had the power to infiltrate the minds and hearts of millions and win them over as converts to the cause.

But *what* cause? What purpose did it serve? Were not the Beamers just another crackpot cult trading on the fears and anxieties of the gullible? Their sole motivation to use the power of mass media to accumulate wealth? That was what – in his ignorance, Cawdor now realised – he had believed, and had stupidly dismissed them as being of no consequence.

He opened the wadded ball of paper and smoothed out its wrinkled surface. 'Please don't, I beg you, do anything to spoil this for Daniella and me. I'll never forgive you. I hope and pray that one day you'll receive the Message, and with it will come true understanding.'

Reading again the words of the postscript made his limbs turn to water. A deadening sense of helplessness and impotence overcame Jeff Cawdor, as if the lifeforce had been siphoned out of him. 'I'll never forgive you', his wife had written, as stark a warning not to interefere as she was capable of delivering.

Was there nothing he could do? Nothing at all?

Abruptly, Cawdor left the kitchen and went up the stairs and entered his workroom. His red leather-bound address book was on the desk. He opened it, and from the clear plastic compartment inside the cover took out the card given to him by Doctor Khuman. He closed the address book and placed the card on top. He sat down at the desk and reached for the phone.

* * *

Pacing the executive suite, Mara BeCalla spun round on her stiletto heels, spots of colour burning beneath her high cheekbones. 'We had a deal, Mr Graye.' She pointed a scarlet fingernail at him. 'Now I find out you're bringing some woman in from nowhere and promising her celebrity status on *The Lovebeams Show*. Promoting her in place of me, goddamnit! And I don't like that.'

Graye sat behind the long, polished, teakwood desk. The beams of twin tracklights angled from above made a death's head of the narrow skull and its cavernous eye sockets.

'Is that a threat I hear, Miss BeCalla?' His voice had a flat, metallic quality, as if issuing from some cold soulless machine. 'Your position within Grace MediaCorp is entirely dependent on my prerogative. You would be wise to remember that, and also not to abuse the privilege you have been granted.'

Mara BeCalla faced him, hands on hips. 'What privilege?' she demanded, green eyes blazing. 'From how I look at it, this Cawdor woman is the one getting all the privileges around here. You pluck her out of total obscurity – from some crummy radio phone-in out in the sticks – and give her a shot on prime-time global TV. I'll tell you this, Mr Graye, it's very plain and simple what I'm asking for. What you *promised* me.'

Graye was silent for a moment. His black eyes glittered with an icy malevolence. Mara BeCalla didn't underestimate his power; she was both afraid of and fascinated by it. But she didn't intend to let his power intimidate her, or cheat her of what had been agreed between them.

The thin pale hand motioned to her. 'Calm yourself and sit down, Miss BeCalla –'

'I don't feel calm.'

'You will,' Graye assured her, 'when you have listened to what I am about to say.'

Mara BeCalla sank back in the chrome and steerhide chair in front of the desk. Her body remained tense, and her eyes still smouldered. Beyond the slanting wall of tinted glass, way off in the distance, a smudge of light that was Fort Lauderdale glowed like a small silver coin. Through the vaulted apex of the pyramid, stars glimmered and winked in the warm winds blowing off the ocean. The faint whine of jet engines could be heard as an airliner made its final approach to Miami Airport.

'Have you never wondered why the influence of the Beamers is so powerful, Miss BeCalla? So pervasive? How we are able to make thousands of new converts every day?'

Mara BeCalla said dryly, 'I assumed it had something to do with the truckloads of melibrium you distribute free to kids in colleges, schools and youth organisations. The stuff looks and tastes like candy, but its effect is more pernicious than tooth decay.'

'No, no – in that you are mistaken. Melibrium eases the path to enlightenment. Makes young minds more receptive to new thoughts and ideas. Simply a means to an end.'

'As well as relaxing their sexual inhibitions,' Mara BeCalla said with a sardonic smile.

Graye ignored that. 'The reason is simple. We inhabit a world made in the image of our Saviour and Redeemer. It is Kersh who creates everything around us. Through His influence, our Message falls upon fertile and receptive ground. He is everywhere and in everything, the vital lifeforce, as universal as the air we breathe.'

'But *this* woman,' Mara BeCalla broke in. 'Why her? What does she have to offer?'

'As with millions of others,' Graye went on, curbing her impatience with a raised palm, 'Sarah Cawdor and her daughter are not immune to the influence exerted over this world by our Saviour and Redeemer. It serves His purpose that they shall be brought into the fold. You have to understand, Miss BeCalla, why it is absolutely necessary to bring them here.' He leant forward, the words a rasping whisper in his throat. '*We must have this woman and her child in our power*. Only then can we repeat the cycle of events begun centuries ago. And if we do that – as we must – then Cawdor is lost. He will be trapped for ever in the same endlessly repeating circle of events. Unable to disrupt it; unable to change it.'

'I find it hard to believe that one man could threaten the mighty Grace MediaCorp empire.' Mara BeCalla's gently mocking tone made Graye bristle.

'The danger from Cawdor lies in the distant past – that he dared once to challenge our sacred creed. For that blasphemy he was punished and made to pay dearly. We dealt with his slut of a wife and bastard child and had him chained in the bilges among the rats and the slime where he belonged.'

Graye's fists were clenched on the desktop like knobs of bone. His gaunt face, bleached of all colour, was bathed in a mist of sweat.

The intensity of his hatred shocked Mara BeCalla. She struggled to grasp what drove such naked passion. The danger lies in the distant past? How could something from long ago possibly affect what was happening today? The past was . . . well, *past*. The living present here and now; the future an unknowable mystery yet to be revealed. And why was Graye so obsessed with vengeance on a man who had been defeated?

She said, 'He blasphemed against your religion and was punished for it, so where's the danger? What's happened has happened. The past is dead and buried.'

'That depends on which past we choose for ourselves.' Graye took a deep breath and became calmer. 'The very purpose for which our Saviour and Redeemer Kersh is suspended in the final instant of existence. For it is through Him that we are able to choose our past and keep to the rightful path.'

Staring at him, Mara BeCalla said slowly, 'Cawdor has the power to alter it in some way – is that what you're saying? He can –'

'He can do nothing. He doesn't know how to even begin.'

'And he must never find a way.'

'No.'

'Which means a way must exist.' Mara BeCalla stroked her cheek. 'Somewhere.' Graye leant back into the padded chair, his eyes hooded and opaque. 'So what you're afraid of is that somehow he'll find a way to get through – to Kersh, is that it? Is that what you fear most, Mr Graye?'

Graye didn't like to be thought afraid of anything. To admit it outraged every fibre of his being.

He drew himself erect and said, 'Your mind skims along the surface of a great ocean of ignorance, Miss BeCalla. Cawdor is a threat because long ago he stood against us and was duly punished for his offence. Because of that event long ago he now threatens to stand against us today.'

'He was punished because he stood against you, and now he stands against you because he was punished,' Mara BeCalla said, struggling to understand. 'But that's a merry-go-round. There can be no winner.'

'*We*, the Messengers, are always the winners, never Cawdor, because the threat is always met with due punishment, and thus the circle remains complete and unbroken.'

Mara BeCalla's eyes widened. 'His wife . . . ah yes, I see now.' She averted her gaze, unable to look directly into the glittering depths of those black sockets. 'It was all a pretext, inviting Sarah Cawdor to take part in *The Lovebeams Show*. You wanted her here, so you tempted her with the promise of appearing with Messiah Wilde.'

'A pretext, yes, and a promise too,' Graye said in a voice that was throaty and sly. Despite herself, Mara BeCalla glanced sharply at him. He leant slightly to one side. She watched as he touched a control, and a console deck of buttons and tiny glowing lights swung out from a compartment under the desk. At the press of a button the inner wall of inlaid rosewood panelling parted to reveal a large screen. Graye pressed another button and a picture appeared. His thin body subsided into the chair, pinstriped sleeves hanging slackly as he folded his arms, his eyes on the screen.

Mara BeCalla turned to watch. The camera's view was from high up in a vast chamber, looking down on a circle of figures clad in black robes. Even though their faces were hidden behind black leather masks, with curved slits for eyes, she knew that Graye was one of them, a spotlight making a silvery halo around his domelike head.

As the camera began to move in, another hooded figure, this one robed in white, joined the circle of figures surrounding a rectangular slab of black marble. On the slab was the naked body of a teenage girl, spread-eagled, secured at wrists and ankles by stainless-steel clamps. Her eyes were open but heavy-lidded, the expression in them glazed, as if she was drugged or had just awakened from sedated slumber. But it was her long blonde hair, elaborately braided and trailing down over her white shoulders, that triggered the spark of recognition in Mara BeCalla. For this was the young girl – Josie – she now recalled, whom Messiah Wilde had brought up on stage as the Chosen One.

The scene was in total silence. So at first Mara BeCalla assumed there was no soundtrack accompanying the picture – until the girl's mouth opened and produced a low shuddering moan that ended in a strangled sob. Josie was staring straight up into the camera lens, her cloudy expression gradually clearing as reality seeped into her brain. Then she whimpered, and her eyes welled with huge brimming tears that leaked down the sides of her face and into her hair.

Mara BeCalla was startled by a movement at the head of the table. It was the pale blur of Graye's hand as it delved inside his robe and reappeared holding a knife. The blade was two feet in length, its edge honed to razor sharpness, its tip like a dagger's point. As the knife was raised high in the air, Mara BeCalla instinctively reared back in the chair and turned her head away, but not quickly enough. Her peripheral vision caught the flashing gleam of the blade as it arced downward, and then the sudden spurt as the throat gushed open, covering the white body in a thick red blanket.

She flinched at the sight. Even though she knew it was staged – a clever special effect – it was so horrifyingly realistic that she let out a gasp.

On the soundtrack she heard choking and gurgling that

died away to a soft, steady glugging, like that of a wine bottle being emptied.

Graye pressed a button and the image snapped off. He touched another and the rosewood panelling slid shut. He turned to Mara BeCalla, waving a hand to the hidden screen.

'Now I trust you will understand why there is no reason to fear Sarah Cawdor as a rival. The true purpose of our invitation, as you saw, is not to seek the participation of the mother, but of her daughter.'

Mara BeCalla was puzzled. 'You want her daughter to become the Chosen One?' She looked in confusion to the panelling. 'But why her when you have an actress to play the part?'

'Actress?' Graye said.

'That was faked, of course, wasn't it? Not possibly real . . .' She swallowed because her mouth was very dry.

'There would be no point at all,' Graye said with a sigh of asperity, 'if it was faked and not real.'

Mara BeCalla's face felt numb, as if she had been struck hard.

'The ceremony performed by the elders of the Temple is sacred to our creed,' Graye informed her sternly. 'Our converts would know the difference at once were we to hoodwink them with camera tricks and cheap fakery. We must keep faith with our flock.'

'You transmit that . . . "ceremony" over the airwaves?'

'A live broadcast goes out on a restricted satellite channel available only to our followers. Who of course pay a special rate to gain access to the channel,' Graye added matter-of-factly.

'But her family – the parents of that young girl. What can you say to them when she doesn't return?'

'Many young people choose to join us of their own free will. Some of them are sent on evangelical missions to all parts of the world. Their activities abroad are recorded on a video, which we send to their family and friends on request, at no charge. The parents of this girl will also receive a video showing her in some country or other – or rather her image digitally enhanced and transposed into a foreign setting. Our technology is state of the art, Miss BeCalla.'

Graye slid the console deck out of sight and stood up, the twin tracklights from above bleaching his face to bone white and black shadow.

'Your concern about Sarah Cawdor was quite foolish and unnecessary. You have no rival, Miss BeCalla. You are happier now, I trust?'

Happier?

The numbness in her face seemed to have spread throughout her entire body so that Mara BeCalla was unable to move from the chair. The images on the screen were etched into her brain, as if they had physically scarred the soft tissue. She felt despoiled by them; overwhelmed by revulsion that soured her stomach like acid. Of course she had known – because Graye had explained it to her – that this glass pyramid and its teeming inhabitants served a religious cause. That the purpose of Grace MediaCorp was to spread the Message worldwide and make converts of the millions who tuned in every day to watch Messiah Wilde. And she had known also, or rather sensed, a thrilling kind of dark power that lured and fascinated her.

What she hadn't guessed at in her wildest dreams was the depths of evil depravity in the black soul of this cult. Yet she had seen the evidence for herself, starkly presented in all its gruesome and gory detail. And the true horror of it was Graye's blithe assumption that Mara BeCalla would want to take part, to use her striking looks and talent as a TV performer to help him spread the Message and make thousands, perhaps millions, of new converts.

Raising her head, she steeled herself to look straight and unflinchingly into the empty pits of his eyes.

'I can't do it. I can't do as you ask. It's impossible.'

Graye gazed down at her. To her consternation, he seemed neither angry nor alarmed by this rejection. His silence unnerved her; Mara BeCalla pressed on. 'I have made it clear to you that I don't share your beliefs. I have no intention of being converted. I can't help you, Mr Graye. I take back my word.'

'I can't return it to you, Miss BeCalla, because it isn't mine to give. When you pledged your support, you gave it not to me but to our Saviour and Redeemer Kersh. You are committed –'

'No, I'm not.' The revulsion inside her fuelled a steely determination. 'Not to a mystical nobody who lives in the nether world of your imagining. Forget it, Mr Graye. I'm through and I mean it. You can tell Kersh that for me.'

Graye swayed forward over the desk, a looming shadow. 'Cleanse your heart of blasphemy, woman! Do not take the name of our Saviour and Redeemer in vain!'

'Not my saviour if I don't believe in him.'

'Is that so?' Graye hissed, his mouth a snarling black maw. 'Perhaps the time has come to put your unbelief to the test.' He came round the desk, beckoning to her with a peremptory hand. After a moment, Mara BeCalla got up and, more curious than fearful, she slowly followed him to the slanting wall of glass. Night pressed against the building, broken only by the distant hazy smudge of light and the wavering stars above.

'Look.'

She strained to see what he was pointing at, his long, bony arm raised towards the heavens. Staring until her eyes started to ache, she searched the void of the night sky, finding nothing. 'What am I supposed to be –'

'*Out there.*'

There was only a vast expanse of starlit emptiness. But then something flickered in the far distance – a flash of blue sheet lightning. It lasted an instant and was gone. She heard Graye intoning deep and sombre within his chest, like a bell tolling under the sea. The blue lightning flared again, brighter this time. Mara BeCalla involuntarily sucked in a sharp breath. Illuminated by the crackling glow, an immensely high column of granite soared upward to the stars. Its sides were smooth and polished, reflecting the flashes of lightning, and in the blue glow she saw a domed roof of glass radiating beams of light like a ghostly lighthouse of the future, warning spaceships of the earth's presence.

Under his breath, Graye was mumbling over and over, 'Our Saviour and Redeemer Kersh, watch over us, we beseech you . . .'

On the edge of the parapet the tiny figure of a man was leaning on the granite balustrade, gazing off into the distance. He seemed oblivious to their scrutiny, to anything below, alone and remote at the peak of his high tower. With a lazy sweep of his hand he brushed back a strand of lank, thinning hair, then picked up a glass and took a long drink. He did everything as if eternity stretched before him. As if, Mara BeCalla thought, he had all the time in the world.

Graye's eyes were closed, his head uplifted, his breathing harsh in his flared nostrils.

Standing beside him, Mara BeCalla felt a shiver crawl down her spine. She *had* underestimated him after all, the power he wielded. Graye had cast a hypnotic influence over her, projected this hallucinatory vision into her mind. It was the only rational explanation for what she was seeing. In reality there was no granite tower rising to dizzying heights in the night sky. There was no man up there on the balcony, calmly sipping a drink and gazing off into the distance. It was all a trick, she insisted to herself, just a damn clever trick . . .

Even so, Mara BeCalla felt her heart pounding. She could use a drink herself right this minute. This image of a man in a tower – why did it fill her with such dread and apprehension? Was it a memory? A long-forgotten fear buried deep in her past that was reaching out to reclaim her?

'Does the light of truth shine upon you?' Graye asked in a sibilant whisper. 'Do not resist; let it enter, my child.'

The light of truth? What truth was that?

Staring up at the man in the tower, Mara BeCalla felt dazed, her senses befuddled. Another image shimmered in front of her, obscuring her vision. It was unmistakably the same man. But here he was behind a sheet of glass or plastic, lounging back in a chair, dragging deeply on a cigarette. There was a mocking sneer on his lips, and he slowly winked an eye that was milkily opaque.

Nice, honey. Touch yourself. Know what I mean?

Hearing these words in her mind, Mara BeCalla underwent the experience of being transformed into another body, another time and place, another existence entirely. She knew she was in a state prison, visiting a convicted killer on Death Row. It was hot, and she could feel the torpid movement of air stirred by the fans above. The man was watching her face through the plastic screen as he did something to himself – devouring her expression with greedy lust as he made her do something to herself. In this different existence Mara BeCalla felt her body respond to her own fingers, the sudden rush of hot juices sending a quiver through her thighs and stomach, followed by the long slow release as she drifted into a pleasant languor.

Not a dream or hallucination or hypnotic trance; Mara BeCalla was convinced of that. The experience had happened for real. The man was Frank Kersh, serving his final days in Angola State Penitentiary. And the woman was . . .

The woman was May-Beth Gaskins of Dubach, Louisiana.

Another separate existence flashed before Mara BeCalla's eyes. She saw herself as in a mirror's clear reflection: a short and thick-legged girl, verging on plump, with a plain round face and mousy hair that frizzed up in the heat. She saw the single dusty street of Dubach where she had been born and grew up, the bitter taste of failure on her tongue even by the age of seventeen. The dismal prospect of a future that was already charted, settled, done. A dark avenue of closed doors stretching to oblivion.

I can promise you another life, May-Beth, the one you secretly desire.

The voice was that of Preacher, speaking to her in the silver trailer with its tattered posters. No longer was she the beautiful and talented Mara BeCalla, driven by ambition. In her place was that pitiful, dowdy, downtrodden creature, May-Beth Gaskins. She had become that other person, living another existence. The girl she had once been and left behind.

The flickering blue lightning was fading in the night sky. In moments it had vanished. The column of granite and the blazing arc of light radiating from its peak were gone, and Kersh with it. Nothing remained except the field of stars, trembling in the rising currents of warm air.

Mara BeCalla turned her back on the wall of glass. She felt dizzy, and her heart was beating hard and fast. What she had seen out there – or *thought* she had seen – had not shaken her half as much as the image of Frank Kersh lounging behind the toughened screen in the humid prison visitors' room with the fans wafting the air overhead. Even more horrifying was the knowledge that came with it. She had escaped from whatever fate had in store for May-Beth Gaskins; she had been given the chance to forge her own destiny as Mara BeCalla. But what had been given could be taken away. Her tenure on the life she had now, in this living minute, was poised in the balance. To stay in the world as Mara BeCalla – or to endure a life sentence in the dumpy body of a plain girl with mousy hair and an empty future.

Her soul shrank from that. It was too horrendous to dwell upon.

She would sooner kill herself than go back.

Turning to Graye, she looked him squarely in the eye. 'You were right. I know that now because I've seen the light of truth.'

Whatever feelings she might harbour, deep down, about Graye and the cult of the Messengers, Mara BeCalla had no other choice than to offer them her total commitment. She *had* to help them in whatever way she could. Because their failure would plunge her back into that other existence she had glimpsed a moment ago in the spasm of blue lightning as it played about the tower of granite and glass.

Into the abyss of the unthinkable.

The peaceful, idyllic view ought to have calmed his nerves and soothed his mind, but something strange was happening. It had started with a tingling sensation in the fingertips of Jeff Cawdor's left hand which then spread through the hand itself to his wrist. At first he thought it might be the sign of a heart attack, or a warning that he was about to suffer a stroke. But the tingling stayed in his hand, didn't move any further up his arm.

The Troth Foundation was housed in a rambling, turreted building of weathered grey stone. It was fronted by a flagged terrace at ground level which extended from tall narrow windows to a stone balustrade on which carved lions, unicorns and other heraldic creatures stood guard. They had a spectacular view. Undulating lawns, like folds in green velvet, sloped down to a grove of beech and golden oaks, and the flat gleaming surface of a slow-moving river could be glimpsed between the curving flanks of two hills. The river meandered south through lush meadows and past lightly forested slopes, eventually feeding into Indian Lake, about twelve miles distant.

Cawdor had driven up the previous evening, keeping to I-87 for most of the 164 miles. Once past Glens Falls he turned east to skirt the northern tip of Lake Luzerne. It was late when he arrived, and Doctor Khuman was not there to greet him. Instead, a middle-aged woman who exuded a delicate sachet fragrance of sandlewood, greying hair coiled into a bun and shrewd brown eyes set in a maze of fine lines – Mrs Brandt as she introduced herself – showed him to his room. There was a cold tray set for him, with cheese and ham, and a large vacuum jug of coffee. Mrs Brandt didn't apologise for Doctor Khuman's absence, or even mention him. She wished Cawdor good night and informed him that breakfast would be served any time after eight o'clock.

He had slept surprisingly well. Probably the three-hour drive had tired him out, Cawdor reckoned. He had devoured the bacon and eggs, hash browns, toast, and a bowl of peaches and melon brought to him on a trolley, wondering if it was the country air that had sharpened his appetite. The morning was fresh and pleasantly cool, though he could feel the gathering warmth of the sun right between his shoulder blades.

As he sat there on the terrace, puzzling over what might have caused the tingling in his hand, something welled up inside Cawdor – the same feeling he had had at Gil Gribble's apartment – like a black snake uncoiling itself in the pit of his stomach.

That first time it had been about Sarah. A dreadful, creeping realisation – *conviction* in fact – that she was in mortal danger. The feeling took hold of him again, but now it included Daniella too, as well as his wife.

Cawdor shut his eyes and concentrated hard, struggling to give form and meaning to the black snake of panic fear writhing through his guts. No image came to him; no specific danger reared up, full-blown and terrifyingly real, in his mind's eye. Was it a plane crash? An automobile accident? A building on fire? A street mugging, an attack by a raging psychopath? The various scenarios of injury and harm and death flashed in front of him, but none had validity or gave shape to the crawling panic in his chest. It remained vague and nameless: simple naked fear that something dreadful had happened to Sarah and Daniella. Or was going to happen – he wasn't clear about that either.

Cawdor opened his eyes. He stared unseeingly at the distant hills. He was remembering what happened last time. How he had driven home recklessly from Gribble's apartment to find that Sarah was perfectly OK. He had almost killed himself in a car smash for no reason. The terrible apprehension he had felt for her safety and wellbeing was a false alarm, a big fat fake emotion that had him, literally, running scared. The memory of this brought blessed relief, and he felt his body relax. He leant back in the chair, the tension draining out of him, letting his eyes linger over the restful scene.

Don't let paranoia grab hold, he told himself. Your

emotions are all screwed up. That's why you're here, seeking help to sort out this mess of confusion. Get a grip on yourself.

Cawdor looked round as a shadow fell across the stone balustrade.

'Good morning. Mrs Brandt tells me you ate a hearty breakfast. I hope you slept well also.'

Doctor Khuman's face was very dark against his crisp white coat, which was dazzling in the sunlight. He wore it unbuttoned over a bottle-green shirt with open collar, his hands stuffed casually in his pockets.

'First off, Doctor Khuman, I want to apologise,' Cawdor said, 'for calling you in a rush yesterday and, well, kinda springing this on you. It wasn't very considerate of me.'

'Jeff, I am so pleased you did!' Doctor Khuman's shoulders went up. 'Do please call me Satish. You are most interesting to me, to my line of research. And this is true –' he held up a slender brown hand '– since we spoke the other day I have thought of little else. In truth, *nothing* else. I asked Annie, after we met, to do some digging in the anthropological library at Columbia, I was so keen to follow it up. I am hoping she will have something to show me very soon, perhaps even today.'

Cawdor was puzzled. 'Digging for what?'

'If I knew that, Jeff,' Doctor Khuman said with a faint smile, 'there would be no need to search for it.'

'It's what's happening now I need help with, Doctor Khu– Satish. Not something that happened long ago in the past.'

'To understand the present, we must first understand the process by which it evolved. The past, present and future are indissolubly linked. Except in this particular instance . . .' He trailed off, stroking the lean line of his jaw.

'What?'

'There appears to have been a dysfunctional element in that process.' He studied Cawdor intently through his silver-framed glasses. 'You sense that too, yes? As if events have suddenly and arbitrarily changed course?'

'If by that you mean I don't know what the hell's going on, you've hit the nail on the head,' Cawdor admitted with feeling. 'The world's gone haywire. I've been married eighteen years and now I find I don't even know my own wife. Or my daughter. And how come I seem to remember meeting you, one day at my office, and yet you insist we've never met before? What I want to know, Satish, is how there can be a memory in my head of something that never happened. Can you explain that?'

Doctor Khuman leant against the balustrade and folded his arms. He said quietly and calmly, 'Oh yes, I can explain it.'

Cawdor was astonished. 'You can?' he said, gaping at him in the sunshine.

Doctor Khuman nodded. 'The explanation is very simple. You remember it because it *did* happen.'

'But . . . you don't.'

'Two versions of events that contradict one another – so which is the "true" one, that's what you wish to know. Yes?'

Cawdor nodded, though he wasn't sure he was ready for an explanation that the Indian regarded as simple and he himself thought of as a logical impossibility, defying common sense.

Doctor Khuman confirmed his fears when he said, 'Both are true, Jeff. Or, to be more precise, both have an equal chance of being true. Neither one is more probable than the other.'

'Does that mean yes or no?'

'It means either/or.'

Cawdor's face was all frown. 'You've lost me.'

Doctor Khuman said gravely, 'I hope very much we don't lose you, Jeff.' He blinked his large brown eyes, became abstracted for a moment. 'Ah yes, yes . . .' He fumbled in the pocket of his white coat and took out a Penguin paperback, which he handed to Cawdor. 'You haven't read *Siddhartha*, so you said, and I think you might find it interesting, and – who knows? – enlightening. Remember I spoke to you about it?'

'That's one memory we both share, thank God,' Cawdor said dryly.

'Yes, the Buddhist vision of the world as a perfect, embracing wholeness, obeying the laws of cause and effect.' Doctor Khuman pinched together his finger and thumb to form a circle. 'But somewhere broken in one place, a sort of gap.' The finger and thumb parted a fraction. 'In modern terminology, what might be called a –'

'Dysfunctional element?'

Doctor Khuman smiled. 'I think perhaps you *do* understand.'

'I think I'm beginning to,' Cawdor said.

They had been treated like royalty from the moment they boarded the plane at JFK: waited on hand and foot in ambassador class, served Cristal champagne in Waterford cut-glass goblets followed by a six-course meal with French wine (a single glass for Daniella, Sarah insisted, let down with mineral water) and afterward relaxed in soft leather seats as wide and deep as armchairs while the three flight attendants fussed around them with pillows, offered magazines, and then hovered attentively to provide whatever service they desired. A bronze-coloured limo with smoked-glass windows had awaited them at Miami Airport, a hood pennant with the Beamers' crest in gold and black fluttering in the warm breeze. They had been driven straight to the headquarters of Grace MediaCorp north of Fort Lauderdale, which for Sarah was the most amazing building she had ever set eyes on – a pyramid made of glass that flashed the Florida sun in a thousand splintering shafts of light. In the rear of the limo, she had reached across and squeezed Daniella's hand, which was damp with nervous excitement like her own, in spite of the air conditioning. Her daughter's cheeks were flushed, her eyes unnaturally bright, her chest rising and falling under the pale-lime blouse with its delicate lace neckline and ruched sleeves finished with matching lace trim. Outwardly, Sarah appeared more composed;

inwardly, she was churning with the selfsame emotional cauldron. On the plane she had sucked on a melibrium lozenge, slipping it into her mouth as she dabbed her lips with a tissue, but it didn't seem to have the calming effect she wanted.

Two handsome, tanned, strapping young men in short-sleeved white shirts and slacks with knife-edge creases took them on a conducted tour of the building. Stepping out of the glass-walled elevator at each of the levels, Sarah and her daughter were literally dumbstruck by the scale and complexity of the operation. On every floor, in all four directions to the slanting walls of glass, hundreds of people in cubicle workstations were quietly and diligently getting on with the task of disseminating the Message via every possible medium. It made Sarah feel rather small and humble. Her own radio contribution, of which she'd been so proud, was feeble in comparison, a mere drop in a vast multimedia ocean that spanned the globe.

Sarah remembered growing just a tad impatient at one point. Two hours into the tour she asked one of the tanned young men how soon it would be before they met their host. And what about the broadcast? Shouldn't she be preparing herself, getting ready to take part? With an easy confident smile that seemed bred into him, the young man answered her questions politely. At the present time, he informed her, Messiah Wilde was busy with rehearsals in the studio. They would meet him later that evening, as soon as the show was over. He told Sarah that she may have misunderstood, because the show she was to participate in was not tonight's, but tomorrow's: the schedule had been purposely arranged so that she had time to relax after her flight, and in the morning she could face a fresh start. There wasn't a thing to fret about, he assured her. Everything had been taken care of, down to the last detail. Everything was perfectly in order.

And indeed it was.

She and Daniella were escorted to a luxury VIP viewing suite where they watched the transmission of

232

The Lovebeams Show. It was the confessional format called 'My Secret Sin' this evening – one of Daniella's favourites – with Messiah Wilde roaming around with a hand mike, firing questions at the row of people on the stage and asking members of the audience for their comments and opinions. As the camera framed each of the participants, a caption appeared on the screen to explain the sins they were confessing to: LIED TO PARENTS, CHEATED ON HER HUSBAND, BEAT HIS WIFE, ABUSED SMALL CHILDREN, HAD LEWD THOUGHTS, USED TO MASTURBATE, KILLED KITTENS FOR FUN. Sarah was glad that her daughter liked to watch 'My Secret Sin', because it combined entertainment with education and spiritual uplift. The point of it was not to hold anything back, but by openly confessing the deepest, darkest secrets to purge the soul and set an example for others of how sinners could be brought to the light.

Sarah was very moved by it. There was a lot of evil in the world, masked by self-denial and hypocrisy, and it did the heart good to see these people baring their hidden desires and lustful yearnings in public.

Afterward they were shown through to the hospitality suite, where a buffet supper was laid out for the participants in 'My Secret Sin'. The room gradually filled up and was soon buzzing with lively conversation and the shrill, fragile laughter of released tension. Many of the senior staff were there, and a tall, tanned, athletic young woman with the Beamers' crest on the breast pocket of her crisp white blouse, who had taken on the role of chaperone, made the introductions. It transpired that Sarah was quite a celebrity in her own right. Many of the people she spoke to were regular and enthusiastic listeners to *Take Five*. One man, whose name she didn't catch in the bewildering flurry of names, faces, handshakes and compliments, told her that the mental image he had formed from the sound of her voice, picturing her as a beautiful and intelligent mature woman, fell far short of the living reality. She had missed her way in not taking up a career in television. Sarah blushed like a schoolgirl.

He went on to say how delighted he was that she had consented to appear on the show with Messiah Wilde.

'His appeal, of course, is to our female audience. We have our chorus line, as I like to call it,' he joked, 'which works very well for, let us say, decorative purposes, but we need more than that: strong physical attraction combined with a penetrating mind and an eloquent turn of phrase. Qualities you possess in abundance, Mrs Cawdor.'

'I'm very flattered,' Sarah said. It sounded as if he was offering her a permanent job.

'Your husband is a lucky man to have such a talented wife.'

'I wish he thought so,' Sarah said miserably.

'Oh? You mean he doesn't approve of the work you do?'

'He actually disapproves. He's one of those, I'm afraid, who has yet to receive the Message. I hope and pray one day he will.'

'Amen to that,' the man said sombrely, his rumbling bass voice reminding Sarah of the tolling of a bell in some chamber deep undergound. He reached out and touched her shoulder comfortingly, and she felt briefly the bony grip of his long fingers. When his tall thin figure moved off into the crush of people she was left with an impression of quiet charm, sincerity, and wisdom.

Sarah looked round for Daniella and almost fainted on the spot. She was standing over by the bar with a group of the 'My Secret Sin' participants, a dreamy, almost dazed, expression on her pallid face as she gazed up into the dark soulful eyes of Messiah Wilde. A shaft of something very near to jealousy pierced Sarah. Her daughter was along for the ride, not to become the focus of his undivided attention. The sharp pain soon passed and was altogether forgotten when she was taken over to be introduced. The first meeting, shaking his hand, smiling up at him, answering his questions, seemed to go by in a blur. In a curious way she didn't feel to be part of herself. It was as if an actress was standing in for her, playing the role of Sarah Cawdor for the evening, mouthing her lines.

234

Probably the shock, she realised, of being in the living, breathing presence of Messiah Wilde Himself. Enough to make any warm-blooded woman feel to be lost and adrift in a world of fantastic unreality. There was a sensual aura about him that excited her; she couldn't deny it. She was aware of a hot dampness between her legs, and her breasts seemed confined inside the fitted jacket of her linen suit. She watched his lips as he chatted with the group, hardly able to take in the sense of what he was saying. He was pleasant and courteous to everyone, with an English reserve she found captivating. Submerged beneath his refined accent she thought she detected the faintest trace of a gentle Irish lilt, which surprised her. Once again a feeling of giddy unreality swept over Sarah: the here and now of being within touching distance of him, of breathing the same air.

There was a greater shock in store. And then it really did seem as if her life had been transformed into magical make-believe.

Looking into her eyes, so that Sarah felt to be drowning in the depths of his, Messiah Wilde invited her and Daniella to be his guests in his Palm Beach house.

7

'How far back into the past?'

'How far back do you want to go? Four hundred years? Five? Six? These guys have been around quite a while.' Annie Lorentz sorted through the clippings, photostats and printouts spread out on the desk in Doctor Khuman's study. She found what she was looking for. 'This is the earliest reference I came up with. 1292. There's an engraving, so you can see what they looked like at that period.'

'Where's this from?'

'The *Codex*. Forbidden access to the great unwashed for centuries. The name Cawdor mentioned – the Shouters – was in use during the eighteenth century, though they've had dozens of names. Their proper name, if you can call it that, is the Messengers of the Fall from Grace.'

'A religious sect, obviously,' Doctor Khuman said.

'Sounds like it,' Annie Lorentz agreed, 'though it's hard to say exactly *what* they were – or still are, for all we know. Five elders ran the show. They always took the names Graye, Whyte, Greene, Browne, and Blacke.'

'Colourful bunch, if not very original,' Doctor Khuman observed.

'Some of their rituals were quasi-religious, but they seem to have dabbled in just about everything else as well. During the Middle Ages they were court advisers to the British monarchy. They were in Italy when the Medicis were coming into prominence, mid-fourteenth century; and in France round about the time of the Revolution. Further back still –' she rooted through the results of her research '– you find them popping up all over the place, but always on the sidelines, never centrestage. Greece, the Ottoman Empire, the Balkans, Russia . . .'

'All of which had revolutions and holy wars,' Doctor Khuman said.

'So have most places at one time or another, Satish,' Annie Lorentz pointed out. 'What are you searching for – a conspiracy theory? The Messengers of the Fall from Grace as perverters of the course of history?'

'When sects or groups perpetuate themselves for hundreds of years, Annie, they have powerful interests to protect. They wish to impose their influence on the right people in the right places. And their name, of course; no ambiguity there.'

'Guess not, Satish. Whose grace did they fall from, you reckon? God's?'

Doctor Khuman gave her a steely stare. You could never tell with Annie if she was being serious or whether her sarcasm was on the prowl.

'Any trace of them recently?' he asked.

'I did a quick check on all the religious groups, but there are hundreds of them, any of which could be the Messengers in disguise.'

'Well, not quite *any*,' Doctor Khuman objected. 'Unless the Pope is called Graye.' Leaning back in the chair, he took off his glasses and massaged his eyelids with long, slender fingers. Annie Lorentz sat on the corner of the desk, swinging her leg in its shapeless cord, watching the bowed head. He was a curious mixture, Doctor Khuman. She had never truly fathomed him. Part medical scientist, part faith healer, part Jungian psychotherapist. Not forgetting his early days as one of the pioneers in prosthetic surgery.

He looked up, blinking slowly. 'Mystics and madmen . . .'

'What's that, Satish?'

'Something I remember from the work of RD Laing. You know of him?' Annie Lorentz shook her head. 'A Scottish psychologist. He wrote somewhere, "Mystics and schizophrenics find themselves in the same ocean, but the mystics swim whereas the schizophrenics drown." We're all of us adrift in the same ocean, according to Laing, and those at the furthest extremes of perception – the mystics and madmen – possess insights denied the rest of us.'

'And which one is Cawdor?'

'I only wish I knew.' Doctor Khuman rubbed his pointed chin. 'You see, Annie, I'm afraid that if I push him too hard, and too fast, we might never learn of the journey he's on. And if I don't push hard enough he might never learn of it himself.'

'What journey?' Annie Lorentz said. She slid off the desk and ambled over to the window. 'From the past to the future? We've all of us got a one-way ticket for that trip, too.' She looked through the Venetian blind, narrowing her eyes from the glare. Cawdor sat on the sunlit terrace below, gazing towards the hills and the river. He hadn't moved in the hour since she arrived, shortly after midday.

'But that is precisely my point,' Doctor Khuman said. 'Cawdor's trip is circular. He has a return ticket.'

'I don't believe in time travel,' Annie Lorentz stated flatly. 'It's one big paradox. Say you go back and murder your own grandfather. You'd never have been born and wouldn't exist in the present. But, if you *didn't* exist in the present, you couldn't have gone back to murder your grandfather, and therefore you *would* have been born. So

237

– having been born, you could go back and murder your grandfather, but if you *did* murder him . . .'

Annie Lorentz turned to him, cross-eyed, and Doctor Khuman grinned at the tortured expression on her face.

'Ever experience a coincidence, Annie?'

'Sure.' She shrugged. 'Who hasn't?'

'Yes, we dismiss them, don't we, as being of no importance. But on a deeper, intuitive level they may be very important, giving us a glimpse of a different level of reality. In fact, we dismiss our intuition far too lightly,' Doctor Khuman said, the thin beams of sunlight flashing on his glasses as he rose to join her at the window. 'Not so the Buddhists. They have as much faith in our intuitive powers as in our reasoning intelligence. Actually, they rely more on intuition than on reason to guide them. They believe it gives them a glimpse of the underlying reality of which this –' he wafted the air, indicating the desk with its spread of papers, the cluttered bookshelves, the shadowy corners of the room '– is only the surface, the superficial outer shell.'

'That why Cawdor interests you so much? You think he might be getting these "glimpses" which are denied the rest of us?'

'I believe so,' Doctor Khuman said devoutly.

Annie Lorentz peeked through the blind. 'Gotta say, Satish, he looks ordinary enough to me. What did you mean, that if you pushed him too hard too fast we might never learn anything?'

Doctor Khuman was silent for a moment, brooding. 'I have to somehow force these memories out, or they may lie buried for ever. But if I do it too quickly, or in the wrong way . . .'

'What?'

'Mystics and madmen,' Doctor Khuman said – and this time Annie Lorentz understood.

'Is there a risk?'

'Yes.'

'Is he aware of it?'

'No. That is, I don't think so.'

238

'I'm glad I'm not in your shoes, Satish.' Annie Lorentz gave him a piercing ice-blue stare. She looked again through the blind at the motionless figure on the sunlit terrace, sitting now with his eyes closed. 'Or Jeff Cawdor's, come to that.'

'Ready for some lunch? Annie Lorentz is here – she'll be joining us.'

A smiling Doctor Khuman appeared on the terrace. He had changed from his white coat into a lightweight green cotton jacket that came complete with wrinkled folds and sagging pockets. He frowned as Cawdor got to his feet, seeing him flexing and rubbing his left hand. 'Everything all right, Jeff? What's wrong with your hand?'

'Nothing. Gone to sleep, I guess.' Cawdor looked around, breathing in deeply. 'This is a wonderful setting. You choose the location for its therapeutic value?'

'No, no, this isn't a clinic and I'm not a doctor of medicine.'

'What are you a doctor of?'

'Well, my doctorate is in the field of psychoanalytical research, Jungian branch. But I have dabbled, and still do, in many other areas of inquiry.' He bent down to pick up the paperback lying next to the chair. 'Don't forget this.'

Cawdor accepted the book. 'This being one of them?' he asked, studying the cover.

'Not only Buddhism. All religions, cults and beliefs interest me greatly,' Doctor Khuman said, extending his hand to usher Cawdor towards the house. 'The search for spiritual truth and enlightenment is mankind's oldest aspiration. It seeks to answer the eternal questions of who we are, why we're here, and what is our place in the grand scheme of things. Those are the only questions really worth asking, don't you agree?'

'And you think I'm gonna be much help to you?' Cawdor asked sardonically.

'First, Jeff,' Doctor Khuman said, putting his hand on Cawdor's shoulder as they walked along the terrace, 'I want very much to help *you*. If I learn something in the

239

process, well and good, I shall be grateful. But let us deal first with the most important thing, which is to seek answers to your questions. The eternal questions will have to wait a bit longer.'

'This'll take more than one afternoon, by the sound of it.'

'Slightly more,' Doctor Khuman agreed with the twinkle of a smile.

'Just that I'd better leave a message at my office,' Cawdor said, entering the house through a stone portal with a pointed arch. Today was Saturday. He hadn't given much thought to how long he might be away, just assumed he'd be back in time for work Monday morning. 'I didn't tell my partner I was taking a trip. What do I tell him – get back Tuesday or Wednesday?'

Doctor Khuman nodded. 'Three or four days should be sufficient,' he said, his voice hollow and echoing in the tiled passageway, 'for us at least to make a start.'

Before they went into lunch, Doctor Khuman asked Cawdor if he'd care to freshen up first. They were standing in the large hallway, huge embroidered draperies with tasselled fringes hanging on the grey stone walls, the ornate plaster ceiling eighty feet above supported by arched wooden beams on granite pediments. The rambling house was a curious composite of styles and periods: old English baronial and East European Byzantine with a dash of medieval gothic thrown in for good measure. 'The dining room is along here, the door at the far end,' Doctor Khuman said, pointing down a long gloomy corridor. 'Come through as soon as you're ready. Annie and I will be waiting.'

Cawdor went up the wide, curved stone staircase to the second floor; that morning, before coming down, he'd had to memorise where his room was located to be certain of finding it again.

He hadn't brought much with him. It had taken less than ten minutes to stuff a change of clothing, toiletry articles, and a few bits and pieces into the leather valise he used as an overnight bag. Mrs Brandt, or another member of the staff, had been in, he saw, and made the bed and tidied up. He took a folded shirt from the valise, shook it loose, and laid it on the bed. Deciding to have a quick wash and change into it, he wondered whether it was sitting on the terrace in the sunshine that had made him hot and sticky, or more likely the crawling panic fear that had gripped him like a fever. But he'd gotten over that, Cawdor thought with relief, unbuttoning his shirt as he went into the bathroom. It was wise to nip these weird fancies in the bud before they went haywire and took over.

Three times the size of the one at home, the bathroom contained a porcelain washbasin with elaborate brass faucets and a cast-iron tub a giant could have bathed in, with wrought-iron feet in the form of lions' paws. A single large sash window admitted the northern light, and the chessboard floor of two-feet-square black and white tiles added to the chill austerity. Everything was sanitised and spotless; everything, that is, except for the glittering fragments of mirror scattered next to the moulded pedestal of the washbasin.

Cawdor halted as if the empty space in front of him had instantly materialised into a solid wall. He stood there, his unbuttoned shirt hanging down, the sticky perspiration on his chest turning cold as ice.

His shaving mirror – *this* shaving mirror – had been broken once before. He could see it now, lying in pieces on the floor of his own bathroom back home in Franklin. The morning after, however, the unbroken mirror was still there on its shelf. It had been a bizarre dream, or so he had told himself then; yet, immediately afterward, everything began to go wrong: with Phyllis, his wife and daughter, his premonitions of some terrible disaster.

For the second time the mirror was broken – its circular chrome frame with a few fractured pieces clinging to the inside rim among the debris. But earlier that morning it had been intact. He had stood here in this bathroom, using the magnifying face to shave with.

Dreading what he might find, Cawdor forced himself to kneel on the black and white tiles. From somewhere, the fragments were catching and reflecting images of light and colour and movement. With trembling fingers he picked up one of the pieces, scimitar-shaped, and stared through his own ghostlike reflection into the world beyond the mirror. The images shimmered and dissolved into one another, and then separated again – and the shock hit him that he was seeing his dreams reflected there. He picked up another piece, and another, and saw within each fragment the same shifting, shimmering world, each fragment containing the whole.

Behold in this mirror –

The thought came from nowhere.

– all your past and future times.

Jeff Cawdor didn't know how or why he knew this, but his entire history lay scattered before him in these fragments. And also the history that had yet to be made.

For a while back there (Kersh can admit it now) he was spooked. Got himself all worked up and jittery, to the extent that he wasn't sleeping too good. Real bad dreams – strapped in the electric chair, staring at a fly on the back of his hand. If I fry, little fly, you fry. Fried fly. So damn real, in fact, that he could feel the raw skin prickling where they'd shaved his temples to attach the electrodes.

Sprawled on the white couch, drink in hand, Kersh allows himself the expansive luxury of a mild twinge of regret. After all, he concedes, it sure spiced things up – got the old brain box a-buzzing. The nerve-ends twitching. Boozing and watching TV and shafting Sue Ellen are fine and dandy, but even a steady diet of that gets pretty boring after a while. At least worrying about Cawdor kept him on his toes.

But hey now – he grins – let's not go overboard. Be thankful for what you've got, Frankie boy. Let's not forget that Cawdor was the one person who could have screwed all this up. Baby Sam was right about that – and right to warn him, too. Give the stinking bag of pus some credit.

In his spare moments Kersh has puzzled over a couple of things. How, for instance, did he get to know about Cawdor in the first place?

OK, through Baby Sam, yeah. But Baby Sam was voicing to Kersh what he knew already. So how did he find out about Cawdor? It was a knotty problem, one that Kersh wrestled with for ages until the answer came to him in a dream. In this dream he was in a hot cramped space that stank to high heaven. He could hear the swirling rush of water through the timber planking. In the light of a flickering candle he saw a circle of figures surrounding a woman. Not that Kersh in his dream was merely an observer; he was active in it, too, a participant in these events. The woman's name was Saraheda Cawdor. She had a husband named Jefferson, and a son, Daniel. And the whole thing had been as real as his dream of the electric chair. Fact was, Kersh came to realise, his dreaming life was just as real as his waking life here in the penthouse. Sometimes he confused the two – that maybe the penthouse and his presence in it was a dream, and his dreams the true reality.

That's what gave him the idea, and solved the mystery.

His *dreams* were the answer – that's how he knew about Cawdor. When he awoke from them he had a gut feeling, kind of a hunch, about what was happening out there, and that's where Baby Sam came in. The knowledge was there all along, buried deep in Kersh's dreams; the scumbag was there to spell out in plain language what the dreams meant.

Then all Kersh has to do then is pass the warning on to the Messengers by tuning into the right channel. Like right now he sees them kneeling in a gloomy chamber somewhere, bowing and chanting and calling his name over and over. This in itself is worth the price of admission: watching these guys hanging on to his every word, looking to him for guidance. Sheeeit.

Kersh is cock-a-hoop that he managed to figure all this out for himself, considering the fact that brainwork was never his strong suit. And this stuff is so damn hard to get a handle on, makes it feel like the top of his head is coming loose. He's always been that way – acted first, thought second. Maybe that's been part of the problem. He killed that dumb kid in the gas station without thinking once, never mind twice, about it. So what the hell. The jerk had it coming to him.

Make my day!

Kersh can't help but laugh aloud at this, head thrown back, glass spilling liquor. He wipes his one good eye with the back of his hand, still chuckling. None of that means jackshit now. Here he is, boy, sitting pretty. This swell penthouse on top of the tower, plus the woman of his dreams (whenever he feels the need) to share it with him. Everything, in fact, he ever wanted. No strings attached. The Messengers had delivered as promised and hadn't demanded a single favour in return. Kersh has wondered about that too. Tell the truth, it bothers him a little, because in his experience you never get something for nothing. There's always a payoff. A squaring of accounts somewhere down the line.

But this time he's clear and running and free as a bird. This time Frank Kersh has come out on top, just where he ought to be. And he means to stay there.

He slides off the couch and pads up to the bar, the black silk robe flapping loosely. The sensual feel of it against his skin makes him think of Sue Ellen. But he's not in the mood right this minute. And not being in the mood, naturally she doesn't appear. Kersh has come to realise this – that he has to really *want* something for it to happen. If he genuinely desires it, then – bingo! – it's his. It appears. Merely thinking about it won't do the trick. Which is just as well, because he wouldn't like to encounter some of the stuff he dreams about. There's a lot of funny – that is, weirdo – garbage buried down there that rises to the surface when he's asleep, and Kersh isn't keen to come face to face with it – if it has a face. He suspects it hasn't. A nameless, formless shape, like the smell of fear, that just hangs there shivering on the edge of his awareness.

Even thinking about it now makes him feel uneasy. Spoils his relaxed and benevolent frame of mind. Snap out of it, Frankie, he chides himself. Don't spoil the party. Everything's under control.

He freshens his drink, takes a belt, strolls out on to the balcony. There's no breeze, but the air feels cool and fresh. The pale slice of moon is still in the same spot. He'd start to worry if it wasn't. No change. That's what Kersh wants. Everything to stay *exactly* as it is this minute – the moon, the stars, the carpet of glittering lights. This is fine. This is just dandy.

Those poor saps down there don't know what they're missing. Like rats in an endless maze. Following each other nose to tail, round and round and never getting nowhere. And to think he used to be one of them. Most people are so stupid, you can hardly give it credit. Example. Kersh has never understood why everyone gets upset when there's an earthquake or an airplane crash or some so-called 'disaster'. There it is, splashed all over the front pages and on the TV bulletins, everybody going around with long faces saying how awful it is, and isn't it terrible, blah-blah, those poor people, 50 killed, 200, 2,000, whatever.

What the fuck was so terrible about it? The planet was crawling with people, swarming over it like lice. What was 50 less, or 50,000, or even 50,000,000? Look on the bright side. It meant more space, more opportunities, more of everything for those who were left. You could spread out a little, breathe in some air that hadn't been breathed in and out by a zillion other anonymous lice. How could you feel sorry or sad for people you'd never known and never even heard about until they were involved in a 'disaster'?

Kersh can't recall ever once feeling sorry. His only reaction was 'Tough crud. Glad it was you and not me.'

That's how most people really and truly felt, deep down, though of course they'd never admit it. Instead they wept crocodile tears and went around shaking their long faces at one another, saying, 'Isn't it awful; isn't it terrible?' Terrible my ass. Now what would be terrible was if it was me instead of them.

Same bullshit about the 6,000,000 Jews. So what? Kersh had never noticed any lack of Jews around, even after they got rid of 6,000,000 of them. They were all over the damn place. Heads of multimillion-dollar corporations. Politicians.

Journalists. Authors. And about 90 per cent of show business, it seems to Kersh. Christ, you could wipe out another 6,000,000 and not even make a dent. Not that he has anything against Jews in particular; it was all this crap about the so-called Holocaust that pissed him off. He's lost count of the number of TV documentaries he's seen about it. More like *not* seen, because the minute they come on he switches channels. Sooner watch a re-re-rerun of *I Love Lucy* than another fucking Holocaust special.

He remembers how sick he'd been when he found out that the Marx Brothers were Jewish. He thought the Marx Brothers were great. They broke him up. After that he couldn't stomach them.

Kersh leans on the rail, sipping his drink. He leans right over and looks straight down. This is some mean motherfucker of a tower block, he thinks. Must be two fucking thousand storeys high. A long way down. And a long way up. Nobody coming up here in a hurry, brother, no sir. It's a comforting thought, and its warmth spreads through him like the liquor warming his gut.

Plus he's got Baby Sam and the gang down there. His private little army of guardian angels. Tell the truth, Baby Sam scares the living shit out of him. Not because of who or what he is – a disgusting sack of seeping brown sewage on feelers – but because Baby Sam reminds Kersh of those dream phantoms of his. That murky stuff shivering on the edge of his consciousness. Like as if Baby Sam came to him in a nightmare and then appeared before him in the flesh.

Kersh shivers. Sheeeit, don't even *think* about it. Kersh takes a gulp of his drink and doesn't.

SHATTER'D PIECES OF MIRROUR

1

The heavens were in turmoil. Gilbert Gryble brooded on the significance of these planetary disturbances, and wondered if the cause could possibly be the massive and mysterious 'black bodies' hypothesised by Michell, exerting their powerful influence on the stars in their courses.

On two successive nights now he had observed several dozen blazing meteors. And the planet Venus, brightest object in the sky, had been obscured, as if wreathed in vapour. Most disturbing of all, towards the western horizon, in the direction they were travelling, lights had flared up brilliantly for just a few seconds, and then been extinguished. Gryble searched his star charts in vain. What did these phenomena portend? Were they signs capable of interpretation, if only he had the means and knowledge?

Gryble was disquieted by it all. It seemed to him that the discord in the sky was a mirror reflection, seen darkly, of what was happening on board ship. The fear was palpable. People shunned one another. Children no longer played games on deck, but stayed close by their parents, sullen-faced. The officers and common seamen went grimly to their tasks. There was no open worship, as before, just huddled murmurings by lamplight, furtively hidden from the general view.

The *Salamander* was infected by a general plague of the spirit, Gryble ruminated. The ship carried with it the smell of the charnel house. Not everyone believed Cawdor and his frenzied accusations. But even those who didn't could sense the malignant mind fever that hung over everything, as ever present, as inescapable, as the stench of the privy.

When at first his wife and son couldn't be found, and he had roamed the ship searching for them, Gryble had feared for Cawdor's sanity.

Like an automaton, Cawdor had stalked through every deck, peering into every face, shaking people from their beds, tearing aside the flimsy shelters they had erected for privacy and disturbing them in all manner of circumstances and occupations. Indeed, he had the look of a madman. Everyone shrank from his stare, which was that of a man possessed. And his constant repetition – 'My wife, my son, have you seen them? Have you seen them?' – was like a dirge, until eventually he was mumbling the words mechanically, without meaning.

Captain Vincent had already instituted a search of steerage and the middle part of the ship which had produced nothing. Cawdor didn't respond to this. He neither accepted the result, nor rejected it. He went off alone and did it all again, himself. He went through the middle part, with the minimum courtesy of at least rapping on the cubicle doors before he barged inside. The bulk of the passengers tolerated this, watching in silence as he looked in every corner, under the beds, even rummaged through their trunks and chests. Anywhere that might conceal a woman or a boy, and some places that conceivably couldn't, unless they had been dismembered.

It was when Cawdor turned his attention to the upper decks of the quality end that the trouble started which was to finally snap the captain's patience, invoke his wrath, and bring about Cawdor's downfall.

An officer had been posted at the head of the companionway next to the mizzenmast, to keep watch on Cawdor's movements, and another at the double hatch leading off the quarterdeck. They had been polite with him, reasonable, and quite firm. All the cabins on the upper decks had been investigated by the first lieutenant,

Mr Tregorath, personally, and he was satisfied they contained no person they shouldn't. There was really no need for Mr Cawdor to trouble himself. In any case the captain absolutely forbade any intrusion into the private affairs of the ladies and gentlemen.

'Surely, Mr Cawdor,' said one of the officers, a young midshipman, who made the mistake of smiling sympathetically, 'you can't seriously accuse anyone up here of the act of concealment. The ladies and gentlemen have given their solemn word that they haven't laid eyes on your wife, or your son.'

'I don't doubt it for a minute,' Cawdor replied. 'And I believe them. I want to see for myself, that's all,' and a second later stepped over the midshipman, who was staring at the spinning mizzenmast with glazed eyes and wondering why the deck had suddenly tilted to the vertical.

Cawdor didn't get the chance to see for himself. Four seamen were despatched to block him, and they were none too gentle in their methods. He was put in his cubicle, bruised and bleeding, with two men guarding the door, while Captain Vincent debated what to do with him.

It was at this point that Gilbert Gryble had requested to see the captain, to plead on Cawdor's behalf, and been turned down. The captain knew the facts of the matter, thank you most *kindly*, and he was in no mood for instruction or persuasion; Cawdor had been warned already about his conduct, and now must suffer the consequences of his disruptive, unacceptable behaviour.

Gryble puzzled over this 'warned already', when one of the officers reported it to him. When, and for what reason, had Cawdor been warned before? In Gryble's experience Cawdor was a man of decent character and genial disposition, rather stolid by nature, who spent a good deal of his time cramming architecture and building practice. Except for the sole occasion when Cawdor had intervened to save the young man from injury, and possibly death, in that bizarre ritual, his conduct had been unremarkable.

But it seemed that the captain had his own sense of justice, and it was a harsh one, Gryble thought bitterly.

Too harsh. Almost vindictive. For what man in Cawdor's position, driven to the point of extremity, wouldn't have reacted in so violent a fashion?

Good God, his wife and child gone! Wiped from the face of the Earth as though they never existed! Enough – more than enough, surely to God – to send any man to the edge of sanity and beyond?

Saraheda and Daniel were not on the ship, that much seemed certain, Gryble acknowledged.

They were by now many miles behind, and many miles deep.

Misadventure or foul play? They had vanished three nights ago, and no alarm had been raised. Captain Vincent had interrogated the officer of the watch, Gryble had heard, who had reported no incident and no disturbance during that night. It was a mystery, and would remain so, unless a witness was found, and none had come forward.

Of course, if it *was* foul play, then it was unlikely that anyone would volunteer information, because they would be implicated in the deed. Either they were directly responsible, or if not should have at least alerted the watch to this nefarious, suspicious activity. That avenue of speculation was a dead end, Gryble concluded. Such a person, or persons, would clamp their mouths tight as man-traps.

Misadventure then? Yet, the more he examined the possibility, the less tenable it seemed. *Two* people falling overboard, and not a cry to be heard? Why were they on deck at all, in the middle of the night? And odder still, Gryble pondered – where the devil was Cawdor while these events, accidental or intentional, were taking place? Fast asleep in his bed? Otherwise engaged? Gryble couldn't conceive of any activity that would distract Cawdor to the extent of wantonly neglecting his wife and son. He was such a loving husband and dutiful father that Gryble found this aspect of the affair the most worrisome and baffling of all.

That, and the brooding atmosphere on the ship, and now the discord in the heavens, all conspired to fill him with dread and foreboding.

The voyage had started out with such hope and high expectation – an adventure in the New World! Pioneer settlers with their eyes firmly fixed on a glorious golden future! Opportunity! Freedom! Achievement! Those had been the resounding watchwords.

Words that now rang in Gilbert Gryble's head like so many cracked bells.

2

Gryble had to grasp the iron hoop with both hands and use every ounce of his strength to budge the heavy wooden trap door. He heaved it open, taking care not to let it crash back on its hinges. Even from down here, in the murky depths of the vessel, below the waterline, the noise might be heard on the upper decks. Gryble didn't care to be hauled before the captain and charged with gross disobedience.

He peered over the edge. The lantern's weak light made no impression on the black void below. He heard the swirl and slap of water, smelt the noxious odour of putrefaction. Something had died down here, and was in the process of decay.

'Cawdor! Are you there? Where –'

A face seemed to swim up to him, floating in the gloom. Red-rimmed eyes blinking in the lamplight. The voice was a hoarse whisper. 'Who is it? I can't see.'

'Gilbert Gryble. I've fetched something for you to eat. I couldn't manage soup, but there's salted pork, hard biscuit –' His round face contorted, now that his eyes had adjusted to the darkness. 'Holy Mother of God, Jefferson, this is a hell-hole. I imagined it to be foul, but this is beyond belief . . .' He gulped back his nausea. 'Reach up and take it. Here. Quick. I mustn't tarry!'

There was a rattling noise.

Gryble stared. 'Suffering Saints, man, are you chained too? Why didn't the captain have you flogged and keel-hauled and have done with it?'

'I can't stand, Gilbert – my arms are fastened. Use the ladder.'

Gryble searched and found the ladder, tilted it through the trap, and climbed down the slippery rungs. Water swirled round his ankles. He swung the lantern, and as he did so there was a flurry of sleek wet bodies sliding into the water and surging off into the further reaches of darkness. Gryble's testicles shrank, retreating defensively into his body. Rats. He shuddered, feeling his stomach churn with fear and disgust.

Cawdor had made a place for himself on a bank of heaped gravel next to the curved side, a tiny peninsular hemmed in by dank green seawater which sloshed about with the motion of the ship. The rushing of the sea itself could be heard, inches away, brushing past the keel. Cawdor's feet were in an iron brace, fastened by chains to the side planking, and a loop of chain from the brace to his wrists prevented him raising his hands above chest height.

'Here, Jefferson.' Gryble waded on to the gravel, holding out the food wrapped in a cloth. 'I cannot stay more than a minute.' He bent forward, lowering the lantern to see into Cawdor's face. 'Are you all right?'

'Do I look all right?'

'Forgive my stupidity, Jefferson.'

Cawdor shook his head. He held up a slice of pork. 'Instead, I thank you most humbly for your kindness. Have you brought anything to drink? I'm more thirsty than hungry.'

'Water.' Gryble took a flask from his pocket. 'Laced with brandy. Or perhaps t'other way round. How often do they feed you?'

'Twice a day. Morning and evening, as near as I can guess. Down here, time is one long night. It doesn't march; it stands perpetually at ease.' He paused to take a deep swig. 'That puts fire into me. Thanks twice over, Gilbert.'

Gryble smiled wanly. He looked almost ready to weep. 'Jefferson . . .' He swallowed a lump in his throat. 'You must accept that Saraheda and Daniel are gone. Lost at sea. There can be no other explanation. They cannot be on board still, or they would have been found.'

252

'Yes,' Cawdor said, calmly munching the pork. 'I agree.'

'You do? You accept that they were lost overboard?'

'No. Thrown overboard. Murdered.'

'By whom?'

'A man named Kershalton.'

'But *how* do you know?'

Cawdor looked into the darkness, his face haunted. 'I was warned by the Indian, Satish Kumar, that the Shouters and Kershalton were plotting against me. I took the warning lightly. I should be damned in hell for it. Perhaps this is my due punishment, or even less than I deserve.'

'Did you speak to the captain about this? He could have had this man Kershalton brought before him and put to rigorous questioning.'

'No.' Cawdor closed his eyes wearily. 'I could think of nothing but that Saraheda and Daniel were on board, alive, somewhere, waiting to be found. I couldn't accept ... the alternative. I refused to accept it. Until now.'

Gryble swayed backward as the ship lurched, and nearly fell into the scummy seawater. Hurriedly, he shuffled up on to the gravel hill. The hairs on the back of his neck were standing up like bristles at the thought of the hordes of rats out there watching him beyond the pale, yellow orb of lamplight.

'I must leave you, Jefferson. If I'm seen I'll be prevented from coming again, but I *will* come again, I promise i' faith.' He shook his head angrily. 'This is a monstrous injustice, whatever you say you deserve. Kershalton should be festering here in this stinking cesspit, not you!'

Lifting the lantern, he turned away, and Cawdor clutched his sleeve with a grimy hand.

'Thank you for rekindling my hope, my friend. I was beyond feeling anything but shame and despair.' Cawdor knelt up. 'There might be a chance, a faint chance, that the terrible truth of this will see the light, and that justice will prevail. The captain is a strict man, but not a mountebank. If he can be made to see just cause, he will make it his business to conduct a proper and fair investigation.'

Gryble sighed and shook his head wearily. 'I've tried

already to see the captain. He refuses point-blank. His mind is shut.'

'There might be a way to open it.'

'How?'

'Speak to his first officer, Mr Tregorath. *His* mind is open. And he is disposed to believing in me, I have heard.'

'What should I say?'

'Tell him about the threats Kershalton made against me. Against my family. Satish Kumar will confirm it. Then ask him to put this new evidence before the captain. If you can convince Mr Tregorath, I'm certain he'll do his utmost.'

Cawdor watched anxiously as Gryble stepped into the water and darted fearful glances all around him as he waded to the ladder. He quickly hopped up two or three rungs.

'Will you do it?' Cawdor asked.

'Yes, of course. I'll speak to him directly.' But Gryble was doubtful. These were suspicions, rumours, not hard facts. It would be difficult enough persuading the first lieutenant, let alone Captain Vincent. 'I'll do my best, Jefferson. And I'll come back tomorrow and tell you his opinion.'

Shivering all down his spine, Gryble climbed out of those dreadful, swilling, rat-infested bilges and lowered the trapdoor. It felt like he was sealing Cawdor in his tomb. He didn't know if he had the courage – or the stomach – to face it again.

When Gryble had gone from the lower hold, the feeble lamplight disappearing up the companionway, a small figure squeezed furtively out from between two of the huge water casks that were ranged in rows several deep. Six Fingers cocked his head, listening to the fading footsteps. He counted up to twelve on both hands, counted again, and yet a third time, before starting silently up the companionway on the calloused pads of his six-toed feet.

Gryble emerged on deck to find the *Salamander* in a tumult of frenzied excitement. There was another vessel alongside!

She was the *Briton Protection*, a fourth-rated frigate converted to merchantman, homeward-bound from Savannah with a cargo of cotton and leaf tobacco.

Lines were strung and messages passed. News spread rapidly among the passengers thronging the deck that twelve of the thirteen colonies were mobilising an armed militia to fight the Crown. A 'Continental Congress', as it was termed, had met in Philadelphia, only several weeks past, and issued a petition to His Majesty's Government insisting that there should be no taxation without representation.

Gryble spun from one group to another, picking up titbits here and there, unsure whether to be alarmed by this fresh development or if it was merely a storm in a teacup. Any talk of rebellion, of course, was pure nonsense. A few thousand raw settlers versus the sovereign might of a world power – why, a couple of detachments of British Redcoats would reduce them to mincemeat in a matter of weeks!

The meeting was brief. After ten minutes or so, the *Briton Protection* drew away, her sails billowing as she caught the freshening westerlies, her crew and passengers lining the rails and waving farewell. Gryble watched until she had faded into the dusk.

Someone mentioned that the frigate had been at sea less than a month, which meant that, given fair weather, the *Salamander* was now only weeks away from the continent of America.

He overheard someone say – jokingly he hoped – 'Look well if the minute we step ashore we're taken prisoner and marched straight to the scaffold. Halfway round the world to have your neck stretched!'

'What!' his companion exclaimed. 'I'll join with 'em!'

'That's treason talk. As a loyal British subject you have a bounden duty to stand up for king and country.'

'Aye, but which country? I'll tell you now, straight, the Crown has no claim on my loyalty and affection. That's the reason I shook the dust of old England off my feet – to be a free man. If there's to be a scrap, I know which side I'm on.'

Gryble went down to his cubicle to prepare his supper, made uneasy by this conversation. Damnation! He'd journeyed all this way to participate in a great scientific revolution, not to get embroiled in a petty squabble between the Crown and the colonies.

With his thoughts centred on this gloomy prospect, and his mind buzzing with morbid speculation, Gryble clean forgot about Cawdor in his wretched stinking prison and the promise he had made him.

'You heard it plain?'

'Plain as daylight. I listened just as you tole me, Franklin.'

'And it was my name he spoke. No mistake?'

'It was dead on your name.'

'Did he say how he come by it? What stinking rat's spilt his guts?'

'He had a warnin', so he says.'

'Warnin'? Who from?'

'He give another name, a foreign 'un. Says this foreign chap warned him to beware. He forgot it. Anyway, he paid no mind.'

'What foreign chap?'

'I forget.'

'Well, fuckin' remember it, you bastard son of a whore, or I'll squeeze yer knackers till they squeak like cherry pips.'

'Coo – Coo – summat or t'other – Ouch! I'm tryin'! I'm tryin'!'

'Never mind. What did ginger 'ave ter say?'

'Gryble jus' took it in, gob open. Oh aye, then Cawdor says to tell the first lieutenant to tell the captain – somethin' like that. Then ginger says he will, straight off.'

'Tell him what?'

'About what Cawdor was warned about and took no heed. Get the captain to haul you on the mat till you spills yer tripes.'

'Shite and corruption! Well, now. Did he? Well, now. We'll see about that, Six Fingers. Aye, we'll see . . . I'll do for that bastard once and for good. Cut off his cock-robin and ram it down his throat till he chokes and see what he says then. Aye, that's a pretty notion . . . I think I'll do it. I think I will, i' faith.'

Gryble sat on the edge of the bed, staring wide-eyed at his white feet protruding below the hem of his nightshirt. His conscience wouldn't let him rest. The image of Cawdor in the black bowels of the ship hovered before his mind's eye, a painful and loathsome phantasm. After supper he'd remembered what he had promised to do, and resolved that first thing in the morning he would approach Mr Tregorath and put Cawdor's allegations to him.

But sleep had proved impossible. The phantasm wouldn't be banished. In fact it magnified itself in his imagination until Cawdor's arms and legs had been gnawed to bloody stumps by packs of scurrying, insatiable rats. Now they were burrowing into Cawdor's stomach, sharp little teeth tearing at his intestines.

Gryble got dressed, putting on his shirt and breeches over his nightshirt. He kissed his Bible and went out.

The senior officers' wardroom was on the middle deck, beneath the captain's stateroom and private quarters. By strict marine etiquette Gryble wasn't allowed there, except by invitation or prior appointment made via a junior officer. He went directly there all the same, and for a minute or two stood fretting in the passage outside, clasping and unclasping his hands, turning away and then coming back again.

He took a deep breath, closed his eyes, and knocked.

The wardroom steward who answered, a thin, sallow fellow wearing a blue-and-white-striped apron down to his knees, at first refused to interrupt the first lieutenant's dinner, until Gryble insisted that it was 'a matter of prime, urgent importance'. Behind the steward, Gryble glimpsed several officers sprawled round a table strewn with the aftermath of a meal; decanters of brandy, rum and port doing the rounds; a thick fug of tobacco smoke standing like a solid blue wall under the polished brass lamps. Gryble spied Doctor Chapman there too, his soiled collar undone, lolling half out of his chair, his eyes bloodshot and bleary.

'What's all this to-do, sir?' Mr Tregorath asked, eventually materialising out of the blue fog. He belched softly, swaying in the doorway.

As soon as Gryble mentioned Cawdor's name the first lieutenant shook his head, holding up his hand to cut him off.

'There's no more to be said on that score. I suggest you return to your quarters, sir, and forget about it. The matter's done and settled.'

'You're a fair man, Mr Tregorath. Cawdor places his trust in you to see justice done. Won't you give him the opportunity to speak, and consider what he has to say?' Gryble's voice was high-pitched with pleading. 'There is new evidence concerning his wife and son, and their ... disappearance. Cawdor believes he knows who was responsible. At the very least he deserves to be listened to.'

'His actions are not those of a rational man, Mr ...'

'Gryble.'

'Mr Gryble. Tearing about the ship in a frenzy. Causing alarm and disquiet among the passengers. Assaulting an officer in the prosecution of his duty. It cannot be tolerated, sir. We have a duty to keep the ship on an even keel, in every sense.'

'I realise that, of course.' Gryble wrung his hands. He had a sick feeling in the pit of his stomach – that he had lost already, that he was failing Cawdor. He was clutching at straws. 'But, if the passengers were to believe that a murderer was roaming free, would that not cause unrest, leading to panic? They must be reassured, Mr Tregorath, for the welfare of the ship and their own peace of mind.'

The first lieutenant closed his eyes and opened them again, rather wearily. With an abrupt gesture he beckoned Gryble inside, and then led him through the wardroom and into a narrow compartment adjoining it. None of the officers paid Gryble any attention. Mr Tregorath closed the door and indicated a chair. He pushed aside bundles of documents and perched on the corner of a writing table, belching again as he folded his arms.

'A gentle word of warning in your ear, Mr Gryble, sir. I must caution you at once against starting such a malicious rumour. Unless, that is, you are keen to join your friend Cawdor in his purgatory. As you will know, I hope, Captain Vincent gives short shrift to breaches of conduct, whether they be civilian or to do with the management of the ship. He has, as we say, a short fuse.'

'Cawdor seeks only a fair hearing. My God, Mr Tregorath, his wife and child are dead! How is a man expected to react under such circumstances? How would you?'

'I'm not married.'

'That's beside the point.'

'Yes, it is.' Mr Tregorath yawned and scratched the back of his head. 'Let me put my cards on the table, Mr Gryble. This is strictly between ourselves. If you repeat it, I shall deny it.'

Gryble hunched forward anxiously, kneading his palms.

'I have my own suspicions about this affair. These arose from a sequence of events some time ago – I shall not go into them now, but they involved Cawdor and a female member of the sect called the Shouters. Anyway, that aside, possibly there is some justification in Cawdor's claim that his wife and son met with foul play. I would not refute it.'

'Then –'

'However! However . . . these are solely my opinions. I have no facts to back them. Nor any solid evidence with which to make a case. Cawdor now says he knows the culprit's identity. But that is merely Cawdor's word against another's, who would doubtless deny it, and in the captain's eyes Cawdor's word is as bogus as a nine-penny piece.' The first lieutenant spread his hands. 'You see, Mr Gryble, where we find ourselves – in a maelstrom of accusation and speculation, surrounded by a vacuum of hard fact.'

'But the man has been done a bitter injustice,' Gryble said heatedly.

'Several injustices.'

'And yet you refuse to do anything to rectify them!'

'If I could,' Mr Tregorath responded with a flash of irritation, 'I would. But I am not the captain, and it is the captain's prerogative to arbitrate in these matters and come to a decision. He has made his decision. What would you have me do, flout his ruling and find myself on a charge of mutiny? Perhaps you won't rest, Mr Gryble, until all three of us are chained together in the bilges. Then we will have the satisfaction of congratulating one another on our unswerving sense of justice and steadfast principles.'

Gryble hung his head. 'I don't know what else to say. You are Cawdor's last hope.'

There came a shout of laughter from the wardroom. The officers, it appeared, didn't believe in stinting themselves. Someone started singing a bawdy song, and other voices joined in.

The first lieutenant swung his leg down from the table and banged his fist on the partition. The drunken singing tailed off.

'They'll not be content till they wake the captain. And, God knows, he is not the most charitable of men, even when not plagued by the piles. I must go through, Mr Gryble, and exert a steadying influence.'

Gryble stood up, feeling wretched. 'The root of all this lies with the Shouters, does it not? Cawdor stuck his nose into their affairs and they cannot abide it. So they employed somebody called Kershalton to do their dirty work.'

The first lieutenant paused, his hand on the doorknob.

'Kershalton is the man Cawdor accuses?'

'Yes.' Gryble blinked up at him. 'Didn't I say?'

'No, you did not.'

'Do you know the fellow?'

'I know of him. He is a rogue, right enough. We only learnt of his history a week out, otherwise we should have ejected him at Plymouth.'

Gryble felt a flicker of hope. 'Then for pity's sake have him apprehended and brought before the captain, Mr Tregorath! At least make him answer these charges. Please, sir, I beg you!'

'I confess, this puts another complexion on the matter.' The first lieutenant frowned, plainly racked by indecision. He snapped his fingers several times. 'But proof – what proof is there? If I am to approach the captain, who is heartily sick already of Cawdor and his doings, I require something of more substance than the frenzied ramblings of a grieving man. As I told you –'

'He is not frenzied, nor is he rambling,' Gryble protested. 'He is as reasonable as you or I.'

'Is he indeed?'

'Why, yes . . .' Gryble's voice sank to a feeble whisper. He stared miserably at the floor.

'You are aware, I take it, of the captain's edict, Mr Gryble? The man is in solitary for a grave misdemeanour. A notice was posted to that effect, to be read by all.'

'I am aware of it.'

'I hope so.' Mr Tregorath opened the door. A draught of tobacco smoke and alcohol fumes eddied in. He put his hand on Gryble's shoulder, ushering him through to the door of the wardroom. 'I fully appreciate that your motives are sound, Mr Gryble, in trying to help your friend Cawdor. But you see the difficulty. However, let me sleep on it. Perhaps in the morning –'

'Hey, Nick, settle this argument!' someone bawled out, addressing the first lieutenant. 'The quack here says the colonies can raise a militia five thousand strong. I say they'll be lucky to raise five hundred – most of them convicted felons at that!'

'Pipe down,' Mr Tregorath snapped, 'or I'll raise a lump on your head. It's time you turned in.' There was some muttered grumbling.

Doctor Chapman rose unsteadily to his feet, hanging on to the edge of the table to prevent himself from falling. He seemed anxious to say something, but then apparently forgot what it was.

At the door, the first lieutenant lowered his voice. 'Pay particular attention to my warning about spreading rumours, Mr Gryble. As it is, the ship is in a nervous enough state without tales of murderers roaming free. If I hear any, I'll know where to come.'

Gryble nodded glumly.

'Don't be so downcast. I promise I'll try to think of a way to help Cawdor. At least he can't get into more trouble where he is. It won't do any harm to let him stew there awhile.'

'Unless the rats get to him first,' Gryble muttered gloomily.

4

The rats were keeping their distance, for the time being. Cawdor had flung the last few scraps of salt pork, which he couldn't eat anyway, as far as his chained hands would permit. There had been a sudden scurrying, splashing rush to get them, squealing cries as fights broke out, and then snivelling, salivatory sounds in the darkness as the winners devoured their spoils.

Cawdor leant back against the planking, feet drawn up, hands cupped defensively over his groin. The sea drummed at his spine. He didn't mind it, indeed welcomed it. One more mile. One more mile. One more mile. One mile less. One mile less. One mile less . . .

For minutes at a time he dozed, lulled by the continual surge and thump of water. Then he came to, only to drift off again. When he heard the creak of the trap door he didn't know whether he was awake or dreaming. A pale shaft of light appeared; the ladder slid down, making the rats scurry off into the further darkness.

Like the rats, Kershalton kept his distance. Holding the lantern high, he first inspected the dank wooden chamber. Above him, ropes looped down from the bulkhead, attached to a block-and-tackle which swung like a pendulum with the motion of the ship. At his feet, the water swelled up in a scummy green wave to slap at his calves, receded, rose up again.

He turned then for a closer look at Cawdor, squinting with his good eye, and there was a pallid gleam of light on metal as he slid a knife from his belt, holding it point uppermost for the quick thrust under the ribcage.

'How do, squire? You've landed yersel' in a bit of a pickle.'

Cawdor had pushed himself upright, half-standing, half-leaning. The chains clinked as he raised his hands to his chest.

'My word, not fit for a gentleman, this, is it? None of them little comforts of hearth and home a wife provides, eh? Bet you miss 'em. The comforts, I mean.' Having judged the extent to which Cawdor's movement was restricted, he circled round, keeping Cawdor on the side where his good eye was.

'Know what I think?' Kershalton confided. 'A carcass wouldn't last ten minutes down here with them.' He jerked his head back towards the darkness. 'They'd pick it clean and crunch the bones. You can say that for 'em. They don't waste much. Very economic.'

Kershalton tested his footing on the gravel slope. He needed a good purchase. He didn't intend to slip at the vital moment. He said, 'Pity of it is, yer lad happened to get in the way. Don't believe it if yer don't want to, but it's the gospel.' He grinned ruefully, shaking his head. 'Come lookin' for his mother! A very bad time to pick. Very misfortunate. Must've been in his stars. They do say, if it's in yer stars, yer knackered.'

By lowering one arm, Cawdor released sufficient chain through the foot brace to raise the other. He held this arm up as far as it would go, using the taut chain as a shield. Even so, the chain was only inches away from his body. One swift jab in the right spot and that would be it. And he wanted so much to kill Kershalton that his bowels ached with the longing.

'Shitehawks,' Kershalton growled, his eyes growing big and round. 'What a stupendous poke! Six lengths she took, all the way up to the bollocks, and never so much as a whimper. Took 'em all and was ready for more. Still –' he shrugged, and smiled, the wide-eyed innocent '– what am I tellin' you for? You've been there once or twice yersel'. Excellent snatch, squire. First-rate.'

The pain was too much to bear. Cawdor squeezed his eyes shut. He screamed. Kershalton was ready, waiting, and went for the heart under the lower edge of the ribcage, thrusting upward. Cawdor jerked the chain. It missed the blade but caught Kershalton's wrist, dragging it sideways. The point of the knife ripped through Cawdor's shirt, causing a deep gash in his side. Kershalton switched angles and jabbed to the right. Cawdor whipped the chain across. There was a clang as it deflected the blade. Kershalton again went for the heart. Cawdor twisted desperately, trying to ram the chain in Kershalton's face, but was brought up short by its length. But neither could Kershalton get close enough. Every time he jabbed, Cawdor whipped the chain across.

It was a furious, grunting, desperate, maddening stalemate.

Kershalton stepped back into the water, chest heaving, face streaming with sweat. He hawked deep in his throat and spat a slimy gob at Cawdor. That missed too.

'Against grown men you're pretty puny,' Cawdor panted. 'Women and children are your mark. Come on. *Come on*!'

But Kershalton was reconsidering. He had the man at his mercy. It was a question of ways and means. He swung the lantern round, his eye glittering, and then he smiled. He waded over, reached up and caught the block-and-tackle in mid-swing. He reached up higher and yanked the rope, so that the heavy block dropped a couple of feet. He sighted with his good eye, calculating the trajectory, and put his arm, his shoulder, his entire body weight into the shove.

The solid teak block weighed about half a hundred-weight. Cawdor saw it coming, but hampered by the foot brace he could shuffle only a few steps. It came at him like a battering ram. He felt it whistle past his ear and heard the boom as it struck the side planking and rebounded.

Kershalton threw back his head and laughed. This was

good sport! Better than a shy at the fair, and nothing to pay. With Cawdor both target *and* prize.

He took fresh aim, and heaved.

The block came straight at Cawdor. He'd never avoid it in time. He went down on his knees, face in the gravel, covering his head with both arms.

Boom!

It crashed above him and swung back. Kershalton hauled on the rope, lowering the block still further. Now it was at waist height, and easier for Kershalton to get his body behind it. This time he took a run, his face contorting as he put all his rage and hatred and fear into one mighty effort. The block swung. Cawdor saw it hurtling towards him and knew he couldn't move fast enough or burrow deep enough. All that he could do, which he did, was to throw up his left arm protectively and curl himself into a tensed, compressed ball.

The block missed Cawdor's head by the merest fraction, wrenched his arm back, and broke every bone in his hand, smashing it to a soggy pulp against the planking.

Kershalton cackled with glee. His good eye lit up with wild delight as he saw Cawdor clutching his shattered hand to his chest, head bowed, moaning and gibbering with pain.

'First prize to me, squire! Now we'll see who's man enough. Yer wife got a length of hard cock; now it's your turn for a length of cold steel. But I'll wager yer won't enjoy it half as much!' He pulled the knife from his belt and waded through the surging water, pale lips pressed thinly to his teeth.

Helplessly, Cawdor raised his head, his eyes clouded by the inferno of excruciating agony raging through him, nursing his broken hand like a sick infant, a shapeless, boneless mess of mangled tissue.

'Franklin!'

'What's the matter?'

Kershalton's head spun round. He stared up, mouth agape, at Six Fingers' upside-down face hanging through the trap door.

'Quick, get out! Someone's here!'

'Shitehawks!'

Kershalton lunged for the ladder. His scrambling shadow disappeared with the lantern; the trap closed, leaving the chamber in pitch-blackness.

There was a pattering of feet above, and then silence, except for the bilge water lapping sluggishly against the gravel heap upon which Cawdor lay bleeding to death.

5

'Well, Mr Tregorath?' Captain Vincent barked, seated behind his desk. 'You have the opportunity. Say your piece.'

'First off, sir, may I give the order to have Jefferson Cawdor removed to the sickbay, where he can be attended more properly?'

'No, sir, you may not. Proceed.'

The first lieutenant glanced at Gryble, who was standing stony-eyed next to the doctor. In the morning light Doctor Chapman's face had a grey, sickly pallor under its cracked mosaic of tiny broken blood vessels. He kept his hands behind his back, under his coat-tails, where the tremors wouldn't show.

'Come along, Mr Tregorath, I haven't got all day.'

'Captain Vincent, sir, in all conscience, and in view of what's happened, I feel we owe it to Cawdor to give him a fair hearing. He has serious charges to make against this man Kershalton, in the matter of Cawdor's family as well as in this brutal and unprovoked attack. We cannot surely allow –'

'Is that the royal "we" or the collective "we", Mr Tregorath?'

'Beg your pardon, sir.' The first lieutenant gave a small, bleak smile of apology. 'Of course what I mean is that the captain must decide on the appropriate course of action, given the facts as have been presented to him. But you will, sir, allow that these new circumstances require further consideration.'

'Do they?' Captain Vincent inquired, with an air of mild

surprise. 'How so? The man was given a reprimand and a firm warning – in your presence, Mr Tregorath – and followed it by disruptive behaviour and an assault on one of my officers. Those are the "facts", sir, and nothing has altered them.'

Gryble's hands twitched involuntarily. He had been cautioned by the first lieutenant not to speak until invited to do so, but this was almost more than flesh and blood could bear. He opened his mouth, but the first lieutenant spotted it and shot him a stern look.

'But for Doctor Chapman's intervention, sir,' Mr Tregorath went on swiftly, 'Cawdor might not even have survived the attack.' He indicated the doctor, whose slack, stooping figure alongside the first lieutenant's lean height seemed pathetic and ludicrous. 'After all, the man was in ship's custody. And his injury was quite horrendous, as Doctor Chapman will testify.'

Now that the doctor had been mentioned, Captain Vincent was regarding him as one might inspect a side of rancid beef.

'Praise be for the good doctor,' he said with heavy irony. 'Where should we be without his sober judgement? I know that your duties are onerous, sir,' he went on in the same tone, 'but I wasn't aware they extended to visiting miscreants in the bottom hold in the dead of night. You might have fallen and hurt yourself.'

Captain Vincent made it sound as if this wouldn't have been much of a calamity.

'I was in the wardroom and happened to overhear Mr Tregorath and this gentleman talking about Cawdor. I became concerned. I felt I owed it to him to . . . to . . .'

He moistened his lips and gestured vaguely; his hands quivered like tuning forks.

'Owed him? Owed him what?' the captain asked sharply.

'Mrs Cawdor assisted me, and I felt . . .'

'What?'

Doctor Chapman drew himself up. He smoothed his shabby black coat, which was shiny with grease. 'I thought them a decent, wholesome family. I was sorry for Cawdor in what had befallen him. I felt an obligation to help him.'

'A decision taken after cold, rational, lucid reflection, no doubt,' the captain remarked dryly.

'On the contrary. I was drunk.'

'Drunk? You amaze me, sir.'

'It is as well I was,' Doctor Chapman stated quietly, doggedly. 'Otherwise I should not have gone, and Cawdor would have no further use for the hand I cut off, nor the rest of him, because he would be dead.'

'Killed by this fellow Kershalton,' Captain Vincent said flatly.

'Yes, sir,' the first lieutenant affirmed.

'And the sole testimony is Cawdor's word alone.'

'Yes –'

'Without witnesses.'

The first lieutenant's lips tightened.

'The word of a confirmed liar and molester, in fact.'

Gryble could stand no more.

'What? Is he supposed to have smashed his own hand with the block-and-tackle? Cut a gash that long in his side? He mutilates himself, cripples himself, in order to accuse someone and cause them mischief, is that your contention?'

'Mr Tregorath, I am not accustomed to being spoken to in those terms in my own cabin on my own ship. If this gentleman persists, have him thrown out and shut away.'

'He is excitable, sir. Understandably so.'

The first lieutenant gave Gryble a fierce, penetrating glare.

Gryble was, literally, hopping mad. He wanted to reach out and grab this leaden dumpling of a captain and shake some common sense and decency into the cannonball he called a head.

'Now then.' Captain Vincent sat back, stubby arms folded across the double row of brass buttons. 'Have you questioned Kershalton about these allegations, Mr Tregorath?'

The first lieutenant seemed surprised. 'No, of course not, sir,' he answered at once. 'Not without first seeking your authority to do so.'

'Well, I have. I sent Mr Turner to fetch him an hour ago, when you requested this inquiry. He is an uncouth rogue, to be sure, and not right in the noodle, I fancy. I examined him closely. He afforded me a full account of his whereabouts last night, with the names of several witnesses, who have since corroborated his version.'

The first lieutenant stared down at the captain, his jaw dropping. 'You've talked to him?'

'I have just said so, Mr Tregorath.'

'Why, yes. Yes. And ... he provided a satisfactory alibi for his movements?'

'Satisfactory to me,' Captain Vincent said. 'He was at prayer.'

'He was at prayer.' The first lieutenant repeated it in a tone of slow, numbed astonishment, as if speaking a foreign language.

'He informs me that he is a member of the group, or sect, known as the Shouters. Elder Graye has confirmed to me that Kershalton was engaged in a ceremony of worship during the exact period that Cawdor claims he was assaulted by Kershalton.'

The captain leant his elbows on the desk. His gaze swept keenly from the first lieutenant to Gryble, passing over Doctor Chapman as if he didn't exist. 'Now then, gentlemen. The choice is a simple one, it seems to me. Whether to take the word of a man proven to be a liar, or that of a respected and learned religious leader. Without hesitation, I know which I choose.'

'But what about Cawdor, sir? He did suffer a grievous attack, there is no question of it.'

'I accept that.' Captain Vincent nodded. 'By a person or persons unknown. But the case against Kershalton is closed.'

6

Time had lost its meaning. The voyage in the dark seemed endless, as if each minute, each individual second, was an eternity from which he would never escape.

His life from now on would be spent in this creaking, stinking pit, with the sound of the rushing, scudding ocean outside, and inside the peevish squeals and slack wet snivellings of the rats.

It would go on and on, for ever and for ever.

Except for the doctor, who came to change the dressing on the raw stump of his wrist, no one visited him. The seaman on duty in the upper hold barred entry to anyone without express permission, signed by the captain and stamped with his seal.

Without the passage of time, the future had ceased to exist. And Cawdor couldn't think about the past. If he did think about it, he felt his mind sinking towards madness. No future; no past. Just the ever present continuous eternity of the single, unique second he was at this moment inhabiting.

So when the rats became bolder, paddling nearer, shiny pointed noses thrust above the scummy water, twitching at the scent of fresh blood seeping through the dressing, Cawdor was unaware of them. He was aware of the monotonous drumming of the sea against his spine, but that was like the tidal forces of his own heartbeat, relentless, lethargic, eternal.

He wasn't aware when the first, boldest, dripping-wet rat crept up the gravel slope, head flattened, sniffing cautiously, picking up the smell of human body heat.

Something touched his hand.

Cawdor found himself gazing into a pair of liquid brown eyes. He continued to gaze, blankly, without comprehension, until Satish Kumar said, 'I did as much as was permitted, but it wasn't enough. Perhaps it was foolish even to try. A man's karma is inviolate and immutable. It can be altered by himself alone, in the act of rebirth. Forgive me for my arrogance and presumption.'

'Forgive *you*?' Cawdor laughed weakly. 'If I'd listened and paid heed instead of being stupid and stubborn, I wouldn't have betrayed my family. But I suppose the best advice in the world is of no use to an imbecile,' he said bitterly.

'Let me see your arm,' Satish Kumar said. He held the bandaged stump in both palms, examining it intently.

'I would have imagined your philosophy to be more concerned with matters of the spirit than with bodily ills, Kumar.'

'If a man lies wounded by a poisoned arrow he does not seek to know who shot it, or its length, or what it is made of. First he requires the poison to be extracted and to be made well. We must face what is before us, as it is; only by direct and personal experience do we learn, not by evading it.'

'Some of us learn too late. What good is the lesson then?'

'Self-pity is a most corrosive force, Mr Cawdor.' The Indian gently released his arm. 'It rots the will and destroys our ability to achieve good karma. It must be resisted.'

'Is that what ails me?' Cawdor asked moodily. Sour bile curdled within him. 'You think I feel nothing but self-pity?'

'No. You also feel grief, remorse, sadness, a sense of injustice, and the desire for revenge. But self-pity you cannot afford. It corrupts every thought, blights every action.'

Satish Kumar suddenly smiled.

'There is a way forward. Not only in this life, Mr Cawdor, but in the next, and the one after that. There are innumerable lives.'

'Your faith is not mine,' Cawdor reminded him.

'We are all of the one universe.'

'But if I don't believe . . .'

Satish Kumar shrugged. 'You may not know that you believe. The important thing is to tread the right path. The Noble Eightfold Path, as I remember telling you.'

'And what is that?'

'Eight steps, which are Right Understanding, Right Thoughts, Right Speech, Right Action, Right Means of Livelihood, Right Effort, Right Concentration, and Right Meditation. The path is not unique to the Buddhist belief.

Other people in other cultures have recognised its virtues. Your English dramatist William Shakespeare expressed the same philosophy, in different terms, in his play *Hamlet*. "This above all. To thine own self be true, And it must follow, as the night the day, Thou canst not then be false to any man." '

'You spoke of karma and rebirth. Tell me about those.'

'Karma means simply a person's actions or deeds. These are causes which give rise to effects. Your great scientist Isaac Newton expressed it in his Third Law of Motion: that for every action there is an equal and opposite reaction. As in the material world, so it is in the lives of men. The universe itself is an effect of our actions upon it. Each separate, discrete part affects all the other parts. We are all integral and interdependent, one with another. Or, as Buddhism would have it, the karma of one is the karma of all.'

'Then my actions affect everyone and everything,' Cawdor said, struggling to understand.

Kumar nodded. 'And the actions of everyone and everything else affect you. Further – and as stated by Newton's Third Law – the consequences of your own actions will react upon you, via the universe, with commensurate force. You cannot escape them, whether you go to the ends of the earth or to the depths of the sea.'

'And rebirth? Is it a literal fact in your religion that after death we are reborn?'

'The body, of course, ceases to exist at death. But the karma of the individual does not die. It is passed on.' Satish Kumar paused, frowning a little. 'Such a concept is hard for you to grasp, I understand that. Imagine a lighted candle passing its flame to another candle. The old candle is discarded but the light lives on: the same and yet different. The essence of Jefferson Cawdor, his karma, does not die with the death of his body. It lights another candle, and another, and another. Innumerable candles.'

'Towards what end? Is there a purpose to this endless lighting and relighting of candles? Where does it lead us?'

'If we faithfully follow the Noble Eightfold Path,' Satish Kumar explained, 'we finally achieve nirvana, which is the state of supreme enlightenment. This is beyond anything you or I have experienced, or will experience in this lifetime. It is a casting off of the self, the ego, so that we no longer regard ourselves as separate, but become one with all things, merging with the cosmic dance. To attain it, having traversed the Noble Eightfold Path, means we have mastered and overcome the weaknesses of the flesh, all selfish craving, all the intoxications and hindrances which tempt and frustrate us. This is nirvana, the state of blessedness, the end of woe.'

'That isn't possible. Not for me. Never.' Cawdor's eyes were cold and brutal. 'My total being aches to end Kershalton's life by the most painful means I can conceive. To see him die in agony would bring me the most glorious, thrilling satisfaction.'

The yellow lamplight flickering across Kumar's smooth, impassive features gave his skin the quality of fine, supple kid leather, without a wrinkle or a blemish.

'Why?'

'*Why*?' Cawdor uttered a harsh laugh. The laugh seemed to stick in his throat. It turned into a choking sob. 'Because the future has become a black void. Kershalton and the Shouters have done for me.' He drew a shuddering breath. 'You say no man can escape the consequences of his own actions – what of *their* actions against me? Against my wife and son? Let me see this cosmic retribution you speak of strike them down. Then your philosophy will make common sense – to me, now, in *this* life, not the next!'

Satish Kumar shook his head sadly. 'You have not understood, Mr Cawdor. Causes and their effects do not turn full circle in the span of a single lifetime. A man's life is but a raindrop in the vast ocean of time.'

Cawdor wiped his eyes with the heel of his hand. 'I see. I must wait for the candleflame to be passed on to eternity, must I, before the account is settled?'

'There will be no settling of accounts, ever, if you maintain your existing state of mind.' The Indian grasped

Cawdor by the shoulder. 'Do you hear me? Please listen carefully. The chain of karma – of cause and effect – will never be broken, Mr Cawdor, unless you decide to break free of it. It will repeat itself, and continue to repeat itself, a perpetual cycle of events to which you are bound, as feeble and helpless as an ant, for evermore. But understand: this is not Nemesis, or fate, or destiny, or providence. *A man writes his own destiny by his own thoughts and actions.* That which is yet to be depends on the deeds now being done. The future is not wrought in stone, or at the whim of God, or the gods. There is within you the power to break free, to sever the links of the chain, if only you will realise that it binds you.'

'I've told you,' Cawdor replied dully. 'What I see before me is a black void. There is no future to be written, by me, the gods, or by blind destiny. The candleflame is snuffed out.'

'It cannot be.' This was uttered quietly and calmly, not as a contradiction, but as a simple statement of fact. 'Your body was born; therefore it will one day die, as will mine. But the spirit of karma is immortal. It cannot be destroyed by an act of will. It has been passed on to you, for this brief mortal span, and in turn you will pass it on to your future selves. You cannot obliterate the future; it is inside you, waiting to be brought into being.'

Cawdor stared into the blackness. Almost against his will he found the Indian's words comforting. But he didn't want to be comforted; he rejected their comfort, because he didn't deserve it. He deserved to be where he was; it was his rightful due, left here to rot. Good riddance to bad rubbish.

'These people,' Satish Kumar said, 'the ones who call themselves the Shouters . . .'

'Yes.' Cawdor dragged his thoughts back from the abyss. 'What of them?'

'They too possess a karma, which lives on, is passed on. They are an equal and opposite force which must be resisted. They are known by many names. In the past I have heard them called the Messengers of the Fall from

Grace. Now they choose to call themselves the Shouters. In the future it will be something else.'

The Indian's eyes were very large and glistening. As he looked into them Cawdor found himself suddenly wondering how Kumar had been able to get past the seaman in the upper hold. A bribe? But Kumar wasn't a wealthy man by any means – he was travelling steerage. And it would have taken a considerable sum for the seaman to disobey the captain's orders and risk a flogging.

'I told you once, Mr Cawdor, that men of good faith must do what they can to oppose the forces of evil. A balance has to be kept, or else everything is chaos.'

'You've chosen a poor disciple, Kumar.' Cawdor smiled bleakly. 'A defective candle to carry the flame. My "good faith" as you call it has less effect on such grand schemes than a stream of gnat's piss.'

'No – forgive me – you are quite wrong. By his smallest positive action a man can raise himself, however little, above his own personal failings. And, because he is part of the whole, that too is lifted, and made greater, as a consequence of his actions. No contribution is too small or insignificant.'

'What if the man is unworthy? What if he feels his contribution is less than insignificant? Indeed, less than nothing?'

'No man is unworthy, Mr Cawdor. He has the freedom to choose which path to follow. Shall it be the path towards self-deceit, darkness, pandering to his own petty cravings, the indulgence of his selfish ego? Or is it the path towards enlightenment? Man is man because he knows good from evil. He is unique in this respect. He knows the difference and has the power to choose between them. You, Jefferson Cawdor, have that power. How will it be used? Foolishly or wisely?'

From a leather pouch at his waist, Satish Kumar produced a small bundle of cloth, and held it in the pale slender palm of his hand.

In spite of himself, Cawdor felt a stirring of curiosity.

'The paths towards nirvana are many. Each man must

decide for himself the most suitable one to take.' Kumar held out the little bundle. 'Here. In these fragments you will see the choices that lie before you. Take them.'

'What is this? Witchcraft?'

'You say you have no future. Here are many futures – rather, each splintered piece contains a reflection of the whole future seen anew from a different perspective.'

Cawdor opened the bundle. Shards of broken mirror lay on the ragged square of cloth, casting myriad splintered reflections which dazzled the eye. He could see nothing but light.

Then, to his surprise, Satish Kumar chuckled softly, and Cawdor felt he had been tricked. 'I see nothing here. Just a broken mirror and a hundred bright distortions –'

'Quite so. The pieces of mirror reflect nothing until they are observed. I shall leave you to observe them, Mr Cawdor.'

The Indian rose to his feet. His tall, thin shadow was thrown across the bulkhead. Cawdor stared up, bewildered and disbelieving. The trap door was shut. There was no ladder.

'Remember,' Satish Kumar said, raising a finger. 'Each piece contains the whole, and also a fragment of the whole. What you will see in each fragment is a singular version of events to come, all equally possible, all equally plausible.'

'But you said that the future cannot be foretold. A man writes his own destiny by his own thoughts and deeds.'

'That is true. What the fragments reveal are the infinite possibilities that await you. Observe each fragment closely. One of them will lead you on the path to nirvana.'

Kumar smiled and raised his hand in farewell.

His shadow on the bulkhead thinned. It became a single black line, and when Cawdor examined it more closely he saw that he was looking at nothing more than a thin caulked gap in the deck planking above his head.

But the lamp was there, next to him on the gravel heap. The cloth was spread in front of him, still, the bright shards glinting like a pile of cheap trinkets.

Cawdor smoothed the cloth with his hand. There was something written there. Bending over it, he strained to read the words in the dim, wavering glow.

'Behold in this shatter'd mirrour all your past and future times.'

Not time singular. Times. Infinite possibilities.

Handling the sharp, jagged edges with extreme care, Cawdor picked up one of the tiny fragments and held it up to the light.

7

From prow to stern the decks were crowded, the forward rails packed tight with expectant, exuberant faces. Seamen clambered into the rigging and cheered. Some of the passengers wept with relief and fell to their knees to thank the Almighty, while others joined together to sing His praises.

29 October 1774.

After eleven weeks and three days at sea, the New World sighted at last!

The cry from the crow's nest of 'Land Ahoy!' came a few minutes after midday, though it wasn't until an hour later that the hazy brown smudge that was the coastline of North Carolina became visible to the unaided eye of those on deck.

A cask of rum was breached and, with the exception of the Methodists and others of a strict religious persuasion, everyone on board drank more than a measure or two. Even Captain Vincent accepted the beaker offered to him by Mr Tregorath, and toasted his officers and crew. A fiddle player struck up; jigs were danced; women kissed; children hugged; backs were slapped; and the general air of carousing swept through the ship until it seemed that the *Salamander*, buoyed up on rum and other high spirits, was skimming along ten feet above the waves.

For the moment, no one gave a thought to the rumours of civil unrest and even outright rebellion by the colonists. Only one blessed thing mattered. Soon they would be rid of this cursed salty capricious domain (better left to the fishes, and welcome) and have both feet planted, God be praised, on the terra firma of their new homeland.

The continent of America!

Gilbert Gryble stood on the quarterdeck, alongside Mr Paine. They had shaken hands and wished one another well, but were now silent, wrapped in their thoughts, watching the revelry on the lower decks.

The sun was hot, and Gryble's head swam a little from the liquor, which he wasn't used to. The ship was now sailing parallel to the land, on their port side, and every time Gryble looked at it he felt a nervous shivering in his buttocks and the backs of his thighs. He hadn't expected it to appear so foreign and exotic. They had sailed for miles along the coast and not seen a single settlement or habitation. In his mind's eye he had pictured bustling seaports and neat little towns, roads, smoke curling from farmhouse chimneys, cultivated fields, all spread out and set apart; in other words England on a slightly enlarged scale. But this was bigger and emptier – vaster – than he had ever imagined.

It was a wilderness, in fact. And there were red savages in it, seven feet tall, with painted faces. Gryble began to wonder if he hadn't made a serious error of judgement. Would there be much need of a cosmographer here?

He couldn't help thinking about Cawdor, though he tried hard to avoid it. Too many violent emotions twisted his stomach into knots. He couldn't recall ever feeling such rage, such bitterness. The dreadful injustice of what Cawdor had suffered left him in a state of tortured emptiness and impotence, like a wrung-out dish rag.

He couldn't think of Saraheda and Daniel at all. No, not at all. He simply couldn't. His heart came up into his gullet and choked him, and he started weeping and couldn't stop.

Kershalton guzzled down another cup and reeled backward against the foremast, giggling and dribbling like a madman. Six Fingers made a grab to save him from falling, and Kershalton swatted him aside, mumbling, 'Gerrout from under me feet, yer freak bastard son of a whore.' He belched and farted at the same time. 'Lemme be. Lemme be. Gerrus a drink.'

He straightened up, head wobbling, using his arm as a prop against the foremast, and turned slowly to look towards the landward side of the ship. Why wouldn't the bastard coastline stay still? First it tilted one way and then the other. Stay still, bastard. Let me take a good gander at you.

'Thas North Calorina,' he told Six Fingers, pointing. 'North Caranalina. Canalrina. Oh fuck it. Thas where we're goin'. Over there. An' we'll be gentlemen. Anythin' we want we can 'ave.' He swept his hand out expansively. *Any fuckin' thing*. For services rendered. Payment is due us, Sam, m'lad. An' we've earned it. We 'ave earned it.'

He tried to strut about, and ended up staggering.

'Money to burn. Here you are, my good man. Think nothing of it. Another bottle, landlord. Make it two. And your fittest wench. One with bosoms out to here.'

'Some more grog, Franklin.' Six Fingers held up the brimming cup.

Kershalton aimed for his mouth, and on the way spilt half of it down his shirt. He drained what was left and flung the cup away.

He squinted with one bleary eye at the group in the middle part of the ship. The Shouters stood in their long grey robes, hands clasped devoutly, gazing into the middle distance. As Kershalton watched them, Elder Graye slowly turned his head and looked directly at him. Their eyes met.

Kershalton grinned, and winked with his dead eye.

In the boisterous and happy tumult on board, no one observed this exchange, except for one person.

On the upper deck, the Spanish Woman stood apart from the rest, watching with cool, green, gold-flecked eyes. A faint curve of a smile touched her lips, shadowy as a brushstroke.

She didn't flinch, or lower her gaze, when the shaven, knoblike head of Elder Graye rotated in her direction and he fixed her with a piercing stare from eyes deep-set beneath the bony ridge of his brow.

He continued to stare at her, brutally, like an act of physical penetration, and she returned it, coolly, almost mockingly, unintimidated.

Abruptly, Elder Graye snapped his head away, and appeared to take a sudden interest in the coastline. At that precise moment, as circumstance would have it, the ship altered tack and began to veer to port, the sails filling with a warm southerly breeze as the *Salamander* headed for landfall.

JOURNEY INTO LIGHT

1

A soft tapping on the door awakened Sarah. Drowsily, she raised her tousled head to find herself lying in a king-sized bed under a single sheet of black silk. The heavy drapes were partially open, a blinding shaft of sunlight making the rest of the room dim and shadowy. Through the closed sliding windows which gave access to the brick-paved patio she could hear the faint lisp of the ocean. Then, like a pack of quarrelsome children, sea gulls set up a chorus of ugly, raucous cries as they swooped over the house.

Sarah sat up and rubbed the sleep from her eyes. The knowledge of where she was filtered slowly into her brain, like a halting message coming from a great distance. She was in the Palm Beach home of Messiah Wilde. She was clear about that much, because she remembered that he had invited Daniella and herself to be his guests. But she couldn't remember how they had got here. The last distinct memory she had was of being among a group of people in the crowded hospitality suite, watching him and listening, in a mesmerised way, while he chatted to them about this and that. And now it was morning and here she was. Alone in a strange bedroom. Her suitcase had been brought in and laid flat down on a trestle stand near the wall of black closet doors with red surrounds. The entire room was decorated in the same colour scheme: black drapes with red trim, black carpet with the Beamers' symbol picked out in red, a thin red stripe on the edges of the shiny black furniture.

The tapping came again, louder this time. Sarah had asked the person to enter before she realised she was naked, and quickly crossed her arms, holding the black silk sheet against her body.

'Good morning, madam.' A small, brown-skinned man, Indonesian perhaps, wearing a white jacket came in wheeling a trolley. From a widow's peak his hair flowed straight back like a glossy black cap. He brought the trolley to the side of the bed and removed the white linen cover. He bowed slightly, averting his elliptical eyes. 'If you require anything more, madam, please use the telephone. Thank you.'

He went out, quietly closing the door. Sarah wouldn't have minded eating breakfast outside on the patio, but she felt too lazy and disinclined to move. Her throat was parched, and she had a raking thirst. She poured a tall glass of orange juice from the ice-cold pitcher and drank it down. It tasted so wonderful that she poured another and sipped it between mouthfuls of scrambled eggs, crispy bacon, and wheat toast spread thickly with butter. She was, Sarah discovered, very hungry, and even thirstier, filling the tall glass for the third time and gulping it down, before subsiding, replete and contented, on to the pillows. She felt revivified, her mind clear and sharp, though her limbs were suffused with a pleasant languor after the meal.

It was only then that her thoughts turned to Daniella. She tried to recall if they had travelled here together to Palm Beach, but that was no use because she couldn't even remember leaving the Grace MediaCorp building last night. And something else hit her. Sarah touched her naked shoulder. Had she undressed herself, or had someone else put her to bed? And, if so, who?

Lying back on the pillows, trying desperately to remember, Sarah was startled when, without any warning, the door opened and Messiah Wilde came silently into the bedroom. He was wearing a robe of black silk that clung to his shoulders and was loosely swathed across his chest to reveal a deep V of his pale, lightly muscled body down to the navel. He stood at the foot of the bed, regarding Sarah with a crooked smile of amusement. Then he chuckled and gave her an impish wink.

'Glad to see you haven't lost your appetite, my dear. Anything else you'd like? More juice?'

'No.' Sarah shrank down, holding the sheet to her with numbed hands. 'Thank you.' She tried to avoid looking at his crotch, which was directly in her eyeline; at the folds of silk rippling over a long hanging shape. 'Where's my daughter? I want to see Daniella.'

'Daniella isn't here.'

'Where is she?'

Messiah Wilde raised his dark eyebrows, as if surprised by her question. 'At the studio, of course. She has to get ready.'

'Ready?' Sarah frowned. The frown felt stiff on her face, similar to the numbness one feels after an injection at the dentist's. 'I don't understand.'

'Daniella is the Chosen One on tonight's show. It's a great honour for her. You should be proud.'

'But, I'm on tonight's show,' Sarah said, articulating the words as if her mouth was filled with large, round, smooth pebbles. 'Not Daniella.'

Messiah Wilde's lips split open in a wide smile and his head went back. She saw his white throat quivering in a dry chuckle. 'No, no, no, my dear. We like tight young cunts, not camel's lips puckered by the ravages of time.' His head snapped forward. The smile vanished and his eyes suddenly narrowed to slits. 'Have some more juice, why don't you?'

Sarah's stomach turned over. She could feel the dull seismic thud of her heart. Her mind was bright and clear – unnaturally so – yet her body was leaden and inert. His meaning was obvious: the orange juice had been spiked. And she had drunk three full glasses of the stuff. And, though his meaning about Daniella was a mystery to her, Sarah was chilled to the marrow of her bones.

Sarah lay palpitating against the pillows, arms crossed over her chest, hands like frozen claws clutching the sheet to her body. The numbness was spreading; she tried to move her right foot, just the tiniest fraction. Nothing.

'What's the matter, my dear? Why so modest? Isn't *this* what you came for?' He jiggled his hips and the hanging shape in the folds of silk swung from side to side.

Sarah formed the words slowly, as if her jaws had been wired together. 'Tell me, please ... what you mean ... about the Chosen One. You won't ... harm my daughter ... please ...'

Messiah Wilde spread his arms wide.

'Of her own free will Daniella became a convert of the Beamers. She is among the most blessed, my dear, being the Chosen One to serve in the sacred rites of our Temple. Your daughter will be revered by millions of people throughout the world. The ultimate sacrifice is the supreme accolade.'

Sarah swallowed painfully. 'What ... will ...' She ground out the words, one by one. 'You ... do ... to ... her?'

'Oh don't worry, you won't miss anything: it'll be taped,' Messiah Wilde informed her. 'We'll let you see a copy.'

He leant towards her, the wavy curtains of black hair framing his face. His eyes bored into Sarah with such intensity that she could feel heat on her face, as if a furnace door had been opened. Dim embers in their dark depths grew brighter and brighter until they glowed fiery red. She tried to tear her own eyes away from their mesmeric power, but the drug had numbed them in their sockets. They were glassy and unblinking. And now everything in the room seemed heightened – sharper and more vivid than real life. Sarah's brain speeded up. Sensory impressions swirled around her in a bright jangle of colour and light and movement, while her body lay stiff as a corpse under the thin sheet she clutched to herself with frozen hands.

Messiah Wilde parted the black robe. Kneeling on the bed, he uncrossed her arms and folded back the sheet to expose her breasts, rising and falling rapidly, and gave a long, slow wink.

284

'First the mother, then the daughter,' Messiah Wilde murmured huskily, his nostrils flaring as his breathing became harsh. 'Daniella, poor sweet, won't enjoy it half as much. These young girls never do. But you, my dear, you have dreamt of this moment, haven't you? And now your dreams are about to come true. Just imagine . . . just think of all the women who would envy you, and yearn for the blessing about to be bestowed upon you by Messiah Wilde Himself!'

'Messiah Wilde Himself made the decision,' said the clean-cut young man. He had a smooth round face, blond hair brushed neatly from an arrow-straight parting, and smelt strongly of aftershave. 'When he saw you last night after the show, and talked with you, he knew you were the one.' He favoured her with a smile that was brimming with enthusiasm. 'Bet you're thrilled, huh?'

'Yeah – uh – yes,' Daniella said uncertainly. 'But – uh – did he ask my mom about it? Does she know he picked me? I mean, I thought she was gonna take part in tonight's show.'

'Hey, don't worry so about it!' the clean-cut young man chided her good-naturedly. 'Everything's jake. She'll get her shot some other time. And your mom'll be in the audience, cheering you on, proud as gosh almighty.'

Looking through the glass walls made Daniella's head spin slightly at the sight of the levels moving rapidly past the elevator. She'd awakened late that morning feeling muzzy, in a strange bedroom of black and red that she knew must be in the home of Messiah Wilde. She knew it because he had invited them to stay there as his guests. There were gaps in her memory that stayed stubbornly blank, no matter how hard she tried to fill them. Anyway, this servant had come into the bedroom, a small Asian-looking man in a white jacket, and told her to get dressed at once, someone was waiting to take her to the Beamers' building. When she asked after her mother, the man shrugged his narrow shoulders and muttered something in a foreign tongue. She asked the black chauffeur the same question, standing by the bronze limo in the driveway, and all he could do was shake his head and mumble, 'Don't have a clue about that, miss. My orders say to drive you to HQ, that's all I know.'

The clean-cut young man who met her in the reception hall had an answer ready. Her mother would be along later; she was having brunch with Messiah Wilde while they discussed some new material for Sarah's radio programme. In the meantime she, Daniella, had a busy day ahead of her, preparing for tonight's show. Grinning at the bewildered expression on her face, he dropped the bombshell:

Daniella Cawdor was to be the Chosen One.

The news sank into her brain like a delayed-action depth charge. She was still grappling with the idea and trying to come to terms with it as the clean-cut young man led her into the coffee shop on the first-floor balcony. There he bought her fruit juice, a double cheeseburger and a Twinkie bar, and a glass of milk (which was what she asked for), and sat opposite her sipping a mineral water, a beaming smile on his round, well-fed face.

'You do realise what a privilege this is, don't you? Many are called but few are chosen. You're a lucky little girl.'

'I know that,' Daniella said. Her head was clamped in a vice, and the waves of his pungent aftershave wafting over her made it difficult to eat. In fact she felt faintly nauseous. She bit into the cheeseburger, which tasted like warmed-over cardboard.

'*Very* lucky. *Very* fortunate. What a story you're going to have for the guys back home in ... where is it you're from?'

'New Jersey.'

'Back home in New Jersey, right.' The clean-cut young man was nodding earnestly. He had a habit of staring at her with his large bright-blue eyes, the whites so white they had a bluish tinge to them, that Daniella found rather intimidating. They seemed to her unclouded by a single thought; or maybe there was just one *single* thought in them and nothing else.

She said, 'I can't eat any more, guess I lost my appetite,' and pushed the cheeseburger aside.

'Don't you want your Twinkie?'

'No thanks. You have it.' He ate it in two bites, chomping it with large square teeth which made her think of white tombstones. She dabbed her lips with a paper napkin. 'You sprung it on me out of the blue. I'm still in shock,' Daniella said, giving him a tentative smile. Everything was happening so fast that she was finding it difficult to get her bearings. Yesterday had been a nonstop whirl, and meeting Messiah Wilde on top of it all had been pure fantasy. The countless hours she had spent in her room playing the *Beamers of Joy* video, his dark soulful gaze filling the screen, had transformed him in her imagination into a figure of mythical proportions who inhabited another realm. In her wildest dreams Daniella had never dared to believe that she would one day meet this wonderful being in person and experience the aura of his actual presence.

But now her dreams were coming true. Not only had she met and talked with him, it was just sinking in that she was going to appear live with Messiah Wilde on *The Lovebeams Show*.

The elevator stopped at level nineteen and the clean-cut young man took her by the elbow and guided her out. This level was different from the others, Daniella saw: not open-plan offices but corridors of dark-grained wood panelling and thick carpets softly illuminated by concealed lighting. She walked along beside him, her heart beating fast.

'Where are we going?' she thought to ask.

'Oh, my, a whole bunch of things to do. Publicity shots, make-up tests, costume fitting, pre-show briefing – when you're chosen to step up out of the audience you have to know how to react, what to say, and you have to look right too. I mean, you look just fine, great,' the clean-cut young man amended hastily, 'but appearance is all important in front of a mass audience. Television is a cruel medium.'

'What do I have to do?' Daniella asked nervously. 'I don't want to make a fool of myself.'

'Don't fret yourself so,' the clean-cut young man reassured her, tapping lightly with his knuckles and opening a door to a room of spotlit mirrors, high-backed chairs and women in white smocks. 'After the pre-show briefing you'll be word perfect. And when they've done with you here,' he said, giving her a gentle nudge in the back to step inside, 'you'll look like a movie star.'

Had it moved or hadn't it? Sarah blinked a mixture of tears and sweat from her eyes and squinted down at her right foot. For the past fifteen minutes she had been using every ounce of willpower to get the damn thing to move even the tiniest, minutest fraction, and because she lacked any physical sensation she had to keep staring at her foot to see if anything was happening. Had it really twitched just then, or was she so desperate she had fooled her imagination into playing tricks on her? She screwed up her concentration and tried again, her naked, inert body shiny with sweat, spread-eagled like a white cross on the black silk sheet as he had left it when he was finally done with her.

Sarah had seen his eyes flare redly with blinding intensity, felt the heat of them upon her like a scorching sun, and then the glare in them had dwindled and died, and they had resumed their dark, brooding impassiveness as he pulled away from her, sated and spent. She had held back her tears while he was doing it, a fierce cold pride keeping her stony-faced, but when the door closed and he was gone they poured out unceasingly until she felt to be drowning in them. They were tears of rage, not self-pity, Sarah kept telling herself – rage and more rage and yet more rage, a flood of *rage* boiling out of her.

She had lain for a long while waiting for the drug to wear off, expecting the tingling of life to return at any minute to her leaden limbs. She was still waiting. The drug had left her senses sharp and alert, and she could move her eyes to watch the shaft of sunlight growing thinner and more upright as the sun rose higher, but her physical self had no more feeling or animation than a statue. That's when she summoned up every fibre of her resolve, urging her right foot to respond to her command with even the tiniest spasm of willed movement. Staring down, her hair clinging wet to her forehead and neck like rats' tails, Sarah shrieked in her head, Move yourself, goddamnit, give me a sign you're alive and not dead down there! One feeble twitch, that's all I'm asking for. You can do it if you try. Do it for Daniella. One feeble twitch for Daniella, that's all you have to do. So do it for her, you bastard. Do it, goddamnit, do it! Do it!

Her right foot moved, suddenly jerked with a galvanic action, like a corpse on a mortuary slab returning to life.

Sarah lay back on the pillows, resting for a moment, chest heaving for breath. She was almost blinded with sweat, squeezing and blinking her eyelids to clear her vision. She looked down, focusing her concentration, and this time she got her foot to move not once but three times – to the left, to the right, and back again.

Encouraged, she set her mind grimly to the task. Progress was agonisingly slow. Every few minutes she had to rest, the furious effort of concentration draining her mental strength until her brain felt like a wrung-out sponge. She was able to flex her right leg now, and tried to use it to lever herself over towards the left side of the bed. The phone – black with a fine tracery of red – was on the left-hand bedside table. After three abortive tries, she succeeded, flopped over on her side and lay there panting, her body a limp dead weight, her arm sprawled out across the cover as if it didn't belong to her. There was no life yet in her fingers. They were next on the agenda. She had to activate them and get movement into that stupid useless arm in order to reach out, bring the receiver near her mouth, and punch the dialling pad. And, if there wasn't a direct connection to an outside line, what then? Sarah shut that unthinkable possibility out of her thoughts. She couldn't let herself be distracted now: she needed to channel every bit of mindpower she possessed into the very simple and excruciatingly difficult action of reaching – for – the – phone –

Time became elastic. It ceased to have any proper dimension, even when measured against her thudding heartbeats. Minutes or hours elapsed; Sarah had no means of judging the steady tick of their passing. She existed in a single extended moment as she watched the first slight tremors twitching through her fingers, her hand curling and uncurling as slowly as the petals of a flower opening to the sun, and then her elbow gradually straightening in tiny spasmodic jerks until her arm was reaching out at full stretch.

Her hand grasped the receiver. She couldn't feel its rounded plastic surface, her nerve-endings still traumatised by the chemicals in her veins. Using her hand as a mechanical claw, she lifted the receiver and placed it on the pillow next to her head. Sarah closed her eyes, offering up a prayer as she heard the dialling tone in her ear. *She was in touch with the outside world*. Reaching out again to dial the number, she had a sudden seizure of panic. What was today? She couldn't remember. Where would Jeff be – at his New York office or at home in Franklin? Think, you dumb bitch, what day is it? Then she did remember; it was Saturday; he was at home, that's where he'd be.

She listened, her ear nestled close to the receiver, to the ringing tone purring over a thousand miles away in New Jersey. He wasn't answering; the house was empty; he wasn't there. And then her heart leapt when the purring stopped and was followed by a click as the connection was made.

'Jeff.' It came out a rusty croak. 'Jeff, it's me!'

'Hello,' said the blessed familar voice. 'This is the Cawdor residence. There's no one here to take your call right now but, if you'd like to leave a message, please do so after the tone. We'll get back to you as soon as we can.'

In an agony of suspense, the breath rasping through her parched lips, Sarah waited for the tone to sound.

It came at last, the long beeping tone, and stopped short in the middle, interrupted by a loud click, as if a plug had been pulled.

The line went dead.

Sarah lay huddled on the crumpled silk sheet, her forehead touching the silent phone, not enough emotion left in her to even cry.

2

Thunderstorms rolling in from the Atlantic meant that the DC-10 was fifteen minutes behind schedule. Eventually it touched down at Miami International at 7:20 p.m. in driving rain that was whipped along the runways by winds gusting up to fifty miles an hour.

Travelling in the forward business-class cabin, Cawdor was one of the first in line as disembarkation began. Unencumbered by any hand luggage, he had only the clothes he stood up in, which was how he had departed the Troth Foundation a few minutes after one-thirty that afternoon.

It had seemed to Cawdor – standing in the bleak, cold bathroom on the second floor, the shards of mirror scattered on the black and white tiles around his feet – that the earth was in upheaval. He had to clutch hold of the washbasin to steady himself as the bathroom tilted crazily, and him with it. The black snake of premonition, coiled in his stomach, the one he had felt earlier on the terrace and dismissed, wasn't a fake after all. Not this time. The danger to Sarah and Daniella was real. He had to act immediately. Clenching his fists to his chest to still their trembling, Cawdor knew this with total certainty. He stood there for a full minute until his breathing was under control. By then the sweat had gone cold on his forehead, and suddenly he felt very calm and committed, resolute and filled with purpose.

Five minutes later he was marching down the staircase, car keys in hand, and, without seeing anyone or even saying goodbye to Doctor Khuman, Cawdor climbed into the Olds and pulled away down the gravel driveway, leaving behind the building with its greystone turrets and miniature towers bathed in warm sunshine.

From the small town of Griffin he had picked up the I-87 intersection between Glens Falls and Saratoga Springs. Thankfully there had been no hold-ups on the interstate all the way south through New York state. Keeping to a steady 65 miles an hour, and with only a single stop for gas, by four o'clock he was nearing White Plains. There he was faced with a tough choice. JFK or Newark? At the gas stop he should have called to find out which airport had the earliest flight to Miami, and cursed himself for not thinking of it. But Cawdor was loath to delay himself further by stopping again and finding a phone, conscious of the minutes ticking away in his brain like an unexploded bomb. He came to the decision, praying it was the right one, that JFK was the better bet, likely to have more Florida flights, and turned east off I-87 to join I-95 a few miles south of New Rochelle.

At this point he was 22 miles from the airport.

Taking the Clearview Expressway toll bridge over the East River, Cawdor followed the parkway past Belmont Park Race Track, avoiding the more direct routes, which he knew from experience would be clogged with traffic, and reached JFK at 4:25 p.m., a few minutes under three hours since leaving the Troth Foundation.

There wasn't one flight for Miami due to leave shortly – there were two. In his haste Cawdor had nearly purchased a ticket for the first flight out, with BryanAir, when he realised it was via Atlanta and included a thirty-minute stopover. He moved three desks down to the Delta counter and waited impatiently in line, hands clenched, palms clammy, praying there would be seats still available. A family of five was in front of him, and it seemed to take the ticket clerk an eternity to process the father's request for economy class to Chicago O'Hare, and she could guarantee *absolutely*, couldn't she, that they would be serving a vegetarian meal on the plane?

Clutching his ticket at long last, Cawdor headed for Gate 14, and was ushered through separately with the other business-class passengers. He had missed lunch, and not eaten a bite since, and although he wasn't remotely hungry he accepted the early dinner tray and made himself finish the turtle soup and took a few mouthfuls of sirloin steak and croquette potatoes before his stomach rebelled. He refused the free alcohol offered him, and drank only sparkling mineral water. In the adjacent seat, a balding man with pouchy eyes saw no good reason to stint himself. After his third bourbon the man tried to strike up a conversation, and wasn't deterred until Cawdor plumped up the cotton pillow and sank into it with eyes closed. Cawdor had no intention of falling asleep – he didn't believe himself capable of sleep – but within less than a minute he was so exhausted he had drifted off.

His dreams were filled with guilt.

It had no name or form at first, this guilt, although Cawdor knew without question that he was the guilty one. He had failed in some vital respect. He had betrayed his family; no, not betrayed them: he had placed them in jeopardy through a stupid and senseless action on his part. But what? In his dream he scurried through dusty hallways and probed empty rooms, searching frantically for an answer. He was to blame all right, but what had he done? Cawdor loved his family too much ever to want to harm them. Saraheda and Daniel were his very life's blood, more precious to him than –

Saraheda and Daniel. It was his wife and son on board the ship, and the dreadful fate that had befallen them: that's why he was racked with guilt. And the reason was simple.

Because upright and virtuous Jefferson Cawdor, paragon of courage and high principles, had intervened in a dispute among the brethren of the cult of the Shouters. Leaping into the circle of bobbing heads, he had rescued a young disciple who was being shouted to death. He had stood up to the leader too, that bony, austere figure in a hooded robe who had been grotesquely interfering with a young girl. Had wrestled him to the deck of the sailing ship and threatened to break his neck if the old lecher so much as touched her again. Oh yes. Brave and indomitable Jefferson Cawdor, defender of the weak, champion of the underdog . . . and look where his self-righteous and vainglorious posturing had landed them! His wife despicably abused, and – with their son – flung over the side, while he himself was shackled and left to rot in the stinking bilges.

Cawdor's guilt was no longer nameless or formless. It blazed in his mind like a firebrand. For his arrogant belief in the justness of his cause, Saraheda and Daniel had paid the ultimate price.

Not only that: the burning hatred that Cawdor's intervention had inspired in the religious cult had left a legacy of revenge that had pursued him and his family over two centuries, from that day to this. Just as Saraheda and Daniel had paid a terrible price, so now the same retribution was to be exacted from Sarah and Daniella. The Shouters, or the Messengers as they had become, never forgot, never forgave.

The guilt gave another twist, like a knife in his side. Why hadn't he made sense of those strange and unsettling dream images of the past before now? Was he just plain dumb? For weeks he had been troubled by them, but he hadn't understood the stark warning contained in those broken shards that what had happened before was about to happen again. If he hadn't been so blind and stupid he might have saved his wife and daughter. He ought to have delved deeper and tried to uncover their real meaning. But of course, Cawdor realised, this was precisely the reason he had opened himself up to Doctor Khuman, to help him discover what all this weird stuff *meant*.

And he had departed the Troth Foundation without a word before any help could be given.

This was part of his guilt-ridden dream too, and as Cawdor awoke in the softly humming cabin he knew the reason why he had to leave so abruptly. The mirror lying in pieces on the bathroom floor was a final warning, and one he couldn't ignore.

Jeff Cawdor had never been more certain of anything in his life.

* * *

Striding up the tunnel-like ramp into the terminal building of Miami International, he had to restrain himself from breaking into a run. It was now seven-thirty. How far was Fort Lauderdale – twenty, thirty miles? He could hire a car, ask at the rental desk for directions to the headquarters of Grace MediaCorp, and be there in under an hour, by eight-thirty at the latest. Sarah and Daniella, Cawdor assumed, were at the studio; he couldn't think where else they might be. Suddenly he was struck by a thought that made him falter in his tracks. This breakneck timetable he was following, calculated to minutes and even seconds, depended on the assumption that *The Lovebeams* TV show went out live. Maybe it was recorded earlier in the day. By now it could all be over. Did it really matter so much, Cawdor asked himself, that he get to the studio before the show started, whether live or recorded? He didn't have a reason why this seemed so vitally important; he only knew that the inner momentum directing and driving him to act told him it was.

Cawdor checked his watch, overwhelmed by a sickening despair. He wouldn't get there in time. Eight-thirty, even if he made it, would be too late. He lengthened his stride and broke into a trot, and then he was running through the interminable, endless labyrinth of Miami International Airport to get to the main concourse and the car-rental desk.

3

Tonight he was a dazzling figure dressed all in white: white double-breasted suit, white shirt and a white silk tie, white buckskin shoes with silver buckles. The spotlight followed him across the stage, and so did 2,000 mesmerised pairs of eyes. He carried a hand mike, darting from this person to that along the semicircular row of young people facing the audience, conducting a session of 'Spirit Talk', in which they were invited to divulge what difference the Beamers had made to their lives. For some it was a joyous revelation, filled with smiles and laughter; for others a highly

295

charged, traumatic experience that had them hunched over and weeping as they recounted how the Lovebeams had entered into them and transformed the world from a place of misery and doubt into a golden paradise of hope and promise.

'Tell all the people, Jodie,' Messiah Wilde encouraged a plump girl with a blotchy, red complexion and lank brown hair sheared off in a fringe just above her glasses, 'how you felt before you joined the wonderful worldwide kinship of Lovebeamers.'

'Ah'd no confidence in myself, no self-respec',' Jodie said tearfully in a southern accent that almost required an interpreter. 'I thought I was no-account trash, no friends, nobody'ud pay me no attention, boys especially. I was a loser in all departments. Life weren't worth the livin', I tell ya the honest truth.'

'You were a nail-biter, Jodie.'

Jodie nodded her bowed head.

'You had bad breath.'

'At school they all used to say my breath stank.'

'Like a . . .' he prompted.

'Like a hound dog's fart.'

'So what nickname did they give you?'

'That was it – "Hound Dog's Fart",' Jodie said, her three chins quivering. She wormed a twisted tissue under her glasses to wipe her eyes.

'Hound Dog's Fart. Don't be cruel, you should have told them. Ha ha. But to be fair, Jodie, you weren't clean in your bodily habits, were you now?'

'Do I have to – have to say, in front of . . .' Jodie's face crumpled and the tears ran down over her blotchy cheeks.

'Don't be a spoilsport, Jodie! You told us back there; you have to tell the people out front, including the millions watching at home. Fair's fair, you know.' Messiah Wilde patted her fat white knee.

Jodie mumbled something into her chest.

'What was that? We didn't hear.' He pushed the mike under her chin.

'I said I didn't used to always change my underthings,

least not every day. When my Daddy run off we was broke, with hardly a cent, and we couldn't afford to buy new stuff and things –'

'Washing costs nothing, Jodie. You should always clean up your own mess, especially if others find the stink offensive. Now, shouldn't you?'

Jodie nodded miserably, her hands grovelling in her lap.

With a wink and a smile, Messiah Wilde bounded up, twirled round and told the audience with a chuckle, 'You see how unhappy and pathetic Jodie was before? As she said, a loser, pure trash. Take a good hard look at her.' He pointed back. 'Life was just one long vale of tears until she tuned in and turned on to the Beamers. Now isn't that a lesson for all of you out there? I *know* you're feeling unhappy and insecure. I *know* you're hopeless at relationships, don't feel attractive to the opposite sex, are worried sick about your appearance and lack of personality and social skills.'

He placed his hand on his heart and looked into the camera with a pained sympathy that was achingly sincere. 'Me, Messiah Wilde, I know and understand exactly how you're feeling out there, right this minute.' His voice went down a key, as he mouthed softly, 'You can change. I make this promise to you – yes *you* – here and now. Allow the Lovebeams into your heart and, believe me, you'll be amazed at the transformation in yourself. You won't even recognise the creature that was the timid, frightened old you – that's my vow and pledge to every single one of you.' He gave a long slow wink, and a sigh like a gently falling wave rolled through the audience. 'Give it a try. Open up and let the Lovebeams shine in.'

There was a moment's deathly hush and then the audience responded to the flashing APPLAUSE sign with whoops and screams and wild applause. Smiling ecstatically through her tears, Jodie was applauding as fiercely as anyone. With a graceful wave of his hand, Messiah Wilde skipped upstage and disappeared through a billowing cloud of dry ice, to the accompaniment of a heavy bass-guitar soundtrack.

The stage lights dimmed and a voice over the public-address system announced a twenty-minute intermission while the set was rearranged for the next segment of the show. 'Messiah Wilde will be right back with you,' he assured them. 'And, remember, someone, somewhere out there, is the Chosen One on tonight's show!'

Sitting beside her, the clean-cut young man leant over and nudged Daniella with his elbow. 'Hear that? Your star spot's coming up – twenty minutes and you're on!' He grinned across to the young woman in the regulation crisp white blouse and pleated skirt seated on Daniella's other side, next to the centre aisle. Their eyes met and she nodded. The kid would do just fine, her look said. No tears or tantrums. The clean-cut young man returned her nod and sat back, folding his beefy arms.

Outwardly, Daniella seemed placid enough, her eyes dreamy and faraway, a small expectant smile on her face. During the day she'd taken three (or was it four?) melibrium, fed to her by her chaperones, and she felt slightly adrift from her surroundings, as if all this was happening at one remove. But her excitement was for real, because her mouth was parched dry and every now and then she had to take a huge gulp of air to steady herself. Not long now!

Conscious of this great honour, she was quietly determined not to let anyone down, especially after all the time and care they had taken with her appearance. They had brushed out her long gossamer-fine fair hair and gathered it with a garland of primroses at the nape of her neck. For hours they had worked on her face, reshaped and dyed her eyebrows, tinted her lashes, and applied a smooth coat of very pale make-up so that under the lights she would glow with a soft angelic radiance. Her lips were painted blush pink and lightly glossed. The cream satin dress they had chosen was tightly fitted over her breasts, with a wide oval neckline that barely covered her shoulders, and below the waist it comprised layer upon layer of cream organdie trailing almost to the floor, giving a semitransparent effect that would show the silhouettes of her long legs against the brightly lit backdrop. On her feet she wore satin slippers, rather like ballet pumps, trimmed with artificial primroses.

Looking at herself in the mirror, Daniella had been surprised to find that her final appearance reminded her of a bridesmaid – or even of the bride herself.

She sat up straighter in her seat as the stage lights came back on, heart suddenly thumping like mad, her mother's absence completely forgotten now. She had asked both her chaperones several times about Sarah, and their replies never varied. Not to worry, her mother would be around somewhere, they assured her with a smile, probably watching from a VIP booth at the back of the studio. And she would be so proud of her little girl, up there in front of millions of people. The main thing to remember, they emphasised, is that this is *your* moment, so go ahead and *enjoy* it.

Daniella jumped with shock as the introductory soundtrack of thudding drums and screeching guitars blasted out from the speakers. Rolling clouds of dry ice tumbled in from both sides of the stage. The platform in the centre began slowly to revolve. As the black staircase with its thousands of sparkling lights came into view, a squealing chorus of swooning lovesick cries shrilled through the auditorium.

Daniella's left wrist was in the tight grip of the young woman, her right in the big freckled hand of the clean-cut young man. He put his lips to her ear.

'Ready?'

Staring glassy-eyed at the stage, pupils dilated, breathing rapidly through flared nostrils, Daniella jerked her head up and then down again.

Palm trees were thrashing about in the wind whipping fiercely from the ocean. Some of their large green fronds had been torn off and sent whirling across the highway, and one of them plastered itself like a slimy sea creature against the passenger-side window of the Honda Civic. Cawdor had the wipers on fast speed, which was only just enough to give him adequate vision in the deluge of rain slanting in almost horizontally from right to left. A small bonus was that the atrocious conditions had cleared most of the traffic off I-95. The foolhardy few braving the storm had their headlights on full beam, white fingers of light poking through a dense wall of lashing rain and flying vegetation.

If a palm frond slapped itself across the windshield, Cawdor thought grimly, he wouldn't stand a chance. At this crazy reckless speed he'd be off the road in seconds. It was a dangerous gamble already, the tyres trying to maintain their traction through sheets of wind-whipped water and sending up plumes of spray in the car's wake.

He risked a glance away from the rushing highway to check the time on the dashboard clock. A minute or so after eight. The clerk at the car-rental desk, whom he'd asked for directions, had assured Cawdor he couldn't miss seeing the distinctive glass pyramid of Grace MediaCorp, even from a long distance. But there was no chance of that, not in this watery murk. On the map, the clerk had circled the location, five miles north of Fort Lauderdale, west of Oakland Park, so Cawdor knew he couldn't be too far off.

Body tensed up close to the wheel, he peered out and saw the sign for Hollywood Airport and route 84 connecting with US 1. By his own reckoning he was two exits away from the turn-off point.

Those were the longest five miles he had ever driven in his life. When the floodlit sign for Oakland Park finally appeared through the swishing wipers he thought it must be a mirage. He slowed and came off the interstate, and followed the long concrete flyover that took him back across the highway. A few minutes later he was driving beneath a huge Beamers symbol of anodised silver, gleaming through the downpour in a battery of spotlights. Reflecting green arrows pointed him to a large open parking lot. Two smaller parking lots were marked EMPLOYEES ONLY, while the larger one, apparently, was reserved for audience members attending the shows. A paved walkway with a flapping canvas awning on a metal frame led to an entrance, above which THE LOVEBEAMS SHOW glowed in red neon. At the end of the walkway, in an area crisscrossed with yellow markings, were thirty or more buses and luxury coaches. Most of the drivers were inside their vehicles, sheltering from the rain. A small group of drivers, who from their peaked caps and green blousons belonged to the same company, were huddled protectively under the canvas awning, smoking and drinking sodas.

Cawdor drove past the buses and parked the Civic in the first free space nearest the covered walkway. He switched off and sat gazing through the smeared windshield with a stupid look on his face, which was how he felt.

For the past several hours, right up to this moment, his entire concentration had been focused on getting here in time. His goal – the glass-walled building that now confronted him – had been the final destination, an end in itself. Only of course it wasn't. He was outside in the parking lot, not *inside* where he wanted to be. There was no doubt in Cawdor's mind that there would be guards posted. A large building such as this, permitting access to the public, couldn't risk not having a tight security cordon. Say he strolled up to the entrance without a valid pass, the guards would simply wave him away. Or worse – should they get suspicious about a guy trying to gate-crash the building – it might enter their heads to detain him, even lock him away somewhere pending further investigation. That was precious little help to anyone, and absolutely none at all to Sarah and Daniella.

Just how the hell was he going to get inside? Bluff his way in? Sure, Cawdor thought sourly, piece of cake. Nothing easier than to pass off his driver's licence as police ID or press accreditation or a visitor from Mars . . .

Minutes dragged by while he sat there at the wheel, a blank look on his face. There had to be a way. Somehow. Cawdor took out his wallet. As well as his credit cards he had 85 dollars in notes.

Maybe there was a way after all . . . Maybe the only way.

Negotiations didn't take too long. He was amazed, really, how little time they *did* take. The only concern the driver expressed as he pocketed the 85 dollars was getting his cap and blouson uniform top returned to him within the half-hour, when the buses were scheduled to depart. Cawdor said he'd be back in ten minutes, at the most fifteen – just as soon as he'd located the person he was looking for. Shirtsleeved arms wrapped tightly to his body, huddled in the group for protection against the gusting rain, the driver was pretty explicit: he didn't give a hoot about the reason, fella. The less he knew, the better. But be damn sure and get his cap and blouson back to him by departure time or the company would dock his pay.

As Cawdor stepped inside the glass-walled enclosure at the entrance, the peaked cap pulled down over his eyes, the blouson zipped up to hide his jacket, his brain was racing with a dozen scenarios. He was trusting to instinct, unsure even at this stage how he was going to handle it when the moment of truth arrived.

It was arriving right now – in the shape of three hulking great security guards manning the desk in the small lobby that led through to the building's central reception hall. One was seated behind a curved desk, shielded by a perspex barrier, a clipboard in front of him. The other two lounged in the background with hard, impassive faces that failed to hide their boredom. Any diversion was welcome, and all three paid attention as the bus driver hurried forward and stood there breathing heavily, clearly agitated, rainwater dripping off the peak of his cap.

'I've gotta find Mrs Gribble, her kid's throwing up in the bus. She's gotta come see to him this minute –'.

'Who?' the seated guard frowned. 'What's wrong? What's the problem?'

'There's this sick kid in my bus!' Cawdor burst out, jerking his thumb. 'Kid wasn't feeling too good earlier, so I said he could stay with me while his mother watched the show. But he's real bad now, burning up like a furnace.' He became indignant. 'And I'm not going to be held to blame. Not my fault.'

'What's the name again?'

'Mrs Gribble. Redhead, about thirty. Big woman.'

'She's here in the audience?'

'*Yes*,' Cawdor ground out.

'OK, calm down. I'll have her paged.' He pressed a button and swung a swivel mike over.

'Listen, ain't my responsibility if the kid croaks, understand me? I did my level best –'

'All *right*, I get the point,' the guard said testily. One of his colleagues leant over and tapped his watch. 'Right, yeah,' the guard said. He looked up. 'The show's about over,' he told Cawdor. 'All right, you can go through. Wait by the elevators – you'll see 'em come up.'

'Thanks.'

The magic eye activated the inner doors of smoked glass, which sighed open to admit Cawdor to the marble-floored hall, which was now filling rapidly with chattering, laughing people. He halted and stood watching numbly as more of them spilt out of the elevators, a knife twisting inside him. Whatever the dreadful thing was that had driven him compulsively to get here – it had happened. He was too late. He had ignored the premonition when the black suffocating wave had first swept over him on the sunlit terrace. Now the payoff. The price to be paid for being such a blind, stupid, ignorant fool.

With forlorn, diminishing hope, Cawdor scanned the faces for a sight of Sarah and Daniella, even while aware it was all in vain. And then, as he stood there, a kind of frenzy took possession of him. He pushed through the groups of people and made straight for the elevators in their column of glass and steel.

'You were splendid,' Messiah Wilde said to Daniella. 'And you looked absolutely wonderful up there. Don't you think so?' In his black silk robe, slippers of soft black leather on his bare feet, he reclined on the dark-red couch in his dressing room, a crystal glass of Jameson's Irish Whiskey in his hand. He smiled up at the two chaperones, and raised his dark eyebrows to elicit their agreement.

'Oh, she was great,' said the clean-cut young man, nodding vigorously. 'Terrific.'

Daniella sipped 7 Up through a straw and gave a modestly demure smile. Reflected several times over in the bright mirrors, her face was a ghostly luminous oval with glassy grey-blue eyes as big as saucers. She caught sight of her own image and it seemed to perplex her, as if she were looking at a stranger named Daniella Cawdor.

Messiah Wilde thanked the two chaperones for taking such good care of Daniella and dismissed them. As the door closed, he lazily rose to his feet and freshened his drink at the bar in the corner alcove. His long, narrow, silk-clad back was towards her, but he could see her face, wan and vacant, in the diamond-shaped mirrors behind the bottles.

'What's the matter, pretty pussy? Why so sad?'

Daniella made an effort and perked up, blinking. 'Uh, sorry . . . Just my head, it feels . . . kinda fuzzy. I guess it's the excitement and the audience and being on TV and everything . . .' Her voice tailed off to a whisper.

'Becoming the Chosen One a bit too much for you, eh?' He turned to her, grinning, swirling his drink so that the ice cubes clinked. 'Well, it's not over yet, pretty pussy.' He took a swallow and winked at her over the glass.

'But I thought . . . Isn't that it?' Daniella said.

'Certainly not, pretty pussy. Your big moment's yet to come. You really believe we went to all that time, trouble and expense for one lousy shot on TV?' Messiah Wilde was shaking his head. 'Oh no, pretty pussy, indeed not. We have a little extra something planned. Hell of a lot of fun, believe me. It'll kill you.'

'I don't know what you mean.'

'Of course you don't, pretty pussy. It's a surprise.'

'Will my mom be there? I want to see her.'

'Well, now.' Messiah Wilde appeared to be considering this, eyes thoughtful as he gazed off into space. 'She might, and then again she might not. But – the more I think about it – not.' He shrugged, and gave her a look of commiseration.

'Can I see her . . . please?'

'Haven't I just told you, pretty pussy slut bitch tart? The answer is no. N. O. *Nein*. Nix.'

Daniella drew herself in, her legs twined together under the chair. Her face wore a puzzled, cloudy expression. 'What are you saying? Why did you call me those names?'

'Don't get upset. No harm done. No bones broken.' When he saw huge tears welling in her eyes, Messiah Wilde said with a pained sigh, 'Can't you take a joke? Don't you have a sense of humour? Don't you know I'm teasing you? Can't you tell, pretty pussy virgin cunt?'

Daniella shuddered, as if something clammy and malignant had crawled over her skin. She tried to get up out of the chair, to stand on her feet, but even this small effort, it seemed, was too much.

Messiah Wilde finished his drink and put the glass down on the bar-top. 'Nearly time to go. You ready, sweet tits?' He loosened the belt on his robe and opened it down the front. Daniella turned her head sharply away from the pale body and its thick patch of pubic hair. She forced her eyes tight shut. Tears spilt out and ran through the make-up that covered her cheeks.

Messiah Wilde slipped out of the black silk robe and tossed it on to an armchair on his way to a wall-length closet. He took out another sheer silk robe, this time a white one, with a hood, and pulled the shroudlike garment over his head with the hood hanging down at the back. He turned, the robe whispering against his skin, and said to the girl sitting there with eyes clenched shut, 'But it's a fact, and I won't deny it, pretty pussy. Your mom's a gorgeous juicy fuck. Tell you the truth, I came like an express train. And did she take it? Every last drop. What a woman!'

Daniella bent forward and covered her ears. She was trembling from head to foot. The bodice of her dress vibrated with the pounding of her heart.

Smoothing down his robe and arranging the folds in the wide voluminous sleeves, under his breath Messiah Wilde was humming, 'We're off to see the wizard, the wonderful wizard of Oz.'

Then he turned to her, shaking his head. 'Come on, pretty pussy, don't be such a wet blanket.'

Next to the alcove bar in the corner there was a wall of dark-grained wood. He slid open a panel. Behind it was a small cubicle, his own private elevator, its interior of studded black leather gleaming in the soft glow of concealed lighting. When he turned back, face lean and stern, dull sparks of red kindled in the dark depths of Messiah Wilde's eyes. 'Ready, baby doll? The party's about to begin.'

4

The elevator took him down five levels and slid smoothly to a halt. The indicator on the illuminated panel read STUDIO. Outside the elevator doors Cawdor dithered, trying to make up his mind. Identical corridors branched off the hallway. The audience had gone, and the hallway was empty except for two people dressed all in white – a tanned blonde girl and beefy young man – who stepped past him into the elevator as he was coming out.

There were no signs to guide him. Choosing at random, Cawdor set off down one of the featureless corridors. At a T-junction it divided into two more corridors, as anonymous as the first one, and Cawdor became alarmed, fearing he was heading in the wrong direction. Or simply getting lost. He took the one to the left, again at random, and forged ahead, heart hammering, the filtered air making the back of his throat dry. The corridor ended in a pair of swing doors. He pushed through. Several large observation panels were set in the wall. Beyond them, to his relief, was the dark cavern of the studio, a quiet bustle of activity under the dimmed stagelights.

Cawdor took off the peaked cap and wiped his forehead. He hoped to God he'd guessed right. Because, if his wife and daughter weren't around here someplace, he wouldn't know where else to start looking.

The camera and sound operators were packing away their equipment, the technical crew winding up cables. High above, shadowy figures on the lighting gantry flitted about like spiders. All were too preoccupied to notice Cawdor as he came down the metal stairway into the auditorium and made his way on to the side of the stage. Behind and either side of the stage was where the scenery flats, turntables and props were stored. Here there were signs aplenty – BAY 4, SCENE DOCK A, SWITCH TERMINAL, VTR CONTROL, F/X FACILITY – but they served only to confuse rather than enlighten him.

The backstage area was starkly functional: caged globes on bare grey walls, matt composition floors, a maze of low-roofed corridors extending into the depths of the sub-basement. Slowly, Cawdor turned and stared about him, looking one way and then the other, fists clenched at his sides.

This was pretty damn hopeless. He wasn't lost, because to be lost you had to have some idea where you were going; know what you were actually seeking. His frustration was compounded by the fact that he didn't know either of these things. The same inner compulsion drove him on this quest that had made him rush headlong from the Troth Foundation. It had no logic to it, obeyed no rules of rational behaviour. There was no reason he could articulate to explain this desperate mission, none at all, except for the panic fear and the sense of foreboding that consumed him like a fever.

He had to find Sarah and Daniella. That was all he knew.

Sarah had been a guest on the show, so she must have come backstage afterward, and Daniella with her, presumably. Back to where – the hospitality suite? A dressing room? Or, it occurred to him, had they been taken elsewhere in the building? God alone knew how many floors there were in this vast pyramid of glass. He could search and search and never find them. Cawdor's hopelessness grew like a monster until he felt lost in its shadow, engulfed by his own despair.

307

Sweat trickled down from the tight headband of the cap. He was perspiring heavily but daren't risk unzipping the blouson in case he ran into the security people. He had to have some cock-and-bull story to fob them off with, no matter how implausible.

Again he chose a corridor at random, because it was the only choice he had. Two of the technical staff in brown coveralls walked by, skeins of wiring looped round their shoulders. They didn't spare him a glance. Cawdor quickened his pace. He arrived at an intersection, with more signs and arrows pointing in all directions, none of which were any help. He turned left, for no good reason. Any reason was as good as the next, which was none at all.

At the next corner, forgetting caution completely, he'd taken two or three paces into the corridor and was striding on before he caught sight of uniformed figures loitering about twenty feet away. Cawdor ducked back swiftly from view. He removed the cap, swabbed his forehead with the heel of his hand, and peeked out. The two guards hadn't spotted him; they were still whiling away the time, he saw. He saw something else. A few feet beyond them lay a strip of red carpet with gold edging. Cawdor followed it with his eyes from the four-way intersection to the end of a short corridor and a set of double doors. There was a sign on the wall, adjacent to where the guards were standing. He leant further out and squinted, trying to read it, but his angle of vision was wrong and it was too far away. One of the guards stretched and swivelled round on his hips, and Cawdor whipped back out of sight.

Pressed against the wall, he waited for a shout or the sound of running footsteps. None came. But the breath was still locked tight in his chest, his body tense. Cawdor knew he'd found the clue he was looking for. Red carpet meant celebrities; it was not for the comfort of security guards or for backstage blue-collars to trample over.

Cawdor looked at his watch and waited, fretting as the seconds ticked by. Nothing else he could do. Whatever tale he might concoct, however plausible, he was damn sure the guards would never let him through. They were far more likely – absolutely deadly certain, in fact – to escort him back up to the reception hall and march him outside double quick.

He looked at his watch again. Another eternal minute dragged by. If this was their allotted station, guarding the short corridor leading to the double doors, then they were never going to move, Cawdor realised. And he could be standing here all night, enduring the agony of endless waiting.

Was there another way in? Suppose he went back the way he had come and tried a different –

From along the corridor came the squawk and crackle of a radio transceiver. Cawdor pressed close to the corner and strained to listen as one of the guards unhooked it from his belt and thumbed a button. 'Say again.' Impossible to make sense of the reply. The bare corridor distorted the tinny voice, which was already blurred by static, so that it sounded like an alien in a blizzard.

'Yeah, unauthorised person. Got that. Male or female?' the guard asked. 'Bus driver? Last sighted where, what level?' He listened some more to the alien. 'OK, we'll check out the elevators first on level five, then work from there.'

Cawdor peeked out with one eye, stomach tensed, ready to retreat should they head this way. The corridors, empty and featureless, afforded no hiding place: avoiding detection would mean running like a bat out of hell. To his relief the guards took a different direction, and he heard their footsteps fading away down the echoing corridor.

Moving with swift silent strides, he reached the sign that read PERFORMERS AND GUESTS: GOLD PERMIT ACCESS ONLY, and kept on going along the short corridor, the red carpet underfoot.

He tested the doorknob, half-expecting it to be locked, then turned it fully when he met no resistance. There was a click, and one half of the double doors opened. Cawdor stepped through, softly closed the door behind him, and turned to find himself in a carpeted corridor with subdued lighting and silver-framed prints of celebrities on the dark-green walls. Several doors opened off it.

'Come on, don't be difficult, sweets. There's nothing to fear.'

Cawdor froze at the sound of Wilde's voice, huskily cajoling yet underlaid with chill menace. This was the third door Cawdor had tried. Now he stood listening, his ear pressed close to the edge of the door, which was open the merest crack. From inside came rapid panting breaths and a subdued whimper.

Moving swiftly and without a sound, Cawdor opened the door, entered a small hallway, passed the open door of a bathroom, and came into the main suite, where he faltered in mid-stride.

It was very odd, because for an instant he didn't recognise either of the two figures. Not the apparition in the white robe, nor the young girl with flowers in her braided hair, her face a ghostly white mask with fogged eyes leaking huge tears.

Holding her by the arm, Messiah Wilde was half-coaxing, half-dragging Daniella towards the elevator. She looked dazed, her movements sluggish, trying to resist with what little strength remained in her watery limbs. Messiah Wilde's arm encircled her shoulders, his mouth whispering in her ear. Cawdor fought the urge to cry out. His swift and silent appearance had gone unnoticed; for a few vital moments he had the advantage of surprise.

Messiah Wilde murmured, 'Your mom will be so proud of you. It's a great honour to have been chosen –'

A knotted fist struck the side of Messiah Wilde's head with such force that he reeled over and went skidding on his back, legs in the air, and crashed into the bar, the white robe billowing around him. Crystal decanters on a silver tray toppled over and smashed, showering him in a pungent cocktail of bourbon, vodka, brandy and gin. Messiah Wilde blinked the stinging mixture from his eyes and shook his head to clear it. He reached up to grip the edge of the bar counter.

Cawdor was too preoccupied with his daughter; she was all that mattered to him.

'Daniella! Daniella, look at me!'

But he realised that she didn't recognise him: in her befuddled confusion she was seeing only a strange man in a peaked cap and a dark-green blouson with TRANS-STATE TRAVEL SERVICE stitched into the black epaulettes.

She backed away, hands raised defensively in front of her.

'Daniella . . . Daniella!' Cawdor stretched out his hand. 'Don't be afraid. Everything's OK. He won't hurt you, I promise. You're safe with me now.'

Her dulled eyes searched his face as the words seeped into her brain. Very slowly and wearily her eyelids closed. Daniella opened them again until she was wide-eyed and staring. In their depths, Cawdor saw reality rekindled: he saw his daughter emerging from the nightmare.

'Dad . . .?' she mouthed faintly, astonished. 'How did you find me? How did you . . . Oh, Dad!'

Daniella fell forward and collapsed into his arms.

'How charming. Family values aren't dead. Loving Pop to the rescue.'

Messiah Wilde was leaning his back against the bar, supported on one elbow, a litter of broken crystal at his feet. His left cheekbone was obliterated by an inflamed swelling. 'Like the get-up, Pops.' His hand moved stealthily across the bar counter towards the alarm button set two inches below the inner rim. 'Let me guess, you entered a Marlon Brando lookalike contest and came third.'

'Where's my wife?'

'I wouldn't know. Not here.' Messiah Wilde shrugged, looking around the dressing room. 'If that isn't stating the obvious.'

His fingers crept over the edge of the bar counter.

'I think you do know.'

'Well, I might,' Messiah Wilde admitted. 'But whether I'm going to tell you, Pops, is another kettle of fish entirely.

311

Now, if you'd had the grace to ask politely in the first place . . .'

Cawdor laid his daughter down in an armchair. He picked up the silver tray from where it had rolled to and brought the rim of it down on Messiah Wilde's reaching arm, breaking a number of the small bones in his wrist and nearly severing the main artery. Blood splashed over the white robe. Cawdor batted the silver tray into Messiah Wilde's face as if he were swatting a fly, and there was a melodic *boyyyyong* followed by the dry crackling crunch of bone and gristle as his nose was squashed flat. He slid down, legs splayed among the broken crystal, a star-shaped spatter of blood emanating from the red splodge in the centre of his face, his limp and ragged-edged wrist bent at an odd angle. Cawdor tossed the silver tray aside, knelt down and lifted Messiah Wilde's head by its long black hair and wrapped his fingers round the pale throat. Specks of blood and tissue were flying from the flattened nostrils with each snorting breath. He was choking and gurgling on his own blood.

'Tell me where she is,' Cawdor said, 'or ten seconds from now I'm going to kill you.' He pressed his thumb against the jerking windpipe. 'Feel that? It's the last thing you'll ever feel. *Where is she?*'

But when Cawdor shook him by the hair his eyes rolled crazily and stared emptily at the ceiling before his eyelids drooped shut. There seemed no point in strangling somebody who was semiconscious and already choking to death.

Cawdor wiped his spattered hands on Messiah Wilde's robe. There were spots of blood all over the front of the blouson, as well as the strong whiff of spirits. He pulled his daughter to her feet, and with his help she was able to walk to the elevator. Daniella slumped groggily on the leather-bound bench seat while he closed the inner gate. He turned to the panel, and then stared in dismay – there was no button marked FIRST FLOOR or GROUND FLOOR. He traced his finger from the top floor – 29 – downward, and then from the lowest sub-basement level – marked with a T – upward. They met at a button marked P, and

Cawdor pressed it, hoping to God it was the right one, and wondering what the hell P might stand for. Parking? Private?

The elevator rose rapidly and whined to a halt. He opened the gate, looped his arm round Daniella's waist, and half-carried her into a short passageway that had a steel door at the end, reinforced with bars of solid brass. Should it lead into the reception hall, or to any other public place, he had some fast talking to do. The cap and blouson came off: they were a positive danger to him now that security was on the lookout for a bus driver. He straightened his tie and smoothed the creases in his jacket. He was presentable enough, Cawdor reckoned, and should have no problem mingling unnoticed in the crowd; that's if there *was* a crowd, and the audience hadn't boarded the buses. One more problem remained, however.

'You OK to walk?' He couldn't risk carrying her: they would be spotted at once. 'You have to walk on your own. Can you do it?'

Daniella raised her head. She looked deathly tired, dark rings under her eyes. 'Hold my hand, Dad, and I'll walk,' Daniella said.

'Sure, honey.' Cawdor hugged his daughter. 'The two of us are gonna walk straight out of here, not a thing to worry about.' He held her hand, which was icy cold with shock, in his. 'Ready? We're on our way, Tonto.'

Daniella nodded. 'OK, Kimo Sabe.'

She was coming back to him. Cawdor could have wept.

Instead, he opened the door.

There was nothing there. Total blackness. Were they still underground? What did 'P' stand for – the pit?

He went forward, holding her hand, the other out-stretched into nothingness. The air felt different – warmer, clammier. Something rattled above his head. Cawdor looked up, startled, and in that moment lightning forked through the sky in a split-second flash that imprinted everything on his eye like a photograph. They were inside a perspex tunnel. The rattling sound was the drumming of rain on the rounded plastic overhead, drowned a moment later by the rolling boom of thunder. Through the rain-smeared plastic walls he saw the darkened bulk of the glass pyramid rising behind them. They were outside. Messiah Wilde's private elevator led to this perspex tunnel that led directly out of the building.

Cool fresh rain hit them, driving hard into their faces, and rain had never felt so good. They ran together, hand in hand, soaked through in less than ten yards, towards the floodlit glow of the public parking lot, visible above a row of thorn bushes and young palms being lashed by the fierce wind. They came upon a chain-link fence, no more than five feet high, and once over that were in the parking lot itself. A few buses were still loading, lined up to take the last of the passengers sheltering beneath the covered walkway.

Most of the cars had gone. The Honda Civic stood on the expanse of rain-swept asphalt. Gasping for breath, soaked to the skin, father and daughter climbed inside.

5

It had torn him apart, driving off into the night knowing that Sarah was still somewhere inside, perhaps held against her will, but the compulsion to get Daniella away from that hateful place overwhelmed all else. Maybe when she was at a safe distance, and secure (a motel?) he could get his thoughts in order and formulate some sort of plan. For now, heading towards the coast for no other reason than that was where the road went to, his mind was in a ferment of such virulent and poisonous rage that he felt almost demented.

In the grip of it, Cawdor didn't notice for a dozen miles or so that Daniella was huddled and shivering in the seat beside him, chilled by the cold night air. He turned on the heater and held her hand for warmth and comfort. He could hardly bear to look at the primped and prettified effigy they had made of his daughter, even though the rain had washed away most of the white make-up and flattened

314

her hair to a sodden cap, tangled strands sticking to her shoulders. A limp petal or two were all that was left of the crown of primroses.

He squeezed her hand. 'Don't worry about your mom, Daniella. I'll get her out of there.' His tone was assured, defiant, but he thought it wise not to add that he hadn't the faintest notion how. But he would do it, by Christ he would. 'First we'll find you a place to stay, and then –'

'I don't think she's in there.'

Now Cawdor did look at her, tearing his eyes away from the rain sweeping towards them through the headlights. 'But weren't you together? Both of you appeared on the show, didn't you?'

'No. It was just me. I haven't seen her since . . .' Daniella struggled to reconstruct the past 24 hours. 'She was with me last night, at a party after the show. Then . . . I think . . .'

'What?'

'I . . . I'm all mixed up.' Her face was creased with the effort of trying to make coherent sense of her befuddled memories. 'Last night I stayed at his house, near the ocean –'

'*His* house,' Cawdor said, staring into the driving rain. He should have finished the bastard when he had the chance. 'You stayed at Messiah Wilde's house?'

'Yes. I didn't see her, but I think Mom stayed there, too. That's right, that's right.' Daniella leant forward, nodding rapidly. 'He invited us both to stay at his home; that's right, he did. The rest is kinda hazy and . . . all I remember is waking up in this bedroom with a view of the ocean. And there was a servant – small, brown, Asian I think – he came in and told me to get ready. I had to leave right away.'

'You didn't see Sarah before you left.'

'No.'

Cawdor wiped first one sweaty palm on the seat cover, and then the other. He said quietly, 'Where's the house, Daniella? You remember?'

'It was . . . it was . . .'

Cawdor bit into his lower lip to stop himself urging her to remember, because he could tell she was already straining as hard as she knew how. He waited in an agony of imposed silence, the passage of time marked by the beating wipers.

'It was in Palm Beach.'

'Palm Beach,' Cawdor repeated. There was a sign up ahead. I-95. The coastal highway stretched the entire length of Florida's eastern seaboard, from Miami in the south to Jacksonville in the north, and then on into Georgia. Along that route, thirty miles north of here, was Palm Beach.

It was so sudden that Cawdor couldn't believe the evidence of his own eyes.

One minute the car was enveloped in a raincloud, the headlights feebly attempting to probe the dense murk, and quite literally one minute later the visibility had cleared so that he could see stars in a clear sky, the headlights picking out just a few damp patches on the road ahead. The edge of the storm's footprint lay directly east to west, almost exactly midway between Fort Lauderdale and Palm Beach. Unused to the bizarre, capricious nature of tropical storms, it seemed to Cawdor that the heavens must be playing tricks at his expense.

Maybe though, this once, he thought with rising hope, in his favour. Daniella's recollection of where Messiah Wilde's house was located, except for the fact that it fronted the ocean, was vague: trying to find it in a raging storm would have stacked the odds against them, whereas in this suddenly calm and clear evening there was at least a sporting chance.

'Any of this familiar to you?' he asked her as they drove down the main thoroughfare, past the large tourist hotels with their white stucco façades. On the opposite side of the street, away from the ocean, people were sitting outside cafes and bars, enjoying the balmy breeze rustling the fronds of the tall palm trees. As he expected of Palm Beach, they were a fashionably dressed, well-heeled crowd, and the Porche 911 Turbos, Camaros and Dodge Vipers in the parking lots confirmed their wealth and status.

'I don't think so,' Daniella said, staring out miserably. 'I just remember these big houses with lawns out front, set wide apart. Some of them had high walls and gates.'

'Does this house have walls and gates?'

Daniella bit her lip, struggling to remember. 'It had a wall . . . but not very high, with bushes planted along the top. The wall was sort of dark grey and shiny and . . . yes, smooth. Like the rocks had been cut and polished and fitted together like a jigsaw.'

A granite wall with bushes growing on top, Cawdor thought in despair. He might spend a whole week scouring Palm Beach and never find such a place. Here were million-dollar homes on every block. And time, above all else, was the crucial factor. Messiah Wilde might have recovered by now and alerted his security people. If Sarah *was* being held at Wilde's house, surely his first act would be to warn whoever was holding her there.

Cawdor knew he couldn't waste even a few hours on a futile search.

He had to find Sarah *now*.

He drove slowly along a curving road that had wind-blown sand heaped in the gutters. To his left were four-storey condominiums with balconies and wrought-iron railings; to his right large and impressive houses whose rear aspects overlooked the beach. Although the road was well lit, the globes on their slender steel posts gave everything a bland appearance, washing out all colour. It was possible to tell if the walls surrounding some of these properties were light or dark, but not much else.

Every now and then he glanced at Daniella, desperately wishing that something might register, waiting for her to leap up and point out a landmark or a feature that had been forgotten until she set eyes on it again. He waited for it to happen, growing more anxious with each passing moment, but it didn't.

The road reached the crest of a small rise and curved

downhill, loosely following the contour of the shoreline. There it intersected with a busier, four-lane highway that Cawdor guessed was possibly US 1.

He pulled away from the STOP sign, crossed the highway, and drove into a Texaco station. He didn't enter the gas lane, but parked near the window of the building where he could keep watch on the car, determined not to lose sight of his daughter for even a single second.

Inside the brightly lit store area he asked the cash clerk, a plump, grey-haired matronly woman seated behind a screen of toughened glass, if he might look at the phone book. There was a problem. The phone book was too fat to slide underneath the cash slot. Cawdor indicated the door at her side. 'Can you pass it through?'

'Not allowed to open it, sorry.'

'So how do your customers get to find a number?'

The matronly woman shrugged. 'I can see that's not much help, but . . .'

'It's no help at all,' Cawdor said acidly. He saw her bridle, and said, 'Please, this is very important –'

'I don't make the rules. Take it up with the company.'

'OK, yes, you're right. Look, I'm sorry I snapped at you. I need the address of someone. This is very important to me. Will you please check it for me? Please.'

'Least you had the decency to apologise,' she sniffed. 'After all, it ain't my fault. What name?'

'Wilde,' Cawdor said, and spelt it so that she understood there was an 'e' at the end. The chances that he was in the phone book were slim to nonexistent, but Cawdor clung to the remnant of this slender hope because he was hanging on by his fingernails to nothing else.

There were nearly two full pages of Wildes, three columns per page. The woman looked up at him. 'Do you have a first name or initial?'

Even if he was in the book, he wouldn't be listed under the self-deluding stage name of 'Messiah'. But he had no other name that Cawdor knew of. 'Look under "M".'

The woman's blood-red fingernail traced down the column. ' "M" for what? Looky here, you got all these –'

she angled the phone book for him to see '– must be thirty, forty or more.'

Cawdor stared at them through the glass screen until they blurred in front of his eyes. He said numbly, 'I don't know. I'm not sure it's actually "M".'

The woman made a resigned clucking sound. 'Well, there you go. Can't help you, I'm afraid.' She looked round, as if someone might be lurking behind her, and tore out the page. She folded it and pushed it through the slot. 'Best I can do.'

Cawdor unfolded the page. Checking out nearly forty addresses in a town he didn't know . . . impossible. He said, 'Thanks for your help. I don't know this person's full name because he's a TV celebrity. More than likely it's a fake name anyway.'

'Oh my, you fall over celebrities in Palm Beach every day of the week! Dolly Parton has a place here, Sharon Stone, and that country singer guy, er – yeah, Glen Campbell. Ex-president Ford. Bob Hope has a home here,' she said, and then frowned into space. 'Or he used to have.'

'Messiah Wilde?' Cawdor said.

The woman widened her eyes. 'Oh, *that* Wilde. Is he the one you're looking for? Yes, he lives in Palm Beach. Gotta house up on Rowen Oak Drive.' She plucked a gratis Texaco street map from a metal tray and after studying it for all of three seconds circled a beach-front area in ballpoint. She pushed it through the slot.

'Five minutes from here, north off US 1.'

She sat back in her chair after he'd gone, staring at the smudge of fading condensation on the glass screen where he'd planted a kiss as a token to her.

There were four houses on Rowen Oak Drive. The second one Cawdor came to had a four-foot-high wall of granite slabs topped by a neatly trimmed hedge. It was an effective barrier, permitting a view from the pavement that was limited to one end of the steeply gabled roof. Pencil beams of light shone through tiny chinks in the hedge, so he knew the garden was floodlit. But that didn't matter.

What did matter was that he had identified the house. He walked back to where he had parked the car. Daniella wound the window down.

'You still OK?' Daniella nodded. 'I've found it,' Cawdor said. 'I won't be gone very long. Keep the door locked and the window shut. If Sarah's still in there, I'll bring her out. If she isn't,' he went on, knowing he shouldn't be saying this, but saying it anyway, 'I'll burn the place down.'

He squeezed her hand, watched her wind up the window, and then went back across the road and walked in the opposite direction, away from the house. Driving up he had seen the wooden sign that said JETTY in the headlights. It pointed to a sandy track that ran adjacent to the perimeter fence of the first house and led down to the beach. There was barely a ripple on the ocean. In the pallid light of a crescent moon he saw the white fringes of tiny waves as they flopped tiredly on the hard sand. A couple stood arm in arm on the wooden jetty, looking into the far distance, where flickers of lightning appeared through a huge dark mass of thundercloud. Other solitary figures strolled along the waterline, the dark leaping shapes of dogs endlessly circling them.

The wooden fence of the first house extended along the beach, and the boundary of Messiah Wilde's property was marked by a palisade of anodised steel posts, their tops sheared off to form points. There was a gate of metal mesh, chained and padlocked. Cawdor moved further along until he could see the house through a gap in a row of juniper bushes and flowering shrubs. The upper floor was in darkness, but lights were burning downstairs. He could make out a brick patio by the splash of light that fell on it from sliding doors of glass, and he saw a shape moving within, though male or female he couldn't tell.

The fence was a real ball-breaker. If he attempted to scale it he'd rip his hands to shreds; or worse, impale himself on the vicious spikes. He looked up and down the beach, as if the empty expanse of sand might offer up an answer. Failing that, he needed divine inspiration. He turned round in a complete circle and looked back towards the jetty. The couple had gone. Cawdor stared at the black outline jutting out into the lapping waves and then he started to run. He had already seen what he needed when he came on to the beach – just too slow and too dumb to have realised it.

Laid end to end on the sand, frames of slatted timber provided a walkway from beach to jetty. The separate frames weren't even joined together or fastened to the ground. He heaved one of them to an upright position and lugged it up the beach, staggering under its weight. Using the slatted treads as rungs, he climbed up the fence, and with a final leap cleared the row of spikes and landed in the soft sandy earth.

The row of bushes afforded cover until he was thirty feet from the house. Beyond them was the lawn, sloping up to the brick-paved patio and illuminated by two large floodlights on metal tripods at either side of the garden. Cawdor began a close scrutiny of each of the many windows before he decided it was a pointless waste of time. Whether or not he was being observed didn't alter the fact that he had to reach the house. Waiting for the right moment made no sense at all. Once he had figured that out, everything became simple. He rose from his crouching position and ran swiftly and silently over the grass, aiming instinctively for an area of blank wall between a darkened window and the sliding glass doors where he had glimpsed someone moving. The brick was warm to the touch, radiating the stored heat of the sun. His face pressed close to the wall, Cawdor edged sideways and peered into the room. It was a bedroom done out in a colour scheme of black and red, he saw, with table lamps casting pools of light, and Sarah was sitting on the end of the bed wearing a lightweight grey sweater, bluejeans and low-heeled suede pumps that matched the sweater.

She didn't notice when he stepped into view. She sat hunched and still, pale to the lips and with a dull glaze over her eyes. Cawdor tapped his fingernails on the glass. When she did see him Sarah lurched to her feet, but there was something the matter with her legs, because she took only a couple of paces before stumbling and falling on all fours. She stayed there, looking up at him with dulled, exhausted eyes. Cawdor inspected the edge of the aluminium frame for an external catch or handgrip; there was neither, and had there been it would have made no difference. The sliding doors were secured by six key-operated brass bolts, he now saw, one in each corner and two in the centre. The triple-density safety glass, of the type used for department-store windows, was as solid and unyielding as steel plate. It would take a battering ram to break through it.

Cawdor tipped over a large, round earthenware tub and wrenched out the roots of the flowering shrub growing in it. He scooped out most of the earth and rolled the tub across the patio. Inside the bedroom, Sarah was kneeling by the bed, a safe distance from flying glass. Cawdor gripped the tub at the rim and the base and strained to lift it. He got it as high as chest level, nearly toppling forward under the stupendous weight, and with a last grunting heave raised it above his head. With the stiff-legged gait of a robot he managed three halting steps and thrust the tub with all his strength at the sliding doors. The glass resounded with the deep bass boom of a gong; the tub bounced off; and the doors shivered and reverberated like the buzzing of a thousand angry bees, not even cracked.

Again Cawdor took hold of the tub by the rim and base. But he knew at once from the trembling in his arms that his first mighty effort had taken too much out of him. He hardly had suffcent strength to raise it off the floor. Instead he rolled the tub to the edge of the brick patio, lined it up, and set it rolling with a kick start, then speeded up the trundling momentum by pushing with both hands. The door vibrated under the impact, and this time the glass gave off a false note, more like the dead clunk of a lead bell. There was an explosive retort as loud as a pistol shot, and a crack appeared from top to bottom.

All it took then was a single kick, delivered with the heel of his shoe: the sheet of plate glass split down the middle, caved inward and crashed into the room, huge jagged shards tumbling over the carpet.

Cawdor dived through the gap. It was only then that he saw the man standing in the doorway. He was small and swarthy, with jet-black hair, wearing a white jacket, and he was holding a gun. There wasn't time for Cawdor to react. But from somewhere, fuelled by a surge of anger, Sarah found the strength to react for him. From her kneeling position she reached out for a shard of glass and in the same movement sent it skimming like a deadly dagger across the room. The servant swayed back and vanished behind the door. If he hadn't, the shard of glass would have buried itself in his forehead instead of in the door. He cautiously reappeared, his dark eyes fearful, and got a fist in the teeth. The blow sent him sprawling back into the hallway. Cawdor stamped down with his heel on the man's wrist. The servant let out a howl, and the gun skittered across the carpet. Cawdor kicked him in the side of the head to emphasise the point, stepped over him and picked up the gun. He was unfamiliar with guns of any description, but he knew enough to aim one and pull the trigger.

The servant lay on his side in a foetal crouch, both hands pressed to his head. He was moaning and jabbering something that sounded like a plea for mercy. Cawdor wasn't in the right frame of mind to listen. Grabbing a fistful of white linen jacket, he pulled the small man to his feet and jabbed the gun barrel hard into the hollow at the nape of the skinny neck.

'Anyone else in the house with you?'

The servant shook his head, rolling the whites of his eyes up at Cawdor.

'I didn't hear you.'

'No, sir,' the servant croaked through bloody lips. A fragment of tooth was stuck to his pointed chin.

Cawdor pushed the door fully open with the toe of his shoe. Sarah was on her feet, but only just. She was trying to say something in a slurred drunken voice, her eyes welling with tears.

'It's OK, it's OK,' Cawdor said. 'Don't try to talk.' But she carried on, and watching her lips he realised the name she was struggling to form. 'Daniella is all right,' he said. 'She's outside in the car, waiting for us.' With an effort he forced himself to smile, in order to encourage her, and Sarah's faltering and feeble attempt to return it broke his heart.

It was obvious to Cawdor that she couldn't walk unaided. The gun jammed against his spine, the servant was more than willing to assist her, and with Cawdor supporting Sarah's other arm the three of them moved through the house to the front door. Cawdor opened it and then stiffened, hearing the approaching wail of a siren. Had smashing the window triggered off an alarm at the local precinct? He stood tensely, listening as the siren swelled and then faded away down US 1.

'Where's the control for the gates?'

The servant pointed to a varnished wooden cabinet on the wall.

'Open them,' Cawdor said. He raised the gun at arm's length and touched the man's glistening forehead, a fraction below the widow's peak of black hair. 'And don't be tempted to press anything else. Just the gates, understand me?'

He stood close behind as the servant opened the cabinet door and flicked a toggle switch. Through the still evening air came the faint whine of hydraulics. The small man took up his burden once more. They went down the driveway and along the road to where the Honda Civic was parked. Daniella saw them coming. She jumped out and helped her mother walk the final few yards. They were both weeping and hugging one another as Cawdor opened the rear door for them to climb in.

The servant backed away, sucking his torn lip and nervously rubbing his thin brown hands. The fear of imminent death was in his darting brown eyes. Cawdor went round the car to get to the driver's side, walking right by him as if he didn't exist. He started the car, turned on the lights, manoeuvred the car through a three-point turn and drove off, leaving the man standing there with an expression of slack and incredulous relief.

Cawdor came out of Rowen Oak Drive and eased into the flow of traffic heading north on US 1. His hand was sticking to the wheel, and he now noticed blood oozing from a gash where his hand must have snagged against the splintered edge of the glass door. The cuff of his jacket and the sleeve of his shirt were sodden with it. He bound the wound in his handkerchief, tied a clumsy knot, and pulled it tight with his teeth.

Just south of Melbourne – 85 miles further on and an hour and a half later – he picked up the interstate again. It was pretty quiet at this late hour, ideal for making good time with no hold-ups. Cawdor had got the idea fixed in his head, as if there was no remotely feasible alternative, that he was going to drive nonstop all the way back to Franklin, New Jersey.

Of course this was out of the question. A thousand miles or more without sleep or food just wasn't feasible. But it wasn't until they were approaching Daytona Beach at ten minutes to one in the morning that reality set in, and the impracticality of what he was attempting finally struck home. Cawdor was well aware what drove this manic compulsion. It was the overriding desire to get Sarah and Daniella as far away as possible from the Beamers and Messiah Wilde and Grace MediaCorp and everything connected with them. As if the mere act of putting distance between them was of itself a cleansing, healing process. Every mile a gradual withdrawal from their clutches; every route marker a wrenching free from that dark aura of evil.

It had been occupying his mind for several minutes before Cawdor realised he was dwelling on revenge. Not revenge for its own sake, of the 'eye for an eye' variety: this organisation had to be exposed, and the pernicious influence it was peddling stopped dead in its tracks. His motive wasn't purely personal. Through their global communications empire the Messengers were spreading the gospel of their creed to millions. They were infiltrating young minds and making converts not only in America but the world over. To the outsider, perhaps, they seemed harmless enough: a media corporation with its own satellite channels and spin-off interests in publishing, music recording and the Internet. And there, Cawdor recognised, was the crux of the problem – convincing a government agency, or someone in the media, that what lay behind Grace MediaCorp and the respectable corporate front it presented to the world at large was nothing less than a ruthless quasi-religious movement whose aim was mass enslavement to a corrupt ideology. Who would believe such a fantastic claim? How and where could he even begin to make himself heard?

And then, out of the blue, Cawdor thought of a way.

A starting point, at least – someone with power and influence in the higher reaches of government.

He was thinking of a Republican senator named Cobb who was related by marriage to Don Carlson. Senator Cobb was a high-profile politician, regularly on TV and in the newspapers, and though Cawdor had never met him he knew that his partner and the senator sometimes attended family gatherings and got along well together. With Cobb on their side, it was a better start than Cawdor could have dreamt of.

With his mind now a little calmer, and clearer, he realised there was no need for this headlong flight through the night. He pulled off I-95 at Daytona Beach and followed the directions of the first sign he came upon, which happened to be for the Best Western Americano Beach. Ten minutes later he pulled into the forecourt of the white-stucco, five-storey hotel overlooking the ocean.

Cawdor switched everything off and eased back, trying to release the tension in his neck and shoulders. After a moment he turned in his seat to look at his wife and daughter. They were wrapped in each other's arms, which was how they had ridden since leaving Palm Beach. Sarah leant forward and touched his cheek. She brought his face

closer and kissed him. Cawdor had no deep and meaning-
ful words to say, because none existed that were adequate,
so he simply smiled at her in the darkened car.

'Do you know how this feels?' Sarah asked him, speaking slowly, the sentence dragged out. Cawdor plainly didn't.
Sarah said, 'It's like coming back into the light after a long,
dark journey.'

Cawdor sighed and smiled. He was very, very happy.

All of a sudden Kersh is getting bad vibes. He can't sleep.
He can't eat. He's even stopped screwing Sue Ellen, which
is a very big sign that something is going wrong. And he has
a real nasty feeling it's up to him to put it right.

Damnit, he's kept to his side of the deal! Given the
Messengers everything they wanted – created his vision of
the perfect world – and they've gone and made a hash of
things. So what now? They expect him to fix it, sort the
mess out alone?

Well, not quite alone. A crafty smile transfigures Kersh's
narrow face. Don't get uptight, Frankie boy. After all, he's
got Baby Sam to help him. That leaking brown sleazebag
will come up with something really ace, Kersh feels sure.
One or two little surprises. Oh, yes indeedy. Cawdor has a
long way to go yet. A long way to go.

Kersh gets up from the couch, slapping his fist into his
palm, filled with new resolve. He pads to the bathroom and
sluices his head with cold water. He needs to think clear
and straight. No more booze and no more screwing until
the situation is under control. He stares at himself in the
mirror, water dripping from the lank tails of his plastered
hair, trying to read the expression in his one good eye.

Maybe just a faint gleam of fear? (Cawdor *is* a threat, no
sense denying it.) But Kersh is glad to see another expression there, too. The sly glint of old that convinces him
he can fight his way out of any corner because there's
nothing he won't stop at, not a single trick he won't pull, to
get Frank Kersh out of a jam. The rest of the punks go so far
and no farther. They turn soft and squeamish, don't have

the guts to follow through. That's where he's different. He's prepared to go all the way – and then some. It's as though something clicks in his brain and he shifts into overdrive. All bets are off. Let her rip. Take it to the limit and never look back, as Bob Dylan might say –

Kersh glimpses something moving behind him in the mirror. He swings round, a blood-red wave of terror clamping his chest tight so that he chokes and gasps for air like a beached fish.

Christ, for a split second there he thought Cawdor had snuck up on him. Practically gave him a bowel movement on the spot. He leans weakly against the washbasin, nervous spasms shooting up the backs of his thighs and making his buttocks quiver.

'So you got the message,' Kersh says, trying not to make too much noise breathing.

'I came running,' Baby Sam says, squatting in a watery brown puddle just inside the bathroom door. 'In a manner of speaking. What's up?'

'What's *up*?' Kersh snarls. 'What d'ya think – we're being attacked by the Easter Bunny?'

Baby Sam extends a claw and scratches the place between his head and torso where his chin should be. 'Take it easy, Frank. Cawdor's still in the dark. He'll never break through into here. He doesn't know how –'

'You –' Kersh points a finger '– had better fucking well make sure he doesn't. But he's got a whiff something's screwy. That's what my gut feeling tells me, and it ain't never been wrong. So what are you going to do about it, scumbag?'

'No call to get personal, Frank.'

'Let me put it this way,' Kersh says, his voice softly hissing. 'If you don't come up with an idea, and pretty damn quick, I'm going to use you for football practice and punt you off the balcony out there. You get my drift?'

Feeling the strength return to his legs, Kersh strides past Baby Sam into the living area. Baby Sam squirms round and flops after him, lidless eyes bright and anxious to please, leaving a trail on the carpet.

'Trust me, Frank,' he whines. 'Have I ever let you down?'

'I don't know. Have you?'

'You're here,' Baby Sam points out. 'And in one piece.'

That's true, Kersh concedes. He's still king of the heap. And it's also true, as the scumbag says, that Cawdor don't know jackshit. A big fat zilch. He begins to feel a little more easy and relaxed. Even so, he reminds himself, don't forget there still *is* a problem. Somewhere there's a weak spot – the other world bleeding through into the one he, Kersh, has created – and Cawdor has stumbled across it. How else could he know his wife and kid were in any sort of danger? He has to put a stop to this before it gets any worse and Cawdor really sees the light.

'Any ideas, Frank?' Baby Sam asks, stroking the white fur of the couch with one of his feelers.

'Why is it always me has to come up with the ideas? You're supposed to be the protection.'

'Yeah, but you call the shots. You're the brains.'

True. Kersh modestly shrugs and sighs. Always was and always will be. Everything depends on him. A feeling like a cold blade sliding into his stomach brings home the truth of this. *Christ Almighty, everything does.* That's a fact – they need him more than he needs them. Without Frank Kersh they're nothing.

Swallowing down his fear, he says, 'We gotta dream up something. Something that'll stop Cawdor in his tracks.'

'Like what for instance?'

Kersh strokes his jaw and starts to smile. From out of nowhere he's had a brilliant idea. 'The wife and kid, he thinks he's saved 'em, right? OK, swell, we let him go on believing it.'

'Huh?' Baby Sam says, mouth hanging open. 'I don't get it.'

'Cawdor's saved 'em, so he thinks,' Kersh explains patiently, 'and, by sticking his nose in and interfering, he gets 'em killed. It's perfect.' He rubs his hands. 'Shit, it'll totally destroy him.'

'Still don't get it, Frank. How we gonna work it?' Baby Sam gnaws at his lipless mouth.

'I don't know how.' Kersh stares off into space. 'Gotta give it some thought.'

'Don't take too long, Frank. I mean if he's, you know, getting ideas already –'

'Don't lecture me, scumbag!' Kersh spits at him. 'Just get back down there and do your job. I don't want that mother-fucker sneaking up on me while you're jerking off in a corner somewhere. Earn your keep and leave me to handle the tough part.'

When Baby Sam has trailed off, sullenly, without a word, Kersh paces to and fro over the thick shag-pile carpet, cracking his knuckles and muttering to himself. He knows he's on to a good idea; it's just how to make it work that's giving him a headache.

He goes to the bar and reaches for the Jack Daniel's before remembering his strict no-booze rule until this is over. He slams the bottle down and turns away from the bar, catching sight of the sickle moon hanging there above the darkened city. Pasted to the starry night sky, unmoving, never moving, immoveable . . .

Seeing the sliver of moon puts another thought into his head.

Where time doesn't exist, one second stays the same second for ever. In this everlasting second, Kersh has all the time in the world to think and to plan and to act. And as Cawdor also inhabits this world – the world Kersh created inside his own head – what's to stop Kersh himself from not just thinking and dreaming what to do, but stepping in there and *doing*? Getting things done.

Holy shit. That's it. So simple, now he's thought of it, Kersh is amazed it never occurred to him before now.

Kersh can't help but grin. That's the best idea he's ever had. He's a fucking gold-plated genius, no question.

A slimy feeler touches his bare ankle. It's Baby Sam, back again, looking up at him with worried bloodshot eyes. 'If ya don't do somethin', Frank, it's curtains.' He says 'coituns' like Jimmy Cagney, and even sounds like him. 'Give him time, he's gonna come and getcha. Ya gonna sit there like a dummy and let him? From me to you, I'm tellin' ya, better shape up, or we all of us gonna take the dive. Ya gotta dream somethin' up, and make it *fast*!'

Kersh is angry, but he knows Baby Sam is right.

And he knows why Baby Sam is right. Because Baby Sam is the place where the dream phantoms come from. The weird imaginings that even Kersh doesn't want to think about, and certainly not dwell on.

He says, 'Take it easy, I figured on a way. Leave it to Uncle Frank.'

'Really? You positive?' Baby Sam is so nervous and excited he emits a wet fart on to the shag-pile carpet.

'Absolutely. Guaranteed to wipe him out, no question.'

But there is a question. A big one. Leaving the protection of the tower, where he's safe, means that Cawdor can get to *him*. In here he's untouchable, invulnerable. Out there he isn't. Is it worth the risk? Graye and the Messengers should've stopped Cawdor before he got this far, that's what burns him up. But if they can't, or won't, it's all down to him, Kersh knows, staring at the moon and reaching for the Jack Daniel's.

Yessiree. Time to make an unscheduled guest appearance in his own show.

FLYING DOWN TO ZERO

1

A TV camera crew had set up shop next to the panoramic window overlooking the floodlit observation deck; it was fronted by a glossy blonde creature holding a stick mike as if she intended to throttle it. Cawdor couldn't see who she was interviewing, but as he entered the first-class departure lounge with Sarah and Daniella he heard an excited female voice behind him squeal, 'It's Linda Gray! Denny, look – Linda Gray!'

Although the celebrity's name sounded familiar, Cawdor couldn't put a face to it.

They got themselves settled, and Daniella said she wanted something to read on the flight. Cawdor turned to watch his daughter as she went over to the newsstand. His anxiety was irrational, he knew that – this prevailing fear of her being out of sight, even for moments at a time. But he couldn't help it. Three weeks had elapsed since their return home from Florida, and it seemed to him a miracle that his family life had resumed its pattern of old, exactly as before. True, for the first few days Sarah had been silent and withdrawn – more so, in fact, than Daniella, which surprised him. But then both of them seemed to suddenly snap out of it, as if recovering from fever, and he kept being reminded of what Sarah had said that night, parked in the forecourt of the Best Western hotel in Daytona Beach. Like coming back into the light after a long, dark journey.

It had been a long, dark journey for him too. As if the three of them had been in the grip of a collective frenzy. For a while back there the world had gone haywire. The analogy occurred to him that it was like a circuit that had shorted – throwing the system out of kilter – and then the circuit had mysteriously righted itself. The juice was flowing again, the three of them plugged in together as father, mother and daughter, a proper family once more.

Their planned vacation to Europe couldn't have come at a better time, Cawdor felt. A complete change of scene would do them the world of good: long golden days in which to relax and enjoy themselves and velvet-soft evenings dining out under the stars, drinking the delicious local wine he remembered from his last trip to Italy.

His attention was distracted from Daniella by a gaggle of reporters and photographers. It was getting to be more like a media feeding trough around here than a departure lounge, Cawdor thought with annoyance. He watched the pack as they closed in on a man in his sixties, built like a quarter-back run to seed, with snow-white hair cropped close to his pink scalp, the squashed nose of an ex-boxer, and a florid face that was mostly jowl.

It took Cawdor a split second to recognise him, and he blinked in stunned surprise.

Byron T Cobb. Senator Cobb, with his homespun Kansas farmer's drawl, whose cousin was married to Don Carlson. Cawdor had spoken to Don already about seeking the senator's help, and Don had E-mailed Senator Cobb's office with a personal request to set up a meeting. The response had been favourable. The senator was more than happy to meet Cawdor upon his return, in three weeks' time, from a foreign trip in his role as chairman of the Senate House Committee on External Pro-American Affairs. A foreign trip, it turned out, on which he and Cawdor were sharing the same flight to London. The coincidence seemed to present a heaven-sent opportunity. Now wasn't the right moment, but maybe during the flight he could introduce himself as Don Carlson's partner and bend the senator's ear a little, prepare the ground and grab Senator Cobb's interest.

It was a good omen, and Cawdor felt buoyed up with optimism. Reason in itself to order a large brandy from the white-jacketed attendant hovering nearby.

'What happened to the strict no-booze rule?' Sarah inquired, sitting back in the low, squat armchair that resembled a piece of Henry Moore sculpture. 'You always insist on staying teetotal when you're flying.'

'Celebration.'

'Celebrating what?'

Cawdor grinned at his wife but decided not to tell her the real reason until after he'd had words with the senator. 'Our family vacation – what else?'

Sarah gave him a look and beckoned the attendant. 'Make it two. With a ginger ale on the side.' She pointed a finger at her husband. 'If you're gonna get smashed, you got company, mister.'

'Good scout. Knew I could rely on you,' Cawdor said, and gave her a solemn wink.

In a tailored cream-coloured suit over a royal-blue silk blouse, wearing a single strand of pearls with matching earrings, his wife looked positively stunning. She had acquired a light tan from sitting in the garden these last couple of weeks, and her skin glowed richly against her shoulder-length fair hair, which was touched here and there with silver streaks from the sun.

Sarah smiled into his eyes. She didn't feel like smiling. But she was so thankful, deep in her heart, that he had no inkling of the despair that lay behind the façade. Every minute of every day she had to live with the terrible memory of what had happened to her, and the sickly dread of what might yet happen. She had told Jeff everything about her enforced stay in Messiah Wilde's house – everything except the single fact that really mattered. She couldn't bring herself to tell him that. At first it was because she was afraid of what he might do. The scenario played itself through in her mind with all the stark melodrama of an afternoon soap: her husband hellbent on revenge, taking a gun and shooting the evil

334

bastard, and ending up on a murder charge. Then that fear had been replaced by another, eclipsing her alarm that Jeff would be driven to murder.

It was that she might be pregnant.

Sarah was on the pill, and she hadn't missed her period, not yet. Physiologically there was no reason why she shouldn't be perfectly all right. She kept telling herself this, repeating it like a comforting mantra, but the terror refused to give way to logic. It was implanted deep within her, as she feared Messiah Wilde's evil seed might be, germinating at this very moment, cells splicing and multiplying and growing inside her body.

She smiled again, brightly, as Cawdor held out his glass, looked deep into her eyes and murmured, 'Bottoms up, kiddo.'

They clinked glasses.

'Happy landings,' Sarah said.

The 747 flew steadily on through the night.

Dinner had been eaten, the lights dimmed, and everyone in first class had reclined their seats to stretch out and get some sleep.

Cawdor was drowsing in his aisle seat, a blanket tucked up under his chin, when he became aware of movement in the cabin. He opened his eyes to find that several other people had been disturbed also. Then he heard Senator Cobb's unmistakable drawl, sounding choked and outraged. 'Jee*suss*, I don't believe this! What in hell ya think ya playin' at, boy?'

'Shut it, fat man. When I wanna hear you, I'll ask.'

He was tall and gaunt, with sharp features, a plume of brown hair brushed back from a bony forehead and growing thick on his neck. He was the dead spit of the young Clint Eastwood, even wearing a fur-lined sleeveless suede jacket with rawhide tassels front and back. His voice was a tight-lipped low growl. The fearsome muzzle of the large handgun in his fist was less than an inch from the senator's hairy nostrils.

'Get up. Come on – up – outta your seat.'

Now most of the passengers had awakened, and those who hadn't were coming rapidly to their senses.

Sarah dug her fingers into Cawdor's arm. Next to her, in the window seat, Daniella was looking round quizzically, aware that something was happening but not sure what. Then she saw the gun and her whole body stiffened. Sarah looked at her with warning eyes and a rapid shake of her head.

A woman gave a nervous trill that sounded oddly like a laugh. The young Clint Eastwood glanced at her sharply and put a finger to his lips.

Senator Cobb was on his feet, his face a furious purple mask. It was taking all his self-control not to lash out. He said, 'Listen, you asshole punk, this is an airline of the United States, not some tinpot Mid-East ramshackle outfit you can –'

His head jerked back as young Clint shoved the barrel of the gun into the loose fleshy pouch of his throat.

'I said to be quiet.' Young Clint's eyes glinted with a dangerous light. 'Now *be* quiet.'

With the gun at the senator's throat, young Clint backed along the aisle to the curtained-off doorway that led to the flight attendants' compartment. Everyone prayed for an arm with gold braid on its sleeve to come through the green curtain, lock itself round the gunman's neck and throttle the life out of him. Instead, a thin freckled arm in a blue work shirt rolled up to the elbow appeared, and with it the blunt snout of a machine pistol, which was thrust into Senator Cobb's belly. The senator was taken inside. Young Clint listened through the curtain, nodding, and muttered something in reply. He turned to face the cabin.

'Passports. Up here to me.' His sharp, narrowed eyes scanned the seats, row by row. 'I wanna see thirty-six passports.' When they had been collected he passed them through the curtain.

Cawdor was holding Sarah's hand, and she was holding Daniella's. Careful not to make any sudden movement, Cawdor turned his head. Daniella was sitting very still, her face drawn and pale under its light tan. Her eyes were very large and glassily bright. Cawdor smiled at her. Daniella's tongue crept out and moistened her lower lip, and she smiled back, her cheeks stiff, chin quivering. Cawdor stared hard at her. We're going to be OK. Keep it up, girl. It'll be all right. Trust me.

Daniella nodded. She believed him and trusted him. Cawdor believed it, too. They were going to come through this. Every fibre of him willed it. These people – terrorists, hijackers, whatever they were – wouldn't harm anyone, providing they got what they were after. It wasn't in their interests to kill over 300 innocent people. They had nothing to gain by such a senseless, futile act.

He piled up the reasons in his mind, building a shaky edifice of belief on shifting sand.

In the quietly humming cabin the man with the uncanny resemblance to Clint Eastwood stood like a statue, feet braced, the gun held close to his chest. If he was sweating, it evaporated in the swirl of air conditioning before it had time to show. He looked calm and in control. But his dark eyes were never still. They raked along the rows of faces, watching for telltale signs. Cawdor forced himself to look straight ahead. He knew to avoid direct eye contact. An inquisitve glance could be taken as an insolent challenge. Don't forget, he told himself, these people are keyed up to breaking point. They're dicing with death and they know it. They can snap at the slightest thing. So don't give them an excuse. *Any* excuse, even an imaginary one.

Senator Cobb hadn't reappeared; there had been no sound; and from memory Cawdor visualised the layout up there. The first-class passengers had entered via the forward door and passed through the flight attendants' compartment. There was a food-preparation area, folding seats for the cabin crew, storage lockers, and various small cubicles off to the sides. Further forward, a short narrow passage led on to the flight deck itself, which was hidden by a thick blackout curtain. And behind that curtain? Cawdor wondered. Was the captain flying with a gun to his head? There had been no announcement, so maybe the rest of the airplane was in blissful ignorance. Had the captain spoken over the intercom, warned the attendants in the body of the plane not to enter the first-class cabin? Cawdor thought of all the people back there, the hundreds of other passengers, snoozing peacefully, dreaming their sweet dreams.

We're going to be OK. It'll be all right. Trust me.

Cawdor stuck to the rule, eyes front, as the young Clint lookalike came down the aisle in his suede jacket with the dangling tassels. He was holding a passport and glancing at faces. The passengers shrank into their seats. Sarah clutched Cawdor's hand convulsively as the gunman stopped at their row. He studied the passport photograph, then Cawdor's face, and jerked the barrel. 'Up front.'

'No – no!' Sarah wouldn't let go.

Cawdor prised her fingers loose. He spoke quietly and evenly. 'I have to do as he says. Take care of Daniella. Don't worry. Everything's going to be fine. Believe me.'

He squeezed Sarah's hand and stood up. He could feel cold air down his back where the sweat had dried. The barrel prodded him in the spine as he went up the aisle, and he was aware from the slight tilting of the floor that they were descending.

The curtain was held aside for Cawdor to step through. Six or seven people were crowded into the compartment leading to the flight deck. There was the black steward who had served Cawdor his dinner, along with other members of the crew: the captain, flight engineer, and two female flight attendants.

Eyes bulging, a strip of insulation tape across his mouth, Senator Cobb had been crammed into a corner of the forward bulkhead next to the external door, hands taped at the wrists. The veins on his temples stood out, blue against his cropped white hair. He looked a prime candidate for a heart attack.

A slim, attractive, dark-haired woman in her mid-twenties was casually holding two grenades, one in either hand, as if she'd picked them off a supermarket shelf and couldn't decide which to buy. Cawdor was trying to work out how many of them there were. Including young Clint, three, he reckoned – or four if there was another standing watch over the copilot at the controls. His speculation was ended by a vicious jab in the back. Cawdor stumbled forward. He was brought up short by the blunt muzzle of a machine pistol being waved under his nose. Cawdor looked down the blue steel barrel into the eyes of the man in the blue work shirt, a head shorter than himself, with thinning fair hair and a badly pitted complexion that a scar along his cheekbone did nothing to improve. One of his eyes had a curdled milky appearance.

'Your name Cawdor, am I right?'

'Yes.'

'You gonna cause me trouble, fella?'

'I don't intend to.' Cawdor tried to keep his voice neutral. No hostility, no bravado, no fear. Zero provocation. But his heart was suddenly hammering in his chest. This man in the blue work shirt was somehow familiar to him. He'd seen that crafty pitted face with its milky eye somewhere before.

The man waved his gun towards Senator Cobb. 'This sonofabitch won't talk on the radio. But I guess you will, Cawdor, because your wife and kid are with you, huh? That so? You talk on the radio, tell 'em what we want, OK?' He was grinning now, as if enjoying himself, raising his sparse eyebrows. 'If you don't, I kill them. And I'll do it, fella, believe it.'

Cawdor nodded. 'All right. Whatever you say.'

There was some confusion then as Senator Cobb decided he'd had enough. He barged forward, face puce above the tape covering his mouth. Cawdor couldn't figure him. Was he trying to be a hero?

The man in the blue work shirt wrestled the senator back and pushed him against the external door. The barrel of the machine pistol all but disappeared in the senator's stomach.

'You wanna go through there? *You wanna go through*?' the man yelled, giving him a back-handed slap across the face. The senator's eyes bulged, a maze of broken blood vessels. 'I'll do it myself, you sonofabitch. You'll have thirty thousand feet to think about it –'

'Open that door and we all go.' The grey-haired captain spoke through thin, bloodless lips. 'You know what'll happen at this altitude if there's a pressure leak?'

The girl said boredly, 'Let's cut all this crap and get on with it.' She was still juggling with the grenades in a manner that made Cawdor's blood run cold. They might be fake, but they looked only too real.

'Are we gonna make Santiago in one hop or not?' the girl said to the man in the blue work shirt, who seemed to be the leader. 'What do we tell these guys, Frank? We going for it or what?'

Santiago? Cawdor thought. Which one? Chile? Brazil? Mexico? Panama? The Dominican Republic? How many other Santiagos were there?

'He says we have to land,' the leader said, referring to the captain.

'I don't believe him,' the girl said. She shouted suddenly at the captain, 'This plane has enough fuel for *London*, you lying bastard! You make London, you can make Santiago.'

'We can't, not without refuelling,' the captain said. 'We'd already covered over a thousand miles before we changed course. And we now have a headwind instead of a tailwind. That can make a difference of three, four, maybe five hundred operational miles.'

'What if we tell you to fly on anyway?' the girl said.

'Then we'll crash.'

'You're lying.'

'My flight engineer, Mr Goldman, will show you the gauges. You can see for yourself.'

'How would we know?' the girl said angrily.

The captain shrugged. He was either extremely cool or a damn good actor. 'Those are the facts, miss. I'll do everything I can not to jeopardise this aircraft and its passengers. There's no alternative. We have to land.'

'Where?'

'First I have to check our fuel and plot a new course.' The captain glanced at his flight engineer. 'What would you say, Ben? Tampa?'

'No!' The girl shook her head violently. 'Outside the United States. Do you think we're stupid?'

'All right,' the captain said calmly. 'Don't get excited. Let me look at the maps with my flight engineer and we'll give you the available options. It's got to be either Florida or somewhere in the West Indies.'

'Colombia,' the girl said. 'You can make Colombia.'

'No, we can't. Not possible. That's another thousand miles, at least –'

'A'right, *a'right*,' snarled the man in the blue work shirt, getting ratty. He looked around the crowded compartment, as if unsure what to do next. Finally he decided, jabbed a finger and ordered the girl to go up front with the captain and flight engineer and work something out. She followed them, juggling the grenades.

The man placed an expensive-looking soft leather bag in the middle of the floor and opened it for Cawdor to see inside. It was packed with gelignite. From his pocket he took out a flat plastic device with buttons, like a TV remote control. 'This –' he held it under Cawdor's nose '– activates that.' He pointed to the bag. 'And that goes on your seat down there in the cabin. Unerstan' me, fella? Yeah? Get the picture?'

He waggled his thumb over the button.

Cawdor stared into the man's one good eye. He had the bizarre notion that at any moment he might wake up. This entire situation had the feel of a dream – and at the same time a kind of fateful quality. Had he known what was going to happen, and blindly, stupidly ignored his gut feeling? But if he had known, he told himself, he would never have boarded the airplane with Sarah and Daniella in the first place. There had been no premonition, or he would have acted upon it.

Something else was bothering him. These people were heavily armed, with guns, grenades and explosives. They had executed a daring mid-flight hijack of a major airline's

341

747, which must have required meticulous planning. And yet they didn't seem to have considered for longer than ten seconds what came next. As if they had decided to do it on the spur of the moment. Let's go hijack a jumbo jet. Hey, guys, swell idea.

Young Clint took the leather bag and placed it on the vacated seat next to Sarah. He reached into his pocket and dangled a pair of handcuffs in front of her. Standing in the doorway, Cawdor was made to watch as young Clint attached one bracelet to the handle of the bag and snapped the other round Sarah's wrist. She wouldn't look at him. She sat very straight and still, the circle of pearls glowing faintly above the dark-blue silk of her blouse.

The gunman curled his finger at Daniella.

Cawdor went stiff, fists clenched at his sides.

The machine pistol jabbed hard into his ribs. 'Easy, fella, you don't want the lives of three hundred innocent folk on your conscience.' The man sighed in Cawdor's ear. 'She's very young. And very pretty. Takes after her mom.'

'Please don't hurt her.' Cawdor's voice was trembling, husky with fear. 'I'll do anything you ask.'

'Hurt her?' said the man in the blue work shirt, sounding surprised. 'I ain't gonna hurt her, fella.' He shook his head and chuckled. 'Naw. Gonna give her a damn good time.'

2

It was beyond endurance. But there was nothing he could do except endure it. Cawdor closed his eyes and held his body rigid while the man in the blue work shirt with the pale freckled arms did everything he felt like doing in front of her father.

He had her in the small cubbyhole with a sink on one side and a row of lockers on the other. Daniella had resisted until he struck her across the head with the metal fretwork butt of the machine pistol. After that she went quiet and docile, not even whimpering. He laid the weapon on the draining board of the sink to give him a free hand. In his other hand he kept hold of the remote-control device, arm stretched out at a safe distance from the grunting, thrusting action.

Leaning in the doorway, young Clint now and then interrupted his watch on the passengers to glance over his shoulder. His face never altered its expression – jaw clamped, eyes squinting – at what he saw, not even the sight of the naked girl. Senator Cobb was slumped in the corner near the door where he had been pummelled and kicked, belly rising and falling with the exertion of breathing through his boxer's flattened nose.

'Come on, honey lamb, you can do better than that. Shake those hips now. Lemme feel some *movement*.' With one hand on her buttocks, the other outstretched, he was doing a parody of a tango step, his thin bare rump jigging from side to side, pants round his ankles.

The younger flight attendant had turned away in revulsion, her blonde head pressed into the steward's shoulder. He encircled her with his arms, averting his eyes from the spectacle and gazing into nowhere with bleak despair.

'Baby, baby, baby,' the man in the blue work shirt crooned softly. 'I do declare there ain't bin nobody else but me. This snatch is spankin' brand-new, honey. You're as tight as a mouse's ear. Oh, Lordy, praise be!'

He snuggled up close, cheek to cheek, his tongue worming wetly in her ear. Daniella's head lolled back, thumping against the curved bulkhead with the force of each stroke. She was still dazed from the blow of the gun butt, which had left a rising weal of orange and purple down the side of her face.

Cawdor could have closed his eyes or looked away. He forced himself to watch. He was storing up pain. He hoarded it greedily. The amount of pain he was able to contain within himself, and not go instantly mad or berserk, seemed to him quite amazing. He could take a world of pain and not flinch. It was feeding him.

And so he watched the man in the blue work shirt with an unblinking gaze as the bared teeth nibbled at the arch of Daniella's neck. Heard the breath hissing from his nostrils, the grunting from his throat with each thrust.

'First time with a real man for sure –' Pausing to gather strength for the next one. 'Bet I can make you come – your first time off, baby – trust old Frank to give you the big O – He got just what you dreamt of, sweet honeycup.'

He ducked his head round, peering through the tangled strands of Daniella's hair and his own, the remote-control device held at arm's length while he continued to pump away.

Still and silent as a statue, Cawdor watched him, piling up pain upon pain. The others in the small compartment, just as silent and still, formed a tableau of waxwork figures. The man in the blue work shirt grinned at that, grinned through Daniella's hair, and concentrated once more on the business in hand.

A few moments of eternity later, with a gasp through clenched teeth, it was over.

A moment after that he was hitching up his pants, ignoring the girl as she slid to the floor and lay in a disordered heap.

'You disgusting animal!' The young, blonde stewardess squirmed round in the protective embrace of the steward, flecks of spittle flying from her lips.

'I am, ain't I?' the man in the blue work shirt agreed. 'Red-blooded animal, that's me. You want some, baby?' He rubbed his crotch and leered at her, tongue vibrating.

Cawdor was suddenly aware of the other stewardess. Tall and slender, her dark hair trimmed above the ears and brushed sleekly back, she was staring hard at him, willing Cawdor to look at her. Their eyes locked. Cawdor saw her eyes drift sideways to the machine pistol on the draining board. A step – maybe two – and she would be within reaching distance. It didn't concern him whether she knew how to operate it. She had seen a way and had the nerve to go for it; he trusted the faith she had in herself.

Cawdor gave the slightest of nods.

'Gimme coupla minutes to get the lead back in my pencil,' the man in the blue work shirt was saying, 'and

I'll show you what an animal feels like.' He glanced at Cawdor. 'You look kinda sick to me, fella. Whassa matter, flying give you the gip?'

'For what you've done,' Cawdor said quietly, 'I'm going to kill you.' He needed the man's attention on him, away from the stewardess, and this did it.

The man in the blue work shirt rounded his one good eye in mock alarm. 'Holy Moses, you don't say. Well, I can see you're upset over somethin', fella. But that –' he jerked his thumb to Daniella's crumpled form '– was just a piece of tail to me. 'Sides, it had to happen sometime pretty soon. She was ripe for it. And, if it's any con-solation, you have it on good authority that no pimply sleazeball's bin tamperin' with the kid afore now. I can vouch for that.'

Behind the man's head, Cawdor could see the steward-ess edging towards the draining board. There was no real plan. It would rely on speed and instinct. The instant that Cawdor saw the stewardess go for the gun, he would make a grab for the remote-control device in the man's right hand. Keep it simple – nothing fancy, no frills.

Forget his daughter lying bruised and raped by the sink, forget that every atom within him was shrieking to lash out and smash the man's face to pulp and gouge the one good eye from his head. God willing, that would come later. No time for that now. Just act.

But he still needed the man's attention on him and nowhere else.

Cawdor shook his head. 'You won't press the button. It'll blow this airplane out of the sky and you with it.'

'Wanna try me?' Grinning, tongue between his teeth, the man held the device in the palm of his hand, a finger poised above it.

'I don't think it's even connected.'

The stewardess was within arm's reach. So slowly that the movement was imperceptible, her hand started to rise away from her side.

'That's for me to know, fella, and you to find out,' the man in the blue work shirt said. He seemed to relish the situation, toying with his victims, and Cawdor was happy to let him. 'You think you can get me all riled up, is that it? You think I'm so dumb I don't know what game you're –'

The stewardess went for it. Cawdor saw the pale blur of her hand. But from the corner of his one good eye the man saw it too. He snatched up the machine pistol from the draining board. Cawdor lunged towards him. The man reared back. More as a reflex than a deliberate action, his finger touched the trigger. A sudden and very loud staccato hammering filled the compartment. The machine pistol jumped and jerked erratically in his hand, discharging half a clip. Three shots went wide; the rest hit Cawdor in a scattered random pattern. His body folded up as if all the joints had become detached and he went down, clutching a bloody hole in his right side.

A thick blue haze filled the air. It swirled upward, sucked in thin vapour trails into the air-conditioning vents. By some freak chance, against all the odds, not one of the bullets had punctured the outer metal hull of the aircraft. The 747 remained intact and airtight.

Treading carefully because the floor was slick with blood, the man in the blue work shirt sidled around the hunched body. Daniella was cowering against the bulkhead, her knees drawn up. Above the knotted fist covering her mouth, her eyes were rinsed out, vacant with shock.

'Lucky break for us, Frank,' young Clint said in a relieved voice. 'Damn lucky. You could've shot a hole in this bird.'

The man whirled round. 'I fuckin' didn't, did I? So shut your face.' He waved the machine pistol threateningly at the stewardess. 'Another move like that, honey, you get it in the gut.' He jabbed the muzzle into her stomach, then leant against the bulkhead, his eye flicking everywhere, never still.

'Jesus, look at the state of these, Frank,' young Clint complained, examining the soles of his high-heeled cowboy boots. 'They gonna be spoilt.'

346

The floor was a mess right enough, blood leaking everywhere, and getting messier by the minute. It was a problem. Impossible to dump the body outside the aircraft at this altitude. Already the floor was swimming. The man in the blue work shirt beckoned to the steward. He pointed to the floor. 'There gotta be a trap here someplace. Open it up.' Standing over the kneeling steward, he watched him remove a small floor panel with a stainless-steel bolt key. Through the black square hole, like through the opening door of a freezer, air from the baggage hold clutched everything with icy fingers.

Waved on by the machine pistol, the steward slid the body across the floor and dropped it into the black emptiness. He replaced the panel and stood up, hands congealed and sticky, his trousers sodden, a ghostly pallor beneath his dark skin.

'Satisfied now? Huh?' the man in the blue work shirt demanded of young Clint. 'There ya go. Another problem solved.'

Through a moonless night, some 400 miles off the coast of North Carolina, the 747 flew on a southwesterly heading at 16,000 feet. Calmly and deliberately, the young copilot, First Officer Greg Richards, was nudging the aircraft lower, imperceptibly losing altitude. He had one aim in mind. To achieve the lowest permissable height for commercial aircraft, thereby equalising the cabin pressure and outside air pressure. There was still a long way to go.

Sarah had wrapped her daughter in a blanket and was cradling her in one arm. Mercifully, the girl had drifted off into a shallow sleep, which every so often was broken by a convulsive shudder and a dry sob. In the aisle seat next to Sarah, the leather bag was a black ominous bulk, her arm resting across it because the handcuffs confined it to this one position. Another shuddering spasm jerked through Daniella, and her mother hugged her tighter.

There was a party going on in the forward compartment. At gunpoint the steward broke open a catering pack of Carlsberg Export, and everyone, with the exception of

Senator Cobb, was made to drink, whether they wanted to or not. The man in the blue work shirt insisted on it. He seemed to be in high spirits.

'Come on, blondie, tip it down,' he told the stewardess, who was holding a can of beer but not drinking. And, as she raised it reluctantly to her mouth, he whacked the underside of the can with the gun barrel so that beer foamed out and splashed over her face. Blood streamed from her lip where it had been split by the metal tab.

He ogled her wet blouse, which was clinging to the faint outline of her bra. 'You an' me get it together later, huh? Let old Frankie boy show you the way.' He did a bump and grind in front of her. 'Jigga-jigga-jigga-jigga-jigga.'

The captain hid his expression while he drank, his hand wrapped around the beer can, almost crushing it. He glanced stony-faced at the flight engineer, and as he did so a movement in the corner caught his eye.

Senator Cobb had worked his hands free of the tape and was on his feet. He ripped the insulation tape from his mouth, and it flapped about, stuck to his fingers, as he charged forward.

'No deals with these scumbags!'

The man in the blue work shirt didn't have time to turn before there was an arm round his neck trying to tear his head off.

'No deals, you hear me, captain?' The senator's voice was a hoarse screech. 'I'm ordering you to land this airplane on US territory. We don't do deals with chicken-livered terrorist bastards – never. We don't give in, hear me? Do it! Land the plane! Do as I say!'

The man in the blue work shirt, choking in the powerful grip, was almost on his knees. The machine pistol dangled from his hand. He reached up to claw the arm from his throat and dropped the remote-control device on the floor.

Instinctively – as if it was the device itself that was about to explode – everyone threw up their hands and scattered out of the way. All but Senator Cobb, purple in the face, who wouldn't let go. He carried on choking the life out of the man.

Moving to one side, young Clint raised the powerful handgun. He lined up to get a clear aim of Senator Cobb's white-haired head. The steward lashed out, and the gunman went skidding on the slimy floor, his legs shooting out from under him.

It suddenly seemed as if the cramped compartment was filled with more bodies than it could hold. The senator was yelling at the top of his lungs, shouting for help, mingling with the screams of the blonde stewardess, hands pressed to her face with blood pouring through her fingers.

The steward looked around frantically. The device was somewhere on the floor, but he couldn't see it. He dropped to his knees, searching desperately among the confusion of feet and legs, his hands smeared with blood. He winced as a shoe struck his wrist on the point of the bone. He lowered his head almost to the floor. And there it was. The remote-control device. Lying face down near the senator's scuffling foot. The steward's arm went out at full stretch, and as he strained forward, hand splayed to grasp hold of it, a heel came down and crunched the plastic case.

The 747 staggered.

Then it lurched to the left.

The sensation inside the forward compartment was of the floor coming up to meet them with terrific, bone-jarring force, like being in an elevator that had come to a dead stop.

The green curtain streamed out horizontally in a sudden howling wind that sucked it into the first-class cabin. Then everything tilted steeply as the nose dropped and the jumbo fell, engines screaming.

The steward climbed up the floor, struggling to free himself from the tangle of bodies. He managed to grip the frame of the doorway and haul himself forward. Above his head, the curtain rippled and cracked like a green flag in a gale.

Inside the cabin, rows of oxygen masks dangled on white plastic tubes, like undersea creatures swaying in the current. In the split-second catastrophe of the blast there hadn't been time to use them. The air was thin and cold as if it had blown straight off a mountain top. The steward gulped at it, whirling black spots before his eyes, his lungs starved of oxygen.

Then he had to hold on tight. The howling wind snatched at him as the pressurised air evacuated from the cabin. It tried to drag him towards the space that had been three rows of seats, towards the hole of torn metal ripped in the side of the aircraft. Someone was waving to him. It was an arm in a sleeve of dark-blue silk – just the arm, severed at the shoulder, caught on a shiny sliver of metal – waving, waving.

Now he can relax. *Really* relax. Those 2,000 volts casting a blight over his future are a thing of the past. It's what he knew all along deep down in his gut, Kersh realises. Stick with it, buddy, and it comes out right in the end. Never give in.

That could be his personal motto, Kersh thinks. Never Give In. Not forgetting, of course, the great Frank's 'I Did It My Way'. That too was his own personal philosophy. He'd always been proud of the fact they shared the same first name. Seemed kind of a lucky charm, two very similar guys with the same name, battling against the odds and winning through – like twins, maybe, or soul mates.

Feeling so good he doesn't even need a drink right this minute, Kersh steps on to the balcony. Same old moon stuck to the sky. That's just how he likes it. He gives the moon a wink for good luck: as long as you're up there, I'm down here. Everything's jake. He wonders idly if he could get old Frank up here with him for a chat. They had so much in common, it might be fun. Crack open a bottle of wine (the red Italian stuff) and chew the fat. Talk over the good old days, a couple of seasoned campaigners who'd lived through some tough times and made it to the top, despite the odds stacked against them. He'd enjoy that, Kersh thinks, and he'd bet Frank would too.

They'd become the best of buddies. Kersh can see it now. Frank sprawled on the white couch, twirling a glass of wine, asking Kersh's opinion on his songs. And Kersh would tell him. Straight out, no bullshit. Frank would listen and nod, taking it all in, because he respected Kersh's opinion, knowing also that Kersh wasn't in the least put out because Frank was a big-shot movie and recording star. That's how Kersh was – talk to Frankie boy the same way he'd talk to anybody. Yeah, Frank would respect that.

He grips the metal rail, cool to the touch, and gazes out at the city. His city. Cawdor's wife and brat are down there somewhere. They're down there for the simple reason that he, Kersh, wills it so. It had been a gamble, sure enough, confronting Cawdor like that. It could have turned out different. *How* different Kersh isn't clear about. Suppose Cawdor had gotten hold of the machine pistol and shot him, instead of the other way round? Would he now be dead and Cawdor alive? But, if he *had* died back there on the 747, Cawdor and his family and all the rest of them would have ceased to exist. Because they were living in Kersh's world, the one he had created. The Messengers had given him that power, and in return they were given the world they wanted. That was the deal. And now, with Cawdor out of the way, they were free to go right ahead and spread the Message around the world.

Kersh gives a sudden grin as something strikes him. What happened on the airplane *had* to happen. It couldn't have been otherwise. Cawdor, poor sap, was going through the motions, jumping through the same hoops because he was playing the game with Kersh's rigged deck. There was no way Cawdor could possibly win. No way he could have stopped Kersh having that little bit of fun with his teenage daughter. In fact, now he comes to think about it, Kersh realises, he can have a little bit more fun with her. Hell, a *lot* more fun. All he has to do is tell that foul scumbag, Baby Sam, to get her up here to the penthouse. Whenever he feels like it. And why not that stuck-up bitch of a wife as well? He can shaft the both of them together. Three in a bed. If he's in a generous mood (which he is right this minute) he can let Baby Sam sit and watch.

Better yet, Kersh thinks (another fucking brainwave!) he can sit and watch while Baby Sam gets it on with the two of them. The little runt would go apeshit at the chance. Jesus, where do these brilliant ideas keep coming from? They just pop into his head from out of nowhere. He's a genius, that's for definite.

Of course that's why the Messengers picked him in the first place. They must have known he was one cool dude fizzing with ideas. Or it was a damn lucky guess. But for him, Kersh knows, their asses would really be in the blender. Cawdor was just starting to latch on. He kept on getting the odd peek at things but never got the whole picture. On the airplane, for instance. The way Cawdor was looking at him, Kersh would have taken long odds that the guy kind of half-recognised him. Which meant that Cawdor must have remembered him from somewhere previously. That somewhere else had to be here – in the tower penthouse – because he hadn't stirred out of the place.

Mentally, Kersh wipes his brow. It had been *that* close. Because Cawdor must have somehow got a glimpse of him right here on this balcony. He doesn't know how this is possible. Unless Cawdor had more tricks up his sleeve than Kersh gave him credit for.

For a second he feels a clutch of panic at his throat. But it's gone as fast as it came. Cawdor's all washed up. He got that way the moment Kersh pumped six slugs into him and had him tossed into the cargo bay. Goodbye and amen, fella.

Kersh winks again at his old friend the moon and strolls back inside. He's in a good frame of mind, and this makes him feel hungry. In the kitchen he whistles a jaunty 'Heartbreak Hotel' as he prepares a monster double cheeseburger with all the trimmings and a pickle on the side. From the fridge he takes a can of Bud and a couple of Twinkies. He can't remember the last time he ate. It must have been some while ago because he's ravenous. Mouth bulging, a smear of ketchup on his chin, he takes his meal into the living area and settles down on the long, curved, white sofa.

Above him, the glass ceiling gives a view of the stars. The rosy glow of the lamps dotted here and there makes him feel comfy and secure. Kersh takes a big bite, munches slowly, and swills it down with a long draught of ice-cold Bud.

Life sure is sweet, he thinks. Couldn't be better. And the beauty of it is, it's never gonna change. Nothing will *ever* change. No sickness or disease, and no old age. He doesn't even need a haircut – never will. The lack of a heartbeat panicked him at first, but now he can live with it, no sweat. Fact is, he's come to realise, another heartbeat is the last thing he wants. He's existing in between heartbeats, and the next one could be his last. Kersh smiles to himself because it strikes him as funny. Whereas every person lives in mortal dread of their heart stopping, Kersh doesn't want his to start. Just keep on doing what you're doing, he tells it, which is nothing. This really tickles him and he guffaws, spraying out bits of mushy cheeseburger on to the carpet.

Hot damn, Kersh chuckles, he's A1 copper-bottomed fireproof.

Because how can you kill somebody who doesn't have a heartbeat to begin with? Simple answer is you can't. You can't take away something he doesn't have, because it isn't there to be taken away. So stands to reason you can't threaten old Frankie Kersh with destruction. He's gone beyond that. He is, in fact, fucking indestructible.

Kersh stuffs in the last of the cheeseburger and munches it through a broad grin.

Kersh the Indestructible. He likes the sound of that.

PART THREE

LOST ZONE

What we call the beginning is often the end
And to make an end is to make a beginning.

TS Eliot
'Little Gidding', *Four Quartets*

GHOST IN THE MACHINE

Doctor Straus said, 'Two still in there we can't get at. I conferred with my colleagues here, and with Doctor Bleckard at the Cornell School of Medicine, and the concensus is we leave them be. Safer that way.'

'*Two*?' Gil Gribble's face was a study in anxiety mingled with plain bewilderment. 'How many times was he shot, for chrissakes?'

'Six bullets penetrated altogether.' Doctor Straus puffed smoke from a curly pipe. Tall and lanky, with thinning silvery hair, he spoke in a staccato fashion, his Adam's apple jerking like a yo-yo on a piece of elastic. 'Left shoulder, left hand, both of which made exit wounds. Two in the lower abdomen, which have been removed. And the two we prefer to leave alone. One in the lower left chest cavity; the other lodged close to the spinal column. Doctor Bleckard advises most strongly against surgery. We could damage a vital organ. Even more serious, in the case of the spinal column a dislocation to the mid-thoracic region might easily cause paralysis.' He leant forward, both elbows on the desk, and gave a slight shake of the head. 'In other words, do more harm than good.'

'He can recover with two slugs inside of him?' Gribble asked, his voice squeaky with disbelief.

'No reason why not.' Doctor Straus was very matter of fact about it. 'If there is no disruption of vital function –

and in particular the sheath of the central nervous system is intact – his chances are excellent. You'd be surprised, Mr Gribble, at the number of people walking around with quite large foreign bodies inside them – some they're not even aware of.'

'OK if I see him?' Gribble asked.

'No reason not to. But I'm afraid that's all you can do at present – see him, I mean. Apart from his physical injuries, your friend is in a state of traumatised shock. The condition is very like that of a coma. Mind and body shut up shop, so to speak, to allow a period of recuperation and recovery.' Doctor Straus set his pipe down in an ashtray and heaved his lanky frame up from the leather chair. 'Come, I'll take you along.'

They went up three floors in the elevator to the ninth floor of Mount Sinai Hospital, where the intensive-care recovery unit was situated to lessen the constant roar of noise from Fifth Avenue and 100th Street. Gil Gribble was in a state of shock himself. He had been for three days past, ever since the news bulletins had reported the emergency landing of the crippled 747 at a US Navy air base north of Jacksonville, right on the Florida–Georgia state line. It was the first officer and copilot, Greg Richards, who was the hero of the hour. Due to his reducing altitude after the hijack occurred, the aircraft had been under 15,000 feet at the moment of the explosion, and this fact alone had averted a major disaster and the loss of over 300 lives. Luckily, all four engines had retained full power, which enabled Richards to swing the 747 due west and make landfall in under thirty minutes. The O'Neil Naval Air Station was the nearest landing strip long enough to take the 747, and with great skill he had brought her down safely, with only a burst tyre, which observers said was nothing short of a minor miracle in light of the bizarre weather conditions prevailing at the time.

Flying conditions had been perfect, which was what made the circumstances so bizarre.

Because, as it loomed out of the night, the entire base

saw that the aircraft was sheathed in blue static lightning. It was as if, some reported, the 747 was encased in a kind of force field. Nobody could explain it. Even experienced Naval pilots on the base, familiar with chain-ball lightning at high altitude, admitted they'd never seen anything like it.

The emergency services had responded by encircling the 747 and spraying it from nose to tail in foam. Confusion had followed, as many of the passengers, believing the airplane to be on fire, had leapt out on to the runway through the shattered fuselage, not waiting for the deployment of the escape chute. As well as suffering shock and hypothermia from the flight, over a dozen of them had an assortment of broken limbs, and three had died as a result of fractured skulls.

In the pandemonium, the security forces had been unable to seal off the area effectively. There were bodies everywhere, people lying around screaming in agony, and in helping the injured it had been impossible to make any distinction between passengers and hijackers. It was even speculated that the hijackers had been aided in their escape by feigning injury and being taken by ambulance to the local hospital. By the time the captain and flight crew were able to provide an accurate description and an identity check was carried out, not one of the three, possibly four, hijackers had been detained or accounted for. It took an hour and twenty minutes after the emergency landing before a tight security clampdown was imposed on the base – which was an hour and twenty minutes too late.

It had been Don Carlson who had saved Gribble a trip south. Gribble had been on the point of flying down to Jacksonville when Jeff's partner at UltraCast had called to say he had arranged a private air charter to transfer Cawdor to Mount Sinai Hospital in New York City. There they had some of the top surgeons in the country, and Don Carlson had already spoken with Doctor Theodore Straus, the senior consultant, who had agreed to take personal charge of the case.

In one sense, purely selfish, it came as a relief to Gil Gribble to learn that his friend was in a coma. He had dreaded breaking the news (should Cawdor not be aware of it already) about what had happened to Sarah and Daniella. Their terrible fate in the context of Cawdor's own incredible survival, it seemed to Gribble, was like a monstrous black joke played by an evil deity. Sooner or later, of course, Cawdor would *have* to learn of it, but for the moment, thank God, he had been spared the agony, and so had Gribble; he much preferred later to sooner.

'Are you a work colleague of his?' Doctor Straus inquired. They were walking along a corridor with a green rubbery floor which was oddly yielding underfoot. The rooms on either side had observation windows set in the walls. Some of the Venetian blinds were partly open so that Gribble got glimpses, like a running tableau, of shadowy rooms and patients in various stages of nursing care. Most were sleeping, or comatose, he wasn't sure which.

'I'm an old friend of the –' Gribble's voice cracked. 'The family.' He coughed and shook out a red-spotted handkerchief to wipe his nose and hide his emotion.

Used to dealing with distress, Doctor Straus had evolved the strategy of simply ignoring it.

He paused for a moment at the glass-walled cubicle of the nurses' station, had a word with the duty nurse while Gribble hung back, then glanced over the clipboard chart she handed him. From Straus's expression, Gribble discerned nothing either way about Cawdor's condition. The doctor beckoned him on. Outside the door, he took two paper masks from a wall dispenser and showed Gribble how to fasten and adjust the sticky-backed tapes. They went in.

The only illumination came from a single cowled wall lamp on a bracket. The figure under the white sheet looked bloated and enormous, absolutely motionless. But then Gribble realised that the sheet was draped over a cage. Wires trailed down and across the floor to monitoring equipment on a trolley. Blips and traces moved on a blue screen. Doctor Straus bent over the patient. His silvery brows came together in a frown as he studied Cawdor closely. He made sure the tubes and drip feeds were properly in place and then stood back, stroking his chin through the mask. Gribble tiptoed forward on the rubbery floor. There wasn't much to see. He might have been looking at a dead body. There was no sound of breathing, and the raised sheet hid any movement of the chest.

The face, unmistakably Jeff Cawdor's face and remarkably untouched in spite of his ordeal, was unearthlily pale.

Gribble starcd at him. He felt he ought to say something. He'd heard that the voice of a loved one or a friend could penetrate into the consciousness of someone even in a deep coma. Didn't they sometimes play the patient's favourite music? He gently cleared his throat to speak, with not a clue what to say, just anything to make human contact, and Cawdor opened his eyes.

Gribble nearly fainted. His legs buckled and he swayed backward. He would have fallen for sure if Doctor Straus hadn't grabbed his shoulder. It was like seeing the eyes of Frankenstein's monster blink suddenly into life. Gribble gasped, 'Oh my God . . . Oh sweet Jesus!'

The eyes were dulled and unfocused. They weren't looking at him, Gribble realised, or at anything. Then he saw the lips twitch in a tortured parody of a grin and he nearly passed out again. Doctor Straus held him.

'It's all right, take it easy. That sometimes happens. It's an autonomic reaction of the nervous system. The mind's autopilot cuts in and operates the body's mechanical processes.'

'You mean he don't know he's doing it?'

'Your friend is unconscious, Mr Gribble.' But Doctor Straus was frowning again as he looked towards the monitor screen. 'However . . .'

'What?'

'I'm not entirely sure. Except the EEG patterns are not consistent with traumatic shock syndrome.' Doctor

Straus knelt and followed the traces with a manicured finger. 'These peaks, you see? Levels of brain activity are abnormally high for someone in his condition. As I mentioned before, the mind closes down all but the most vital functions in order to protect itself. This is by no means the regular pattern.' He looked up at Gribble. 'Does Cawdor have any history of epilepsy? Psycho-kinetic dysfunction?'

'Ain't got a clue, doc. He never mentioned it.'

Doctor Straus got up, shaking his head. 'At the appropriate time I'd like to carry out a brain scan. Can't risk it until he's in better shape, though. No evidence of physical injury to the cranium, but there might possibly be internalised damage caused by shock syndrome and lack of oxygen. He was in the depressurised cargo hold for over an hour, I'm told.' Doctor Straus indicated they should leave. In the corridor he stripped off his mask and said thoughtfully, 'Those EEG readings. Similar to what one sees at peak dream times when the brain is at its most active.' He gazed down sombrely at Gribble. 'Let's hope that's the explanation. Your friend is dreaming.'

Gribble didn't understand. 'Why? What if he ain't?'

'If he isn't, Mr Gribble, those readings could indicate possible brain damage. In which case – his physical injuries aside – there's nothing we can do for him.'

'But he'll recover, doc, won't he?'

'Damage to the brain is irreversible, Mr Gribble. Permanent. For ever.'

Gil Gribble glanced through the Venetian blind. In the dimly lit room with its flickering blue traces the figure seemed to be floating under the shroudlike sheet. The eyes were closed once more, Gribble saw, in the ghastly pallor of the face.

'So how do we know if Jeff's dreaming or not?'

'We won't know,' Doctor Straus said, turning away, 'until he wakes up.'

'Let us give profound and humble thanks to our Saviour and Redeemer. The way has been prepared and made straight. The circle is unbroken and shall remain unsundered. May the blessings of the Beamers be upon Him, and keep Him safe in His tower of granite and glass.'

Elder Graye arose from his kneeling position and bowed to the stone slabs in the shape of an 'M'. The semicircle of figures in their black robes bowed also, the prayer of thanksgiving a mumbled drone on their lips.

As he departed, Graye glanced across the chamber. The creatures behind the thick wall of greenish glass were quiescent: they had been fed fresh meat recently and were basking contentedly under the artificial sun of the halogen lamps. So recently that the jaws of the alligators were still shiny with rivulets of blood, and the boa constrictor drooped heavily on its branch, weighed down by the lump that stretched its skin to a pearly sheen. They had shared the meal between them, savouring every morsel. It was regrettable, Graye felt, that a replacement for Wilde would have to be found, but unavoidable. Not only had his handsome looks been spoilt by a broken nose, he'd also been encumbered by the deformity of a withered hand that had been almost severed at the wrist.

But there were other candidates, Graye was confident, who with proper grooming could host *The Lovebeams Show*.

Changing into his dark suit of grey pinstripe, he went up in the private elevator to his office at the peak of the pyramid. Through the angled smoked glass the sun was a dull purple ball low in the sky. It was growing late, but for him the time of greatest activity. As night fell over the Americas, other continents were awakening to a new dawn. Unresting during the hours of darkness, he would place calls, send faxes and E-mails to Africa and the Middle East, to India, Eastern Europe and Russia. The global reach of Grace MediaCorp was expanding – established on some continents, a fledgling on others – and the work had to go on, day and night, unceasingly, to bring the Beamers of Joy and their Message to every living soul on the planet.

The way had been prepared and made straight, the circle unbroken, thanks to their Saviour and Redeemer.

Kersh had done everything that was expected of him. Indeed he had done more. Recognising the danger Cawdor presented, he had intervened personally, and decisively, and at great risk to his own wellbeing. Leaving the safety of the tower had been a foolhardy act born of desperation. Graye hardly dared contemplate what might have happened had the outcome been different – if Cawdor had not been defeated. For that would have meant the end of Kersh, and his failure would have wrought destruction upon them all. Total annihilation of their dreams.

But the gamble had paid off. Kersh had triumphed, and the battle had been won. The way had been prepared and made straight. Now Graye's work could proceed unhindered. So, with rejoicing in his heart, he relished the night ahead, beaming the Message to the faithful.

Seated at the desk, his back to the flattened oval of the sun balanced on the horizon, he didn't see the dark clouds slowly gathering, obscuring its face. Against this panorama, the silhouette of Graye's head was a dark asteroid, his eye-sockets like craters of deeper, darker shadow.

He looked up sharply as the bronze-panelled door opened. For anyone to enter without being summoned, or without receiving his express permission, was not only unheard of, it was unthinkable.

Graye's finger strayed to a button on the console beside him.

Mara BeCalla's heels cracked like pistol shots on the marble floor. As she strode towards him, her tall statuesque figure seemed to shimmer before his eyes; for an instant it was transformed into the short, dumpy form of a round-shouldered girl with a pale, pudgy face surrounded by frizzy hair. Graye's outstretched finger curled into his palm.

Then Mara BeCalla was standing in front of the desk, clasping a black leather purse in both hands. Her green eyes studied him for a long silent moment. An icicle of doubt, of trepidation even, pierced through the man behind the desk. He might have dismissed it as fanciful were it not for that flickering change in her appearance: seeing, or rather sensing, the aura of May-Beth as Mara BeCalla crossed the floor. The membrane separating those two selves – whether or not she herself was aware of it – was ominously thin, and did not bode well.

Graye folded his hands in his lap and waited.

Mara BeCalla then did something outrageous. She sat on the corner of his desk. 'Your scheme for Sarah Cawdor and her daughter didn't come off, did it, Mr Graye? Evidently Cawdor knew more than you bargained for. He had forewarning and was able to enter this building and rescue the child, thereby preventing the ceremony taking place. You could say he outsmarted you.'

'You mean that he possessed some knowledge of the past?' Graye shrugged this aside. 'A few fragments, perhaps, imperfect and incomplete. Had Cawdor known the whole, he would never have embarked on that final, fateful flight. In his ignorance he did so, not understanding that our Saviour and Redeemer had the power to intervene.' Graye smiled thinly. 'So you see, Miss BeCalla, we were not "outsmarted" as you put it. This feeble attempt of yours at scoring cheap points is quite misplaced and also a waste of my time. I have work to do.'

His finger moved towards the button.

'Go right ahead.'

Her cool rejoinder had the opposite effect, making Graye pause. Mara BeCalla met his piercing stare unflinchingly. She said, 'What if he did outsmart you and you don't know it? But go right ahead, Mr Graye. If you want to go on believing Cawdor is dead, go ahead and press it.'

In the silence, Graye withdrew his hand, which formed itself into a bony fist. 'Cawdor was killed. He was shot several times and thrown into a freezing baggage hold. He didn't survive. It isn't possible.'

'The facts you state are correct,' Mara BeCalla agreed airily, 'though your assumption isn't. Cawdor did survive.'

'Impossible.' Graye's thin body inclined towards her, his eyes dark and hooded. 'What is this nonsense? Have you any evidence? And, even if you have, why should I believe it? Have you seen the man alive?'

'No, I haven't seen him.'

'Then what proof have you to make this preposterous assertion?'

'An eye-witness account.' From her purse Mara BeCalla took a hand-sized microrecorder and placed it upright on the desk. 'Before I had my own show I started out as a TV news reporter. So, to earn my corn and safeguard both our interests, I thought I'd do a bit of double-checking. I traced the copilot, First Officer Greg Richards. This is an interview I did with him. He insists that the man who was shot during the hijack was found alive in the baggage hold. The man received emergency medical treatment in the sickbay at the Naval base, where he was kept for fourteen hours, and then transferred –'

'You trust him?' Graye interrupted harshly.

'He had no reason to lie.'

'I didn't suggest he was lying, Miss BeCalla. But that he was mistaken. Did you speak to the Naval doctor in charge of the case?'

Mara BeCalla tightened her lips. 'No, I did not. Security was on red-A alert and it was impossible to gain access to the base. I happened to meet First Officer Richards in the lobby of the Orange Park Resort Hotel, which is directly across interstate 295 from the O'Neil Naval Air Station.'

'You "happened to meet" him?'

'We had a few drinks in the Cypress Gardens Bar. After the third Tom Collins he was most cooperative.'

Graye's pointed tongue flicked out to moisten his hard, thin mouth. He was becoming agitated. 'Did he say if Cawdor was lucid or dysfunctional? Were there any signs of personality disassociation?'

'I didn't ask. I'm a journalist by training, Mr Graye, not a psychiatric nurse.'

'Let me hear the tape.'

Mara BeCalla picked up the microrecorder. But instead

366

of switching it on she crossed her legs and lazily swung her foot, gazing past him to the flattened purple sun in its wreath of storm clouds.

When Graye spoke there was a weary stoicism in his voice. 'Very well, Miss BeCalla, I accept what you say. He received treatment at the base. Then what?'

'Moved to New York by private charter plane. Richards said it was Cawdor's business partner, a man named Carlson, who arranged it.'

'Does he know where Cawdor was taken, to which hospital?'

'No.'

Graye pushed back his chair and abruptly stood up. Kneading his veined hands, he turned away and for the first time noticed the storm clouds blotting out the sun. He stared fixedly through the tinted glass wall. 'He must be found. Find him.'

Had Mara BeCalla expected a word of thanks or a sign of gratitude, she was both disappointed and mistaken.

'You're asking me to find him?'

'Why not you? Don't deceive yourself. If Cawdor has survived it will affect your future as much as mine. You have no choice. Without Kersh we have no future.'

This confused her. 'But he's in no danger. You said Kersh was safe unless Cawdor could find a way through, and he can't. That's what you said –'

'On the basis of probability that Cawdor was *dead*. Can't you understand? Cawdor should have died in the baggage hold. The probable outcome was his death, but it didn't happen. So now we are faced with another probability.'

Mara BeCalla felt the blood leave her face. She slid off the desk.

'That Cawdor might . . . succeed?'

'Kersh exists in a place and time beyond our direct influence. He is safe there. He has the power to protect us. But we must do everything we can to protect Him also.' Graye swung round. 'Speak to Carlson as a reporter. Get him to tell you where Cawdor is located.'

'I already have.' Mara BeCalla held up the micro-recorder.

A ghostly smile stole over Graye's face. 'You don't play all your cards at once, I see.'

'I talked to Carlson on the phone earlier today. He refused to give me any information. Just that his partner is being well cared for.'

The smile faded. 'Then don't waste time. We need that information from somewhere. Somebody has to know.'

In the murky twilight that thickened the air between them, the silence stretched on and on. The bloated sun had vanished below the horizon, leaving behind angry massing storm clouds shot through with spikes of fiery red.

2

Perched on the arm of Gribble's tatty couch, Annie Lorentz sipped her coffee from a chipped mug. Watery sunshine of late afternoon washed over the cluttered room from the high narrow windows. Across the street, the stone balustrades and columns of the university library gleamed pale and damp. She'd been working there when she received Gribble's call, following up her research on the traditions and folklore of the Haida tribes of northwest America.

'You're the expert.' Annie shrugged. 'You tell me.'

'I *am* telling you,' Gil Gribble said, his voice high-pitched with annoyance. He jabbed at the screen. 'I didn't put this in. Christ, I don't even know what it means!'

'You don't sleepwalk, do you, Gil?'

'Ha ha. Very funny. Listen, Annie, after I came back from the hospital I worked till late last night, and everything was fine. I switch on this morning and all I get is a screenful of garbage.' He peered round at her in his myopic fashion. 'You're the expert in hieroglyphics and all that stuff. Can *you* decipher it?'

'These aren't hieroglyphics,' Annie Lorentz said.

'You know what I mean,' Gribble sighed. 'This is

your field, after all – dialects and languages and ancient lingo. That's how your mind works, linguistically. I think numerically.'

'Numbers could come into this,' she said, leaning forward.

'Yeah? How?' Gribble scratched his scrub of beard. Forehead puckered, he gazed at the block of letters on the screen:

```
R R T S E D H E S E Y D S N H R D S A E Y E S M E
E E S D N N T N D I A L E I S E E K I C A V E A N
W T A E A U O A N N C R L A R W E E D A D I M E A
O N E E H O R H E N E O U R E O R E E R O L O R H
T E B N T B T T S A D W R B K P C S M G T A C D T
```

Annie studied it. 'Well, the first thing is that the rows are all of equal length, twenty-five characters per line. So that suggests some kind of pattern or arithmetic progression. And there are five lines, which might be a clue.'

'There could've been four or six. So what?'

'There could have been but there aren't,' Annie Lorentz said patiently. 'That's what. Quiet a minute.'

Gribble obeyed. He guessed that she was working through different groups and combinations of letters to find coherent words. He had already tried that himself, and reckoned he had stumbled on the key. But he wasn't going to tell Annie Lorentz that. It would have blown his excuse for calling her and requesting her help. And, the fact was – apart from the pleasure of her delightful company – he really did need another keen intelligence to help him figure out the meaning.

Annie Lorentz was scribbling on a pad. She'd broken the top line down into five-letter groups – RRTSE, DHESE, YDSNH, RDSAE, and so on – trying to make anagrams of them. Nothing. She crossed them out and started again. After three or four minutes, and as many failed guesses, she muttered to herself, 'Of course, that's it. Gotta be!'

Gribble craned to see the pad. 'You found something?'

'It's a form of mirror writing.' Annie Lorentz tapped the screen with the pen. 'See – reversed and upside-down. Take the first vertical line and recite it backward.'

Gribble's mouth fell open. 'That simple?'

'Simple when you know how,' Annie remarked dryly.

'Well, who'd have thought?' Gribble mused in admiration, and then wondered if he wasn't pushing the dumb act a mite too far. He cleared his throat and spelt out the first line, starting at the bottom.

'T–o–w–e–r.' Gribble then read out the next vertical line from the bottom. 'E–n–t–e–r.' He glanced at her. ' "Tower Enter"? Don't make any sense.' Annie's eyes narrowed a fraction, and he quickly decided to see the light.

'Ah, gotcha! If everything's reversed, these are the *last* words in the sequence. We gotta read it backward, yeah? Start with the right-hand column, not the left.'

'You catch on mighty quick,' Annie Lorentz said in a tone of stupendous astonishment, goggling at him. 'I thought for a minute there we might be here till midnight.'

Gribble bent over the keyboard, avoiding her eyes. 'OK, I have it now, I got it. We'll take the drudge out, let the machine reverse the sequence, and see what comes up, huh?'

He tapped keys. The block of letters scrolled up the screen, and in its place appeared:

THANE	DREAM	COMES	ALIVE	TODAY
GRACE	MEDIA	SEEKS	CREED	POWER
KERSH	BRAIN	RULES	WORLD	DECAY
ANNIE	SENDS	THANE	TROTH	BOUND
THANE	NEEDS	BEAST	ENTER	TOWER

The two of them studied it in silence. Annie Lorentz stroked the tip of her nose. 'There's your answer, Gil.'

'Answer?' Gribble's face showed bewilderment, and this time it wasn't faked. This time he was genuinely mystified. 'None of it makes any sense, Annie. What does "Thane" mean for a start?'

'It's from *Macbeth*. The Thane of Cawdor.'

'Then why does it say "Thane" when it means "Cawdor"?'

'Because "Cawdor" has six letters, and the message is limited to five-letter words. Everything there, for whatever reason, is in groups of five.'

Gribble read out aloud, 'Cawdor dream comes alive today . . .' He paused, then stiffened a little as Annie moved up close alongside. Her face was next to his, and he breathed in her perfume. He kept his eyes glued to the screen, feeling a blush creeping up his neck.

Annie said, 'What he's trying to do, Gil, is tell us something about his dreams.' She went on as if thinking aloud. 'They're coming "alive" – he means coming true. Jeff couldn't speak to you at the hospital, so he had to find another way. And this is how.'

Gribble felt a stirring of excitement, and Annie Lorentz wasn't the only cause. He read on, 'Grace media seeks creed power. Any idea what "Grace media" is?'

Annie shook her head. 'Is there a company of that name? Grace Media . . .?' She suddenly made the connection. 'Hey, remember? In his trance Jeff talked about the Shouters. When I checked up on it, that's one of the names used by an ancient religious cult called the Messengers of the Fall from *Grace*.'

They looked at one another. Annie was high, her eyes sparkling. Gribble beamed back at her. He felt suddenly feverish, what with her presence and their shared excitement. Though he buckled down dutifully and gave it his full attention as Annie worked through the message, line by line.

The gist of it, he gathered, went something like this:

'THANE DREAM COMES ALIVE TODAY' meant that the dreams that had plagued Cawdor over recent months were coming true.

'GRACE MEDIA SEEKS CREED POWER' referred to a cult that was seeking religious domination.

'KERSH BRAIN RULES WORLD DECAY' brought them both to a grinding halt. Who was Kersh? And as for his brain ruling over world decay, that was totally baffling.

With the next line they were back on track.

'ANNIE SENDS THANE TROTH BOUND' surely meant that Cawdor was asking Annie to send – or take him – to the Troth Foundation.

Gribble turned surly. 'How come he asked you and not me?'

Annie patted his shoulder. 'Don't get upset, Gil. "Gribble" has seven letters, 'Annie' has five. He was limited – don't ask me why – to groups of five, and my name fits the bill.'

'THANE NEEDS BEAST ENTER TOWER.'

They studied the last line in silence. In his dream-trance, Gribble recalled, Cawdor had spoken of an immensely tall tower reaching up into the sky. He needed to enter it. That much was plain. But now it was Annie who was at a loss, it seemed from the way she was biting her lip.

'I get the tower reference – that's pretty clear. What the heck is "beast" though?'

'I guess I know the answer to that one,' Gribble said with a smug grin. One up for him.

He pointed grandly to the workbench. On it sat the VR headset in a tangle of cables and wires. 'That's what I call it – the Beast.'

Then it dawned on Gribble what Cawdor meant. The Zone Virtual Reality program was the key to all this. Not just a pile of recalcitrant junk with a mind of its own after all. It had a real function, a true purpose. Maybe this was the very reason he'd invented the crazy box of tricks in the first place.

Annie Lorentz got up and stretched. Gribble looked away as her plaid shirt was pulled taut, outlining her lean boyish figure. He said, 'You realise he can't be moved, not right now? Jeff's one sick guy, according to Doctor Straus. Anyway, he's in good hands at Mount Sinai. We'll have to put this on hold, I guess.'

'You're right, Gil, we'll leave it for now,' Annie agreed.

'I guess there's time for this later. We're not in any hurry.'

Gribble gave her a swift glance. It was on the tip of his tongue to suggest they step along to the Italian place down the street. Or maybe even a bar. He dithered, and by then she had shrugged into her green corduroy jacket, and the moment had been lost. He tried anyway.

'Little early. After five is all.' He got up, rubbing his hands briskly. 'But there's a bar that sells Italian spaghetti round the corner.' That didn't sound right. 'I mean, there's a spot that does Italian beer and spaghetti . . . and stuff.'

He was floundering. It was hopeless.

'I'd love to, Gil,' Annie Lorentz said. 'But I can't this evening, sorry.' She moved to the door. 'Rain check?'

Gribble nodded, dry-mouthed. Smitten and in love.

'Can Jeff receive visitors? I'd like to go see him.'

'Uh-huh,' was all Gribble could manage.

'I adore Italian.'

'Uh. Good.'

'We'll make it soon.'

'Uh.'

Gil Gribble sat for a while in reverie. It seemed to him that she really liked him, incredibly. His imagination took a step forward. Him and Annie Lorentz having dinner together, somewhere intimate and romantic, with candles on the tables. Maybe a gypsy violin (no, back off, that was Cary Grant and Deborah Kerr in soft-focus Technicolor). The two of them strolling in the park. Tossing bread to the ducks. Smiling in the sunshine, laughing in the rain (now he was in Neil Sedaka territory).

He knew his fancies were running away with him, and he didn't mind. He felt happy. Gil Gribble and Annie Lorentz an item. It was a distinct possibility, not just a hopeless daydream. He sat there with a soppy look on his face.

No candlelit dinner with Annie, so the next best thing.

He spent fifteen minutes in the cubbyhole of a kitchen, sweating over the griddle, and emerged with a double cheeseburger topped with onions, and a Twinkie bar and can of Carlsberg from the fridge. His thoughts of a golden future that included Annie Lorentz had given him an appetite. He'd taken a big munching bite, the juice running down his wrist, when the phone rang.

His heart leapt upon hearing a female voice, thinking it was Annie, but he knew at once that it wasn't. This voice was low and husky, breathing into the phone.

'Sorry to interrupt your meal, Mr Gribble.'

Gribble swallowed the mouthful of cheeseburger that had made him sound like a pig at the trough. 'That's OK. Who's this?'

'My name is BeCalla, of SPF. Can you spare a minute?'

'What's that?'

'Oh, sorry. Syndicated Press Features. We're doing a piece on the 747 hijack. You know – the one that landed in Florida? I believe you're a friend of someone who was on board?'

'Yeah.'

'It's a big human-interest story, as I'm sure you'll appreciate. We're trying to trace all the people on that flight, follow up their personal experiences. Can you help me?'

Gribble covered a belch. 'What d'ya wanna know?'

'Your friend, a Mr . . .' There was a rustle of paper. 'Mr Cawdor, I believe? We'd like to find out how he's coming along.'

Gribble became wary. 'Listen, Miss . . . er . . . there's just no chance you can see him or speak to him. He's at a real delicate stage at this point in time. Some slimy bastard shot him all to hell. That's all I can tell you.'

'But he *is* recovering?' The husky voice sounded concerned, which reassured him somewhat. Last thing he wanted was a sensation-seeking reporter making capital out of Jeff's plight.

'Well, we're hoping so. I spoke with the doctor in charge of the case, but it's too soon to say. We won't really know till Jeff – that is, Mr Cawdor – regains consciousness.'

'He's in a coma, then?'

'Yeah.'

'I see. Let's pray he comes out of it very soon.'

'You and me both,' Gribble said. This woman sounded OK. Her compassion had a genuine ring to it. Not all reporters were out-and-out shits, he decided. 'Anyway,' he went on, 'you'll have to excuse me. Thanks for your interest, Miss . . . ah . . .'

'BeCalla. SPF. May I leave my number with you, Mr Gribble? I'd very much welcome and appreciate an update on Mr Cawdor in due course, if it isn't too much trouble.'

Gribble jotted down the number she gave him.

'Thank you so much for your time,' the husky voice breathed in his ear. 'I'm certain your friend will recover. It's amazing what medical science can do these days, especially with a surgeon of that calibre looking after him.'

'If anyone can do it, I'm pretty confident Doctor Straus can. He's the best.'

'He certainly is,' she agreed. 'And thanks again.'

'Don't mention it.' Gribble hung up. Munching his cheeseburger with onions, a smile on his face, he took a swallow of Carlsberg and gazed out of the window, dreaming of Annie.

3

The day after, the weather changed completely. From cool and showery to hot and muggy. It marked the beginning of high summer in the city, when air conditioning would be humming full blast for the next two months, designer blouses and lightweight suits would be on the streets, and the calmest temperaments would start to unravel.

Mara BeCalla dressed for both comfort and style. Her button-through crepe de Chine dress with scoop neckline, fitted waist and full skirt was in a striking combination of jade and tiny dots of white. Her high-heeled shoes matched the jade, and so did her eyes as near as damnit. She turned heads as she walked from the basement parking garage on 98th Street and along Fifth Avenue. Men ogled and lusted; women cast sidewise louring looks of unfair sisterly competition.

The main entrance of Mount Sinai Hospital faced Central Park, across four lanes of dense traffic. Garish sportswear and Day-Glo lycra flashed in the bright sunlight as the joggers, blade-skaters and cyclists circulated through the park in an endless riot of colour. On that side of Fifth there was a straggling line for the Metropolitan Museum of Art; on this side an orderly one for the Guggenheim.

The hospital was vast, the second biggest in the state, taking up one whole block. Mara BeCalla stood in the busy main hall, scanning the board that listed over seventy specialist departments. The American Medical Association directory had located Doctor Theodore Straus at Mount Sinai for her, and a call earlier that morning to the hospital's general-inquiry desk had established that he was chief house resident of Surgical Trauma Wing E-4. She found it on the board and moved to the elevator.

The receptionist on the sixth floor didn't bother examining her press accreditation card too closely; she was far too busy. She said shortly, 'You can't possibly see Doctor Straus without prior arrangement. You media people, I don't know who you think you are.'

'Is he presently in the building, do you know?'

'You expect me to keep track of senior surgical staff every minute of the day?' The receptionist scowled, snatching up a phone that was flashing. She said, 'Hold on,' and covered the mouthpiece. 'He could be in his office, or in the ER suite, or doing his rounds in Recovery.' Her pink-lidded eyes behind round, rimless glasses roamed towards the ceiling. 'But, as you haven't done the courtesy of making an appointment, it doesn't actually matter, does it?'

She turned away on the swivel chair, speaking into the phone.

Waiting for the elevator, arms folded, her slim leather purse under her arm, Mara BeCalla casually took in the pale-yellow signboard covered in a sheet of clear plastic. Her eyes drifted down.

E-4 Wing. Recovery Unit – level 9.

The doors slid open. She entered the elevator and pressed for level nine.

If there was any security on the ninth floor it certainly wasn't obvious. The elevator opened on to a corridor with a green rubbery floor on which her heels were perfectly soundless. She glided along silently like a beautiful ghost. The observation windows, as she passed by, showed the reflection of a golden-skinned woman with a mass of tumbled black hair wearing a shawl of Spanish lace.

Without pausing, Mara BeCalla shot swift glances to left and right through the thin gaps in the Venetian blinds, and checked off the names on white pasteboard cards in the brass door slots.

Dresner . . . Jackson . . . Dugdill . . . Trewin . . . Wildenstein . . . Fisher . . . Perlmann . . .

In some of the rooms nurses were attending to patients, but there were none, so far, in the corridor. This floor didn't have the rush and bustle of a general ward; the work went on quietly and unseen in an atmosphere that was poised precariously on the lip of life and death. Eternity was close by, waiting, heartbeats away.

A nurse appeared from the glass-fronted room of the nurses' station. Mara BeCalla slowed her silent pace, watching as the nurse set off purposefully in the other direction without looking her way. Now she could hear the murmur of voices. She could also see the chill light from a bank of monitoring screens reflected in the large panes of glass fronting the corridor. She stopped. She hadn't yet found the room she was seeking, so logically it was further along.

Striding out, she marched along the corridor as if she had every right to be there, and carried on past the nurses' station without wavering for a moment, eyes to the front. It took half a dozen strides for her to be on the other side and out of view.

The corridor stretched emptily ahead, the green floor gleaming under the frosted globes.

'Can I help you?' The voice was sharp, authoritative. It belonged to a tall, thin, hollow-cheeked woman in the dark-blue uniform of a senior staff nurse. She wore a white starched cap set back on a severe cut of straight grey hair.

She remained in the open door of the nurses' station, her head thrust forward on a stringy neck.

'Do you realise where you are? This is a private recovery unit of the hospital. You can't just walk in unannounced.'

Mara BeCalla hung her head. 'I'm so sorry,' she said meekly. 'But I was told there wasn't much time. And I did so want to be with him when he . . .' She let her hands dangle forlornly at her sides, clutching her purse.

'Told by whom? Are you visiting?' The name tab on the breast of the dark-blue uniform identified her as S/N Kelsall. Staff Nurse Kelsall stepped forward, folding her arms, and saw that the eyes of the dark-haired woman were shiny and moist. Mara BeCalla blinked her long lashes and two perfectly formed tears rolled down her cheeks.

'Are you here to visit someone?' Staff Nurse Kelsall asked, pitching her voice in a softer key.

Mara BeCalla nodded. She tried to stifle a sob, but it escaped. 'My husband.'

'And you are?'

'Mrs Cawdor.'

'That is completely untrue.'

'What?' Mara BeCalla stiffened.

Staff Nurse Kelsall allowed herself a tight smile. 'You have been misinformed, Mrs Cawdor. Your husband is in no immediate danger. His condition is stable. Come in here, please.'

Mara BeCalla followed her into the nurses' station.

Behind the low counter a young nurse in an all-white uniform was seated in front of the bank of screens, drinking from a mug. She turned the page of a magazine and looked up. The senior staff nurse was flicking through sheets on a clipboard. 'Do you have any ID on your person, Mrs Cawdor? I have to ask – it's hospital policy.'

Mara BeCalla made a show of hunting inside her purse, and halfway through shook her head distractedly, as if suddenly remembering. She snatched out a tissue and pressed it to her nose.

'I'm sorry, no, I don't have it with me.' She sniffed. 'I keep my licence in the glove compartment of my car.' She gazed tearfully at Staff Nurse Kelsall.

'I see.' She was a tough nut to crack, this Staff Nurse Kelsall. A hardened professional who had seen it all. 'May I ask who it was said your husband was critically ill, Mrs Cawdor?'

'A very close and dear friend of ours – Jeff and myself. Mr Gribble.'

'Forgive me, Mrs Cawdor, I don't quite understand. Your husband has been here three days now and this is your first visit? Am I correct?'

'Yes. I've been . . .' Mara BeCalla stared down at the wadded tissue in her fist. 'I was travelling in Europe. Mr Gribble finally reached me in Hamburg. I got back this morning on the first flight. A priest very kindly gave up his seat so that I could be with my –'

She bent her head, hawking up wretched sobs. Staff Nurse Kelsall hurried round the counter and took the poor woman's arm.

'Please, don't distress yourself. Come with me, I'll take you to him. Your husband is in D-16. His surgeon, Doctor Straus, is hopeful, Mrs Cawdor, very hopeful. You have every reason to be optimistic.' She led Mara BeCalla into the corridor. 'He really is receiving the best possible care.'

Mara BeCalla wiped her eyes. 'You're very kind.'

Staff Nurse Kelsall smiled her special kind smile. 'Chin up, my dear.'

'Can I see him alone?'

'Yes, of course you can.'

Mara BeCalla managed a brave watery smile.

At the desk the young nurse answered the discreetly buzzing phone and came to the door. Reception was on the line. 'Excuse me one moment.' The senior staff nurse squeezed Mrs Cawdor's arm reassuringly and returned to take the call.

Below, on the sixth floor, the receptionist cradled the receiver on her shoulder. She listened, nodding, and raised her pink-lidded eyes.

'Are you related to the patient?'

'No. I'm a friend,' Annie Lorentz said.

The receptionist relayed the information and said, 'Yes, I have that. Thank you, staff nurse.' She hung up. 'The recovery unit is on nine. You can go up but you'll have to wait. The patient already has a visitor.'

'He has?' Annie Lorentz frowned. 'Who is it, do you know?'

'I'm sorry, I don't.'

'Thank you.'

'You're welcome,' the receptionist said automatically, already busy with paperwork.

Annie Lorentz pressed the elevator button. She waited, examining her fingernails. Was it Gil? Or someone from the office – Jeff's partner maybe? Definitely *not* Jeff's secretary, she reckoned with grim humour.

The bell pinged and the doors slid open.

Mara BeCalla paused – the vivid red of her fingernails spread on the half-open door of D-16 – to look behind her. The corridor was deserted. Staff Nurse Kelsall hadn't emerged from the nurses' station.

She went inside. The room held a muted symphony of sounds. The gentle tick-ticka-tick-ticka of monitoring equipment, the whispering sigh of tiny bellows pumping oxygen through the nose tube, the soft bubbling of purifying fluid in the cyclosis system.

On the outer windows overlooking Central Park the fluted vertical blinds had been angled to mask the daylight, admitting a faint golden haze in which the white humped shape seemed to hover, weightless and insubstantial as a cloud.

A complex arrangement of cables and tubes linked Cawdor to the monitoring equipment and life-support apparatus. With her fingertips she followed the transparent oxygen tube in its taped harness to the pumping bellows, and decided to leave it be. The alarm would sound at once in the nurses' station. Two plastic packs were suspended above him on brackets, drip-feeding plasma and glucose. Another tube was connected intravenously into his forearm, maintaining a flow of purifying fluid to keep the arteries and veins from clogging. Reduce or divert the supply of plasma, glucose and the anti-coagulant and he would expire by slow degrees. His heart and respiratory system would continue to function with only minor impairment and few telltale signs. But eventually they would fail. And they would fail for good, beyond hope of retrieval.

As she worked, Mara BeCalla kept one eye on the monitoring screen. She pierced all three tubes at the lowest point of their loops over the bed, making slitlike incisions with nail scissors for the fluids to drip through and soak into the pillow and bedding. On the screen, the blue peaks and troughs showed no change or variation, exactly as she'd surmised. It was working fine.

She turned her head suddenly, listening hard. She could hear agitated voices in the corridor, and then the sound of rapid footsteps thumping on the rubbery floor.

Mara BeCalla was stunned. How could the staff have been alerted when the screen showed no change – the blue blip tracing the peaks and troughs as before?

At the observation window she peered anxiously through the Venetian blind. Two nurses raced by, followed by a white-coated male orderly pushing a trolley loaded with resuscitation equipment. They vanished out of sight along the corridor. Mara BeCalla smiled. The emergency was for another patient.

A stroke of good fortune for her; an instant death sentence for Cawdor. Nobody would be expecting *two* emergencies at the same time: for several crucial minutes Cawdor's monitor would bleep its distress signal to an empty nurses' station.

Whipping back the sheet from its supporting cage, Mara BeCalla reached inside, tore off every wire taped to his chest, plucked out every tube. She flung the tangle away and seized the pillow from under Cawdor's head and pressed it over his face, using the weight of both elbows to bear down. The body lay limp and motionless, offering no resistance whatsoever.

* * *

Annie Lorentz backed hastily against the wall as the orderly went by with the trolley. Nurses appeared magically from out of nowhere. What had been until a few moments ago a silent and empty corridor was suddenly transformed as all hell broke loose.

Inside the nurses' station, a red cross was flashing on one of the screens, the blue blip tracing a flat line. And now two red crosses were flashing, Annie saw. Two emergencies together. She looked at her watch. Bad timing to have turned up on such a busy morning.

She was undecided what to do – whether to carry on waiting or go away and come back some other time. She decided to do neither. Further along the corridor she found Cawdor's name in the door slot.

She tapped lightly and went in.

Annie regretted it at once, and nearly backed out, thinking she had intruded on a private moment when she saw the dark-haired woman leaning intimately over the bed. So intimate, in fact, that she was right on top of him. He was being smothered not with affection, Annie realised, but with a pillow.

And the woman carried on, elbows sunk deep in the pillow, even while she stared over her shoulder, a feverish glitter in her green eyes.

Annie swung herself round the bed-rail. The momentum helped her gather speed and force for the punch that knocked the woman against the wall. But she recovered faster than Annie expected. So fast that Annie was still reaching out to remove the pillow when the woman came back at her. Locked together, the two of them spun across the room, Annie grabbing fistfuls of lustrous black hair, the woman clawing at Annie's face with her sharp red fingernails. They cannoned into the far wall and bounced off, then whirled round and round in a flurry of arms and legs. The gasping struggle threw them off balance and they toppled to the floor, still in a fierce embrace. Annie's cheeks and one side of her neck were on fire where she had been raked by the nails. Twisting her lithe body, she tried to get leverage to pound the dark head against the floor. But the woman was strong – maybe stronger than she was. Spitting and scratching, they rolled back towards the bed. Annie came out on top, which gave her an advantage. Her fingers got a vicelike hold round the woman's throat. The woman heaved up with her strong torso, like a bucking bronco, the sudden movement throwing Annie sideways. Her head connected with the tubular metal leg of the bed. Annie's vision went black, then exploded into bright glittering fireworks. Her grip slackened as she slumped over, and she was left feebly clutching thin air.

Everything went quiet then except for the roaring crowd that was beating a gigantic drum inside her head. Through a pain-filled haze, Annie glimpsed the mane of tousled black hair through the slats of the blind as the woman sped past the window.

Annie used the bed-rail to haul herself up. Her limbs felt weak as water, and her heart was palpitating madly. She knew that the shock of the struggle would soon hit her like a ton of bricks.

Cawdor's face, when she pulled the pillow off him, was so pale it looked translucent. His skin was cold and clammy to the touch. Annie didn't wait to check for breathing. She searched round frantically for the panic button, couldn't find it, and made a staggering run for the door.

In the corridor a young nurse in a white uniform gaped at her.

'My God, what happened to you – your face?'

Blood from the claw marks was dripping down and soaking into Annie's shirt and corduroy jacket.

'If you want to save a life, now's your chance.' Annie grabbed the nurse's arm and pointed. 'The man in there will be dead in minutes. That's how long you got.'

Annie sat in the office on the sixth floor, her face packaged in gauze wadding. The swelling lump on the right side of her head was clearly discernible through her sleek, razor-trimmed hair.

'He can't possibly be moved from here, don't you see that?' Doctor Straus said. 'How can you even ask that after what's just happened?'

'That's precisely why I *am* asking. If his injuries don't kill him, someone else will try to, I'm sure of it. He has to be moved to a place of safety. Mr Cawdor knows that, insists on it.'

Doctor Straus was baffled. 'He's in a coma, Ms Lorentz, and has been since the moment he arrived. In his condition he can't have communicated anything at all. And who was that woman anyway?' Doctor Straus went on, filling his pipe. 'Why does she wish to harm him? You haven't explained that, Ms Lorentz.'

Annie sighed. 'Because I don't know.'

Doctor Straus wafted away a cloud of blue smoke with a gesture that also dismissed her argument as ridiculous. 'You really expect me to risk a patient's life on the basis of paranoia?'

'You think I'm paranoid?' Annie Lorentz said, bridling.

'I think your reasoning most definitely is.'

'Have you put a guard on Mr Cawdor's room?'

'I've alerted our security people, yes.'

'I'm afraid that's not enough.' Annie Lorentz got to her feet. 'I'd like to make a call. In private, from your outer office, if I may.'

Within the space of fifteen minutes Annie had spoken to Doctor Khuman and Doctor Khuman had spoken to Doctor Straus. Annie didn't overhear the conversation – she had no idea what had been said – but, whatever it was, Doctor Straus immediately made arrangements for Cawdor to be transferred to the Troth Foundation.

An hour later he was on his way.

4

'Jeff – great to see you! Doc Khuman says it's OK for a quick chat.' Gil Gribble dragged a chair forward on the sunlit terrace and sat down, hands clasped between his knees, beaming.

'How ya feelin'?'

'Not too bad, I guess. They've patched me up. I'm all kinds of bits and pieces now. Not sure where I stop and the bits and pieces start.'

When he smiled the hollows in his cheeks filled out. It was as if his skin had been shrunk-fit over his skull. Gil Gribble tried not to stare. Remarkably, the only actual disfigurement he could see was the smooth black sheath of moulded thermoplastic that encased Cawdor's left arm from elbow to fingertips. Propped stiffly on the arm of the wheelchair, Gribble assumed it was a cast of some kind, holding and compacting his damaged hand while the bones knitted.

Gribble squirmed in the chair, rubbing his palms together. Birds twittered in the bushes. Already he seemed to have run out of conversation. Trouble was, he didn't know what to say and what not to say. It was like treading over a minefield in the pitch dark. Doctor Khuman had warned him to be careful about speaking to Jeff of his past life.

'The memories of his wife and daughter, and what happened to them, are too painful,' Doctor Khuman had told him. 'The sudden shock could prove disastrous in his present mental condition. For the moment he is reasonably happy and content.'

And it was true, Gribble thought, as they sat there on the terrace. Cawdor didn't seem too much interested in his past life. He was more concerned with his injured hand, banging the hard sheath against the side of the chair, cursing under his breath.

'Is it painful, Jeff?'

'Not too bad, just itches like hell.'

Despite the pleasantly cool breeze, Gribble found that he was perspiring. Avoiding the minefield sure was a strain. He muttered encouragingly, 'Supposed to be a good sign, so they say. When it itches.'

Gribble got up, awkwardly shuffling his feet, tugging at his wispy beard.

'Doc said just a few minutes is all.'

Cawdor didn't seem to mind if he stayed or went. Gratefully, Gribble went.

Gribble finished the brandy and put the glass on the corner of the desk. At least his hands were a mite steadier. He hadn't known what to expect; maybe if Cawdor had been wrapped from head to toe in bandages, it might have been preferable. In fact, Gribble had been prepared for something worse – permanent disability even. Anything but the empty shell of the man he once knew.

'Another one?' Doctor Khuman offered, indicating the Remy Martin.

'No, I'm OK now.' Gribble sucked his teeth. 'Poor Jeff. I guess it's the medication he's on, huh? Still groggy. You're still giving him painkillers, right?'

'Yes, but their effect is marginal. It seems likely –'

'Marginal? You mean he's gonna stay that way – like a blank slate?' Gribble glanced in alarm at Annie Lorentz, who was sitting in the armchair opposite, one leg drawn up, clasping her knee. 'You been here a few days, Annie. You seen any change in him?'

She shook her head. 'He kind of drifts off into another world someplace, as if he's here and yet not here.' Annie Lorentz's cheeks had healed over, though they still bore faint marks from the deep scratches. 'I don't think he's really aware of his surroundings.'

'He say anything?'

'He tries to, but it's as if he's talking to himself. It doesn't make any sense.'

Gribble turned a worried face back to Doctor Khuman.

'So how long is this gonna last? Weeks – months – what?'

'I don't know,' Doctor Khuman admitted. 'As well as the physical damage, your friend Cawdor is suffering severe psychic shock. For that reason we must proceed with extreme caution. Bringing him safely through it will not be easy. And for him it could be highly dangerous. Terminally so.'

'As in dead, you mean?' Hunched in his chair, Gribble

gazed at the empty glass on the desk. 'Maybe I got the wrong end of the stick here or somethin', but I thought the idea was to bring up all this stuff buried in his unconscious, and then Jeff would be done with it – finito. Am I wrong or what?'

'Unfortunately, Gil, you couldn't be more wrong.'

Gribble was taken aback. 'How so?'

'The buried memories, strictly speaking, belong to someone else,' Doctor Khuman explained. 'Someone in the past who was one of Cawdor's previous selves.'

Gribble sighed heavily. 'Sorry, doc, I can't buy that stuff about previous selves or lives or whatever. I just can't.'

'Do you have another theory to explain what's happened to him?'

'If I've lived before I sure don't remember it.'

'Of course not.' Doctor Khuman made a weary gesture. He did look tired, the skin dark and puckered under his eyes. Probably just as worried as he was, Gribble realised. And he didn't have all the answers either: theories but no real answers. 'Physical memory requires a physical brain,' Doctor Khuman continued. 'The brain you have now is not the brain you had before. That other brain died when your body died.'

Gribble was floundering. He wondered what the hell any of this had to do with the state Jeff was in – and, more importantly, getting him well again. Time was passing and all they were doing was sitting here drinking brandy and discussing abstract philosophical concepts. He wanted to be *doing* something, not blowing hot air.

He said shortly, 'You either swallow that guff or you don't. Question of belief, nothing else. You telling me Jeff is locked into something and can't break free?'

'His past and his future.'

Gribble threw up his hands. 'We're back to that. He's going round in circles, is that it? Tell me, doc, does Jeff himself know this? He know what's happening to him on this merry-go-round?'

'I think so, yes.'

'How come?'

'Why do I believe he knows?' Light winked on his silver frames as Doctor Khuman tilted his head. 'Remember how insistent Jeff was that I'd visited him in his office, yet I had no memory of it? Let's suppose that meeting *did* take place. How to explain it? Because Jeff remembers it from a different, a separate, existence. Something must have happened to him *after* that meeting – a disruption of some kind – which diverted him along another path. This path of the here and now. So what he's looking for is a way back to that other existence, but he doesn't know how. That's the crux of the problem. How to devise a way that will access him into timespace.'

'You mean spacetime.'

'I mean timespace.'

'There's a difference?'

'All the difference in the universe. Timespace is concerned with movement, with continual change. We're all of us moving through timespace. What we observe in our day-to-day lives is but one slice through an infinite number of possibilities. We choose to call it reality. But the numberless other possibilities are just as real. They're here, ever present, all around us.'

Annie Lorentz had heard most of this before, but that didn't make her any less lost. 'I've got an infinite number of choices, Satish, is that what you're saying? OK, I'm here, this minute, sitting in this chair, in your office, in the Troth Foundation. Did I choose it or didn't I?'

'Let's say the *you* talking to me now made the choice. That's apparent, isn't it, because you're sitting there right now? But, just as you made a choice, your other selves made their choices too. And maybe,' he added, 'some of them are asking the very same question that you're asking me.'

'Where – in another office of another Troth Foundation facing another Doctor Khuman?' Annie Lorentz said with an impish grin.

'You're getting the idea.' Doctor Khuman nodded, which made her grin fade away. 'Some of those other selves will have grasped it quicker, because those other Doctor

Khumans explained it much better. It's in the nature of timespace that all possibilities are equally viable.'

A glimmer of understanding was alight in Gribble's eyes. He hunched forward, hands clasped together. 'What you're saying, doc, is the same, or similar, I guess, to what I based my interactive VR program on. Probability theory, am I right? The participant has an infinite number of choices.'

'Why do you suppose Jeff sent you the message?' Doctor Khuman smiled. 'He referred to it as the "Beast", which is your pet name, I believe, for the program you devised. That's what I meant when I said he is seeking a way through. How or why Jeff knows this, or hopes it might help him, I'm not sure –'

'Then let's do it!' Gribble burst out, excited at the prospect. 'I got the VR headset and the Zone program in my car. I can set up the whole box of tricks in Jeff's room, no problem. Do we give it a go?'

'Not yet.'

'Huh? Why the heck not? Come on, doc, let's get moving!'

'I'm sorry, Gil, given Jeff's critical physical and mental state I couldn't permit it. We must proceed slowly and cautiously –'

'Just let him sit there, you mean, like a cabbage?' Gribble's face had reddened. 'That ain't helping him any.'

'Do you think I *don't* wish to help him?' asked Doctor Khuman quietly.

'Well, uh . . . No, doc.' Gribble glanced sideways at Annie, a little shamefaced. 'It's just that, well, seeing him that way, a shadow of the guy I knew, it gets to me. And I keep thinking of . . . I mean, I can't forget what happened to –' He stumbled over the words. He wanted to express what he felt about Sarah and Daniella, but emotion choked him into silence.

'That could be one of the reasons why the state of shock persists,' Doctor Khuman told him. 'The memory of what happened to his wife and daughter is too painful for him to confront. So to safeguard itself the mind operates a kind of protective trip mechanism that encases it in mental lead shielding. We must be patient, give Jeff time to assimilate the loss, come to terms with it.'

'I guess you're right,' Gribble muttered, his polite self once more, though in truth he didn't think Khuman *was* right. All this abstract theorising was driving him crazy. Doctor Khuman had Jeff's best interests at heart, that he didn't doubt, but talking round and round in circles instead of *doing* something was getting them nowhere.

Hiding his frustration, Gribble said, 'Somethin' still puzzles me, doc. The message Jeff sent, the mirror writing and the five-letter words . . .'

'What about it?'

'Why only *five* letters per word?'

'That's simple. Because on his left hand, naturally, there are only five fingers.'

'His . . . left hand. The one that's injured?'

Doctor Khuman nodded.

Gil Gribble sighed. 'Well, he'll sure be glad to get rid of that plastic sheath, or cast, or whatever it is. The itching is driving him crazy.'

'The itching is imaginary,' Doctor Khuman said. 'His left hand was smashed beyond repair. I had no choice but to remove it.'

It was on the Tuesday morning, a few minutes after eleven, when his secretary buzzed through to say he had a visitor. Don Carlson was puzzled. 'That can't be right, Helen. I've no one scheduled.'

'You're right, Don, you haven't,' Helen confirmed. 'But I think you'll make time for this one. It's Phyllis Keets.'

Don didn't hesitate. He made time. Because that bizarre episode with Phyllis and Jeff somehow seemed part of what had gone wrong in recent months. In fact, as he recalled, Phyllis's accusation that Jeff had sexually assaulted her was how this nightmare scenario had kicked off. From that point the whole shooting match had gone rapidly downhill on a grease slide with a following gale.

Phyllis was pale and obviously distraught, and the first

thing he did was to sit her down on the couch and ask Helen to bring in some coffee. The second thing he did was to seat himself at a safe distance in an armchair, the ceramic-tiled coffee table between them.

She wasn't crying, but he could tell she had been, and recently, and Don got the impression it had taken a lot out of her, getting this far. She sat with her plump knees pressed together, her hands never still in her lap. 'I can't make you understand, Mr Carlson, how awful I feel at what I did. It was terrible of me. I don't understand it myself.'

'And what would that be?' Don asked quietly, knowing what was coming.

'What I told you on the phone, about... about...' Phyllis gulped in air like a stranded fish. She stuffed a lace-edged handkerchief to her mouth, shutting her eyes tightly. 'It never happened.' Her voice was muffled.

Don said with icy politeness, 'I'm sorry, Phyllis, I didn't hear you,' though he had heard perfectly well.

'It never happened like I told you. None of it did.' She glanced up, blinking rapidly, as Helen placed a tray on the table. Helen caught Don's eye as she turned away, with a 'Want me to stay?' lift of the eyebrows. He shook his head and she went out.

'You know, Phyllis,' Don said, leaning forward with his elbows on his knees, 'this confession is as shocking as the accusation you made against Jeff. For you to come straight out like this and admit it was all made up, a pack of lies, I find quite incredible. Have you any idea of the stress and anguish you caused him? What the hell was it all about? What were you *playing* at, for pity's sake?'

'I was jealous, I guess.'

'Jealous of who, *what*? I don't understand what you're saying.'

Phyllis stared miserably at her clenched hands. 'His wife, Sarah. I was in love with ... I thought I was in love with him, with Jeff. He was always so nice to me. We had fun together – I mean, just laughs, you know, joking and stuff? I thought it was more; I wanted it to be more; but nothing ever came of it. Then I started to hate her. She had him and I didn't. How or why it happened – what I did – I can't explain, Mr Carlson. It was unforgivable.'

Don shook his head in weary despair. He felt so angry and frustrated he wanted to reach out and give the stupid cow a full-handed stinging slap right across her fat pitiful face. It took most of his self-control to resist the temptation.

'Good for you, Phyllis,' he told her bitterly, 'but it's a bit late in the day, wouldn't you say? So why tell me all this stuff now when it's too damn late to do any good? You want me to forgive you on Jeff's behalf? Pat your hand and tell you it's fine, forget it, water under the bridge? I can't do it. Well, I can, but I fucking won't.'

'I don't expect you to,' Phyllis said quietly. She sniffed and dabbed at her button nose. 'I felt so ashamed when I heard what happened to his wife and daughter. Like I was in some way to blame. I can't sleep or eat or nothing. The shame of it never leaves me in peace for a minute.'

'That's tough, Phyllis,' Don said. 'Or do I mean "tough crud"? I think I do.'

'I'm so sorry, Mr Carlson. Honestly and truly, I wish there was something I could do.'

'There is. You can collect your severance cheque on the way out. You know where the cashier's office is.'

'Yes.' Phyllis nodded meekly. 'It's one floor down.'

Don Carlson goggled at her. It began to fit together. He'd speculated to Jeff that Phyllis Keets had suffered a nervous breakdown, and it seemed he was right. The woman was out of her tree. Living on the planet Zarg.

He met her eye nervously as she gazed up at him. 'Is he going to be all right, Mr Carlson? He'll make it, won't he?'

'We hope so,' Don said stiffly.

'I wish I could tell Jeff how sorry I am. And wish him well, too, of course. Such a terrible thing to have happened.' Her face went ugly as she began to weep. The tears traced shiny paths through the thick powder on her cheeks. Now she had started she couldn't stop, sobbing uncontrollably as her shoulders heaved.

Don said awkwardly, 'If it'll make you feel any better, Phyllis, I'll get word to him. OK, will that do? Then you can start eating and sleeping again,' he added dryly.

'Thank you, Mr Carlson, oh thank you.' Before he could react she reached out and grasped his hand in both of hers. He recoiled from the warm, clammy pressure but left it there, enduring the ordeal in stomach-churning silence. 'Tell him, tell him,' Phyllis was weeping and babbling hysterically, 'I never wished him any harm, and what a cruel thing I did, and if I could take it back I would, I'd give anything to do that. Please tell him that, please!'

Don extricated his hand, and it took an effort not to wipe it on his trouser leg. He said, 'I can't tell him personally, Phyllis. He's been moved upstate to the Troth Clinic or some such place. I've already promised Jeff will get your message, and I'll make sure he does. That's the best I can do.'

He thanked the Lord, then, that this seemed to calm her. She wiped her eyes and even attempted a watery smile as she pointed at the jug on the tray. 'Coffee's gone cold. My fault. Sorry.'

'Never mind,' Don said automatically, as he was thinking, Out of her tree without a fucking parachute. She's right here, guys. Just make sure those straps are good and tight.

The elevator doors opened to admit Phyllis Keets to the basement parking garage of the Chrysler Building. She walked past the dimly gleaming ranks of cars and limos to the bulbous-nosed RV with ribbed all-terrain tyres and mirror-reflecting windows. At her approach the side door slid open and an arm was extended to help her inside. The door slid shut with a solid clunk.

Phyllis settled herself on the bench seat and noisily blew her nose into a tissue.

The five figures, attired in dark suits, waited for her to finish. She fumbled in her purse for another tissue, wiped her stained cheeks while they patiently waited some more.

'Are you catching cold?' Graye inquired.

'I had to give a performance.'

'Was it a success?'

'He seemed to think so.'

'What do you think?'

'Oh yes.' Phyllis pushed the crumpled tissues into her bag. 'When the Oscar nominations are announced, check out my name.' She looked up, eyes dry now, stony. 'I found him.'

5

The bed felt solid. The bedsprings creaked as he moved his weight.

Cawdor gasped and laughed weakly. For a horrible moment he'd thought he must be dead, but the creaking bedsprings reassured him he wasn't. He pressed his foot to the floor, and that was solid, too. He moved across the solid floor to the door. The corridor was dark and there was a musty smell – but of course the house was very old, Cawdor reminded himself, with stone floors and arched portals and hanging tapestries thirty feet long.

The floor was gritty underfoot. Mrs Brandt was an efficient housekeeper but sweeping wasn't one of her many talents. He paused in the chill corridor with its flagged floor, uncertain which way to go. Ahead of him in the gloom was a staircase, the varnish on the banister rail worn through to the wood where many hands had scuffed it away. Cawdor climbed the staircase to a part of the house he'd never been before. Unlike the rest of the building, this was more like a hospital. The floor had a rubbery feel to it. The walls were a restful shade of green, with globes in the ceiling casting an even light that didn't hurt the eyes.

There was an acrid smell in the air, as of something burning.

Cawdor paused in mid-stride. A door, slightly ajar, seemed to be inviting him to push it open. He did so and went in.

A figure shrouded in a white sheet lies on a bed, wires

trailing to the floor. The shrouded figure twitches; the torso jerks; the legs quiver. There is the dry crackle of electricity, and the smell of burning is stronger now, stinging his nostrils. Afraid to look, and yet compelled to, Cawdor moves to the bed and pulls back the sheet.

Then freezes, rooted to the spot.

The man lying there – rubber pads clamped to his temples, face tight with pain as the surges of electricity course through his body – is himself. Cawdor stands by the bed, the sheet in his hand, gazing down numbly at his own white, foam-flecked face.

The eyelids flicker and spring open. The eyes are dulled and unfocused. They register Cawdor's amazement, and a sudden nervous spasm jerks the tortured features into what might be a grin.

'Took your time, Jeff . . .' The lips slowly form the words, as if each word is an agony. 'But you finally made it.'

Cawdor reaches out, only to see the image of himself and the hospital bed fading away. The sheet in his hand disperses like pale smoke. The figure in the bed is now a vague blur, hovering in space, like a pencil sketch with only the outlines left.

Leaning against the wall, Cawdor wipes cold sweat from his face. His limbs are shaking, whether through fear or fatigue he doesn't know. He squeezes his left hand into a fist, trying to stop the pins and needles shooting through it.

Cawdor raises the hand in front of his face and examines the fingers. He shuts his eyes. The tingling sensation continues as before, but there's something else. Something he didn't expect.

He can see the hand through his closed eyelids.

The hand is floating, ghostlike, unattached, in midair. He opens his eyes and stares at it.

He turns away and for the first time sees the plate-glass window. It takes up the whole of one wall, like a polished black mirror. He cups his hands to the glass and stares out. Buildings loom, rising up to a starry sky – a slice of crescent moon high above. He looks down below and sees a swamp of industrial waste, belching toxic fumes. And there are people down there, trudging through it, grey-faced, emaciated, wearing masks. Like the lost souls of the damned.

Cawdor stares through his cupped hands.

Who *are* these people?

What city is this?

From the window, Cawdor gazes down into the dark miasmic canyons, and far below he sees a deserted highway. Cluster of lights in the distance. A car pulls in at a gas station. A thin man with lank fair hair takes a gun from the glove compartment and tucks it inside his dark-blue windbreaker. While the attendant fills the tank he strolls inside and browses through the magazines. The attendant returns, a fat red-haired kid of fifteen or sixteen, wiping his hands on a rag. The man with lank fair hair and the bad eye swivels round, one hand free, the other inside his windbreaker. *All the cash you have, sonny. Hand it over. Now.* The kid turns to the drawer. His hand hovers, drifts below the counter. He turns suddenly, burnished blue barrel raised. *Go ahead, scumbag. Make my day.* Grins with gapped teeth. *Take your hand outta there. Slowly.* The man with lank fair hair looks surprised. The look of surprise transfers to the red-haired kid as the man with lank fair hair brings his free hand up and fires from the hip. Sucker punch. The gun was tucked into the back of his pants. The kid slithers on his own blood. His belly is dripping. He does a soft-shoe shuffle and tries a back flip, which doesn't come off on the wet floor. He stares up at the man, remembering his lank fair hair and bad eye and scar for all of three seconds, before another bullet goes through his windpipe and another lodges in his left lung. The man with lank fair hair scoops out the cash drawer and stuffs a dozen Twinkie bars into his pocket. Shakes his head. *Make my day!* What a jerk-off.

Cawdor watches everything – watches the kid slither and drop behind the counter. Watches the man with lank fair hair bundle the leaking leaden body in the trunk and speed away down the dark deserted highway – and can do nothing. The events will not be changed. How can they be changed, when they are taking place inside Kersh's brain?

But, if nothing can be changed, Cawdor thinks despairingly, why is he here? Kersh exists, and while he continues to exist these events will continue to happen, enacting and re-enacting themselves . . .

Behold in this mirror all your past and future times . . .

He looks through his own ghostlike reflection in the gleaming black surface of the window, and suddenly he realises what Doctor Khuman has been driving at since the day they met. History could not be rewritten. What was past was gone for ever. *If it was the only past.* The future was infinite in its permutations, so why not the past?

An infinity of pasts.

Cawdor begins to perceive what Doctor Khuman had meant about the unity of all things – the endless cycle of birth, death and rebirth – being broken in one place. A small gap through which one could enter into something strange and new, not bound by the everyday plodding pace of the here and the now.

There is a way through. A gap exists and, if Kersh could find it, then so can he.

Cawdor stands at the window looking up at the pale slice of moon. It remains stuck there like a piece of silver paper. Around it the stars are fat and brilliant, sparkling against the black velvet sky. Nodding to himself, a slow smile creeps over his lips. He now knows without the slightest shadow of doubt that Kersh is the man on the balcony on top of the tower.

And that Kersh is the man he has to destroy.

Kersh has the uneasy feeling he's being got at. He can't put his finger on when and how it started. Just that things seem to be out of whack all of a sudden.

Stretched out on the sofa, Jack Daniel's on the rocks in one hand, remote zapper in the other, he tries to relax with some favourite entertainment. He knows what he wants to see, and flicks up the picture, boosts the stereo surround-sound to near max, settles back and takes a stiff belt. Spotlights stab down on to the stage. A drum roll starts up, giving him goosebumps, because he's already feeling the thrill of anticipation. Then the applause builds like a wave breaking over rocks as a shadowy figure strides out from the side of the stage, and Kersh can feel the tension shoot through the auditorium like an electric charge.

Nobody beats the King in live performance. Not even Frankie boy, and he was pretty hot in his heyday.

Kersh's grin sags. Liquor dribbles out and drips off his chin.

The tall lean guy with the sideburns and the snarl and the hip swivel has turned into a bloated whale in a sequinned suit with a pasty face made out of Pilsbury dough. He doesn't stand there: he squats, all 275 pounds of him. He doesn't walk: he waddles, hairless chest and flabby gut bursting through the buttons of his shirt. And that curl-lipped snarl has turned into the weak pleading puppy-dog look of a drunk begging for a hand-out.

Kersh can only stare; he's too stunned to do anything else. He doesn't want this. Not only that, he didn't *ask* for it. And anything he wants he asks for and gets. That's part of the deal. Twenty-one-year-old Elvis live in performance was what he asked for, not this pathetic, middle-aged fat slob dressed up like a Christmas tree.

OK, forget it. There are other entertainments on offer. He takes a shower, douses himself in Old Spice, slips into his black silk robe. He's lying there on the bed, rampant as a stallion, ready to fuck anything in lace pants with an ass and two legs, and what happens? Nothing. The door doesn't open and no Sue Ellen comes in. Maybe, Kersh thinks, he's growing tired of her. Getting jaded with the same old routine with the same old broad. So he lies there, trying to conjure up a real firecracker who'll turn him on and light his candle.

He lies there, blank-eyed, waiting, not really aware of the motionless, unchanging stars through the glass ceiling. And after a while he starts to get desperate. He ransacks his brain for a desirable image, and what should pop up but May-Beth, the religious freak who paid him a visit in the Angola State Pen. No, no, Kersh protests, I can do better than that. He doesn't want May-Beth, for chrissakes: he wants a gorgeous fantasy made flesh. A TV or movie star to drift through the door in a pink negligée, pouting red lips and a please-take-me-but-be-gentle look in her eyes.

Kersh anxiously watches the door, dry-mouthed. If it opens and May-Beth walks in he'll go apeshit. What are they trying to do: palm him off with third best? He shuts his eyes, squeezing out any thought or image of her, arms spread-eagled on the bed, fists clenched tight. He's scared now because, if she *does* appear, and he doesn't want her to, that means he's losing control of his own desires. It means that all the cruddy stuff buried deep down there can float up anytime it wants to.

You call the shots around here, Kersh tells himself. You create the universe in your own image – the world *you* want to exist in.

It works. May-Beth doesn't show, which proves he's still in charge and gives him a boost. He's confident again. The corkscrew in place of his spine starts to unwind, and so does Kersh. The stars above grow dim as he floats off on a cloud, feeling warm and peaceful, breathing in the bracing tang of Old Spice . . .

Upon waking, Kersh experiences the most horrible feeling he's ever had in his entire life. There's somebody inside his mind.

As he lies on the black silk sheets, the unchanging spread of stars overhead, a sense of dreadful panic overwhelms him. Somehow or other, Cawdor has gained access to the tower. He's down there right now, many floors below, ransacking his store of memories. How can this be, Kersh wonders, when Baby Sam promised to protect him? No way Cawdor can get through: it's impossible – that's what he was told. But the impossible is happening. It feels like a termite in his brain. A parasite. Right now it's a minor irritant, wriggling away, but pretty soon it will burrow its way into the core of his brain and then . . . and then . . .

Kersh is sweating. He swings his legs down and stands up, his toes deep in the shaggy pile of the carpet. He is very frightened and also very angry. He feels betrayed. Promises were given, assurances made. He was supposed to be safe here in his tower – nothing could ever get to him. And, if something or someone *did* get through, there was always Baby Sam. So where is the sleazebag now, Kersh snarls to himself, when he needs him?

He pads through into the living room. The sunken well of white carpet is splashed here and there with pools of lamplight. Over in the corner the glinting bottles on the mirror shelves wink at him invitingly. He could drown his sorrows, but that wouldn't solve jackshit. It would screw up his head, throw his thoughts into chaos.

Kersh pauses, stares at the bottles.

Maybe that's exactly what he *ought* to do. Get smashed out of his skull. How would Cawdor handle being trapped inside the mind of a drunk? But Kersh has doubts. Suppose Cawdor gets to him when he's muzzy and incapable? He'd be easy meat. Shish kebab on a skewer.

But then another thought strikes him. *This is total bullshit!* Cawdor is living in his, Kersh's, world. Cawdor can't do a damn thing Kersh doesn't want him to do. I could squish him like an ant if I wanted to, Kersh thinks. He exists in a world I created, a world where the Messengers can spread their Message all over the globe. I control the whole thing. For the first time in his life, Frank Rudolph Kersh is calling the shots. Yes! Then what the fuck, Kersh thinks savagely, is Cawdor doing in *his* tower? How the hell did he get through? Cawdor is supposed to be *out there*, in the world Kersh created, dead or dying after six shots were pumped into him and he was dumped in the freezing hold of a 747 over the Atlantic.

But he isn't.

Kersh's balls shrivel and contract inside their turkey-gizzard sac.

It doesn't matter how Cawdor got through, he realises, it's all down to him. If he doesn't stop Cawdor, nobody will. Jee-*zuzz*. As usual it's all down to good ole boy Frank to haul his chestnuts out of the fire.

'Need some help?'

Kersh notices a brown trail on the white carpet. He follows it to the pulsating bag of pus grinning up at him, feelers twitching, squatting in a spreading pool of green-grey emission.

Kersh retches. The smell alone turns his stomach inside out.

He wipes the spittle from his mouth. 'Took your time, scumbag.'

'I only come when you need me,' says Baby Sam. 'Got a problem, Frank?'

'Yeah, he's in here – down there somewhere.' Kersh points at the floor. 'I want him stopped. Can you do it?'

'I can try . . .'

'You can *try*?' Kersh is both furious and incredulous. 'You understand what I'm tellin' you? I don't know how the bastard did it but he's in here and I want him stopped, goddamnit!'

Baby Sam uses a slimy feeler to scratch the place where his nose ought to be. 'That ain't s'posed to happen. What went wrong?'

'I don't fuckin' know! Does it matter?' Kersh aims a kick at him but, being barefoot, is careful not to make contact with the quivering glutinous mound. 'Get down there and do your job. Not just my ass on the line, remember. He gets through, we *all* of us take the drop, you included.'

THE CITY OF PERPETUAL NIGHT

1

Each day was like drifting through a warm fog. He seemed to have few recent memories, and the memories he did have were painful and unwelcome: white figures in masks holding shiny instruments, the soft thud and hiss of machines. The sickly aftertaste at the back of his throat, coating his tongue with a pasty white grime.

There was the shaded room too – sunlight glancing off Venetian blinds and splintering across the ceiling.

Cawdor didn't like this memory. He tried to avoid it. He didn't want to know why. It was too full of pain. If the thorn in the foot hurts, don't put pressure on it. Use the other foot. Better yet, don't walk at all.

But, if his memories were vague, his dreams were vividly alive.

Night after night they came to him, more real than his waking life. He was able to reconstruct last night's dream, for instance, in every specific detail.

He moved out from his room into the corridor, walking, able-bodied, wondering in which direction Doctor Khuman's office was. It was the state of abandonment and neglect as much as the darkness that confused him: the floor strewn with rubble and broken glass. The smell of mildew and decay. The slimy sheen of damp on the walls.

He turned a corner, arms outstretched, shuffling through the debris like a sleepwalker.

There was a door in front of him, at the end of the

corridor. When he touched it his fingers sank into the spongy mass where the covering had rotted away. It was, or had been, a padded door. As the door swings open under the pressure of his hand a breeze of dank clammy air wraps itself around his face. He hears the swish and gurgle of water, and suddenly he is standing in a scummy frothing tide which laps over his boots and swirls about his calves. The floor tilts. Timbers creak and groan. Everything shudders as the sea batters at the wooden walls. Somewhere from the darkness comes a scuffling and squeaking, and Cawdor becomes aware of yellow slitted eyes on all sides watching with a steady, unblinking malevolence. Their human larder has arrived.

But he is mistaken.

It isn't him the rats are watching.

A man is slumped on a heap of gravel, knees drawn up under his chin, iron manacles round his wrists and ankles. His eyes are shut. He might be sleeping, Cawdor thinks, but if so it is a fitful, unsettled sleep. The man's shoulders twitch and jerk. Spasms chase themselves across his face as dark murky dreams swim up to the surface. Now and then he starts violently and his eyelids spring open, only to droop again, the head lolling forward, the tics resuming their game of hide and seek across his ravaged features, grey with fatigue.

Cawdor watches the man's troubled sleep for some time. It is like observing a racial memory. A dream of his own come to life. He is both watcher and watched.

This is the mirror world his dreams have led him into, Cawdor realises, the world he now inhabits. Now he doesn't need to awake; he can continue exploring the mirror world until, at last, it brings him face to face with Kersh. He is relentless and filled with fierce resolve. Nothing will stop him. There is no escape for Kersh – nowhere for him to hide from the consuming desire for revenge that fuels Cawdor like a hard bright flame.

He moves on, confidently. Ahead of him in the gloom there is a staircase, heaps of dust in the corners. As he climbs it he sees that the varnish on the banister rail is worn through to the wood with the passage of many hands. The staircase leads up to a corridor, the walls dim and green under the ceiling globes. Cawdor lifts his head. He can smell something burning, sharp and acrid. Through a half-open door he glimpses a figure lying on the bed, shrouded in white. Wires trail across the floor. The smell of burning is stronger now, and he can hear the dry crackle of electricity.

All this is familar to him. It is too familiar. The same dream as before.

Cawdor moves to the bed. This time he is afraid to look because he knows what he will find. Even though he tells himself it won't be the same, he knows that it will. And it is.

He pulls back the sheet and looks at himself, the rubber pads clamped to his temples, his own face creased with pain as the surges of electricity course through his body. He stands holding the sheet in his hand, feeling the sickness of despair as he gazes down at the white, foam-flecked face.

And as before, as he knows they will, the dulled, unfocused eyes seek him out, and the mouth twists into a tortured grin.

'Took your time, Jeff . . .' The words escape with agonising slowness. 'But you finally made it.'

The image vaporises and fades away to nothing. Cawdor looks at his hand, the fingers curled, still holding the nonexistent sheet – just as it was the last time.

I've been through all this, Cawdor thinks, and it's happening again. I'm not climbing the tower at all. I'm no nearer to Kersh than I was before. I'm going round in circles.

Cawdor cups his hand to the window and stares out. The scene is unchanging. Buildings loom on all sides, rising up to a starry sky. The pale slice of moon hasn't moved. Nothing here ever moves or changes; it just repeats itself endlessly. He feels numb with despair and defeat. How can he break free of this? More than belief in himself, Cawdor realises, he needs help from outside.

Somehow he has to reach out to Doctor Khuman and Gil Gribble, get a message to them. Do they know he's trapped in here? How can he communicate with them?

How?

Cawdor squeezes his left hand, trying to stop the pins and needles shooting through it. The tingling is driving him insane.

He shuts his eyes and sees the hand, ghostlike, floating in midair. Of course – *there is a way*. The way he got through before, to Gribble and Annie Lorentz, when he was in the coma at Mount Sinai Hospital. They interpreted the message and had him moved to the Troth Foundation. That must mean, Cawdor thinks, hope rising again, he *can* communicate with the outside world. Kersh has his allies out there in the Messengers and Mara BeCalla; and so has he – if only he can reach them.

Eyes closed, he pulls together every shred of concentration, willing Doctor Khuman and Gribble to hear him and understand. Please hear me and understand how much I need your help. Raising his hand, he presses it flat to the window and feels a million tiny pins jabbing away in his fingertips. Some form of interaction – an exchange of energy – between his hand and the glass. The tingling increases and shoots up his arm like an electric shock.

What does it signify – that his message has got through? That out there they can hear him, and understand, and help him?

Cawdor opens his eyes and stares through his own dim reflection at the city spread out before him. He waits in the timeless moment for a sign, something to tell him he is not alone. He waits, and nothing happens, and continues to happen. But then, miraculously, he sees a light. No – a cluster of lights – in the distance. Night wind blowing sand across the blacktop. A car pulls in at a gas station. A man with lank fair hair takes a gun from the glove compartment and tucks it inside his dark-blue windbreaker as a red-haired kid pumps gas into the tank. The man gets out, stretches, and ambles towards a wooden shack . . .

The same thing, exactly as before. The same events

happen and keep on happening. And he can do nothing. It isn't Kersh who's trapped in here: it's *him*. It will take an eternity to climb the tower, and even then, at the end of it, he will be no nearer. The knowledge is like a tremendous deadening weight on his spirit.

The circle is unbroken, Cawdor knows, interminably going round and round towards never ending infinity.

From his window Gil Gribble looked at the moon hanging in the summer sky, bright and sharp as a silver dollar, with just one or two faint stars becoming visible as the colour drained away and the darkness deepened over the wooded slopes.

Doctor Khuman's housekeeper, Mrs Brandt, had shown him to the room earlier that evening, and in passing had remarked that it was the one Cawdor had occupied on his first visit. Gribble wished she hadn't told him that. He was miserable enough, and the poignancy of his spending the night in the same room made him even more despondent. He was also feeling guilty. Jeff's condition hadn't improved; in fact he had relapsed into a coma. They should never have transferred him from Mount Sinai Hospital in New York. There he would have received expert medical attention and the best possible nursing care. Moving him here was too great a risk – greater, certainly, Gribble reckoned, than the supposed threat to his life had he remained there. After all, they could have tightened up on security, hired 24-hour protection if needs be. It was a mistake, and he regretted it bitterly.

Gribble turned away from the window and switched on the bedside lamp. He thought he might read for a while. He was fairly tired, but too restless to sleep. He sat down on the bed and then immediately got up again. Maybe a walk in the grounds would settle his nerves. He went to the door, stood dithering there for a few moments, and instead turned about and headed for the bathroom. He wasn't sure why, because he didn't need to pee, but Gribble turned the handle anyway and went in.

His own dim reflection, silhouetted against the glow of the bedside lamp, confronted him in the bevelled mirror of the vanity cabinet. The sight of his round face and tangle of reddish beard depressed him even more. The idea of him and Annie Lorentz becoming an item – what a joke. Where did he get these crazy notions? You only had to look at him to know it was plain ridiculous. What kind of juvenile fantasy land was he living in to even contemplate such a –

Gribble's mind stopped dead. He felt the breath gather in his chest, and involuntarily he held it in as if a sudden shock had seized up both his lungs. Which it had. The bathroom was in semidarkness, the only light from the lamp in the bedroom, and by its glow he saw a row of letters appear on the surface of the mirror.

R R T S E

A second row formed itself:

E E S D N

And was followed by:

W T A E A
O N E E H
T E B N T

It hardly took a moment to interpret the mirror writing, because Gribble knew already what it meant: THANE NEEDS BEAST ENTER TOWER.

As he read the message in the mirror, it seemed to Gribble as though his mind was a flower opening to the sun. The same message, of course, that Cawdor had sent via the computer – but only part of it. Gribble nodded to himself, knowing why, because now he understood. This was the vital part. Trapped in its shell of a body, Cawdor's mind was reaching out to him, striving to communicate this final desperate instruction, or plea, or cry for help.

Gribble wasn't sure which. But that didn't matter.

* * *

Leaning back in his seat, the driver said over his shoulder, 'Albany coming up, sir. Should I stay on 87 or branch west on interstate 90?'

'Take the shortest route.'

'Not sure which it is,' the driver said. He glanced across the darkened cab of the recreational vehicle to his companion, who was peering at a road map spread over his knees with the aid of an angled spotlight. 'What say?'

'Not much to choose between 'em.'

The driver glanced back again, anxious not to make a mistake.

'Use your best judgement,' Graye said.

The driver's companion came to a decision. 'OK. Take interstate 90. Then we head north on route 30 past Great Sacandaga Lake.'

'And the distance from here?' Graye asked.

'Less than a hundred,' the man with the map said. 'Probably nearer eighty.'

Graye leant back in the padded chair, his hands splayed loosely over the armrests. His face was hidden in shadow except when a neon sign along the highway or the headlights of a car splashed briefly across it. Even then his expression was hidden in the deep pits of his bony eye sockets.

Behind him sat the other elders. In the chair next to his, Phyllis Keets stared straight ahead, her round face framed by tiny kiss curls, her lips pressed tightly together. The slight jolting of the ribbed tyres on the concrete highway made her bosom jerk and tremble, causing the silver pin on her left breast to send out faint flashing gleams.

Ahead, a cluster of signs announced they were nearing the divergence of the two interstates: to the north, Saratoga Springs and Glens Falls; to the west, Schenectady, Amsterdam and Utica. The driver signalled and slid into the right-hand lane, slowing the vehicle to take the curve through the underpass which led on to interstate 90.

On the illuminated dashboard the green glow of the clock showed 9:52. At this speed – a steady sixty – the driver estimated they would make Griffin by eleven o'clock. Their final destination was somewhere near there, deep in the Adirondack National Park. He doubted that it would be signed, which worried him, but he had hopes that the Troth Foundation wouldn't be too hard to find in that sparsely populated neck of the woods.

2

Annie Lorentz was perched on the window ledge, one blue-jeaned knee drawn up supporting her elbow, her chin propped on her fist. Her eyes hadn't moved in the past several minutes, had scarcely blinked, and Gribble had a pretty good idea why.

He guessed that she didn't like the shiny black motorcycle helmet he had rigged up with wires. It made Jeff resemble an alien monster from a fifties horror movie. For another thing, she probably couldn't get a handle on the bizarre setup: Jeff Cawdor's physical body right here in front of her, lying prone on the bed, while his mental being was absent, free to roam anyplace it chose. Even into realms that existed only in the imagination. Pretty creepy, Gribble had to admit.

Annie took a gulp of the Irish whiskey that Gribble had thoughtfully placed in her hand. 'Can he hear us?' she asked him. 'Is Jeff aware of people around him in the room?'

'The helmet's insulated to cut out external sound, but some of it might seep in. It'll come through like voices in the head, you know? Not someone actually talking to him direct.'

Gribble was at the foot of the bed, the laptop with its small green screen on a low table in front of him. He had made a bank of pillows to support the VR headpiece and thus take the burden off Jeff's shoulders. His body outlined under the single sheet, Cawdor lay motionless, arms by his sides. Sensor pads were attached to his right wrist and to his left forearm, just above the thermoplastic sheath. From these a series of wires transmitted a constant stream of data, measuring pulse rate, skin conductivity and electrical stimulation of the nervous system. These feedbacks were vital. They allowed Gribble to monitor the stress levels Cawdor might be experiencing, and in theory alert him to any sudden fluctuations that might indicate a potentially life-threatening situation. In theory. Gribble hadn't actually run a test to see if the system would work, but, fingers crossed, no reason why not.

This was another reason he hadn't sought Doctor Khuman's permission: being unable, as Gribble readily admitted to himself, to give the doc a copper-bottomed assurance on the makeshift hardware down to the last nut and bolt. Even less could he guarantee with total confidence that the Zone program would perform as it was supposed to. It was his own personal creation, right enough, but the extensive field trials on a wide variety of human subjects had been somewhat limited. In fact, to just one. Him.

The *main* reason, however, was that Doctor Khuman had already made his opposition abundantly clear, insisting that Cawdor was in no fit state at the present time to undergo such an experience. Reluctantly, Gribble had accepted that professional verdict. He had respected Doctor Khuman's right to make it. No longer. All bets were off. Jeff had asked for his help as plain and direct as if he'd grabbed Gribble by the arm and begged him on bended knee. Even told him *how* he could help. That was more than good enough for Gribble.

He glanced up at Annie Lorentz perched on the window ledge, her fingers wrapped tight round the glass of whiskey, her eyes still fixed on Cawdor. He'd been reluctant to involve her in this, but he had no option, needing another pair of hands to assist in setting everything up. And – though Gribble was even more reluctant to confess it – for moral support too.

She took a sip and blinked slowly. 'How long's this gonna take, Gil? All night?'

Gribble's answer was a shrug; he really had no idea.

He said, 'What you have to remember, Annie, is the passage of time inside the Zone is different to ours. A minute, say, of our "real" time doesn't relate to a minute of Jeff's time.' She gave him a quizzical look. 'Inside the Zone everything moves at the speed of thought,' Gribble explained. 'Jeff might live through a whole raft of experiences – heck, a whole lifetime – that lasts a fraction of a second on our timescale. You know, like in a dream? Like you can fall asleep, see all kinds of stuff, have weird adventures even, and bingo, you wake up to find only a coupla minutes have gone by, maybe even less. That's what the Zone lets you do.'

'Just what *does* it let you do?' Annie frowned at him.

'Well, uh, it's . . . interactive,' Gribble began lamely. He tugged at his beard. He had no problem knowing what it was supposed to do (after all, the Zone was his baby). It was putting the concept into words that gave him a problem. 'With virtual-reality programs you got choices, right?' She nodded. 'But the choices are limited to what's been programmed in. Like you can move at will through a room, say, decide to go left or right or turn around. What you *can't* do is decide for yourself what's in the room or what it looks like or how big it is. Those choices are given, not arbitrary. You're stuck with 'em. Now, with the Zone, you, the player – you get to create the entire mindscape. You project your thoughts and the scenario you imagined comes up right in front of you. You're slap-bang *in* there, seeing, feeling, hearing – the whole experience. But here's the real zinger. Sometimes the scenario you get is not the one you imagined it would be. Sometimes it's different, which is all down to the in-built probability curve.'

'The what?'

'That's the beauty of this program, Annie,' Gribble said, warming to his task. 'It provides an infinite range of variations. Stuff might happen or not happen, like on the toss of a dice. Every time it's different, and unpredictable, for everyone who tries it. All depends on the individual and what they –'

'You've been around Doctor Khuman so much you're starting to sound like him,' Annie Lorentz remarked dryly.

411

Gribble was stung by the comparison. 'Naw, ain't the same thing at all. The doc's slant is religious, not scientific. Philosophy and metaphysics, that kinda stuff.'

'So how do we know what's going on in there?'

Gribble coughed. 'Well, to be honest, we don't,' he had to admit. 'I can keep tabs on Jeff's heart rate and how his nervous system's reacting, but what's actually happening to him is a blind guess.'

'But Jeff can come out, yeah? He can return from wherever he is, anytime he wants to?'

Gribble's response was hesitant. 'Er, well, yeah, I guess so. I mean, I'm pretty confident he can.'

Annie Lorentz sat up.

'What? You're telling me he could get trapped in there? What if Jeff finds himself in a scary situation, for instance? Threatening or dangerous or . . .' But then she calmed down. 'I guess that can't happen, can it, because you're in control, right?' She fixed him with a piercing look of her pale-blue eyes. 'You *are* in control, Gil, aren't you?'

Gribble nodded, fingers crossed under the table.

'Suppose he wants out and can't make it for some reason?' Annie pressed him. 'What happens then?'

'Oh, that's easy.' Gribble gestured to the keyboard. 'We cut the power.'

Annie relaxed. 'Of course. Close down the program. After all, Jeff isn't physically anywhere else, is he? His body stays here even if his mind is –'

'Look!' Gribble was pointing.

Cawdor's left arm had risen, the black thermoplastic sheath held directly in front of the helmet's mirrored visor. It hovered there for several moments, as if Cawdor was studying it.

'Can he see that?' Annie asked in a hushed voice.

The arm floated down, a slight tremor in the empty sheath as it came to rest on the bed.

'I guess so, inside his own world,' Gribble said. 'Wherever that happens to be.'

* * *

412

With long nerveless fingers Graye unzipped the small leather pouch and opened it flat upon his knee. A gold Beamers pin lay there, encased in a sheath of clear plastic. Slowly and with extreme care, he removed the pin and held it between thumb and forefinger.

'You will observe no difference, apart from the colour, in shape or appearance to yours.' Graye jerked his hand. 'Take that one out and put it in your purse.'

Phyllis did as she was told and removed the silver pin. Graye replaced it with the gold pin, pinching the woollen sweater to insert the pointed end through the fold. The point was open at the tip: a tiny aperture connected to a hollow tube filled with a triple concentration of rattle-snake venom, which would only be released when press-ure was applied.

'Don't remove it until you judge the time is right,' Graye instructed her. 'And hold it by the sacred symbol, nowhere else. Aim for his hand or his arm, but the optimum point of penetration is the side of the neck, into the main artery. Do you understand?'

Phyllis nodded. Her round face with its dimpled cheeks and rosebud mouth was expressionless. Her eyes, usually as bright as buttons, were glazed over. She fastened the gilt buttons of her jacket and sat there, docile, hands in her lap.

Graye turned to look through the side window. The high stone walls were a darker shadowy blur in the dark-ness outside. Beyond them, the square bulk of the house was outlined against the night sky, a few lights visible in the upper storeys. A single-track road of pale gravel led to the gates. After parking at this distance under the trees, the driver had slipped from the cab and returned a few moments later to report that the gates were standing open. Apparently no one in the Troth Foundation had thought to close them, or perhaps reckoned they were safe from outside intrusion out here in the depths of the countryside.

At Graye's signal the driver slid open the side door.

'May the blessings of the Saviour be with you,' Graye

said as Phyllis stepped down. 'Let His strength and purpose guide your hand. The neck, remember, is the most vulnerable point. Kersh be with you.'

The dumpy figure moved off along the track, low heels crunching on gravel. A few moments later it had merged into the darkness and was gone. The night returned to stillness and to silence.

Annie Lorentz had dozed off, her head resting on her crossed arms supported by her drawn-up knees. Her sleep was shallow, so that part of her knew she was at Cawdor's bedside while the rest of her mind was thronged with turbulent dream images that chased their own tails in endless circles. Cawdor was also in her dream. He was asking her something – rather, pleading with her – but there was some kind of failure of communication, as if he was speaking a foreign language, and try as she might she couldn't understand him. She kept repeating, 'Tell me again, tell me again,' and, the more desperate his pleading, the more incoherent he became.

Then she was in Gil Gribble's apartment. He was searching for something on the cluttered workbench. He was very agitated, rooting through piles of stuff, saying, 'I know it's here, it's gotta be, I just put it down this second. It can't have gone. Have you moved it?'

'Moved what?' Annie asked him, heart pounding, his anxiety infecting her too. 'What have you lost?'

'It's gotta be here . . . Things don't just vanish into thin air. What have you done with it?'

'I haven't touched it!' Annie protested, feeling guilty even though she didn't know what he was looking for.

Suddenly he gave a cry and pounced on something and held it up. Something small and shiny, but she couldn't make out what he was holding even though she strained to look.

In the next dream she was in a hospital corridor with a green floor. The corridor stretched away to a pinpoint in the distance. She had to get down that corridor, but a nurse with a white starched cap was restraining her. Annie struggled to get free. The nurse was hanging on to her arm with both hands, her grip like iron claws, hurting her. Annie tried to wrench her arm away. Her elbow slipped off her knee and her head dropped forward, bringing her awake with a start.

'Annie.' Somebody was holding her arm, gently shaking her. 'It's getting late, gone midnight,' Gribble said. 'Why don'cha go to your room and get a decent night's sleep?' He straightened up, smiling. 'Nothing's happening right now, and it could take some time.'

She smothered a yawn and looked at Cawdor, the shiny black dome of the helmet giving him the grotesque appearance of half-man, half-insect.

'Is he OK?'

'The output levels are pretty normal so far.' Gribble nodded to the laptop with its tracery of blips arcing sedately across the screen. 'Nothing to concern us. I'm sure he's fine.'

Annie Lorentz slid to the floor, rubbing both shoulders. 'It still bothers me, Gil, that we can't –' Then she stopped, remembering her dream.

'What?'

'Communicate with him. He's here in this room with us and yet he's not here. It's creepy, Gil.'

'I tell ya, Annie, don't worry about it! I'll keep a close eye on things. You get some rest.'

Annie yawned again, picked up her shoulder bag and went to the door. 'If you need me, let me know right away. OK?'

Gribble smiled and gave her a wink. He seated himself at the keyboard and gazed at the screen while he listened to Annie's footsteps fading away. His smile faded with them. Her questions had disturbed him. Every one of her doubts and concerns had hit the bull's eye, and he wondered if his feeble assurances had actually fooled her. He was working blind here, with nothing to go on except a screenful of data that meant whatever he wanted it to mean. Truth was, if Jeff got into real trouble, he couldn't rely on these readings to tell him that for sure. They might indicate, for example, an intense and heightened dream state – which was what Jeff was experiencing anyway – but Gribble wouldn't have a clue whether that was a normal response to imaginative stimuli or whether his friend was screaming blue murder and pleading to be released from some dark torment.

Fretting, Gribble scratched his scrub of beard. It occurred to him – too damn late now! – that he could easily have incorporated in the system a signalling device of some kind: a panic button to be activated if things got too tough. Not a button in the physical sense, of course, because objects inside the Zone had no physical reality; more a mental trigger that would curtail the program and return him to the outside world.

Why the hell hadn't he thought of that before? He shifted uneasily on the hard chair, recalling Doctor Khuman's warning about Jeff's fragile psychological state. He'd spoken about the risk of 'psychic shock': the brain overloading on data, receiving too much input too fast for him to handle it. The result of which would be total mental breakdown.

Gribble looked at his wristwatch. It was ten after midnight. He'd give it till two o'clock, he decided. And if before then the readings went haywire, or even looked like doing so, he'd pull the plug at once.

Hunched forward, mouth set grimly, Gribble followed the gentle rhythm of blips on the screen, his eyes continually flicking up to the figure in the bed, which was entirely motionless except for the slight tremor in the empty thermoplastic sheath.

3

Mrs Brandt must have known that when he awoke it distressed him to see splinters of sunlight on the ceiling, and she had considerately closed the blinds so that the room was in subdued and restful shadow.

Cawdor lay back on the pillow, breathing a long sigh of relief.

The constant bombardment of images, spinning round

and round in a vicious tightening circle, had drained him to the point where he couldn't have gone on for much longer. He had been trapped in that endless, nightmarish merry-go-round, moving forward, so he thought, only to find himself back where he started. The weight of the past had been too great, the reliving of those memories too much to bear.

How it had worked – *how in hell he'd managed it* – getting a message through to the outside, he had no idea; he was just so profoundly grateful that it had. He closed his eyes, flexing the fingers of his left hand. That's how. His hand was the key. Doctor Khuman had picked up the signal he was transmitting and had the great good sense to pull him out of his coma and back to the land of the living. Now, after a rest, his strength regained, he could talk it over with Doctor Khuman and plan a way of getting to Kersh. The man was cleverer than he had supposed, Cawdor realised. Kersh had led him along, letting him gain access to the tower, and then constructed a series of images and experiences that led round and round in circles. That poor wretch in the stinking bowels of the sailing ship. The white-shrouded figure in the hospital bed who turned out to be himself. The red-haired kid in the gas station gunned down in cold blood.

Then back to the ship, the hospital, the gas station; on and on and on . . . It exhausted him even thinking about it.

Cawdor drifted off again into a dreamless sleep, and when he came groggily awake the shadowy room was airless and stifling. He could feel the heat of the sun even through the closed shades.

It was an immense relief, stepping outside, to see, in place of the dark phantoms of Kersh's twisted imagination, a friendly face. Because there, standing on the sun-lit terrace, was the welcome sight of his old friend Gil Gribble beaming at him, his face flushed from the heat, gingerish mop of hair like a fuzzy halo.

'Better sit down, Jeff. You look kinda wobbly.'

Cawdor sank into a chair. Gribble was right. His legs felt rubbery.

'It was killing me in there. I needed to rest.'

'Sure you did!' Gribble grinned. 'Take your time.' He glanced around, as if they might be overheard. But there was no one on the terrace, and the windows of the Troth Foundation were empty. Below them the lawns sloped gently to the sparkling ribbon of water beyond the trees.

Cawdor smiled. 'It's good to see you, Gil.'

'You too, Jeff.'

'How's your cat?' Cawdor asked, his smile broadening.

'Cat?'

'Your cat. What's it called?'

'Oh, yeah. My cat. Schrödinger.'

Cawdor relaxed. 'That's right. Schrödinger. For a minute I thought you'd forgotten.'

Gribble shook his head and chuckled.

Gribble was perspiring heavily, Cawdor noticed, glistening brown beads of sweat trickling down his face; but then it was hot out here in the sun. In fact, so hot that Cawdor felt drowsy. The heat was pleasant on his eyelids. His limbs were aching and he'd like nothing better than to just sit here on the terrace and bask, recover his strength.

Gribble was doing something with the tubular metal arms of the chair. Cawdor opened his eyes to find Gribble fastening leather straps to his wrists. He had no idea where the straps had come from, but there they were. And Gribble's face is now a wet brown mask. His gingerish mop of hair has receded across his skull, vanished in fact, leaving a lumpy cranium. Brown fluid is seeping out of him and dripping sluggishly to the floor. He's shrunk, too, become low and squat, no more than waist height, and he's fastening the straps with feelers ending in little curved claws, six on each extension.

Cawdor tries to move and finds he can't. The thing that was Gribble, transformed into this disgusting creature, is squatting at his feet on a rubber mat, busily securing his ankles to the chair. Why a rubber mat? Cawdor wonders. Because, he realises, the floor has to be insulated from the power surge when they throw the switch.

418

'Take it easy,' the creature says in a squeaky voice as Cawdor starts to struggle. 'All you'll feel is a little tickle. It ain't nothin'.'

The electric chair. Another Kershian memory, stored in that demented brain. Why hadn't he known that Kersh would try something like this? Cawdor curses himself for a fool and an idiot. Hadn't he warned himself to be ready for the worst Kersh could do to him? Of course (glaringly obvious to him *now*) Doctor Khuman and Gil Gribble – the real Gribble – hadn't received his message. Kersh has fooled him into believing they had, let him build up his hopes, all the while toying with him, then setting a trap that Cawdor had walked blindly into like an innocent child.

There is no help from outside. Nothing has changed. He's still trapped inside Kersh's crazed imagination.

The creature has crawled up the back of the chair. Clinging on with its lower extensions, the creature is fastening the strap round Cawdor's neck. It is necessary to do this first, in order to fit the electrodes to Cawdor's temples. 'We're gonna burn your ass,' the creature squeaks in his ear. 'After all the fuckin' trouble you caused Frank, it's only what you deserve. Frazzle you to a cinder. Render you down to a grease spot. Nobody messes with Frank and gets away with it.'

It flops to the floor, excreting more brown liquid, and squirms away. Wires trail from the back of the chair. Cawdor is bound tight, locked to the chair, straining impotently against the straps. The sun that was in his eyes, its heat pressing down languorously on his eyelids, has turned into a bright cowled lamp. There is nothing around it or beyond it but blackness.

'This is neat,' the creature giggles from the surrounding darkness. 'I guess it's what they call "poetic justice". You takin' Frank's place in the chair, I mean. He lives. You fry. Hee-hee.'

He will be annihilated. Obliterated. Cawdor knows that. Not killed in any conventional sense, because in a place of no-time such a thing cannot happen. But all the endless possibilities which he is capable of inhabiting will cease to be. He will become null and void, without past, present, or future. Kersh will continue. Grace MediaCorp will continue. The Beamers will continue. There is nothing to stop them.

'Got a last request?' inquires the creature gleefully. 'Any little ole thing I can do for you? Better make it snappy.'

'Yes,' Cawdor says dully. 'Promise me something.'

'Promise you what?' The creature is instantly suspicious.

'That you'll let my wife and daughter rest in peace.'

'Not up to me. Frank calls the shots around here.'

'Talk to him then. Persuade him to leave them be. You can do that, can't you?'

'I dunno. Frank likes his fun. That's how he gets his rocks off, replaying the golden oldies. *Whoosh!* Out through the side of that airplane at fifteen thousand feet in mangled bits and pieces. He loves that one.'

'You can at least try,' Cawdor pleads.

'Naw, he'll go apeshit. Frank don't like interference.'

'You scared of him?' Cawdor says tauntingly.

The creature bristles. 'Listen, asshole, without me ya know where Frank Kersh would be? Nowhere. He *needs* me.'

'So how come he treats you like a bag of shit? You deserve some respect, don't you, for everything you've done? You're the walking asshole, not me.'

The creature's red-rimmed eyes stare up at Cawdor. 'How come ya know about that?'

'I saw it all.' Cawdor smiles. 'In the mirror.'

'Huh? What mirror?'

'If Frank Kersh is so smart, he'd know about it, wouldn't he? He doesn't – and now you do. You're one up on him for a change.'

The creature is still suspicious, but also intrigued.

'You see stuff in this mirror, that what you're saying? Like what, for instance?'

'Past and future times. Like what's going to happen to

420

you, for instance.' Cawdor nods down to the breast pocket of his shirt. 'Take a look.'

The creature slithers forward and strains up curiously on its globular body. 'You kiddin' me?'

'See for yourself. Then you'll know something Frank Kersh doesn't. A *lot* of things he doesn't. Then he'll have to give you respect, because you're the smart one, not him.'

All eager now, the creature clambers up, its clawed feelers reaching for the breast pocket, salivating brown goo in its excitement. Cawdor waits, letting the creature get near – right up close where he wants it. As the creature stretches up, Cawdor squirms his wrist inside the strap. His hand shoots out and closes round the flabby fold of skin that passes for a neck. Fingers digging deep, he increases the pressure until blood vessels start to burst in the bulging eyes. The lipless mouth yawns emptily and soundlessly, exposing the bloated tongue writhing like a fat blue worm.

'Good boy,' Cawdor croons. 'Undo the strap.' The feelers twitch, claws feebly scratching the leather thong. 'Oh, come on,' Cawdor chides, 'you can do better than that. If you can't, you're a dead white slug. *In ten seconds from now*!'

As Cawdor feels the strap slacken and fall away he straightens his arm, lifting the creature off the floor. The tips of his fingers are almost touching through the pouchy neck. The creature gurgles, but not from his throat. Watery brown fluid glugs from every orifice in its head and body. The thing is being squeezed dry, like a dirty dish rag. Cawdor shakes the carcass to and fro and the sloshing liquid spills over the floor in a stinking brown tide of untreated sewage. Finally he lets the wrung-out, empty sagging sack of skin drop.

Two red eyeballs, like burst tomatoes, stare up at Cawdor from the swilling mess that was the contents of their own body.

'One thing I forgot to mention,' Cawdor says, releasing himself from the chair. 'The mirror broke. And broken mirrors sometimes bring bad luck.'

* * *

There's a lesson to be learnt, Cawdor knows, and if he doesn't learn it now he's finished. Kersh had sent that thing to stop him. It had assumed Gribble's shape. It had even re-created a location, a landscape, that was familiar and reassuring to him. And, after vowing never to be taken off his guard, he'd fallen for it, straight off, without a twinge of foreboding or a moment's hesitation.

From now on, Cawdor tells himself savagely, don't trust anybody or anything. No matter who, no matter what.

And don't expect any help from outside. There's none coming.

He wipes some glutinous residue from the fingertips of his left hand and turns to look through the window. The buildings of the city are dark and silent under the starry sky of perpetual night. The pale slice of moon still hasn't moved. As he stares out, Cawdor is struck by a thought – a revelation – that sets his heart pounding. He must be getting nearer to Kersh than he had imagined. Because Kersh's sending that disgusting creature to destroy him is an act born of desperation; of fear that his sanctuary in the tower is in danger of being violated. And Cawdor realises something else: a sudden startling insight that causes hope to surge through him like a rush of pure oxygen. Up until this encounter on the terrace, the events he has witnessed were from the past. The poor wretch in the hold of the ship, the red-haired kid gunned down in the lonely gas station, even the image of himself lying in the hospital bed – all had come from the store of memories inside Kersh's head.

This encounter was different, indeed unique, because *it hadn't happened before*. Within Kersh's unchanging world, an event had taken place, and therefore change had occurred where nothing ever changed.

In itself so tiny and insignificant, to Cawdor this knowledge is momentous. It means that, at some point he passed through, and without being aware of it, he has entered the continuum that Kersh inhabits. This puzzles him deeply. What brought it about? He sought help from the world outside and no help was forthcoming. Unless . . .

422

Unless Gribble received his message.

Cawdor can think of no other explanation than that Gribble received the message and acted upon it. He activated the Zone program, providing Cawdor with the means to focus and direct the power of his thoughts. While his body lies in a room at the Troth Foundation, his mind has been liberated and given the freedom to seek out Kersh on his own territory. He's made it, finally, into the mirror world where Kersh is living out his eternal last second, suspended in the limbo between life and death.

Whatever he's got planned, Cawdor resolves, I'll be ready. No matter what. Come on, Frank, give it your best shot. Let's see how you do without a gun in your hand and some innocent kid behind the cash desk of a gas station to blast apart.

Gribble rose quickly and went over to the bed. For several moments he had been observing the spasmodic tremor in Cawdor's right hand, the fingers suddenly clenching tight. He didn't know what it signified, and the monitoring displays hadn't indicated there was anything amiss; but he wanted to make sure that Jeff was OK. If he was in distress – or maybe trying to communicate – Gribble was anxious to know about it.

The hand lay open now, fingers gently curled, trembling just very slightly. Gribble squeezed it.

'You need help, or you want out,' he muttered under his breath, 'all you gotta do is give me a sign. I'm here and I ain't movin'.'

Anxiously, he gazed at the black bulbous headpiece, as if in forlorn hope that he might gauge how Cawdor was feeling from its smooth, shiny, blankly anonymous exterior. He couldn't, of course, and knew it was futile. Still, there was no doubting the strain Cawdor was under: tension exuded from his body almost like a powerful scent, was physically evident in the rigid set of his shoulders, the stiffness in his spine.

Maybe these external signals are Jeff's only way of communicating distress, Gribble thought, and I'm just too dumb to recognise a cry for help when I see one. He agonised with himself, uncertain what to do. It would take less than five seconds to break the circuit and bring him out of the Zone. The worst-case scenario was that Cawdor might be at a crucial stage and didn't want to exit the system; but that couldn't be any worse than his being helplessly trapped in there, desperate to get out and unable to do so. While he dithered and did nothing.

Gribble made up his mind. He turned resolutely towards the keyboard. It was then he became aware of the woman standing just inside the open door: short and ample in all departments, a nervous, almost pleading smile on her round face. She wore a navy-blue jacket with gilt buttons over a cashmere sweater, a pleated skirt, and low-heeled shoes that didn't disguise but drew attention to her thick ankles.

'Yes?' Gribble said. He sounded sharp because he thought she might be a member of staff he'd never seen before who only worked nights. He wondered nervously whether Mrs Brandt had sent her.

'You're Mr Gribble, aren't you?'

He nodded warily.

'I'm Phyllis Keets,' the woman said shyly.

The name didn't register with Gil Gribble, though she announced it as though it should.

'We've spoken on the phone, Mr Gribble. I work for Jeff – Mr Cawdor,' she informed him, 'as his personal assistant.' Her eyes strayed to the figure in the bed. Some small bright object inside her open jacket flared in the light from the lamp as she came further into the room. Her shy smile flickered briefly once again, meant for him, though her gaze didn't move from Cawdor.

Oh, *that* Phyllis, Gribble was thinking. His jaw nearly dropped then, remembering that this was the woman who had accused Jeff of sexually molesting her. So what the hell was she doing here? And less important, but just as puzzling, how had she known where to find her boss? Gribble's natural inclination was to be polite, but he couldn't quell a lurking sense of suspicion, if not downright unease. Something didn't add up.

Phyllis Keets said, 'I hope you don't mind my showing

up out of the blue like this, but I was so concerned when I heard Jeff had been moved from the hospital in New York. I mean, really anxious to learn whether he'd recovered from his injuries or had relapsed.' She stepped nearer the bed, frowning. 'Is this . . . some form of treatment he's receiving?' she asked, indicating the black headpiece.

Gribble's nod was guarded. 'Yeah.' Several days had passed since Cawdor left Mount Sinai Hospital, that's how concerned she was. He stared at her for a long moment. 'Jeff's coming along just fine, Miss Keets. Healed up pretty good.'

'I'm so relieved, I can't tell you,' Phyllis murmured, her black eyelashes fluttering, putting her hand to her heart. 'Poor man, all he's suffered, it's terrible.'

'We're relieved too, now he's on the mend. He's getting the best of care here, so there's no cause to fret.' Gribble, ever courteous, tentatively waved an arm towards the door. 'If you wouldn't mind, Miss Keets, this is kind of a delicate part of the recuperation process. I don't want Jeff disturbed at this point in time. You with me?' he said more insistently when she remained standing there, fingers spread over her upper breast, her eyes fixed on Cawdor. 'Miss Keets?'

She came out of her trance, blinking rapidly.

'Oh, yes. Sorry to intrude. I just wanted to make sure he was OK.'

'Well, now you seen for yourself he is. You come all the way up here on your own?'

'Yes.'

'Helluva long drive.'

Phyllis nodded and yet still lingered, which pushed Gribble's irritation very quickly to real pissed off.

Something about the woman that gave him the shivers. A sort of deadness inside, as if she had been programmed, her expressed concern and sympathy rather cold and automatic. He'd formed a mental picture of the Phyllis who accused Cawdor as being jittery and highly strung, wild gestures and hysterical outbursts. He couldn't have been more wrong: shy and demure on the outside, pure ice maiden inside.

He said through tight lips, 'Forgive me, I don't mean to be rude, Miss Keets, but I have work to do.'

Now she was leaning forward, hand on her breast, peering into the helmet's mirrored visor, which revealed nothing except her own distorted image reflected back at her like a bloated balloon, dark eyes and snub nose fringed by tight curls.

'Does he know I'm here?'

'No.'

'Is he sedated?'

'No,' Gribble said again, grinding it out. His natural gentle politeness wearing mighty thin.

'I'm sure Jeff knows,' Phyllis persisted. 'I can feel his eyes on me.'

'No, he doesn't – he ain't aware of anythin' here in this room. It don't exist for him.'

'You mean he's in his own private world, cut off from the outside?' Phyllis said. 'How strange.'

Gribble stared at the carpet, fists bunched impotently. How in hell – apart from bodily throwing her out of the room – was he ever going to get rid of this damn infuriating woman? Dropping heavy hints and pointedly asking her to leave didn't work, which left Gribble at a loss about what to do next.

He sighed and glared at her. Maybe throwing her out was the only –

In the mirrored visor Gribble saw a blur of movement. It was Phyllis's hand looming large as it reached towards Cawdor. Her fingertips were pinched together, holding something that flashed in the lamplight. Staring into the helmet's reflecting curvature, he saw a gleaming golden point aimed at the side of Cawdor's exposed neck. The needle's tip was barely a couple of inches away when the swinging blow caught Phyllis on the upper arm, knocking her hand aside and sending her staggering off balance to land heavily on her knees, one hand at full stretch to save herself toppling over, the other clutching the pin. Gribble had acted instinctively, in a split second, even though he didn't have a clue what was wrong. He still didn't know, couldn't figure it out. Had Phyllis attacked Jeff? Meant to do him harm – with that gold pin she was holding?

Was the woman crazy or what?

Still confused, he craned his neck towards the crouching figure as Phyllis straightened up. Her face was round and bland, her eyes flat and without expression. Again he sensed that emptiness inside her, a vacuity of feeling. She squirmed sideways, and from a kneeling position made a lunging dive towards the bed, aiming the pin like a dart at Cawdor's shoulder under its loose white shift. Taken by surprise, Gribble kicked out erratically. His foot missed her hand, and instead connected with the point of her elbow. There was a sharp crack of bone. Phyllis gave a shrill yelp, like that of an animal in pain, and jerked her arm protectively towards herself. The hand holding the gold pin tightened in a convulsive grip as she rolled on to her side, her full body weight pressing down on the carpet, her clenched hand underneath. At once she heaved herself over, straining to get up. Phyllis herself didn't appear to notice anything wrong, but Gribble could clearly see blood oozing from between her fingers. Oblivious to her injury, she tried another feeble lunge with her bloody hand, and then, it seemed to Gribble, she suddenly lost interest. Shoulders bowed, she sat rocking slightly, her clenched hand with blood oozing out resting limply in her lap.

Then it happened, very slowly to begin with, right in front of him. Gribble couldn't believe it.

The hand in her lap started to grow. He could actually see the hand enlarging itself, becoming huge and puffy and bluish white in colour. It grew and continued to grow to the size of a football. The blotchy bluish-white swelling moved along her arm, forcing the material of her jacket into a stiff fat tube of trapped flesh.

By gradual degrees, as if subsiding into a warm bath, Phyllis lay back on the floor and closed her eyes. She looked peaceful and at rest, perfectly normal in fact, except for the giant hand and arm lying stiffly beside her, fingers poking out of the pale-blue football like gorged slugs.

Gribble had seen pictures in medical textbooks that were very similar – of people who'd died of rattlesnake venom. He wasn't squeamish, and had a strong stomach, but he had to turn away. He might have called Doctor Khuman for assistance; even considered doing so for a fleeting moment before he realised it was too late. Poison of such virulence, acting with such speed, would have killed an ox cold stone dead by now, much less Phyllis Keets.

He slumped down on the chair, face averted from the sight, and looked without seeing them at the arcing green blips on the screen.

4

Nearer.

He's getting nearer, Cawdor is convinced of it. The sensation in his hand – like sparks of pure energy jumping crazily between nerve cells – is proof of that. By this time Kersh's brain is running out of images. Pretty soon the only image he'll have left is of himself in the penthouse. He won't be able to retreat from that; it's his last and only refuge. There's no place else to go.

I just wanted to make sure he was OK.

Swirling in from the surrounding darkness, a woman's voice that sounds familar, echoing as from a great distance. Is the voice from within – or from the outside world, beyond the Zone? Or is it yet one more sly trick to throw him off his guard? By now Cawdor is suspicious of everything. After coming awake in a perfect replica of the Troth Foundation and encountering the fake Gribble on the terrace he is prepared to take nothing at face value.

I can feel his eyes on me.

Cawdor places the voice – it's Phyllis's, he's in no doubt. But identifying it doesn't help; it only adds to his confusion. Is Phyllis in league with Kersh, here inside the tower? If not that, then her presence is bleeding through from the outside, from the shadowy room where his body lies on the bed. But that doesn't seem credible either, because how could Phyllis Keets know of the existence of the Troth Foundation or that he was there?

It's another trick; it has to be. In his desperation, Kersh is trying everything: images, memories, emotions, voices. Even dredging up dream phantoms from the deepest recesses of his own mind – the creature with the slimy sac of a body and scaly feelers.

After Phyllis, Cawdor wonders what Kersh will try next. He has to break Cawdor's spirit, crush him entirely, in order to survive, using any means possible. The more searingly painful and soul-destroying the better. So what else can his sick mind come up with?

A sharp cry, as of an animal in pain, echoes from the surrounding darkness and swirls through Cawdor's head.

Crazily, that too sounded like Phyllis. But he still doesn't know from where. Here inside the Zone or from out there.

A thin shrieking sound insinuates itself into his head. This time, though, not human. It is the whine of jet engines. The instant he recognises it, Cawdor feels his heart seize up. A crawling black panic clutches his insides like a claw of sharpened talons. Because he knows what is about to happen, and he knows he cannot face it. He couldn't endure the annihilation of his wife and daughter over again – blown out through the shattered side of the airplane – and retain his sanity.

Cawdor fights with all his mental strength, resisting the image trembling on the edge of his consciousness. No way, Frank. You had the power once, but you've lost it. The sound fades away; the image is stillborn. Gaining in confidence, Cawdor smiles to himself, quietly triumphant, and it's then that the realisation hits home. If Kersh really has been stripped of his power, maybe this is the opportunity Cawdor has been waiting for. The time to pit his will and belief against Kersh's; the time to prove himself the stronger.

This is it. The one thing Cawdor has been praying for, and the one thing that Kersh fears most. The ultimate test.

Hands clamped either side on the polished black surface, Gribble held his breath as he eased the helmet off, being especially careful not to let Cawdor's head thump back on the pillow when he lifted the helmet free. He set it at the foot of the bed, the skein of cables and wires trailing down to the floor.

Gribble mopped his face with his shirt sleeve. Sweating like a pig. Not the effort of removing the headpiece – tricky though it was – but riven with feelings of guilt at deceiving Doctor Khuman. And, far worse than that, the awful dread churning in his guts that he might have done more harm than good. Real and irreparable damage, in fact, considering the delicate nature of Jeff's mental and physical condition. How in hell could he have acted so *dumb*? He was playing with a man's life as if it was some damn-fool experiment to prove his genius at home-grown amateur gadgetry. It was wilfully and criminally insane to have even attempted such a crazy stunt.

In the light of the lamp Cawdor's face had a waxy pallor. Hardly surprising, Gribble thought. The poor guy had been to hell and back; recovery from such a major trauma was going to take months. He ground his teeth in shame and remorse, wondering why it had taken so long for that simple fact to sink in.

He rearranged the single sheet over the motionless body. Turning away, he purposely kept his gaze averted from the horribly bloated figure of Phyllis on the other side of the bed. It was then he glimpsed the red light flashing on the keyboard.

Gribble spun round and leant towards it, eyes bulging.

The gentle green arcs measuring Cawdor's vital life signs were gone. No peaks and troughs. Just three straight lines, that was all.

Three straight green lines humming softly across the screen to oblivion.

* * *

There was no doubt in Gribble's mind that it was the worst moment of his life. He stood rooted to the spot as Doctor Khuman straightened up and turned away from the bed, tugging the stethoscope loose and letting it dangle in his hand. The expression on Khuman's lean brown face obliterated the last shred of hope, plunging Gribble into the darkest, bleakest depths of despair.

He couldn't look Doctor Khuman in the eye, and neither could he meet Annie Lorentz's frowning stare. Her bewilderment was plain, as she tried to take in both Cawdor's comatose form and the bloated body of Phyllis Keets lying beside the bed.

Gribble had roused her at the same time as he had rushed upstairs to Doctor Khuman's room. Despite the hour, after one-thirty in the morning, the doctor was awake and still fully dressed, reading and making notes. Gribble led the way downstairs, so distressed that in answer to Doctor Khuman's questions he could only shake his head dumbly. Annie Lorentz had followed on, appearing a few minutes later in Cawdor's room as Doctor Khuman was carrying out his examination. She stayed silent: the sombre atmosphere, and Gribble's rigid, fist-clenching stance, made all questions redundant. And the absence of activity on the screen confirmed the obvious.

'Why did you wait before calling me?' Doctor Khuman asked, and his hushed tone didn't soften the accusation.

'Wait?' Gribble was confused. 'I called you right away. The instant I noticed something was wrong I came up to get you.' He made a vague gesture towards the bed. 'It's been only a few minutes, doc, I swear.'

'All signs of life are extinct,' Doctor Khuman pronounced. 'No cardiovascular or respiratory functions whatsoever. Such a condition takes not less than fifteen and as much as thirty minutes.' With the tip of one finger he touched the shiny black helmet, which was still lying at the foot of the bed where Gribble had placed it. 'Is this the cause? You put him into the Zone and he never came out of it. Is that what happened?'

'No . . . No!' Gribble protested. 'I did, yeah, I admit – I

wanted to help Jeff, so I tried out the VR program, but he was perfectly OK in there. I monitored him and he was fine. Annie will vouch for that. There was no sign of any physical lapse or nothin'.'

'Until you noticed it too late on the screen.'

'But that was *after*,' Gribble insisted. 'Not in the Zone. It was when I took the helmet off that his functions failed. That's the honest truth, doc.'

Doctor Khuman closed his eyes. 'Oh my God.'

Gribble was stricken. 'What – What is it?' he stammered, ashen-faced. 'What'd I do? What went wrong?'

'I think he got through,' Doctor Khuman said. He looked down, touching the helmet again. 'I think Cawdor made it. Or had nearly made it, when you took him out. Now God know's where he is. In limbo somewhere, trapped between this existence and ... the one he was seeking to enter.'

Gribble hung his head. 'I got scared, that's why I pulled him out. I thought I'd pushed Jeff too far, that he wasn't in the right physical shape to withstand the strain.' He stared at the floor, tears of remorse welling in his eyes. 'I try to help the guy and make a complete balls-up of everything! What a dumb asshole!'

He felt a hand on his shoulder. Annie squeezed it comfortingly. It didn't make him feel any better. If anything, it made him feel worse, because her consolation only chafed and made more unbearable his sense of stupidity and failure.

Then Doctor Khuman surprised him. 'Your friend Cawdor's physical condition is not a relevant factor,' he informed Gribble with a shake of the head. 'You see, in that other place, the life of the mind where he dwells, he suffers no wounds that were inflicted here, in the outer world. He has two good hands. He is physically as he imagines himself to be – a whole man. It is his psychological strength, his will and determination and self-belief – those are the qualities that are absolutely crucial.' Doctor Khuman regarded the prone body, the face with its waxy pallor. 'He has passed through, beyond the pale, but perhaps he remains there, adrift in nowhere; in the literal sense, a lost soul.'

'But we can do *something*,' Annie Lorentz burst out. 'Can't we, Satish? Can't we help him somehow?' She pointed to the helmet. 'That contraption, Gil's VR program, it worked before. Why not try it again?'

'You don't understand, Annie. It will do no good. What you see on the bed is an empty shell. It would be like fitting the helmet to a dead carcass. The person you knew as Jeff Cawdor has vacated it.'

'So there's nothing we can do?' Annie leant against Gribble and gazed down at the body. Her voice sank to a whisper. 'No way we can reach him?'

Doctor Khuman didn't answer, which was what Gribble had expected all along. The dying ember of hope was finally extinguished. No way through. A dead end. Feeling hopeless and wretched, he watched as Doctor Khuman lifted the shiny black helmet in both hands. The action meant nothing, triggered no response in Gribble. His stare remained blank and uncomprehending even when he heard Doctor Khuman say, 'Yes, there is something we can do, Annie. Where Cawdor has gone, I can go, too. Well, Mr Gribble?' he said, a faint smile straining his lips. 'Would you like another guinea pig for your experiment?'

'Another ...?' His meaning at last penetrated Gil Gribble's befuddled brain. He swallowed a dry lump in his throat. 'I can't do it, doc ... I daren't risk it, not after what happened to Jeff.'

'You are not risking anything, Mr Gribble,' Doctor Khuman said gently. 'I am. And I am quite prepared, and willing, to accept the risk. But of course I need your agreement as well as your expertise. Well?'

Her pale-blue eyes fixed on Doctor Khuman, Annie Lorentz clutched Gribble's arm. 'Satish, you don't mean – the same thing that happened to Jeff might happen to you?'

'I won't deny that it could happen, Annie. Anything is possible. But it is more a possibility than a probability. I'm sure Mr Gribble appreciates the distinction. Isn't that so?'

Gribble's nod was mechanical.

Doctor Khuman's nod was brisk. 'Good.'

Cawdor is blind and lost. He thinks, I'm trapped in here. Going round and round and getting nowhere. Gribble had offered him hope – the belief that entering the Zone would give him the power to defeat Kersh. Back there awhile, out on the terrace, he had been filled with expectation that it was himself and not Kersh who was in control. And then – nothing.

Now Cawdor feels lost and alone and helpless, and knows in his heart the bleakness of utter despair. He has deluded himself into thinking he was getting near to Kersh. *Nearer and nearer* pounded the rhythm inside him, when the truth is that Kersh is as safe and impregnable as ever in his tower. Nothing can harm him because he has created this world in his own image. And, because Cawdor too is part of the image inside Kersh's head, he cannot escape from it.

Cawdor's hand twitches.

Part of the image –

Cawdor's hand jangles with a surge of pure energy.

– inside Kersh's head.

How much nearer to Kersh can he get than that? He's here already. In the blink of an eye the vast gulf that separates the two of them shrinks to zero. He's so near, Cawdor realises, so damn close that he and Kersh are bound together as a single indivisible entity. The difference being that until now Kersh has wielded the power, disrupting the flow of events – which is what Doctor Khuman meant by 'disruption', Cawdor suddenly understands, at their first meeting, that stormy morning in his office. Until now Kersh has called the shots, because of Cawdor's failure to realise that he also possessed the power to influence the course of events. The signs had been there all along. The broken mirror in the bathroom. The dreams of the sailing ship. The night of his drunken stupor when he'd seen Kersh in the electric chair. Phyllis's accusation that he had molested her when the fantasy had existed only in his mind: that had been Kersh too. Sarah and Daniella falling under the influence of the Beamers: Kersh again. At every critical stage Kersh had stepped in and twisted events to serve his own demented purpose. While Cawdor had stood impotently by, the ignorant and hapless victim, not knowing he too had the power to shape events, even when Doctor Khuman had told him precisely that in so many words.

How could he have been so fucking blind? When, right from the start, it was all as clear as daylight? He ought to have acted sooner – he *could* have acted – but for his ignorance. No, not ignorance alone. Stupidity. The signs were all there in the shards of broken mirror on the bathroom floor. Pointing to the future and into the past. God help him, the portents were staring him in the face *and he had done nothing*.

Blind ignorance and wilful stupidity.

For these sins of omission Cawdor has paid a terrible price. He has been stripped of everything he held dear, left with nothing but a broken body teetering on the cusp between life and death. And still Kersh isn't done with him. He can resurrect those same searing images any time he likes, as many times as he likes, replaying the same events in an endless loop to gratify his sadistic pleasure.

Always and for ever, replaying them from here to eternity, each time twisting the screws of torture tighter on Cawdor's rack of guilt and self-recrimination. On and on, for ever, always the same.

And the same. The same. The same. The same.

They decided to use Doctor Khuman's study, three doors along from where Cawdor lay stiff and silent as a waxwork. Before they could begin, however, there was another matter to attend to. Mrs Brandt had been summoned and instructed to arrange for the removal of the corpse of Phyllis Keets. Several things concerning this puzzled Gribble. Was the housekeeper – though without question a resourceful woman – supposed to manage this by herself, or was there help to hand? Even more perplexing, Doctor Khuman didn't ask for, and apparently didn't require, any kind of explanation for the unexpected appearance of Phyllis Keets, nor for her demise. Almost as if, Gribble thought, he knew her identity, and her purpose in coming to the Troth Foundation was no mystery to him.

It certainly was to Gribble. Though for the time being he put such mysteries and speculations on hold: there was more pressing business that couldn't wait.

Seated behind Doctor Khuman's desk, the keyboard and screen in front of him, Gribble made his final preparations. Already wearing the helmet, Doctor Khuman reclined in the armchair opposite, his hands splayed on the leather arms, sensor pads attached to the insides of both wrists. Annie Lorentz sat on the carpet facing him, leaning back against the desk, in her customary position of knees drawn up and clasped in her arms. Gribble could see the top of her head; it was a great comfort to know she was there.

Annie peeked at him over the desk. Her eyes were large and shadowy with apprehension. 'You sure about this, Gil? You want to go through with it?'

'No,' Gribble replied stolidly. 'But I have to. I owe it to Jeff after what happened.'

'That wasn't your fault. Doctor Khuman said as much.'

'He also said that Jeff was trapped in some kind of no-man's-land like a wandering – what was it? – lost soul. I couldn't live with that.'

Annie held his gaze. She turned back and crouched over her knees, eyes narrowed, watching Doctor Khuman with scarcely a blink. Gribble spent a few moments more finalising his preparations. Then he was ready. He pressed the key.

Far away, in the murky depths of the underground passage, Kersh sees a vast shape which glitters faintly. The shape is advancing towards him, filling the passage, its bulbous sides brushing the stone walls. The glittering effect, Kersh now makes out, is caused by chunky rhinestones and hundreds of sequins on a glowing one-piece suit of almost fluorescent white. The suit is split in a V down the middle, revealing a hairless chest that swells to a vast pale belly that overflows a straining belt, its gold buckle encrusted with a rainbow of bright flashing stones.

The head of black glistening hair, which is swept back from thick sideburns, almost touches the ceiling. There is hardly space for the shoulders as the bloated figure waddles forward, wheezing and grunting, the full soft lips set aslant in a crooked grin.

Exact in every detail, from the rings arrayed on both hands down to the last sequin on the costume, the figure is from life – except twice or even three times life size. It has been expanded and engorged to monstrous and grotesque proportions.

It comes on, blocking out the light, filling Kersh's vision with a dazzle of sparkling rhinestones like a field of stars. There's nowhere for him to go, except backward. Retreating, Kersh is hemmed in between the stone walls on either side, the iron door behind, the bloated figure closing in rapidly. A jewelled medallion in the shape of a star hangs down on the pale exposed gut, directly in front of Kersh at eye level. Kersh retreats further. But it's as far as he can go. Squeezed into a tight space, he feels surrounded by and then immersed in a mound of sweating blubber. With his back against the iron door, he feels the pressure increase, and then the suffocating weight and bulk of flesh crushing into him. The edges of the rhinestones are vicious and sharp, drawing blood as they snag at his face. His ribs are creaking, and even by straining hard he can't draw breath. His senses are fading, everything becoming dark and distant as his body is compressed and the air squashed out of him.

Kersh is suffocating in a mountain of flesh.

Sinking into folds of flab.

Fighting himself free and lifting his head to suck in a gasping breath, Kersh's clawing hand strikes the star-shaped medallion. He grasps it and thrusts one of the jewel-tipped points into the quivering mound of white fat lapping over him. The jewelled tip goes deep. But not deep enough. He grinds it in, up to the elbow, then deeper still until his arm is enveloped and being sucked inside. This can go on for ever, Kersh thinks; there's no end to it. But he increases the pressure still more, thrusting the jewelled tip with all his strength into the shuddering mountain. Something inside gives way, ruptures and rips apart, and a shock wave flings Kersh against the iron door, his skull ringing with a thousand crazy bells.

The carcass has exploded.

Lumps of bloodless flesh cling to the ceiling, ooze sluggishly down the walls, seeping with rhinestones and sequins. Tattered shreds of white suit drift to the floor. Ripped apart, the studded belt is scattered everywhere in bits and pieces, and all that remains recognisably intact is the star-shaped medallion with its jewelled points, lying in a pool of simmering fat.

Kersh tries to move. He's stuck to the floor. He heaves, struggling to wrench his feet from the congealed mess. The smell of frying grease reminds him of hamburgers sizzling on the griddle in some smoky hash joint, and he comes awake with flailing legs and the stench of hot grease like stale vomit in his nostrils.

Lying on the sheets of black silk, his body beneath the robe bathed in cold sweat, Kersh experiences the first, and completely authentic, stab of naked fear.

The dream has come to him unbidden: the idol of his teenage years seeking to destroy him. OK, a dream only, that's all (stay cool, man!), but still an image out of left field that he absolutely knows, goddamnit, didn't originate in his own mind.

That's what really freaks him: the fact that he, Frank Kersh, didn't think of it.

For a full minute he can't move. Like in the dream when his feet were glued to the floor. Then he forces his muscles into action, swings off the bed and staggers a few steps before he can gain control of his legs. The knob of the bedroom door feels slimy in his clammy palm. Kersh turns it, then hesitates. He tells himself that the living area beyond is empty. He convinces himself no one is there. But what if he's wrong? What if, shit and corruption, someone is? Edging the door open, he peers cautiously into the living area, does a long slow sweep across the entire room, from the sunken well to the bar, and on to the sliding glass partition fronting the balcony. Kersh closes his eyes and leans against the door jamb, stomach gurgling like a stormwater drain. Thank you, Jesus.

Everything exactly the same. Just as it was before – unchanged – and just as it should be, and will be, for ever and ever. Amen.

At the bar Kersh reaches down the Jack Daniel's, fills a shot glass and throws it back in one. The liquor forges a molten path right down to his vitals, gives his confidence a kick start. He decides that what happened back there was a fluke. Some kind of glitch is all. Rest easy, Frank. You're safe here, he tells himself. Nobody can get through, and certainly not Cawdor – he doesn't know how.

He refills his glass and tosses it back. He's in mid-swallow when his eye happens on something that makes his bowels loosen and his sac of testicles shrivel like a dried prune.

A crack has appeared in the mirror backdrop behind the bar.

Running jaggedly from top to bottom, it splits his image straight down the middle, so there are two slightly disjointed Frank Kershes gaping back at him, drops of liquor dripping from their chins. With the back of his hand, Kersh wipes them off. Unchanged no longer.

Almost skidding off the leather-topped barstool, Kersh spins round to scour every inch of the living area, expecting to see a grinning Cawdor standing there. But the place is silent and empty. The stars gleam steadily through the curved glass dome overhead; the slice of moon is unmoved.

If he's aiming to freak me, Kersh thinks, tough titty. I don't scare that easy. The creep don't know it, but he's dealing with a killer here, a hardened pro like Lee Marvin who can wipe out ten guys in three blinks of an eye. He swings back to the bar and sloshes liquor into the glass. Maybe, Kersh thinks, I can get Lee up here and we can kick some ass. Me and Lee would get along jake. A couple of hard-drinking, heavy-screwing, saloon-brawling hellraisers. Real close buddies standing shoulder to shoulder, wiping out the opposition and then raising our glasses in mutual respect and admiration, Lee giving that famous lopsided grin and growling, 'Frank, gotta say this. You're one helluva guy. A real knockout with the ladies too, you old lech.'

Ain't that the living truth, Kersh admits to himself. A snap of the fingers and any woman he wants comes running –

Sheeeit!

He can't hold back a rebel yell. He's had an idea. Boy, and it's a barnstormer – his best yet. It'll stop Cawdor dead in his tracks. Poor sap won't know what hit him.

Kersh raises his glass to himself in the fractured mirror and his two selves raise theirs to him.

5

He has no other choice but to accept it. Kersh has won. Cawdor can do nothing to stop him. He's no nearer to reaching Kersh than he ever was. It was all a delusion. Kersh has been toying with him since the beginning, leading him on to believe he was moving forward, making progress, when the bitter truth is this: he is at the mercy of Kersh's malicious whim and fancy, endlessly spiralling through the store of images in that demented brain of his.

Like this one. Sitting on the heap of gravel, knees drawn up, feeling the monotonous drumming of the sea against his spine through the timber planking. All around him the rats paddle, their shiny pointed noses twitching above the scummy water, waiting for his heartbeat to stop. The boldest rat doesn't wait. It creeps dripping-wet up the gravel slope, head flattened, sniffing the scent of human body heat.

Eyes closed in the hollow, thudding darkness, Cawdor flinches as something touches his hand.

Then finds himself gazing into a pair of liquid brown eyes.

'I did as much as I could,' Kumar says, 'but it wasn't enough. Forgive me.'

'Forgive *you*?' Cawdor laughs weakly. 'If only I'd listened to you and taken your warning seriously. But I was too stupid to understand. Even when it was shown to me in the broken pieces of mirror, the past and the future laid out in front of me –'

Cawdor stops. He is trembling all over.

'We've been through this before. You and me sitting here, saying the same things to one another.' His heart seems to shrink inside him. 'Will it just go on for ever, the same events repeating themselves endlessly? Do I have to live through the same future again and again? Doesn't it ever *end*?'

'Not until you act to change it.'

'I'm lost in here. I don't know how.'

Kumar smiles. 'Yes, you do.'

'How? Help me.'

'You must break the circle. I possessed the knowledge, it's true, but it is you who has the power to defeat Kersh. That's why I came to your office. To warn you.'

'You remember that?'

'Of course.'

'But before you didn't . . .'

'Because I was trapped in one body. I inhabited a single existence. You saw two of my selves in two separate existences, where I was aware of only one. Don't you understand? When you broke the mirror in your bathroom you entered another world. A probable world of what-might-have-been. A world in which your wife and daughter were abused and then destroyed. But it is only one world out of an infinite number of probable worlds.' Kumar grips his arm. 'You must defeat this evil. If you don't, history will follow the path of the Messengers, and everything is lost.'

'It's too late.' Cawdor stares off into the darkness. 'Kersh has won.'

'No!' Kumar's grip tightens. 'Everything that's happened is in the world of what-might-have-been. But you can change that.'

'Why me?' Cawdor asks, savagely breaking free. '*Why me*?'

'Because the only person who can destroy Kersh is the one who gave him life. That person is you.'

Cawdor jerks back in astonishment. 'Me?'

'Kersh committed murder and was sent to Death Row. The Messengers needed an evil brain to create a world, both past and future, in which they would triumph, and Kersh was perfect. In that world you defied the Shouters on board this ship and were punished for it, along with your family. Because of that, Kershalton survived. He went on to become Kersh, who then murdered the boy in the gas station and was sentenced to death in the electric chair. The Messengers were then able to use his brain to create a world in which they would triumph. In that world you defied the Shouters and were punished by them... And so the circle goes on, and will do so, unless and until it is broken. It encompasses the distant past and reaches into the far future where the corrupt power of the Messengers has achieved complete control and total domination. A world made in the image of Frank Kersh.'

Cawdor turns back to the limpid brown eyes in the narrow swarthy face. 'Can it be broken?'

'The truthful answer to that, my friend, is that I don't know. All I do know is that the possibility exists.'

'How do you know that?' But, even as Cawdor asks the question, the answer comes to him.

Behold in this shatter'd mirrour all your past and future times.

The shards of broken glass had revealed to him the world as fashioned in the warped brain of Frank Kersh. In these fragments he had been permitted a terrifying glimpse of both past and future in a world of what-might-have-been that could become its own self-fulfilling prophecy. A world that exists because it exists in its own world. The circle complete and unbroken. But Kumar has faith that it can be broken, and now Cawdor understands why.

The reason is simple. Because Kersh is afraid. He's afraid because he doesn't have absolute control of the world he created. If he had, Cawdor wouldn't be here now thinking the thoughts he is thinking. Kersh would have obliterated any such possibility. But Kersh cannot rest, cannot be fully at ease, because the possibility exists.

That's what scares him. The possibility.

Beyond the timber wall, the sea roars and shudders. The scummy tide swills back and forth in the gloomy hold, lapping at the heap of gravel. The boldest rat, halfway up the slope, suddenly retreats and slides back into the water as Cawdor climbs to his feet. Kumar rises with him. They stand facing one another.

'I remember something you once said to me, long ago. You said that men of good faith must do what they can to oppose the forces of evil. A balance has to be kept, or else everything is chaos.' Cawdor grasps Kumar's hand in both of his. 'You have shown me the truth of that. I thank you for the gift.'

'Yes – and your reply was to call yourself a poor disciple. "A defective candle to carry the flame." Remember?' When Kumar smiles, his whole face is suffused with radiance. 'But I happen to be an excellent judge of candles. The flame burns brightly, as I knew it would.' He turns Cawdor's left hand over and presses his fingertips into the palm. It is a curious gesture, one that Cawdor doesn't understand. 'Don't forget,' Kumar says softly, increasing the pressure, 'who it was destroyed this part of you. Kersh may yet live – or die – to regret it.'

From the bottom hold of the vessel Cawdor ascends alone to the lower deck, where bodies lie crammed together on hard bunks in a miasma of suffocating heat and noxious stink. He sees the ship's doctor on his knees, tending to some poor wretch. Cawdor passes on. No one pays him any notice. He climbs a ladder of worn rungs to the middle deck. Somewhere here, in one of these narrow wooden cubicles, he and Saraheda and Daniel spent week after week of an interminable voyage to the New World. His wife and son never lived to see the end of it. They met the wrath of the Shouters. On a moonless night in the middle of the ocean the Shouters' murderous accomplice, one Franklin Kershalton, did for them. So be it. Cawdor gathers the malice and hate-filled revenge to him as tightly as he grasps the rail of the companionway and hauls himself up to the main deck and the fresh open air. The stench and heat below are swept away. He breathes in the warm night. The breeze touches his cheek like a soothing caress. Cawdor tilts back his head and looks up to the stars. They blaze in splendour across the heavens. He has never in all his life seen such a display. It is magnificent. More wondrous and splendid than even Gilbert Gryble might have rhapsodised about in his wildest moments of fantasy. But there is something wrong about it. Cawdor stands looking up, puzzling what this might be. The stars do not blink. They gleam hard and cold, without the tiniest flicker, spheres of dead light. Away to the eastern horizon the early phase of the moon is a thin sickle of pale luminescence. To Cawdor it looks fake. Like a piece of silver paper stuck to the sky. So bemused by this strange artificial phenomenon, it takes a while for him to realise that he's gazing upward at the night sky through a dome of glass.

His eye follows the glass curvature downward to a white wall and then to a white carpet. The carpet extends across the floor to three steps leading down to a circular well in the centre of the room. There, on a curved bench sofa of white fur, a man is stretched out at ease, hands folded behind his head, his thin legs and bony knees emerging from a black silk robe.

'Bin waitin' a long time for you, boy.' Kersh grins, the skin crinkling around the eye of blank milky marble. 'But jeez, fella, you finally made it.'

Kersh slides off the sofa, still grinning. 'What's your poison, Jeff? A shot of good ole rye whiskey?' He comes up the carpeted steps. 'Naw, wait a minute. You prefer Irish. Am I right?'

He goes past Cawdor to the bar and reaches down two glasses from the shelf. 'Had fun gettin' here, huh?' Kersh says over his shoulder. 'Jumped through a few hoops along the way. Sure hope it was worth it.'

Cawdor looks around. Everything here is a creation of Kersh's private fantasy. From this penthouse suite to far beyond the glass roof, to the stars and slice of moon. It is always night here, the City of Perpetual Night, constructed from the dark labyrinth of Kersh's imagination. He sits atop his tower of granite and glass, 2,000 storeys high, master of all he surveys. None of this comes as any surprise to Cawdor; he expected it, and calmly accepts it. What does surprise him, and frankly baffles him too, is that Kersh shows no sign of fear, nor even the slightest concern. He has to be afraid that all this will be taken away from him. Has to be.

Why isn't he afraid?

'Crying shame about Baby Sam,' Kersh says, sloshing out liquor. 'You know, I really miss the old scumbag. He always was good for a laugh. Did you have to do what you did?' Kersh shrugs it off. 'Ah, well, guess so.'

He picks up the two glasses and jerks his head towards the balcony. 'Come on, it's cooler out there.'

Cawdor follows him outside.

He halts at the rail, shocked and momentarily dazzled by the vast city of twinkling lights, spread out from horizon to horizon. The sight makes Cawdor draw breath. Way off in the distance he sees a pyramid of glass glowing like a beacon. The sheer scale and power of Kersh's creation is overwhelming. For the first time Cawdor feels a shadow of unease; of corrosive doubt eating away at his resolution and sapping his confidence.

Kersh sweeps out a hand proudly. 'Great, huh?' he boasts. 'All this – everything I always wanted. And wanna know something? No strings attached. One second of my time is all they wanted. The last second, as it happens, so what had I to lose? Hell, sure, they can have it and welcome to it. What use is it to me anyway?'

'What happens when it's over?'

Kersh chuckles. He hawks and spits into space. 'You know better'n that, Jeff. It's never over. Just goes on and on.

And on. Hey, drink your drink.'

Why isn't he afraid? Cawdor wonders, sipping his drink. Maybe he isn't afraid because I'm part of it, too. And, if I'm just another phantom of Kersh's imagination, what has he to fear from that? And why am I leaning on the rail of his penthouse drinking with him? I came here with black revenge in my heart. I came here to destroy him. Cawdor looks down into the abyss. If Kersh fell from here, would it kill him? Is it even possible for him to die in this place of his own creation? Maybe Kersh can't die, Cawdor reflects . . . Not unless Kersh himself thinks it.

'Like I said, this is one sweet deal,' Kersh is saying. 'I just have to dream something up – and I get it! Neat, huh? Anything my heart desires.'

'As you desired the deaths of my wife and daughter,' Cawdor says bitterly.

Kersh is hurt. 'Hell, no, Jeff, that wasn't me! That was them other guys. I didn't mean you no harm – you or your family. It was them religious nuts did all that stuff, the Messengers. Nothin' to do with me.'

If that's true, Cawdor thinks, why did I see Kersh's face in the fragments of mirror? How come I knew about the penthouse, the tower? He stares out dizzily at the millions of lights twinkling below. What if Kersh is the wrong man? Not really to blame? This isn't how Cawdor imagined it would be. Fact is, Kersh doesn't seem such a bad guy after all. He's free with his liquor. He's not bad company. Cawdor might even get to like him.

'Just between the two of us, Jeff, I never could understand what all that religious crap was about.' Kersh leans nearer, confiding. 'See, they never explained it to me. Them guys is weird people – and I mean *weird* – believe you me. Give me the creeps.' Kersh shivers and takes a deep gulp.

'Could be I made a mistake,' Cawdor says in a small voice.

'Well,' says Kersh charitably, 'we all of us do that. Hell, have I made mistakes! I'd rewrite the book if I could. Start over. But that's life, I guess.'

Cawdor is totally confused. Even his own thoughts don't

seem to belong to him any more. He's thinking things that seem alien to him. Why has he come here, seeking out Kersh, if Kersh isn't to blame?

He blinks and stares out at the lights, swirling all around, above, below, from horizon to horizon.

Is it the drink that's affecting him? What has Kersh put in it?

He glances up muzzily as a flash of blue lightning flickers distantly across the sky. Even Kersh has electrical storms. Like the spectacular one Cawdor remembers watching from his office window in New York –

'Yeah, that was me.' Kersh grins, boasting again. 'I can play around with electricity. It's the juice in the chair. It feeds me. I tap into it and –'

He stops dead as Cawdor turns to stare at him.

'How did you know what I was thinking?'

'Huh?' Kersh swallows nervously.

'You read my mind.'

'I did?' Kersh gives a rapid shake of the head. 'Naw, don't think so, Jeff. Coincidence, that's all. Let's have another drink.'

The lightning crackles like small brittle bones being crushed in a huge fist.

'You got me all wrong, Jeff.' Kersh pats his arm. 'We're buddies, ain't we? I'm not such a bad guy after all. I'm free with my liquor. I'm not bad company. You might even get to like me.'

No wonder these thoughts seem strange, Cawdor thinks. They're not mine. They're his. *Kersh is thinking me. Putting these thoughts inside my head.* The bastard's to blame all right.

'Naw, it wasn't me.' Kersh's tone becomes wheedling. 'It was the Messengers all along, like I told you. They used me to get at you. That's the truth, Jeff, I swear.'

Underneath the good-buddy act Cawdor sees that the man is trembling. The good eye rolls up, showing white. His face twitches.

'You're innocent, right, Frank?'

'Yeah . . . Yeah, sure I am. It's them guys you want, not

me.' His voice strains with pleading. 'I got nothing against you, Jeff – or your wife and kid. What happened to them was out of my control.'

'It was out of your control when you raped my daughter. Is that what you're saying?'

'Not me, man, I never did such a thing. Never.'

'You raped her in front of me. That was your mistake, Frank. I saw you do it.'

'But listen, hey *listen*. They made me do it. I had no choice. It was the Messengers, they forced me to rape her –'

Kersh clamps his mouth tight, as if he could have bitten off his tongue. He grips the rail in both hands, then casts a crafty look in Cawdor's direction. 'Anyway, you ain't no fuckin' angel.'

'What?'

'You didn't do a fat lot to protect them.'

'What do you mean?'

'You know damn well what I mean. That night on the ship. Out in the middle of the ocean. Your wife and kid paid the price while you were too busy getting laid. Remember?' Kersh shakes his head, clucking his tongue. 'Talk about fall from grace, Jeff. You fell *way* down, you can't deny it.'

Cawdor doesn't try to deny it, even to himself, because he knows it's true. Inside he burns with shame. And with shame comes a mountain weight of guilt, crushing him, crippling his resolve. Frank is right. He left his family unprotected. He was tempted and led away from the straight and narrow. What right has he to pass judgement on anyone else? OK, so Frank made a few mistakes. But who hasn't, for chrissakes? Hell, Cawdor thinks, have I made mistakes! I'd rewrite the book if I could. Start over. But that's life, I guess.

It's happening again.

He's thinking Kersh's thoughts.

No – Kersh is thinking *him*.

Snap out of it!

Savagely, Cawdor shoves himself away from the rail and straightens up to his full height. He's losing control, becoming confused and lost in the dizzying swirl of lights. His purpose in being here is floating away on the night air. One minute he reckons Kersh might be a decent enough guy who's been misjudged; the next he's stricken helpless with guilt over what he himself did – or rather failed to do. He has to fight these crippling thoughts; he has to beat Kersh at his own game, break out of this mental prison and find the strength to make the evil bastard pay for what he did.

That night on the ship. Out in the middle of the ocean. That's what Kersh had said. Cawdor snatches the image away from Kersh and seizes on it. He sees Kersh and his brat of an accomplice on the deck of the ship under a moonless sky. A boy in a billowing nightshirt appears. There's a struggle. Then they're lowering a soggy, trussed-up bundle into the ocean, followed by the unconscious young boy. His wife and son had been murdered by this swine Kersh, just as Kersh had returned to repeat the act with Sarah and Daniella. Again and again, the endless cycle repeating itself. How many times had it happened, the same scenario re-enacted? How many lives had he himself lived, and in each one lost a wife, a son, a daughter?

The lightning is moving across the starscape in jagged streaks, coming closer. There are no storm clouds: the brilliant flashes of blue light appear out of nowhere, out of nothing. Cawdor turns, fists clenched by his sides, his lust for revenge restored, pure and distilled. Kersh has retreated along the balcony. His good eye gleams, bright with fear and hatred.

I can play around with electricity. It's the juice in the chair. It feeds me.

He means to fry me, Cawdor thinks. It's the only way he can destroy me. If he fails, he will lose everything. His tower will fall; the universe he has created will collapse in ruins. Nothing will remain.

'Know something, Frank? I've only just realised. Behind the bullshit you're nothing but a big fat zero. A cheap petty hoodlum. Mr Three-Times-Loser himself. To think that all along I built you up in my mind as some kind of masterbrain, a Mr Big with balls and brains pulling the strings. And look what I find. It's sad. In fact, it's pathetic. All you really are is a no-count two-bit hustler, a piece of Southern white trash I'd scrape off my shoe as I would a dog turd, and not think twice about it.'

Kersh glances up to the sky, then back to Cawdor. 'You think so, huh? Reckon you're so goddamn smart, don't you, you stuck-up sonofabitch with your "principles" and your "ideals" and your happy-families crap. You ain't no better'n me, Jeff. You just had the breaks is all.'

Cawdor smiles, and a nervous spasm twitches in Kersh's cheek.

'There's only one thing you haven't got, Frank,' Cawdor says quietly. 'And that's guts.'

Kersh gapes at him. '*What*?'

'You're yellow. I can see the streak down your back from here. Women and children, fat simpletons with toy guns in gas stations. That's just about your mark.'

'Oh yeah?' Kersh squares his narrow shoulders. 'You think I'm trash, right? And you're the guy with right on his side. OK, we'll see who's got balls around here.' He curls his finger. 'Come with me, cocksucker.'

Cawdor follows him through the glass doors, back into the penthouse suite. He feels stronger now, more confident, having steeled himself to reject those insidious thoughts creeping into his mind. Keep up your guard, Cawdor tells himself. Never forget for a single instant that this is Kersh's world: he can conjure up dream phantoms any time and in any place he wishes. Take nothing on trust. Believe half of what you hear and nothing of what you see. The guy is a sewer rat: liar, cheat, murderer, rapist.

Kersh goes past the bar to the bedroom door. He halts there, his hand on the doorknob, and glances back over his shoulder. There's a slight curl to his lip that Cawdor doesn't like.

'Not sure you oughta see this. Might stunt your growth.'

'You're a joke, Frank. A bad one. Nobody ever told you that?'

Kersh's expression tightens for a second. The dead eye flares drably with dull fire. 'If I'm a joke, then get a barrel of laughs outta this, fella.'

The door swings open and Kersh steps through, standing to one side so that Cawdor has a view of the bedroom, which is bathed in pink light, like a room in a high-class whorehouse, dominated by a king-size bed with black silk sheets and matching pillows. Cawdor stands on the threshold. He hasn't prepared himself because he isn't afraid; he's been through the very worst of it with the deaths of his wife and daughter, so whatever else Kersh's sick brain can conjure up will amount to nothing more than a feeble shadow of the horrors he has endured. After that, he can endure anything.

Anything at all.

Any . . . thing.

Sarah lies on the bed. She wears a satin negligée cut low at the front, trimmed with lace that barely covers her breasts. The negligée is slit up to the thigh, revealing creamy flesh above the stocking tops and a red suspender belt. Her lovely grey-blue eyes are thickly made up with mascara and purple eye shadow, her lips painted a glossy, garish vermilion. Her hair is dyed platinum blonde and brushed in shining waves that curl over her shoulders. She looks . . . grotesque, artificial, a wooden doll, her delicate features and fine bones hidden behind the hideous daub of a mask.

'Hi, babe. Get some rest like I told you?' Kersh floats out a casual wave. 'Never guess who's here.'

Sarah sleepily raises her head. She looks up, one eye hidden by a sweep of blonde hair. 'Don't fuck around, Frank. Come back to bed.'

'Horny as a bitch in heat,' Kersh says, giving Cawdor a private wink. 'These highfalutin broads all the same. Ice maidens on top; dirty sluts with filthy minds underneath. Honest truth, Jeff, this cock-happy chick damn near wore me out.' He sniggers down his nose, enjoying the look on Cawdor's face, that of a man who has been kicked in the belly by a mule. 'What was it you said, Jeff? Somethin'

451

about a bad joke? This takes first prize, I reckon, and the joke's on you, you pompous prick!'

Cawdor shuts his eyes, fighting to obliterate the image from his mind, pitting his willpower against Kersh's. He opens his eyes and the image is still there. Kersh is grinning at him. The illusion won't go away; doesn't even fade a little around the edges. It stays hard and solid and real – this horrible parody of Sarah stretched out languorously on the bed, a secret plea in her eyes as she gives a sidelong glance to Kersh, her tongue sliding out to moisten her lower lip. Watching her, the woman he loves, Cawdor feels the spirit within him shrivel up and wither; he feels empty and inert, as if the lifeforce has drained out of him. He has no strength to resist. He can't fight any more. He has failed his wife. She has been sucked into the dark, twisted spiral of Kersh's endless fantasy. Kersh can make of her anything he desires, his eternal plaything, a captive in his tower of granite and glass until the stars never fade from the sky.

Cawdor stands there helplessly while Kersh stands there grinning. He can't even summon up the will or the strength to strike out at Kersh – he feels so scoured raw and empty inside, the purpose and resolution that sustained him and drove him on crushed under a mountain of guilt for having failed, so pitifully, to protect his loved ones.

'I did say, didn't I?' Kersh sits on the bed, absently tracing a finger down the contour of Sarah's leg under the sheer negligée. 'That you ain't no fucking angel yourself. Me, I admit my mistakes. Then I bury 'em.' He giggles like a naughty child. 'Or slide 'em into the swamp so the 'gators can have a midnight snack. But that's always been your problem, Jeff. Denial.' He shakes his head sadly and sighs. 'Don't pay in the long run, fella, believe you me.'

'Sarah!' Cawdor finds his voice at last. It sounds cracked and hoarse. She swings the curtain of hair back, her expression lazy and indolent. He stumbles half a step forward. Kersh's hand moves up to stroke her exposed thigh. Reclining side by side, the pair of them observe Cawdor as he sinks slowly to his knees. He presents a pathetic figure, kneeling at the foot of the bed with shoulders hunched and head bowed. Kersh wears a cloudy half-frown, as if trying to figure out what new gimmick Cawdor has come up with. Sarah seems hardly to notice him, as a vague other presence in the room. Or perhaps a dream phantom on the edge of a nightmare.

'Sarah,' Cawdor says again, brokenly. He can't look at her, he's so ashamed, staring down at his clenched white fists. 'I did this to you. I stood against them because I knew they were evil and had to be stopped. Me with my precious cast-iron soul, fighting the good fight against the Shouters, the Beamers – the Messengers in all their guises. But it wasn't me who suffered their wrath, not directly. Their retribution fell upon you. And when you needed me, God curse me, I wasn't there. I was tempted; I was weak; I was led astray.' Tears splash down on his bunched fists. The words are strangled in his throat. 'Forgive me.'

'Bit late in the day, buddy, wouldn't you say?' Kersh sneers at him. 'You had your chance and blew it. Tough titty.'

Cawdor raises his head and stares mutely at his wife. Or rather at the travesty that Kersh has made of her; the apparition he has manufactured to satisfy his lusts and at the same time to extinguish the last spark of any hope Cawdor might have. Because Kersh has hit on the one thing against which Cawdor has no defence. His rat's cunning has located the chink in his armour. That's why Sarah is here – to confront him with the physical manifestation of his own guilt. Guilt as corrosive as acid, eating him away from the inside, destroying his will to survive.

He doesn't expect a response to his plea, and God knows he doesn't deserve one. The brainless painted doll on the bed can't absolve him from his sins or bestow her forgiveness. Not when she's been moulded by Kersh's slimy fingers and shaped into his compliant whore. That's all she is. An image seen in a distorting mirror. Not his wife. Not Sarah.

The doll, the image – the distortion of Sarah – is leaning on one elbow. She is smiling at him, and there are tears in her eyes.

'Kumar was right and I was wrong,' she says.

Kersh violently pulls away from her. 'What the fuck?'

'Sarah?' Cawdor unclenches his fists. '*Sarah*?'

Her gaze is straight and clear, unwavering.

'Good, noble and brave. What you did was all of those things.'

The mountain weight turns into a feather and floats away. Cawdor smiles but is unable to speak. His heart is too full.

'I can't forgive you,' his wife says, 'because there is nothing to forgive. If you hadn't done what you did you wouldn't be the man I loved.'

Kersh jerks up off the bed. His face is white and taut, his good eye staring in disbelief. From above comes the crack of lightning and the rumbling cascade of thunder; the storm is directly over the tower.

The heavens are in turmoil.

The vast dome of sky is seething with electrical activity. Flashing with a billion sparks like the impulses of a psychotic brain. Synapses connecting and interacting in a gigantic network of frenzied dementia.

The spectacle is both awesome and terrifying to Cawdor as he stands at the balcony rail. Awesome in its ferocious and abundant energy; terrifying because he knows he is witnessing the mad chaos of Kersh's brain in the jagged arcs of blue lightning. This *is* Kersh's brain. These are his thought waves, flashing across the dark universe of his conscious mind.

Knowing he ought to be afraid, instead Cawdor feels a strange kind of peace. When the mountain weight of guilt was lifted from him, fear went away also, and with it the desire for revenge. Now his mind is free and unburdened, and his spirit is liberated. Strangest of all, he cannot find it in his heart to hate Frank Kersh any longer. This is very curious, beyond his understanding, and Cawdor is lost for a reason to explain it. Perhaps Kumar would know why. Though perhaps not – Kumar wasn't the infallible fount of all wisdom. He spoke of the circle being broken but was unable to say how it might be achieved. He had expressed his faith in the *possibility*, that was all, leaving the rest for Cawdor to figure out. Yet in his present state of mind, of restful calm, this doesn't have the same burning importance either. It's as if, Cawdor reflects, he has come to accept with equanimity the path of his own fate. That comes pretty near to describing how he feels. Describes it exactly, in fact. Acceptance. Allowing events to unfold as they will, cause and effect to follow its immutable course.

And so he feels no concern or alarm at the sight of Kersh leaning back with folded arms against the granite balustrade, head sunk low on his shoulders. His face flares up, a drab ghastly white, in the flicker of lightning playing around the tower. Malevolence surrounds him like a black aura.

'You and your slut bitch of a wife are trapped in here, you know that, don't you? No way out, except down there.' He waggles his thumb over the balustrade. 'You wanna try it? Maybe you can fly – or fry.' Kersh is actually smiling at the feeble joke. 'Don't say I didn't give you a choice.'

A long finger of destructive energy jabs down from the night sky followed by a crash of thunder. Kersh is enjoying himself. 'Wanna mess with me, do ya?' he goads Cawdor. 'Come on then, cocksucker. Make my day.'

'Quit fooling around, Frank. You might get burnt.'

'*Me*? Wanna bet?'

'You shouldn't gamble, Frank. Three-time losers never win. Haven't you learnt that much yet?'

Kersh spins round and grabs the rail tight in both hands, a rictus of fury convulsing his features. 'You're in the hot seat, not me,' he snarls. 'Watch this.' The cords strain and stand out in his scrawny neck. At once the lightning intensifies, malevolent mind waves raking across the sky. A bolt of lightning forks down, searing the air and scorching the tiles at Cawdor's feet. He staggers back, shielding his head, and stumbles towards the doors. The doors slide shut.

Kersh throws back his head and cackles. His knuckles show white, gripping the rail. 'You're dead meat, boy. A grease spot, hear me? Dead. Nothing. Zero.'

455

The entire tower is enveloped in crackling blue fire, granite and glass streaked with heat marks. Another lightning bolt strikes at Cawdor, almost playfully, toying with him, singeing his hair and eyebrows. He can smell himself burning.

Kersh is having the time of his life. He's in control. This is what it is to have absolute power. Nothing can touch him, or harm him, or hurt him, ever again. Sheeeit, if he knew it was going to be so much fun he'd have gotten Cawdor and his slut bitch up here sooner. He can use the excitement. The thrill of it.

'Hey! Might just keep you two around for a while,' he screams with glee, hanging on to the rail. 'Bring you out now and then when things get a little tame around here.'

With a gaping grin he looks up to the crazy mosaic of light filling the sky. Cawdor thinks he's suffered, does he? The cocksucker don't have the faintest notion what real suffering is. Kersh knows. All his life, the same bitter taste of failure, defeat, humiliation. The women he wanted who sneered at him – and worse, laughed. The high-and-mighty people in their fancy apartments who looked at him as if he was vermin. Nobody ever gave him a decent chance. He never had the breaks. Even his girl, Sophie Molosz, bleached-blonde hair and chipped nail varnish, had deserted him when he was in the Pen. He couldn't even hang on to a cheap piece of tail.

But one thing he can do. What he did to that fat cretin at the gas station who tried to make fun of him. Blow Jeff Cawdor to kingdom come. Yessir. Fry, you fucker. Fry.

The seething mind waves converge and combine to form a blinding blue-white streak of colossal power that lights up the entire sky. It strikes from on high – a shaft of pure energy aimed with evil intelligence and deadly precision directly at Cawdor. Nothing can alter its course. It is unstoppable and instantaneous. In that instant, which seems to Cawdor to expand and stretch to occupy aeons of time, he remembers Kumar's parting gesture. How he had touched the palm of Cawdor's left hand – once smashed beyond repair, now restored to him intact in this other world – and had murmured, 'Kersh may yet live – or die – to regret it.'

He may yet live. Or die.

With his left hand Cawdor grabs hold of the rail as the lightning bolt strikes. It scores a direct hit, suffusing his body with millions of volts. The current shoots through him. It passes down his arm and through the hand gripping the rail. It travels along the rail to where Kersh stands, both hands holding the rail. It welds both of Kersh's hands to the metal. His body stiffens like a ramrod, grows a full six inches. His milky eye explodes out of his head. His good eye melts and runs down his cheek, which is already melting. His lank fair hair shrivels and curls into black ringlets. His mouth widens in a silent scream and keeps on widening as the lips crinkle and peel off, exposing a skeleton grin.

And then the grin is gone, and Kersh with it.

All that remains is the black residue of his hands, fused to the rail, like a sticky spider's web. The rest of him is vaporised in a cloud of sooty particles, which swirl up, wisps from a funeral pyre, and disperse into the night sky. After that, nothing at all. Not even the smell of burning.

The lightning ceases. The myriad twinkling lights below flicker and are extinguished, like the last, fading impulses of a dying brain. In the far distance, the bright beacon of the glass pyramid flares briefly and is snuffed out. Then one by one the stars grow dim and expire. From the balcony Cawdor watches as the sky gradually darkens and the city fades to black. Soon there will be silence and emptiness and eternal darkness. There will be void.

Kersh has entered the longest night of all.

6

Thud.

Kersh slumped forward against the straps. Both hands hung limp, fingertips quivering as the final twitches of his autonomic nervous system died away. The skin at his shaven temples was scorched and blistered. Dried salty tears, like slugs' trails, gleamed on either side of his nose. There was brown stuff on his shirt-front, ejected from his mouth and nostrils.

Above his head the fly buzzed. A sixth sense had warned it to take off from his hand the instant the switch was thrown. It droned around aimlessly and then zoomed off to look for a way of escape from the cork-lined room.

Meacham opened the door with the glass porthole and came in, followed by the doctor. The doctor had performed this service a number of times, though he was still nervous. Ninety dollars never seemed, to him, enough. He waited for Meacham to decouple the power cable, as an extra safeguard, before checking for pulse and heartbeat. Even then you couldn't always be sure. The lingering aftershock did strange things to the nervous system.

The doctor held the flaccid hand for a minute and then went on to perform an auscultation, listening through his stethoscope. The blood was gurgling and settling in the left ventricle, but there was no rhythmic sound. No regular thump of a heartbeat.

'I think we got a bull's-eye.' Meacham stood, hands on the folds of his hips, observing the procedure. He could spot a dead 'un when he saw one.

'Maybe,' the doctor said cautiously. 'We'll check the brain.' He attached a sensor pad to the centre of Kersh's forehead and knelt down on the rubber mat to study the meter reading.

Meacham half-turned, glancing over his shoulder at the tall figure in the doorway. 'Not a thing you can do any more. He's pleadin' his own case now.'

'Then his soul is finally at rest,' Preacher said.

Was that a question or a statement? Meacham speculated. 'I guess so, Father.' He never knew how to address these holy rollers, but 'Father' would have to do.

'No signs of any activity,' the doctor said, rising. He showed Meacham the reading. 'Braindead.'

'OK, doc, I'll put my name to that. Pack your stuff.' He looked round, pursing his fleshy lips and shaking his head slowly.

The priest seemed reluctant to leave, though finally he turned and went out. He nodded to the warden, left the brightly lit anteroom and climbed the concrete steps, his bony hand sliding along the rail where the paint had worn through to the metal.

Kersh had failed them. It was a tragic and devastating body blow to all their plans. The more so, Preacher knew, because Kersh had been the perfect type. Had he succeeded, he might have created a world – an entire universe – in which the Messengers would have had total control. That there was such a world somewhere, waiting to be discovered, but for the time being merely held in abeyance, Preacher was in no doubt.

There were countless alternatives, he was sure, and this very nearly had been one of them.

Why then had it failed? What had gone wrong? Kersh's final second, stretched to infinity, was time enough, aeons of time, in which to create the kind of world that the Messengers desired. But that hadn't happened. No such world had ever existed. It had been stillborn in Kersh's brain.

Something – or someone – had prevented it from happening.

Another power equal to theirs.

Preacher walked along the main corridor of F Cellhouse, past the sign pointing the way to Unit F-2, known as the Block, and was checked through the double security gates by the guards.

This time that other power – whatever or whoever it was – had defeated them. But that was this time.

Next time it would be different, Preacher vowed.

Next time.

The outer compound of baked red earth was bright as day under the gantry arclights. In the far corner, away from the other parked vehicles, sat the silver trailer like a dulled and battered torpedo, torn posters peeling from its ribbed sides. Preacher was halfway there when he felt a pair of eyes upon him. He didn't turn or glance that way,

459

knowing at once who they belonged to, and carried on with measured step.

Next to the chain-link fence, May-Beth Gaskins watched the tall black-clad figure cross the compound and enter the trailer. So much for high-flown prophecy, she thought contemptuously. So much for bullshit promises. She really had fallen for Preacher's fake bill of goods, and now she felt disgusted with herself for being so naive. Another life – a *new* life – that's what Preacher had offered her. Filled her head with romantic dreams that she might become beautiful and famous, powerful and rich. She snorted derisively. Imagine her swallowing that guff when it all depended on a petty hoodlum and three-time loser like Frank Kersh. She must have been crazy. The only legacy Kersh had to offer eternity was a piece of stringy buzzard meat.

One thing she knew for damn sure. No more visits to that ramshackle chapel out on Frog Wash Road to listen to the Messengers spouting their phoney claptrap.

Shaking her head, May-Beth passed through the side gate, leaving the bright arclights for the darkness beyond the compound. A warm night wind brushed her cheek. Overhead, a few wispy clouds floated by, lit by a pale slice of moon like a piece of silver paper stuck to the sky.

TIMESPACE

1

The building shook: it was one of the most spectacular storms he could remember ever having hit New York. From his office window on the 23rd floor of the Chrysler Building, Jeff Cawdor watched the flashes of blue lightning flickering through the dark roiling clouds, felt the shock wave of the thunder in the soles of his feet.

A shiver of awe and wonder rippled down his spine. Made you understand how the ancients could believe that it was the gods up there, hurling lightning bolts across the heavens in an ultimate tussle for supremacy.

Mankind hadn't really progessed that much further, he thought. For all its science and technological advance, there was still a stubborn, deep-rooted belief that the elemental forces of nature were outside its control, and, more significantly, beyond its understanding. Sure, they could be 'explained' in mechanical terms. But there was an intuitive sense – hence the awe and wonder he felt – that they were part of a grand enterprise of which mankind had only an inkling of understanding, had barely scratched the surface. The more we learn, he reflected, the less we realise we know.

A thought straight from a fortune cookie, Cawdor thought to himself, grinning.

The epicentre of the storm was moving on, crossing the Hudson River into New Jersey. The boom of thunder was trailing a few seconds after the flashes, not so deafening as a few minutes ago. Craning to look down, Cawdor could see that the murk was starting to clear. At the height of the storm, Lexington Avenue had been shrouded in grey, from up here the stream of cars and the dots of people as invisible as creatures at the bottom of the ocean.

For just an instant back then, as the shiver went down his spine, he had been tempted to glance over his shoulder. It was the feeling one gets of there being another presence in the room. He had resisted the urge. The rational part of his brain told him it wasn't possible for anyone to be sitting there, because he would have heard that person enter the office. And no one had. No one with a dark narrow face and liquid brown eyes, wearing silver-framed spectacles that winked in the penumbra outside the bright cone of the desk lamp. No one with slender brown hands clasped to his chest, leaning forward with an expression of concerned inquiry. No, definitely not. People simply didn't appear out of nowhere. It defied logic.

And yet, as he turned away from the window, he was conscious of holding his breath. He held it long enough to make sure the chair was empty. Then, seeing that he was alone, Cawdor let it go. Logic had prevailed.

The storm had distracted him from his work, and there was a pile of it to be got through before he went on vacation in three days' time. Don was frantic that he complete the Florida development proposal before he went. Don was due to make the pitch for the $22 million contract, which would be their slice of the hotel and casino complex at Holmes Beach near Sarasota. The design work was finished, but the technical specs were causing problems. For the past week Cawdor and his engineering team had been wrestling – at times almost literally, it seemed – with trying to incorporate the air-conditioning system into a building that at the touch of a button switched from open-air arena to closed auditorium. The management wanted their air-conditioned cake, and they wanted to eat it too.

He swung his leg over the swivel chair and settled himself at the drawing board. The CAD screen displayed the structural stress projections: a three-dimensional skeleton of the building, with a blizzard of numeric notations high-lighted in red covering all the stress points. The figures hadn't added up when the storm had pulled him magneti-cally to the window, and they didn't now, twenty minutes later.

While he worked he let his mind dwell on the promise of Tuscany. Cawdor was half-afraid he'd banged on about it a bit too much and that Daniella wouldn't be all that impressed by the reality, beautiful as it was. Or worse, that she might even be bored. At sixteen she was no longer a child, and yet not an adult, and it was impossible to predict what her reactions might be. They had taken the villa, with its own pool, situated in the hills above Cecina, for three weeks. There would be trips to Florence and Pisa, and the coast was within easy reach. For him and Sarah, visiting museums and art galleries, and discovering the treasures of village churches would be a delight, but they would need to ensure there were plenty of less serious diversions as well. Cawdor was determined that the holiday was going to be fun for all three of them.

The storm still rumbled faintly, way off in the distance. Minute by minute the sky was visibly brightening. Patches of blue had appeared, and the sun was playing hide and seek behind the tumbling banks of cloud being swept inland on a westerly breeze.

Just after four there was a light tap at the door and Phyllis entered. She apologised for disturbing him and held up a sheaf of letters. 'If I'm gonna catch the mails, these need your signature.' She stood near the desk, eyebrows raised, her cheeks dimpling in a smile of entreaty.

Cawdor looked up from the board. 'Sure, I'll sign 'em right away.'

He swung round as Phyllis placed the letters on the blotter and stood waiting, her chubby hands pressed together at her bosom.

'Coffee on the hob?' Cawdor asked, approaching the desk.

'Just made a fresh potful. Like some?'

'Great timing.' Cawdor grinned. 'As usual. Fetch me a mug while I sign these. Thanks, Phyllis.'

He watched her leave the office and then sat down at the desk to sign the letters. He was through signing them by the time she returned with his mug of coffee, black, one sugar, just the way he liked it.

Bright sunshine flooded in, illuminating the clutter on Gribble's workbench like a searchlight. Sitting in his usual hunched posture in front of the VDU screen, he gazed dreamily across West 116th Street at the pale stone edifice of Columbia University Library.

Maybe she was in there right this minute, working away at some impenetrable ancient text, glasses perched on the end of her nose, short red hair like a flaming beacon under the cowled reading lamp. A Lorentz was her name – he'd seen it on the Natural Sciences department board – though he hadn't yet discovered what the 'A' stood for. Angela? Alice? Abigail? None of those seemed to suit her. She wasn't due to become an official member of the faculty until September, but Gribble had seen her around the campus for the past three weeks. He assumed that Ms A Lorentz was engaged in private research, or possibly preparing her doctoral thesis. She'd smiled at him, just the once, in the staff refectory, when he'd been dithering about what to have for lunch: picking up dishes and putting them back again, because he always got flustered when faced with more than three things to choose from.

Gribble knew (everyone had 20/20 hindsight!) that he ought to have grabbed the chance right then, got talking to her, made some witty remark, or, failing that, a dull pleasantry would have done. *Anything* would have been better than clearing his throat and colouring up like a lovesick, tongue-tied adolescent and shuffling off with his tray. How pathetic could you get?

He sighed and blinked and drew his mind back to work. There was always that – and he was damn lucky, he supposed, that he loved it so. Not many could say the same. Be thankful for small blessings, Gribble admonished himself. And anyway, there was always a next time, and next time he *would* find a smile for Ms A Lorentz, and a shaft of wit to go with it, if only he could think of one.

He tapped at the keyboard, quickly becoming engrossed once again with the program he was trying to write. It was purely for his own amusement, and he had been tinkering with it for weeks now. The basic concept was very simple; the execution fiendishly difficult. The idea was for the user – in this instance, G Gribble, Esq. – to enter his own vital data (age, education, circumstances, personality profile, future prospects and aspirations) and the program, which he'd named Delphi, would then chart his 'world-line' for the next five, say, or even ten years. The 'world-line' represented the general direction of a person's life, touching on all important aspects such as career, relationships, illnesses, accidents, and any other major events likely to have a bearing on how the future unfolded.

Gribble intended Delphi to be a fun thing rather than a program with any serious application. But it also might be instructive. Find out where his career was headed, if he was going to win the Irish Sweepstake, whether there was a steady relationship on the horizon – even, fingers crossed, with a tall, slender redhead by the name of Angela-Alice-Abigail Lorentz.

Of course it was all speculative, just one possible extrapolation into the future out of the millions of possibilities that awaited him. Harmless fantasy with a dash of wish-fulfilment.

And yet, Gribble reasoned, *one* of those futures had to be the right one. In a sense it existed already in a limbo of time yet to be, just waiting to happen. That was Delphi's task (when he got the Beast working!): to compute the odds against this or that event happening, and to plot a 'probability curve' for the subject in question. The intriguing aspect of this theory, to Gribble, was that all these infinite probabilities existed side by side. So that, for instance, you could hypothetically live through each one, leading a countless number of separate lives that might vary just fractionally from all the rest. Over the entire spectrum, some lives would vary just a tiny fraction, while others would be totally different from one another. But you'd be living them all, simultaneously and continuously, that was the point.

Was this all a bit far-fetched? he wondered. You could make it work out on paper, get the math right, construct a watertight theory, but what about in practice? Each person had only one life that they could live. There may be millions of other possible lives, but you were aware of only one because you were stuck in your own separate timespace. Timespace? Where had that come from? Had he just coined a new word?

Gribble glanced round, clicking his fingers. A tail wagged. 'Here, boy. Come on, Heisenberg!'

The rust-coloured dog jumped down from the sofa, trotted forward, and licked his hand. 'Want to go walkies, boy? Sniff around a few hydrants? Chase a piece of tail?'

The mutt had a better sex life than he had, Gribble reflected. Sad but true. Sometimes he wished he could change everything, lead a life of excitement, danger even. Well, he thought, maybe in one or other of his probable lives that's precisely what he *was* doing.

'And good luck to him,' Gribble murmured. 'I mean, to me.'

He patted the dog's head, stretched himself, and got up out of the chair. He'd had enough for one day. He'd take Heisenberg for a stroll and stop off somewhere for a sandwich and a beer. What an exotic life he led.

The screen faded to grey as he switched off. Peeping over the Columbia Library, the sun's last rays beamed into the room and flared brightly as they struck an object on his workbench. Gribble picked it up. As with nearly everything else, it was an item that had just accumulated, along with the rest of his stuff. He couldn't even remember if he'd found it on the street somewhere or bought it in a junk shop. A gold pin (not real gold of course) in the shape of a butterfly. Or was it meant to be a bow tie? He didn't suppose it mattered. Nothing special, anyway, and certainly of no value.

Yet looking at it resting in his palm now, Gribble realised he was rather fond of the piece of junk. As if it held a memory for him, or some romantic association. Though for the life of him he hadn't the vaguest notion what that might be.

2

The *Salamander* was prepared and ready to depart. Jefferson Cawdor had stowed his belongings below and now he was eager to see the gap of foul water widen between ship and shore and to wave farewell to the smoky haze of Plymouth. He had few regrets. England was a place of persecution and bigotry. Other sects, besides his own Telluric Faith, were leaving, he had noticed. There were Methodists and Catholics on board, and he had observed a group of monklike figures in black robes standing in a circle in silent prayer. It comforted him to think they were praying for a safe voyage. If they were to be protected and afforded a sound passage, then it followed that so were he, Saraheda and Daniel.

Up on deck there was a frantic bustle, men hanging in the rigging and getting ready the sails for when the vessel reached the harbour mouth. Three men stood at the gang-plank, awaiting orders to raise it. Others leant over the side, coiling ropes as they were released from the mooring blocks.

It was a beautiful evening, the air soft and balmy. Cawdor lifted his face to feel the last heat of the setting sun. Though in the Colonies, he knew, he would get as much sun as he cared for.

'God in heaven!' Saraheda exclaimed, wrinkling her nose. 'Do we have to live with that smell down below for three whole months? I feel nauseous already, Jefferson.'

'You won't once we get going. The sea breeze carries it away.'

'Before they carry me away, I hope,' Saraheda replied darkly.

Cawdor laughed and squeezed her to him.

'What's holding us up?' Daniel asked, hopping impatiently from foot to foot. He looked up at his father. 'We have to catch the tide, you said. Suppose it goes before we're ready?'

'We're ready now.'

'But we're not *moving*.'

'The captain won't miss it, Daniel. He's an experienced seafarer, I'm told. Look! That's the reason.'

Cawdor pointed, and lifted Daniel up to see. One of the ship's officers, in cocked hat and dress coat, was remonstrating with a man in a torn filthy shirt and ragged breeches, lank hair hanging over his face like a clump of matted straw. The man was waving a scrap of paper, though the officer would have none of it. He shook his head, beckoned a couple of seamen forward, and waved the man from his sight.

'Why, see there – they're throwing him off,' Saraheda said. 'Poor man.'

'Why "poor" man?' Cawdor said. 'He might be a felon. Looks like a rogue to me.'

'You oughtn't to judge by appearances,' Saraheda chided him primly, and stifled a whoop as Cawdor pinched her bottom.

Everyone craned to watch as the man was frogmarched to the gangplank and sent staggering down it, almost losing his footing and nearly ending up in the poisonous turd-swilling harbour. Then the order was given, the gangplank raised, and the man stared balefully up at the ship, fists clenched at his sides, his lower teeth showing like a mongrel about to bite.

'He's got a funny eye,' Daniel announced blithely, and Saraheda dug her elbow into his ribs. 'Well, he has!'

'That's not his fault. Shush!'

Daniel fell silent, gladly, because now the *Salamander* was actually moving, turning about, being pulled towards the harbour mouth by longboats. The sails were unfurled, the vast yardage of canvas stretching and filling out, rosily pink in the light of the sunset.

Seeking a better vantage point, Daniel leapt on to a

bale, and spotted something else.

'Mr Gryble! Mr Gryble, you're being robbed!'

A boy of eight or nine, half his backside hanging out, was in the act of removing Gryble's astrolabe from his sack. Evading Gryble's swipe, he hugged the instrument close to his chest and ducked and weaved through the passengers' legs, dodging out of harm's way. Cawdor stuck out his foot. The boy did a spectacular somersault, but as Daniel jumped down to retrieve the astrolabe from where it had rolled into the drainway the boy came up spitting like a wildcat. Daniel stood his ground, but regretted he had a moment later when he received a terrific sock in the mouth. He sat down, spitting out blood and bits of teeth. The boy came for him again, so it was just as well that Cawdor got there first, stepping in between and hoisting the ragamuffin up by the scruff.

'That's the brat who came aboard with Kershalton,' a voice called out. 'Why didn't the captain evict him too?'

The boy was wriggling in Cawdor's grasp. He swung around, snarling foul abuse, and spat in Cawdor's face.

'Toss him over the side. Let him sink or swim.'

Cawdor moved as if to do so, and the boy squirmed and whined, 'No, sir, please. Don't, sir. I'll drown.'

'Let him drown, then. Good riddance to bad rubbish,' a woman said.

Cawdor wiped the spittle from his face, holding the boy at arm's length. 'You'd better calm down, then. And show some decent manners. Or I will feed you to the fishes.'

'Yes, sir. Oh yes, sir.'

He held up both hands in supplication, and Cawdor saw they were oddly shaped, with an extra, withered finger and a curved nail on the outside of each one. 'What's your name, boy?'

'Sam, sir.'

'D'you belong to the man who was thrown off?'

'I don't belong to nobody,' the boy answered sullenly. He jerked his head. 'Least of all a murderer who escaped the gallows by the skin of his teeth. I got my pride.'

Cawdor laughed and set the boy down. At once the

little ruffian grabbed the hand that had been holding him and sank his teeth into it. The boy's eyes grew round. Slowly he drew back, saliva dripping from his open mouth, a look of mortal terror on his face.

'What's the matter, boy?' Cawdor asked mildly. 'Too tough for you? Have another chew.' He offered the same unmarked hand and the boy shrank away.

'Must have skin like bull leather,' somebody muttered.

'Naw, the lad's toothless,' another decided.

'If you misbehave once again on this voyage,' Cawdor said softly, holding up his left hand, 'I'll wallop you with this. I don't think you'd like that.'

Cawdor winked, as if the two of them shared some secret understanding, and turned back to the rail. Saraheda had cleaned the blood from Daniel's face. Cawdor inspected his teeth. One lost; one chipped. 'It'll spoil your handsome looks for a while, but never mind.' He ruffled his son's hair.

'He won't do it again. Next time I'll be ready for him,' Daniel announced.

'There won't be a next time,' his father promised him. 'Believe me.'

'Jefferson, your hand.'

'It's all right.'

'Are you sure?'

'Yes. Positive.'

The lines from the longboats had been cast off and the ship was now clear of the harbour. Above their heads the topsails cracked open and filled with wind. The three of them took a long last look at receding England and then turned away.

Cawdor lifted Daniel up to perch on his shoulder and put his arm round his wife. His spirits were soaring. Flying along with the ship. A new life in the New World! Out there in the Colonies a golden future awaited them. He was convinced of it. Indeed, he knew it for a fact.

Under full sail, the *Salamander* surged forward confidently to meet the open sea.